SOVIET AUTHORS LIBRARY

RADUGA PUBLISHERS

FYODOR ABRAMOV

The Swans Flew By

AND OTHER STORIES

RADUGA PUBLISHERS
MOSCOW

Translated from the Russian
Illustrated by *Andrei Golitsin*

Ф. Абрамов
ПРОЛЕТАЛИ ЛЕБЕДИ
Повести и рассказы

На английском языке

English translation © Raduga Publishers 1986.
Illustrations

Printed in the Union of Soviet Socialist Republics

A $\dfrac{4702010200-050}{031\,(05)-86}$ 007-86

ISBN 5-05-000641-4

CONTENTS

LOVE AND PAIN
in Fyodor Abramov's Stories

Fyodor Abramov's prose is harsh. He is truly merciless with his readers, forcing them to drain the bitter cup of knowledge to the very bottom. But at the bottom we discover a precious sediment—true beauty.

How such prose managed to burgeon on the infecund northern soil is one of Life's great mysteries, and it is also the secret of the writer as well, the fruit of a rare literary and human gift rooted in the kinship between the author and his characters. To see them as they are, he need not stand on tip-toe, nor bend down. He may have lived a large share of his life apart from them, but he has always remained one of them.

Fyodor Abramov (1920-1984) was one of those few writers whose entire personality, character and way of life have been poured, as it were, into their books, finding there a three-dimensional reflection. Not that Abramov's works include chunks of his own biography, nor is it a matter of resemblance between his literary heroes and the people the author knew, though, of course, he did paint his characters from life. But the intrinsic connection is much more profound and organic.

With Abramov, little appeared above the surface. There were not many changes in his external circumstances, but each stage in his development was intense and dramatic.

He was born in the village of Verkola, Pinega District, Arkhangelsk Region. Here, in northern Russia, he finished school, and then went to Leningrad and entered the Department of Philology of Leningrad University. Just think of the implications of this fact of biography: a village lad from the back of beyond is accepted at a famous university. But soon the war began, and Abramov joined the Leningrad Volunteer Corps. Then he was conscripted into the regular army and fought the war to the end. He was wounded several times, received a number of decorations, and in 1945, after

7

Victory, returned to Leningrad University, a war veteran. He graduated from the University in due time, then defended his post-graduate thesis and received the academic degree of Candidate of Philology. For ten years after that he lectured on modern Russian literature at the same university.

Fyodor Abramov's first works of literary criticism and book reviews appeared in print in 1949. He published his first novel, *Brothers and Sisters,* in 1958 at the age of thirty-seven. After that he devoted himself to professional writing to the exclusion of everything else. In answer to his readers' questions, Abramov had this to say about the story of the writing of *Brothers and Sisters:* "In the winter of 1942 I was severely wounded and evacuated from besieged Leningrad to the mainland. After several months of hospitals, I came home to my home village in the wooded country of Arkhangelsk Region to convalesce. It was a terrible time. In the south the enemy had reached the Volga, and here, in my own Pinega country, a battle for bread and for life itself was being waged. There were no exploding bombs and no whistling bullets, but there were death notices striking one family after another. There was need and back-breaking toil. Men's work in fields and meadows was done by worn, hungry women, old folks and adolescents. That summer I saw a great deal of suffering and grief. But I saw even more courage, stamina and Russian generosity of heart."

The life of the Soviet countryside was the key theme of Abramov's activities as a critic and researcher, and it subsequently became the central theme of his creative writing. All his life he remained loyal to this one theme—the Russian village during the war and the post-war years, and he created a single historical character in Soviet literature, that of the modern Russian peasant.

This statement in no way contradicts the fact that Abramov's stories and novels teem with characters as unlike one another as trees of the same species growing in a forest.

The north of European Russia and its people—young and old, peasants and intellectuals, Party functionaries and local administrators—held Abramov's interest overwhelmingly till the last days of his life. His heritage is an example of a writer's ability, while focussing his gaze on a comparatively small segment of society, to rise to artistic analysis of the most important phenomena and most pressing problems in the life of the country, to hear the tread of Time as it were.

This applies, first and foremost, to his tetralogy *The Pryaslins,* which was awarded the USSR State Prize for Literature, and also to his long and short stories, the best of which are represented in this collection.

The tetralogy consists of the novels *Brothers and Sisters, Two Winters and Three Summers, Roads and Byways* and *The House,* and every word in them was dictated by the harsh times they describe. The war against nazi Germany was the severest, most devastating trial, which did not bypass any single Russian, whether he was fighting at the front or working in the rear. The lives of the young Pryaslins are typical, with minor modifications for personal events, age and geography, of the life of every Russian young person during the war, with its hunger, hard, grownup toil, its instinctive longing for carefree childhood, and the death notices which only very few households were spared.

From the pages of *The Pryaslins* arises the collective image of a people who, when subjected to one of the most gruesome ordeals that ever fell to a country's lot, accepted the crushing burden and did not waver or bend underneath it. The author remains faithful to the truth throughout, never once yielding to the temptation of smoothing things over to please some or blackening them to please others. "The book is populated by characters, who are wonderfully alive and natural, and the reader feels personally concerned with the fate of each of them," Alexander Tvardovsky wrote to the author after reading the novel *Two Winters and Three Summers.*

Tvardovsky made special note of the image of Mikhail Pryaslin's sister Liza: "She is a real artistic discovery, and the charm of this image is not comparable with anything else in our present-day literature."

Whether by chance or as a consequence of some deep inner logic, most of Abramov's short stories are centered on an image of a Russian peasant woman. Old Milentyevna appears in "Wooden Horses" as the Russian national character incarnate. This woman, cruelly though she has been treated by life, is wise, kind and strong in spirit. One might have expected her to have become embittered because of the hardships and losses that had dogged her along her life's path. But yet now, in her declining years, this woman who was "pushed into marriage" at the age of sixteen—"into a den of wild beasts"—remains an impressive example of inner beauty.

9

"The herd of wooden horses" reared by Milentyevna—a horse for every house; her father-in-law's words spoken at a dire hour in front of many people: "Thank you for making men of us fools"; her reputation for "quiet patience", firmness and flinty determination—these are but a few gems from that great spiritual treasure store which has been created by "a peasant woman from the dense northern forests, unknown yet great in her active life". Abramov does not often utter "lofty" words. But when he does say them, they are worth their weight in gold.

Profound respect for the Russian peasant, for his historical role in clearing the forests and cultivating the soil of northern Russia, for his self-sacrifice during the war years is combined in the outlook of Abramov, the realist writer, with a sober understanding of the historically limited patriarchal psychology of the peasant and everything that this psychology involves.

"Pelageya" and "Alka", which followed one another chronologically, could well be called "A Story of Mother and Daughter". Like all Abramov's works, these stories triggered off lively critical debate. True to himself, the writer again confronts his reader with crucial moral issues. The purpose and meaning of life in their various interpretations are presented on the example of two women, the baker Pelageya and her daughter Alka.

Pelageya is a woman of rare industry, competence and self-sacrifice. At the same time she is petty, envious and heartless to all with the exception of her daughter, but even her love for Alka is visibly stamped with possessiveness.

Pelegeya's aims in life seem to be irreproachable: she wants to have a full prosperous home so she won't be ashamed before respected people; she wants to bring up her daughter to be a credit to the family name. Yet her own life ends in complete moral bankruptcy, in emptiness and loneliness. Her husband Pavel dies before his time largely due to her hard-heartedness and despotism. "Forgive me, forgive me, Pavel! It was I, I who drove you to the grave!" Pelageya cries when her eyes are opened to the grief she has brought upon herself. The most precious person in her life, her daughter, leaves home after Pelageya practically pushes her into the bed of a scoundrel, bedazzled by his officer's uniform and imagining herself working for her daughter's happiness.

How can such mutually exclusive traits be contained within one person? How are we to reconcile the author's ruthless exposure of his heroine and his obvious love and pity for her?

The explanation is that Abramov followed Pelageya throughout her entire life and was a party to her successes and a witness to her failures. He conceals nothing and is ashamed of nothing. The things that ruin Pelageya's life and are at variance with her inner essence are all traceable to that very "idiocy of peasant life" Lenin spoke of, a mentality that becomes as deeply ingrained as soot and is only removed with as much difficulty and at the price of much suffering. In townsfolk we also find this mentality and refer to it as pedestrianism, consumerism, and the like.

But the time will come in Pelageya's life when she will realise that there is something wrong with her set of values: "What was she to do now, how was she to go on living?" she asked herself. "Whatever she did, it all went wrong, missed the mark." This time will come, but not before Pelageya has buried her husband, not before her daughter has run away from home, not before—and this is really the last straw—Pelageya makes a fool of herself over a plush jacket, which is sold to her as a favour when it has long gone out of fashion. Until then, until all her notions tumble down, her concepts of life, of relations between people, of the traditional rural hierarchy, of advantages and disadvantages remain as firm and unchangeable as the path from her home to the bakery which she has trodden for years two or three times every day and which, after her death comes to be known in the village as "Pelageya's path".

Pelageya is invited to two parties at once—to the birthday of her sister-in-law Anisya and to the home of the local "big wig" Pyotr Ivanovich. Without a moment's hesitation Pelageya chooses the latter. "Pyotr Ivanovich invited folks who counted. He was not the man to pour his wine down the throats of rag-tag-and-bobtail," she reasons. He will have "the men at the top—the chairmen of the rural Soviet and of the kolkhoz..." It was worth her while to chat with every one of them of some business or other or at least to walk "arm-in-arm with Soviet Authority" so that all should see.

The profitable job at the bakery was not presented to Pelageya on a platter. To get it she sacrificed her woman's honour.

" 'If you let me sleep on your hair, I swear to God in a week you'll work in the bakery,' Olesha promised her. 'I'm not jesting.'

11

" 'I'm not jesting either.'

"Within a week she was installed at the bakery. Olesha kept his word... Well, she too kept her word—after the first day she stayed all night at the bakery..."

Enough quotations though! I hope I have made my point clear. Abramov's every line, every word, even though it comes from the heroine herself, seem to pillory her for all to see her shame. One imagines she will never be able to rise again. But no, she never really fell. We are exasperated, resentful, and contemptuous, but at the same time we sympathize with Pelageya and even admire her. Yes, we can't help admiring her intrepid strength, her tenacity, her devotion to her home and hearth that is stronger than life itself, her astute and sober mind, which she uses as a sharp knife to cut through the tangle of prejudice that is pulling her down. And she does cut through, on more than one occasion. And, of course, her most admirable quality is the ability to work, indefatigably and conscientiously, her hunger for work, whatever curses she may heap on her bakery in a moment of weakness. "She had always regarded the bakery as a millstone round her neck, as grinding toil. But it seemed that without that toil, without that millstone she could't breathe." Her harsh intonation softens when she speaks of the loaves she used to bake: "The loaves were pleasant to see and to handle, they seemed to smile at you. Almost flew into your mouth."

And it was not just the loaves, although making bread was the main thing in Pelageya's life, both a job and an art. She actually says to her daughter: "Mine's the most important job on earth, if you want to know. I bake bread, I make life itself..."

Whether it's "sweating" about the house, or "hopping off" into the woods for berries or mushrooms—here, too, Pelageya had no equal. She loved work and detested those who did not work well, did not like working, who did not sense the poetry of work. Never mind that this simple baker-woman did not have the word "poetry" in her vocabulary—all the same her attitude towards work fully deserves to be called poetical. It was poetical in happiness, as when she rejoiced in the fruits of her labour, and in grief, as she watched her bakery going to the dogs because of the bungling lazy way Alka went about the work in her mother's absence: "Twelve loaves, no less, were wet and 'sad', you couldn't say whether they'd been baked in

12

the oven or in the sun."

" 'Is this your first time in the bakery? Didn't you see how your mother did it?' Pelageya demanded indignantly.

"An offshoot" of her own, "a young filly" she could at least reprimand. But what weight did her words carry with Ulka, a grown woman who took her place at the bakery when Pelageya fell ill? "Pelageya left without sitting down. She dared not even cast a farewell glance at the dirty samovar and washbowl, at the stove that had not been whitewashed once since she left. Because she felt as though all of them—the samovar, the washbowl and the stove—were looking reproachfully at her."

The narration in "Pelageya"is thoughtful and unhurried, its music tuned to Pelageya's mood in her last months of life, a mood both sad and light, finding succour in all the good things she had accomplished and blaming herself ruthlessly, though belatedly for having wasted her life on trifles, for having thinned it out like her own glorious hair, once like a wave of gold and now "a wisp of colourless tow". All her hopes were pinned on her daughter Alka: "...if the Amosovs were to rise in the world, she thought, it would be only through Alka. Through her beauty. Through that capricious gold..."

But the beautiful, irrepressible Alka, daunted by her mother's hard life, renounces her mother's passionate dream of "making good". While not hampered by her mother's failings however, neither does she possess her mother's talent for work and love of it. She is truly a restless young filly cantering through life, chasing away, while she has strength and health, the nagging thoughts about the price she will inevitably have to pay for her frivolous superficiality.

Pelageya's life ends on a note of frustration. Nonetheless, the good she has done has not been forgotten by her fellow-villagers, who gave her name to the path leading from her house to the bakery, the path she trod for 20 years. People coming from the city and hearing about "Pelageya's path" asked who was the woman so honoured. "It 'mazed them that a path should be named after a person who lived in our own time. This is like a monument, they said."

Alka's life is only beginning. What will she leave behind for people to remember her by?

"Pelageya" and "Alka" are an elegy about great human potential gone to waste. The author's sympathy for the heroines is so frank, his pain so poignant, that his lament for

13

these misguided lives has not an enfeebling but an ennobling effect on the reader, making him more demanding of himself and others, strengthening his aspiration to reach the ideal.

The gallery of women's portraits in Abramov's stories is as vast and endless as life itself. These stories may be quite long, like "A Disciple of Avvakum", or occupy just two or three pages, like "Hands of Gold", "Polya-Open-Your-Eyes" or "The Happiest Woman". Some of these miniatures were a year, or even several years, in the writing—hence their impact. There would be a fleeting impression that germinated in the depth of Abramov's heart like a pearl in its shell until the little masterpiece came to fruition.

"The Happiest Woman" is a story about a woman who was badly maltreated by her father-in-law but who took him into her house when he lost his sight and was abandoned by his own sons. She did this out of the goodness of her heart, but she firmly believed that this good deed was rewarded by Fate and that because of it she became "the happiest woman in the village": "I had four men fighting in the war, my husband and three sons, and every one of them came back."

Such is the popular concept of happiness, which the author fully subscribes to.

A man of the generation whose youth fell to the years of life-and-death struggle against nazism, Abramov the writer feels the closest affinity for the women of his generation. No, he does not idealise them or put them on a pedestal. Very often, their lives end as sadly as Pelageya's.

But in every one of Abramov's stories you are aware of his profound respect for the ordinary Russian woman who, during the grim years of the war, together with millions of her kind, put her shoulder readily and uncomplainingly to a burden of unheard of heaviness. This, naturally, did not make her an angel who floated into our own time on snow-white wings.

It was as though Abramov felt it was incumbent upon him to say a kind word about his women contemporaries in reparation for the involuntary guilt incurred in regard to them by Time, History and the People. For the benefit of coming generations, Abramov sought to light up with the magic lantern of art the deep-lying truth, the rich beauty of character of the Russian woman.

The heroine of "Jobbely", a peasant woman from a remote northern village, has spent all fifty years of her life

14

working and caring for her family—a typical enough fate. Quite a lot of family and other troubles fell to her lot. But neither the years nor the hardships have broken her spirit. On the day of her fiftieth "jobbely", glowing in the warmth of love and admiration of her fellow-villagers, she blossomed not only spiritually but physically, suddenly becoming younger and prettier than her own daughters, who were "nothing to look at compared with their mother, like dry crusts beside a luscious cake, in spite of their perms and gold rings..." She made merry and danced at her fiftieth birthday with tremendous, infectious abandon. Holidays are rare in the life of a simple village woman, the writer seems to tells us, so don't miss the occasion to admire her at the time when she rises to her full stature!

Abramov was always happy to discover that other people shared his sentiments towards the Russian woman. This is the message of his story "The Blue-Eyed Elephant", telling about an anniversary celebration of a modest clerk-secretary type woman, for which teachers and scholars gathered from all over the country—and not out of a sense of duty but from a sincere desire to be with her.

"I knew many of them personally, having met them at various meetings and conferences, and some I saw for the first time because they lived and worked in the Far East, in Siberia, in the Urals, on the Kola Peninsula.

" 'They had come specially for the occasion, you mean?'

" 'Sure thing! Why, for Maria Tikhonovna's anniversary people would've come from the next world, to say nothing of some far-off corner of this one...' "

The austere, chaste, restrained word-painting conveys an inexpressibly pure and heart-felt "Abramovian" veneration of the Russian woman.

"What mines of spiritual treasure, what wealth of spiritual light! Endless self-sacrifice, an acute Russian conscience and sense of duty, an ability for self-denial and compassion, love of work, of the land, of all things that live on it—you cannot enumerate it all," said Fyodor Abramov of the Russian woman in his speech at the 6th Congress of Soviet writers. These words contained his symbol of faith, a key to the understanding of his entire work. They were an expression of his love and pain.

Boris Pankin

Wooden Horses

1

For many days now there had been talk in the house about the coming of Maxim's mother Milentyevna—and not only talk, either; preparations had been thorough and energetic.

For instance, Maxim himself, who, like most childless men, as a rule was apt to let things slide around the house, had been hard at work the whole of Sunday. He had taken apart and rebuilt the stove in the bath-house, he had repaired the fence, he had chopped for firewood the fir stumps which had lain under the windows ever since the spring and finally, when it was too dark for anything else, had laid a board walk to the porch so that his mother wouldn't have to wade through dew-wet grass in the mornings.

But this was nothing to the elbow-grease expended by Maxim's wife Yevgenia. Everything had to be washed, scoured and scraped throughout house, entry and loft, then the best coloured runners were laid down and the old brass bowl for washing was polished to a fine glitter.

In fact, it had certainly been no secret to me that Milentyevna was coming; yet when the old woman actually did arrive it caught me as unprepared as a fall of snow from the roof.

I was across the river putting down a net when the boat carrying Milentyevna and her younger son Ivan with whom she lived tied up by the village. It was already fairly dark, with mist floating over the river, and my ears rather than my eyes told me what was going on.

It was a boisterous welcome.

The first to come chasing down to the water was of course Zhuk, a small black dog belonging to the neighbours; he had a voice that could be heard for miles and he made full use of it whenever he heard an engine. Then came the familiar harsh jangle of a fastening as Maxim pulled excitedly at the door and ran out. Yevgenia's high-pitched voice called, "Oh, oh, look who's come to see us! " Other voices followed—Granny Mara's, old Stepan's, and Prokhor's. In fact, it looked as though everybody in Pizhma had come running out to meet Milentyevna; and I was the only disgruntled soul who wished her farther.

For many years I had longed to find some quiet rural back-water with all the joys of the wild—hunting and fishing, mushrooms and wild berries. And—most important of all—quietness, with none of those pestiferous loudspeakers which bawl from early morning until late at night in almost every village you can find, and without the metallic roar of machinery and trucks which I had more than enough of in town.

In Pizhma I had found the place of my dreams.

It was a tiny hamlet of seven houses on the bank of a river of considerable size and surrounded by forest— thickets of firs with plenty of game, buoyant pines with mushrooms growing under them. Trails that enticed your feet.

The one drawback was the weather; hardly a day passed without rain. But it failed to damp my mood. I had yet another interest—the house where I lodged.

What a place that was! Of dwelling-places alone there were four: the winter room, the summer room, a loft with a carved balcony and a spare room off at the side. Then there was a well-lighted entry with steps down to the porch, and a store room, and a roomy lean-to shed.

So when my good host and hostess were out (and they were always at work during the day) I delighted in wandering about that marvellous house. Barefoot, without haste. Strolling. To get the feel of times past not only in heart and mind, but through the very soles of my feet.

But the coming of this old lady would put an end to all my explorations, that was clear. And to my museum hobby, the name I gave to collecting old peasant dishes and implements scattered all over the place. How could I bring indoors some dusty birchwood bowl and turn it this way and that right in front of the former mistress of this house? As for other pleasant habits such as lying sprawled out on the bed in the middle of the day smoking the place out with cigarettes—I could just forget them. Nothing doing! Not with an old woman in the house.

For a long time I sat in the moored boat.

The mist already lay thick on the water and the lights in my host's house on the far side were dull yellow patches, stars had scattered over the sky (yes, there was everything, mist and stars) and still I sat, blowing on the flame of rancour.

They called me. Maxim himself called, so did Yevgenia, but I nursed my stubbornness and kept silent. At one time I even thought of going to spend the night at Rusikha, a big village three or four kilometres downstream, but I feared to lose my way in the fog. Even the local people would have had a job to find the track through the pastures, let alone a stranger like myself.

So I sat there glumly in the boat and waited. Waited for the lights to go out on the other side so as to postpone meeting that old woman at least for a little while, till tomorrow, till the morning.

I don't know how long I sat there—two hours, three or perhaps even four. Enough, surely, for them to have had a dozen suppers. But still that light shone through the fog.

I was hungry; coming back from the woods I had been in such a hurry to get off fishing that I hadn't even waited to have dinner, I shivered, my teeth chattered from the damp chill of night; so at last—after all, there was no sense in this—I picked up the oars.

Now the light did me good service. With its guidance I crossed easily without missing my way in the fog, followed the path past the old bath-house and through the kitchen garden to the house.

To my considerable surprise it was silent; had it not been for the bright light in the window one might have thought everyone was asleep.

I stood under the window listening, and finally decided not to go inside but to climb straight up to my loft.

However, when I opened the door the iron fastening made such a clatter that the very house seemed to vibrate, and that spoiled my idea of slipping in quietly.

"You found your way, then?" said a voice from the bed on top of the great brick stove. "God be praised. And there was me, lying here hoping all was well."

"What could go ill?" said Yevgenia with some irritation. She, too, was awake, although she had gone to bed. "She put the light there for you," and she nodded at the lamp standing on the windowsill behind the head of the wide nickel-plated bed. "So's our lodger wouldn't get lost in the fog, Ma said. Like a child, that lodger, wouldn't have the wits to get back himself."

"Nay, but aught can happen." That was the old woman again, speaking from the stove-bed. "One time there was, my master was going up and down the river all night, hardly got himself home. A real bad fog, that was."

Grunting, wry-faced, Yevgenia started getting herself out of bed to give me supper, but food was the last thing I wanted at that moment. Never in my life, I think, had I felt so ashamed of myself, of my foolish sulks, and without even venturing to lift my eyes to the stove-top where the old woman lay, I bolted out of the room.

3

I always wakened early, as soon as my hosts began moving below. Today, however, although the old wooden cottage groaned and trembled in every beam, every board, I made myself stay abed until eight. For today, at least, I would not fail in consideration for an old woman who would naturally want to rest after her journey.

When I did finally descend, however, to my astonishment I saw only Yevgenia.

"But where are your visitors?" I did not need to ask about Maxim; he was at home only on Sundays; after that he went off for the whole week to the tar distillery where he was foreman.

"Gone like the morning dew! " she replied gaily. "Ivan went back home—didn't you hear the engine?—and Ma—of course she's gone off to get mushrooms for pickling."

"Mushrooms? Milentyevna?"

"So what?" Yevgenia cast a quick look at the old flower-patterned clock hanging on the front wall alongside the cherry-wood dish-cupboard. "She went with the first light— not yet five, it wasn't."

"All alone?"

"Mushrooming? And why not? How long is it since I've lived here? More'n seven years, for sure. And never a year she hasn't come about this time. And what doesn't she bring in! Mushrooms, and berries, too. A treat for Nastya."

Here Yevgenia cast a quick secretive glance round, village fashion, and dropped her voice to a whisper. "It's only because of her Nastya stops with Ivan. It's God's truth! She told me herself back in spring when she took him to town to cure him of the drink. She was that sore at him! 'I wouldn't stand it another day with that devil,' she says, 'but I'd be main sad to leave Ma.' Aye, that's what our Milentyevna's like," she concluded with a touch of pride, picking up the poker. "Me and Maxim, it's like as if there's new life in us when she comes here."

That was true, I had never seen Yevgenia so light-footed and active. As a rule, dragging about the house in the mornings in old felt boots and a quilted jacket, she would wheeze and groan and complain of pains in her legs and her back—she had had a hard life, like most village women whose youth had been one of wartime toil. She had made thirteen rafting trips the length of the river. Think of that!

But now—now I couldn't take my eyes off her. It was like a miracle, as though she'd been sprinkled with the water of life. The long poker didn't stir the fire, it danced in it, and the reflection of the flames flickered on her dark, rejuvenated face, on her round black eyes usually so austere, now smiling gently.

I too felt some inexplicable zest for life. I quickly splashed water over my face, thrust my feet into galoshes and ran outside.

The fog was thick—it was only now I realised that it had not been white curtains that blanked out the windows. That fog covered the whole river. I could not see even the tops of the fir trees on the farther bank.

Somewhere over there, on the other side, old Milentyevna was wandering in the cold damp fog with her basket; a quick mental picture of her sent me running to the shed to chop some wood, it might be needed to heat up the bath-house for a chilled old woman.

4

I went down to the river three times that morning, and Yevgenia probably as many, but all the same we missed Milentyevna. She appeared suddenly just as Yevgenia and I were having breakfast.

Whether the porch door was unfastened, or whether we were absorbed in talk I can't say, but all of a sudden the door swung back and I saw her, tall, soaking wet, her skirt tucked up in the old peasant style, carrying two birch-bark baskets full of mushrooms.

We jumped up to take the baskets while Milentyevna herself, stepping rather shakily, went to the bench by the stove and sat down.

She was tired, of course. It showed in her thin, fine-featured face, washed to pallor by the thick fog, and in a faint trembling of her head. Yet at the same time her blue eyes, under slightly drooping lids, held quiet satisfaction and happiness. It was the satisfaction of an old woman who has done a good job well and once more proved to herself and others that she is still of use in the world. I remembered my mother when she was alive, and the glow of satisfaction in her eyes when she came home in the evening after working in the fields, or mowing till she was ready to drop.

Yevgenia, the good daughter-in-law, was up and bustling at once, with remarks like "Here we are filling our bellies and she's done a day's work, that's what she's like, our Granny". She brought in a light tub, ready washed and scoured for salting mushrooms, hurried into the pantry for salt, then out into the kitchen garden to break off fragrant currant leaves, and finally, when Milentyevna had rested and gone into the other room to change, she folded up the colourful runners in the middle of the room, preparing a place for the salting.

"You think she'd take a bite or sup now," Yevgenia rattled on, as though explaining why she didn't start by sitting her mother-in-law down to a meal. "Not for aught in the world! She keeps to the old ways, better not talk of eating till the mushrooms are picked over."

We sat down right on the bare floor, close together. Bright reflections of the sun played round us and the smell of mushrooms mingled with the warm scents of the house; it was a real joy to look at old Milentyevna, now in a dry gingham frock, at her dark veined hands dipping into the bucket, into the tub, into the enamel pan of salt—because of course she entrusted the actual salting to nobody else.

The mushrooms were firm and perfect.

I lifted one after another with great care from the basket and before picking off the rubbish, raised it to the light.

"You'll never have seen aught like these, eh?" Yevgenia

asked slyly—a teasing hint about my own very modest forest booty. "Aye, you go to the same woods, but you can't find the same mushrooms. And no marvel. She's been at home in them fir trees over the river right from her wedding night. And nigh got her belly riddled for them mushrooms, too."

I stared—what on earth was she talking about?

"Why, didn't you ever hear tell of it?" she said, amazed at such ignorance. "How her man shot a gun at her? Come, Ma, tell him how it all was."

"Nay, what's there to tell?" Milentyevna sighed. "All sorts can happen in your own family."

"Your own—but he nigh killed you! "

"If it was but nigh, then it was naught."

Yevgenia's black eyes widened till they were quite round. "Eh, Ma, I don't know. Wi' you it's all upside down and inside out. Maybe you'll be saying next naught happened at all? Maybe it wasn't after that, you got that shaking of your head?"

With the back of her hand Yevgenia pushed a strand of hair behind a small ear with a red earring, and seeing, evidently, that there was nothing to be got from her mother-in-law, began the tale herself.

"Milentyevna was just turned sixteen when they married her off. Maybe she hadn't even her breasts grown yet, I know I didn't when I was that age. And how it 'ud be with a maid after—'twas little thought they had for that, them days. Her father had no eyes but for his son-in-law's house and stock. Only one lad in the house, you'll have it all to yourself. Now, what could you have to yourself with a village full of savages, real wild men?"

"Well, not all of them, maybe," Milentyevna objected mildly.

"Don't you try to defend them. Anyone'll say the same. Savages. Why, I mind it all myself. There was times, on big holidays, they'd come to our village, the whole gang of 'em. Married or not, it made no difference, there they were. Bearded and beardless. They'd go about bawling, pestering all they met, making the place stink, fighting all up and down the village. And at home with none to see them it beat all, the way they went on. Not one of 'em but 'ud think up some daftness. One put on a woman's sarafan, another—it was Martynko-Siskin—went off to the river for water on skis. Summer it was, and hot, and he put on sheepskins with the wool outside. And Isaac Petrovich, his wits went a-wandering, he thought he was a bishop. I heard tell he'd wait for evening, put a dark blue quilt-cover on him and went from house to house singing psalms. Wasn't it like that, Ma? It's right what I say?"

"We've all got our faults," Milentyevna said evasively.

"Faults! What faults did you have, at sixteen, for him to shoot off a gun at you? Nay, it's the breed. All their days in the woods, and no other folks round—will-ye nill-ye, you'll get wild and mad and bad. And they threw a maid of sixteen into that den of wild beasts—live or die, that's your own business.

"Well, Ma thought the best thing she could do was get her father and mother-in-law on her side. Try all she could to please them. And how'd you best please them in those days? With hard work.

"Now, them as is new-wed find plenty to do their first night, but Vasilissa Milentyevna was up wi' the dawn and off over the river for mushrooms. It was autumn, wasn't it, Ma?"

"Yes, seemingly it was." The reply came unwillingly.

"Not seemingly, but right," said Yevgenia confidently. "You don't find so many in summer, but you got a basketful in an hour or two. How long would you be traipsing about the woods with a husband waiting at home?

"So back she came from the woods, right pleased. Not a chimney smoking in the village, all still abed, here she was bringing mushrooms. They'd be well satisfied with her, she thought. Aye, they gave her satisfied. Soon's she'd crossed the river and took one step away from the boat, bang! A shot right in her face. Her lord and master welcoming his young bride."

The sinews on the old woman's wrinkled neck tautened like cords, her stooping back straightened—she wanted to still the tremors which had noticeably increased. But Yevgenia saw nothing of it. She was gripped as strongly as her mother-in-law by the events of the far-distant morning, which she knew only from what others had told her, and her dark face alternately flushed and paled.

"It was God, God saved Ma then. It's just a stone's throw from the kitchen garden to the bath-house. And Ma was just coming to the bath-house when he aimed his gun at her, but likely his hand shook from the drink or it'd have been the end of her. There's shot in the bath-house door still.

24

Haven't you seen it?" This was addressed to me. "Take a look, take a look. When my own man brought me here, what d'you think he showed me first? The house? All his gold and silver? Nay, he led me straight to the bath-house. 'Here's where my father gave Ma a lesson,' he said. There's a wild woodsman for you! And they're all the same, all of 'em. The lock-up's gaping for every one of 'em."

I could see old Milentyevna was tired of the subject, our tactless insistence displeased her. Yet—how can you stop when you're carried away by such a strange story?

"But what was all that rumpus about?"

"The shooting?" Yevgenia liked to call a spade a spade. "Because of Bald Vanka. That devil, God forgive me for calling my father-in-law names, he woke up in the morn— where was it you were sleeping, Ma? In the lean-to? Well, he stretched out his hand—no one there. Out he went, and there she was, his young wife. Coming back from across the river. Well, then he went real crazy. So that's it, he thinks, she went off to Bald Vanka! They'd arranged it! "

Milentyevna, who seemed to have got herself in hand again, enquired not without malice, "And how do you come to know what your father-in-law was thinking?"

"And how'd I not know? Folks told me, that's how. And that Bald Vanka, he used to say, when he'd had a glass, 'Lads, I belong to two villages, my body's at home and my heart's in Pizhma.' He said it right up to the time he died. Aye, he was a handsome fellow, all right.

"Why make any bones about it? Ma always had plenty of fellows after her. She was real pretty. Why, look at her now—you could marry her off tomorrow," Yevgenia flattered, and smiled—for the first time, I think, in all her talk.

Then, with a somehow affected roll of her narrowed sombre eyes she said teasingly, "Though I wouldn't say you showed sense either, Ma. You may have been a bit of a girl, but old enough to know what a man marries you for. Not to have you running off for mushrooms the very first night—! "

Oh, how old Milentyevna's quiet blue eyes flashed! It was as though a thunderstorm passed outside the window, as though a red-hot lightning ball had burst.

Yevgenia wilted in confusion, and I myself didn't know where to look.

For some time we sat there in silence, very carefully

cleaning rubbish from the mushrooms.

Milentyevna took the first step to reconciliation.

"I was looking back on my life today," she said. "Walking there in the woods, but in my mind, walking the long road back. Sixty years it is, now."

"Sixty since you married into Pizhma?" I asked.

"Since I was pushed out into Pizhma, more like," she answered with a tinge of mockery. "It's true, what she said—I never had my youth. And if you put it as they talk now, I didn't love my husband."

"There you are! " cried Yevgenia, not without a touch of triumph. "You admit it! But me—I can't open my mouth, whatever I say's wrong."

"When ye rasp a sore place, even old wood creaks," said Milentyevna placatingly.

The mushrooms were nearly finished. Yevgenia set an empty box on her knees and started picking the berries out of the mushroom trash. She was sulky, but all the same cast inquisitive glances now and then at the old woman, who was back in the past again.

"Old folk like to praise the old times," said Milentyevna quietly, thoughtfully. "But I've little good to say about them. Folks nowadays have got learning and can stand up for themselves, but we didn't have any freedom in our young days. I was married off—would you believe it—for a sheepskin coat and a shawl."

"What—no?! " cried Yevgenia, wildly excited. "That I never heard! "

There was nothing left of her recent annoyance. The avid curiosity of a countrywoman, rooted so deeply in her, pushed back every other feeling and her burning eyes bored into her mother-in-law.

"It was this way," said Milentyevna. "Father was building, he wanted a fine house, he grudged every kopek; and there was me, a maid grown. It would be shame and disgrace if his daughter came out on feast-days without a new sheepskin and shawl, so when the matchmakers came from Pizhma saying they'd take me without either, he gave way."

"But where were your brothers?" Yevgenia interrupted hotly, and turned to me. "She'd good brothers, Ma had. They thought the world of her, they'd ha' done aught for her, they would. When she was wed, and they'd got their own families, still they always helped their sister."

26

"They were away in the forest," said Milentyevna, "cutting wood for the house."

Yevgenia nodded eagerly.

"Aye, then it's clear. It's always puzzled me, how such brothers, the best lads in the village—Ma came from a good house—how they couldn't stand up for the sister they were so fond of. But that's how it was—they weren't there when you was wed."

After that, digging out additional details she had not known, Yevgenia gradually got the talk back into her own hands. And soon Milentyevna's quiet voice was not heard at all.

Yevgenia was completely absorbed in the long-past drama of her mother-in-law.

"It's awful, awful what could have happened." She gestured energetically. "The brothers heard tell he'd shot at their sister and came galloping over. With guns. 'Just say one word, sister, and we'll riddle him like a sieve.' Dashing lads, they were, and hot-tempered. And strong—they'd break a bear in two, let alone a man. But Ma, she just told them: 'Take shame, dear brothers, to come rampaging for naught and getting folk all upset. Our young master was trying a gun, he was going off hunting, and you get dear Lord knows what into your heads.'

"Now, there's wisdom for you—and she but sixteen! " Yevgenia looked proudly at her mother-in-law, whose eyes were on the floor. "Nay, if my Maxim had ever raised his hand to me, I'd never have stood it. I'd have taken him to court and put him away where he belonged. But she—she just shook her head and scolded her brothers: 'What are you interfering for? Where's your wits? It's late now for me to go back when I've a woman's shawl on my head. I've got to make my life here.' That's the turn she gave things."

Yevgenia let out a sudden sob. She really was a kindly soul.

"And her father-in-law—he was nigh ready to kiss her feet for it. Aye, and why not, there could ha' been murder done, that's sure. Them brothers was real blazing mad, wouldn't have thought twice of making an end of Miron. I was but a mite then, and I've little memory of Onika Ivanovich, but old folks remember to this day. Wherever he went, nigh or far, there'd always be a gift for his dear Vasilissa. And if he'd had a drink and they wanted him to stop overnight—'Nay lads,' he'd say, 'I'll get me home, I want to see my Vasilissa the Beautiful.' That's what he always called her when he'd had a drink."

"That's right, so he did," Milentyevna sighed and I thought her old eyes which had seen so much were misty.

Yevgenia evidently saw it too. She went on, "Aye, there's cause to bless the memory of Onika Ivanovich. Maybe he was the only good, decent man in the village. All the rest were real *urvais*.* They're all even called by that name in Pizhma, Urvayev. And my man's father, Miron Onikovich, he was an *urvai* too. And a right one. Now, how'd any other have borne himself after a thing like that? Quiet and canny. But that one was just the contrary way. Never satisfied."

Milentyevna raised her head, evidently she wanted to defend her husband but Yevgenia had the bit in her teeth again and gave her no chance to say a word.

"And no call to whitewash him. All knew what he was like. If he'd had any goodness in him, would he have kept you shut up here in Pizhma ten years and never let you stir a foot out? Ma could never go anywhere—not to festivals, not even to her parents. And she'd have to sit at home in the evening spinning yarn, alone, instead of joining the other women. Jealous he was—awful!

"But that's how it was," Yevgenia shrugged. "There was naught could please him. Well now, was it his wife's fault if all the children were the spitting image of her and none like their father? But he blamed her for that, too, with his 'Whose are them fledglings round my table?' He'd always start on like that when he'd taken a drink. And what did he have to grumble at? He was no beauty, for sure—scraggy and black like a charred stump from the fire, and pitted with the smallpox as if wasps had bored into him. He ought to have been glad and thanked God the little 'uns didn't take after him! "

I don't know whether Milentyevna disliked the way Yevgenia dealt with her past life or whether, like an old-style peasant woman, she was not used to sitting idle—anyway, she rose heavily to her feet and the conversation broke off short.

* A local word meaning lawless, predatory.—*Tr.*

Maxim's house was the only one in the village which faced down to the river; the others all had their backs to it and faced the street.

Yevgenia, who had little good to say for Pizhma, explained it simply.

"*Urvais*. Stick out their ugly arses just to rile folks! "

That was not the real reason of course. The village stood on the south bank of the river, and the houses faced the sun, which was not a very frequent visitor in those forested parts.

I loved that quiet hamlet smelling of the barley hung to dry in fat sheaves on fencepoles. I liked the old-style wells with their tall sweeps and the spacious barns on cone-shaped supports. But most of all I liked the Pizhma houses, big log houses with wooden horses on the roofs.

Actually, a house crowned with a horse is nothing out-of-the-way in the North, but I had never seen a village where every house had one. Only Pizhma. You walk along the narrow grassy path which is all the dearth of inhabitants has left of the village street, and seven wooden horses look down at you from above.

"There used to be more," said Milentyevna, walking beside me. "Our wooden herd came to a score."

Many times already that day I had had cause to marvel at the old woman.

After breakfast I had expected her to think of resting at her age. But when she rose from the table she went out into the entrance, brought back a flat birch-bark basket and began fastening straps to it made of old homespun.

"Where are you going?" I asked. "Not to the forest again?"

"Nay, not this time. I'll go to my elder daughter in Rusikha," she said.

"But what's the basket for?"

"If all goes well I'll go into the woods in the morn, early. The milkmaids go to work on trucks, they'll take me with them. I haven't time to waste, you see, they only let me come a wee while this time, just a week."

Till then Yevgenia had taken no part in the talk, she was preparing to leave for work, but now words came bursting out.

"A wee while, is it? But that's always the way. She's

always on the go, never sits quiet. If it were me I'd lie about all day long, what, then—are people born only to toil and moil all day and every day?"

I said I'd go with Milentyevna to the ferry—the ferryman might be off drinking again and the old woman would need help. But it turned out she had helpers without me. We'd barely drawn level with the stable, an old sagging barn at the edge of the village, when Prokhor Urvayev dashed out with a bandit whistle and yell on a rattling ungreased cart pulled by Thunderer, the one and only horse in Pizhma.

Thunderer had probably once been a spirited horse, but age had reduced him to a skeleton under a hide rotten with mange; if anyone could make that skeleton rattle his bones it was Prokhor, one of the three men still living in Pizhma.

Prokhor, of course, was tipsy as usual and stank of cheap eau-de-cologne.

"Hi, Aunt, Auntie! " he yelled as he rattled up. "See, I don't forget all you did for me. Been waiting with Thunderer since the morn, I knew you'd be going to the ford. Eh? Wasn't I right?"

Milentyevna did not refuse her nephew's help, and soon the cart was rolling over the green mown meadow towards the ferry at a sandy spit.

I returned home.

Yevgenia had gone to help the women gather peas in the field; it was just the moment for me to get down to my own occupations. I had a net waiting across the river, and I wanted to go into the woods, too—when would I find a better day?

But I entered the empty cottage, stood a while at the entrance, then turned into the lean-to.

It was Maxim who had first shown it to me (I had wanted to sleep in the hay-loft) and I remember how I gasped when I saw everything it held.

It was a whole peasant museum!

A horned reel, a hand-loom, a spindle, a painted distaff from Mezen, a scutcher, all kinds of boxes and baskets woven from pine slivers, birch-bark and roots, birch bread containers, flat baskets, the unpainted wooden bowls people used to take with them into the woods or distant meadows at mowing time, torch holders, duck-shaped salt-cellars and countless other pots, dishes, utensils and implements of work swept into a pile like rubbish.

"I ought to throw all that out," said Maxim as though excusing himself. "No use for it these days. But somehow—I can't do it. Those are the things fed my parents."

There were few days when I failed to glance into the lean-to. Not that these old things were new to me, I myself came from a similar kingdom of wood and bark. What actually was new was the beauty with which everything was carved and plaited; this I had never noticed before.

All her life long my mother always had a birch tow scutcher in her hands, but when did I ever notice that the scutcher itself was the colour of flax—a tender soft tint with a silvery sheen? And the birch-bark bread box, how could I not remember its golden glow? It descended onto our table like a long-awaited sun. All I called to mind was what had been inside and when.

Whatever I took in my hand, whatever I looked at—the old rusty sickle with its handle polished by many hands, the soft, melliferous bowl carved from strong birchwood—all of them opened up a special world of beauty to me—a quiet, very Russian beauty, with nothing loud or arresting, all created with axe and knife.

Today, however, after meeting the former mistress of this house, I made another discovery.

I realised that not only axe and knife had made things beautiful. The main moulding and polishing of these scutchers, sickles, baskets, wooden ploughs (yes, there was even one of those antediluvian instruments standing in a dark corner) had been done in the fields and meadows; it had come from gnarled peasant hands.

6

The next morning I saw rain; it had evidently set in for the day.

Like the previous day, Yevgenia and I waited a long time before sitting down to table, thinking Milentyevna might come any moment.

"She wouldn't go far a day like this," said Yevgenia. "She isn't a child."

Time passed, however, and the rain didn't slacken; I never left the window, but nobody appeared on the far bank. Finally I pulled on a raincoat and went to heat up the bath-house; the best thing for her after this downpour would be a steam bath, right away.

The Pizhma bath-houses, blackened by the chimneyless stoves which heat them, stand in a line not far from the river, beneath the kitchen gardens which bask on the rise.

The bath-houses are flooded in the spring and opposite each of them on the lower side log piers are dug into the ground, to hold back and break ice pushing up, in addition, strong hawsers of woven birch twigs run from them to the bath-house so that it stays moored like a ship.

I once asked Maxim the reason for all this—wouldn't it be simpler to set the bath-houses on top, where the kitchen gardens were planted?

Maxim laughed "like an *urvai*", as Yevgenia would have said.

"For better sport. Springtime, we'd all be shooting at them hunks of ice! Oy-oy-oy! With all the guns there! "

My first day there I had noticed the traces of birdshot in the smoky old door; it was pitted all over. Now, heating the bath-house and remembering Yevgenia's story of the previous day, I even tried to guess which were the shots fired that time at Milentyevna, a young bride. It was impossible, of course. And anyway, I had other things on my mind. I was worried about the Milentyevna of today, it must be drearily wet and cold in the woods.

Yevgenia, too, was worried. She could not sit quietly at home, but came out to join me.

"Eh, but I don't know. I don't know what to think," and she shook her head despondently. "Like enough she's gone off to Bogatka—can't be aught else. There's an obstinate old woman for you! Won't take heed no matter what you say. At her age—and out there tramping the woods in this weather——! "

Shading her eyes with a dark hand she peered across the river and went on with greater assurance:

"Aye, that's what she's done, gone off there. It was the same last year, here we were waiting and worrying, watching till our eyes ached, and off she'd gone to her Bogatka."

I had heard about Bogatka, a pasture three or four versts up river from Pizhma, but I had never heard of it being a good place for mushrooms or berries, so I asked Yevgenia.

She opened her eyes wide as she always did when asked something which to her was clear as daylight.

"Mushrooms? In Bogatka? Well, there might be some now, it's all grown over, the forest's moved in, but what it used to be was just grass. Onika Ivanovich, Ma's father-in-law—just he alone used to get a hundred ricks of hay. And she goes there every year, it was with her that Bogatka started. She's got an eye for all that's good. Before she came to Pizhma there was none ever heard the word Bogatka, it was just pasture for the beasts, that's all."

With a jerk of her head Yevgenia indicated the village.

"You see them wooden horses on the roofs? And how many of them? You won't find that many in all Rusikha. And tell me this, did they often use to paint the big gates? Only them as was real rich. But there in Pizhma they're all painted. There was times, going along the other bank at sunset, you'd be right feared, looked as if all Pizhma was ablaze. And all that's from Bogatka,* and it was Milentyevna showed them the riches of it."

I understood nothing. What riches was she talking about? Where was truth and where fantasy?

Thick smoke coming from the entry sent us closer to the small window, where we sat down on a bench under a pole with dry birch-twig switches depending from it.

Coughing from the smoke, Yevgenia eased her mind with a few words about her absent husband for the way he had laid the stove and then passed on to the other men of the hamlet.

"They're all *urvais* hereabouts. I spoke good of Onika Ivanovich yesterday because of Ma, but to tell you the truth, he was an *urvai* too. How'd he not be! Right till his old age he made his old woman put on her good clothes at night. Wi' other folk, they put on their best clothes to go out for holidays or where folks can see them, but he—he had to have her in silk at night. That's the bee he had in his bonnet. And what might a clod of a peasant think of when there was naught in the house but holes and cracks?

"It was Ma. Ma as put them on their feet," Yevgenia concluded with conviction. "It was when she was there that them *urvais* grew into men."

"How, then?"

"How did she put them on their feet? It was that Bogatka. With clearing. Way back till oldest times the North's stood up on clearings. Them as cleared the woods and ploughed

---

* From *bogaty*, rich.—*Tr.*

fields, they got grain and beasts. And Milenty Yegorovich, Ma's dad, he cleared more'n any other in Rusikha. Four grown sons—there was strength and power!

"But in Pizhma those *urvais* had everything upside down. All they thought of was hunting and fishing. But the soil— they'd no love of it. What their grandads had cleared they sowed, that was all. They didn't always have grain enough to last them to New Year. Sure, when there was a harvest of beasts in the woods, then there was singing. But when the woods were bare they went hungry.

"Well, Ma lived like that awhile, and then she saw something had to be done. No good going on that way, they had to work on the land. She'd a clear path to her father-in-law's heart already from that wedding night, so now she started dropping words—drop after drop with 'Dad, it's time to be sensible. Dad, we ought to live from the land.'

"All right. I wouldn't say he agreed exactly, but at any rate he didn't stand in the way. So Ma called her brothers: it's like this and that, dear brothers, come and help your sister. Well, they'd ha' put their hand in the fire for their Vasilissa. They picked a likely place and got rid of the growth, they cut the trees and burned the scrub, and in the autumn they sowed it all to rye.

"So then them *urvais* started scratching their heads. Because the rye that grew—nigh as tall as the firs. You know how it grows when the place has been fired. The hunting ended and the fishing. And they all took their axes.

"And when they did start—well! I don't remember it myself, I was little, but my mother told me about it, how she saw them working on that same Bogatka. I'd be going through the woods looking for the cow, she said, and there was a fire, and that big—up to the clouds. And a lot of naked men jumping round it. I just stopped right where I was, she said, I couldn't take a step. I thought it was wood goblins, what else? But it was *urvais*. Clearing the woods. They'd all taken off their clothes, they got hot, and they didn't want to get them torn, too, it wasn't like these days.

"And the way they tormented their little 'uns—my Maxim tells me about it, times—you'd never believe. Now tell me, can you imagine tying a toddler up like a dog on a string? But that's what they did. They'd fill a cup with milk

34

and put it on the floor, and leave the babe to crawl about all day while Pa and Ma were working. They were feared the little 'uns could set the house afire.

"So that was the *urvai* sort—wild," Yevgenia concluded again. "And why? All their lives they'd never really worked nor yet their fathers before them, they just shot and hunted, you can think for yourself the strength they'd gathered.

"Eh, Ma, Ma. She did it all for the best, but it turned out for the worst. They were sent away as kulaks when the collective farms were started."

The conclusion drew no gasp from me. Nobody's going to marvel in our days about the old story of the chips that fly when wood is chopped.

Yevgenia, however, took my silence ill. To her it seemed like indifference and there was an offended note in her voice as she continued.

"Aye, folks think naught of the old days now. It's all forgot—how the collective farms were set up, and how we went hungry in the war. Oh, I don't blame the young folks—youth's youth, they want to live their own lives, no time to be looking back; but nowadays even the old women aren't like right old women any more. You can see them going to Rusikha for their pensions, each bigger and stouter than the last. There aren't even bones left of their children killed in the war, but all they've got in their heads is to live long, and hoping there won't be war again. But about the woods taking back their fields and meadows—ne'er thought. They're full fed. With a pension coming in each month.

"I asked Granny Mara once: 'Doesn't it go to your heart? Aren't your eyes sore from it? Time was you'd look out of the window and see fields round, now it's all scrub.' But she just laughed. 'All the better, my girl, not so far to go for firewood.' And that's all an old woman thinks of. *Urvai*—a real *urvai*! And my Maxim's the same, just laughing and joking, never mind if the flood comes."

Yevgenia stopped, then sighed heavily.

"Nay, I'm a white crow in our days. Always worrying and bothered. Everything dragging at my nerves. And my heart aches for my mother-in-law. What d'you think? You try and try your best and then it's all your fault. That's what the times were. 'I wouldn't have minded for myself,' said Ma, 'I'd have borne aught. But bring such woe to others.' "

"What others?"

Yevgenia turned quickly to me and her black unwinking eyes blazed again.

"They cleaned out five farms. What d'you think? Back in the Civil War they'd taken the grain from the barns, but when collective farms came they really let themselves go. And with *urvais*, what could you expect? It all added up. If they'd kept quiet and spoken soft, maybe they wouldn't have been touched—everyone knew how it all started. And when folks came to sign them up for the kolkhoz they just said: No! Not for us! We've got our own kolkhoz. So the bosses got real mad at them. Well, it's true four of the men did come back. My father-in-law, Miron Onikovich, he came too though he was sick, but Onika Ivanovich stayed there.

"Eh, but it was awful, all that happened then. The year Ma told me it all I wished I hadn't heard. I could do naught but cry and cry."

Yevgenia sniffled noisily and wiped her eyes with her kerchief.

"Just think, now, the way things turn out, times. Ma was threshing rye in the barn when the thunderbolt fell on them. Yes, in the barn she was," she went on after a moment's musing. "And mighty glad she was, thinking God had given them grain once again. It was fine, big rye that year, maybe the best there'd ever been. And all of a sudden her little girl comes running with 'Ma, come home quick, they're taking Dad and Grandad away!'

"Well, Ma says she knew herself she ought to run. They made quick work of it them days, one-two and a man was gone, but she says her legs just wouldn't bear her, she couldn't keep on them. So she dragged herself to the gate on her knees. It was fearsome. Because it had all come because of her. If she hadn't talked the old man into doing that clearing, who'd have touched *urvais*? They'd always been paupers before.

"And it wasn't with abuse old Onika crushed Ma but with words of kindness. She expected aught but that—to be cursed with words that seared, you know what a man may well say at a time like that, but Onika suddenly went dropped on his knees and he says, 'Thank you, Vasilissa Milentyevna, for making men of us fools. And don't fret,' he says, 'I've no ill against you in my heart. I'll bless you to my last breath.' "

Yevgenia was frankly weeping now and just managed to finish in a choked voice, "So Ma never took leave of Onika Ivanovich. She fell down like one dead."

It was after three when Milentyevna arrived, more dead that alive—but with mushrooms. Carrying a heavy basket that creaked as she walked.

Actually, it was the creaking of her basket that told me of her approach to the shanty under the firs on the far side—I hadn't been able to wait and had crossed over myself.

Yevgenia, who had been even more worried and anxious than I had, started scolding the old woman like some foolish child before she was properly inside the door.

Granny Mara backed her up.

Granny Mara, a stout, red-faced old woman with impudent grey eyes, and Prokhor, had been in several times that day, rather tipsy, and always with the same questions: where was the visitor? Why were we keeping her hidden away?

Milentyevna was wet to the skin, blue and wrinkled with cold like an old mushroom, and the first thing Yevgenia did was to strip off her wet coat and shawl; after that she got well-warmed felt boots from the top of the stove, and pulled galoshes onto them.

"We'll get them wet boots off, and off with you quick into the bath-house."

"And a hot bath's just what she mustn't have," said Prokhor weightily. He was sitting by the small stove, smoking up the chimney.

"Shut your silly mouth!" Yevgenia cried. "You're drunk. You're just talking daft!"

"And why wouldn't I know? It's medicine."

"Medicine! Does medicine say you can't steam yourself?"

"Well now. Maybe she's got pneumonia. What then?"

Yevgenia hesitated. She cast a desperate look at Milentyevna who was sitting on the stove bench, eyes closed, breathing heavily; she looked at me, but I know even less about medicine than she did, and in the end she decided not to risk it.

So instead of the bath-house, Milentyevna was settled on the stove shelf.

All through this exchange of opinions about the bath-house, Granny Mara had been looking amused, wagging her big head in its red sateen kerchief. Now she spoke.

"Well, and where've you been and what have you seen?"

"What I needed, that I saw," Milentyevna answered quietly.

"Aye, but tell us what," Granny Mara smirked. "You'll have been seeking treasure again on Bogatka, I make no doubt?"

"Let be, now, let be," said Yevgenia placatingly, "whatever she sought it's none of our business. Can't you see she hardly dragged herself back, nigh dead! "

Granny Mara laughed a deep laugh, and I saw with surprise that she still had all her teeth—big, strong ones, too.

"Prokhor, weren't you saying they'd started giving kolkhoz members plots, the ones overgrown with scrub, but they didn't say a word about our clearings?"

That started a long, fruitless discussion about clearings and virgin land.

Prokhor turned to me as a man living, as he put it, in the same city as the biggest chiefs who decide our lives, and demanded a clear answer: why was it that in southern districts they were ploughing up virgin land, while up here it was just the opposite, they went in for alders and aspens, as he put it.

I started talking rather uncertainly about agriculture in remote forest districts being hardly worthwhile, and of course Prokhor soon had me pinned down and wriggling.

"Quite correct, quite correct," he said in an artificial voice, apparently mimicking some local speaker. "So now it isn't worthwhile. But in the war, dear comrades? Was it worthwhile, tell me, during the war? With just womenfolk and childer sowing all to the last inch! "

Granny Mara at once backed him up—for some reason she took a delight in pricking me.

At last I guessed the best argument to settle my opponents—a bottle of good vodka. It is true that economical, domestic Yevgenia was not particularly delighted over this way of getting rid of uninvited guests, but when they had emptied the bottle and left, embraced and singing, she let out a sigh of relief.

She summed up her final attitude to the revellers as she

cleared away, because Yevgenia could not stand dirt or disorder.

"Looks like it isn't only fields get neglected but folks, too. Dear Lord, who ever heard tell before that drunken *urvais* could come bursting into Milentyevna's house? The river'd have turned back sooner. Times, when Ma was passing and the childer was being naughty their elders'd tell them, 'Quiet, you imps, Vasilissa Milentyevna's coming,' and when she'd passed they'd say, 'Now you can go wild, stand on your heads if you want.' That's how they used to respect her. Will you have something to eat?" she asked her mother-in-law, who was moaning softly on the stove. "Will you come down? Or shall I give it you where you are?"

"I don't want it, thank you kindly. I'll take something after."

"After when? You've had naught since the morn. Come, have a bowl of soup. We've got good fish stew today, peppery."

"Nay, I ate earlier. I'd bread with me."

Try as she would, Yevgenia couldn't get the old woman to eat, and her spirits flagged again.

"Eh deary-dear, what'll I do with you? Maybe you're proper ill, Ma? I could go for the doctor——?"

"No, I'm all right, it'll pass off, I'll just get warm and then I'll come down. But you—it'd be good if you could pick over the mushrooms."

Yevgenia could only shake her head.

"Eh Ma, Ma—what a woman! Is it time now for you to be thinking of mushrooms? Lie quiet for the love of heaven! And forget all that tramping the woods."

All the same Yevgenia did pick up the basket of mushrooms and we went off into the other room. So that the old woman could rest a while.

8

This time the mushrooms were poor—a wet mixture that was half rubbish. Shrewd Yevgenia drew from this a depressing conclusion.

"Eh deary me, this is bad," she said. "Milentyevna's ill for sure. I've never known her bring mushrooms like these in all my born days." She sighed significantly.

"Aye, so Ma's starting to fail, and there was me used to think she was made of iron. Naught could touch her. Eh, but with the life she's had the wonder isn't that she stumbles but that she's alive at all. Her man—there was something got wrong with his head, three times he tried to shoot himself, how can you live through that? Well, they buried him and then—the war. She'd two sons killed and the third, that's my man, he was listed missing for years, and then Sanya crushed her Ma heart. The trouble she's known in her age. If you shared it among ten it 'ud suffice for all. And here—all on one head."

"Sanya—was that her daughter?"

"Aye—haven't you heard?" Yevgenia laid the bread knife she was using for the mushrooms on the table. "Ma had twelve childer in all, and six lived. Marfa was the eldest daughter—that's the one who married into Rusikha, then came Vassily and Yegor, the ones killed in the war, then my man, then Sanya and last that drunk Ivan.

"Well, Milentyevna saw her lads off to the front, and a year later it was Sanya's turn. She was signed up to float timber on the river. Like the army, war service too. Eh, but she was a lovely maid! I've never seen the like in all my life. Tall, and her skin white, and a thick plait right down to her knees, folks said she was the image of her mother before her, and maybe even prettier. And quiet, she'd never stir a ripple, not like us, always in strife. But it was just that as was her bane. She met a rascal and got a full belly.

"I don't marvel at it, not a scrap, the way it all happened. It's them as spends their lives under their parents' wing and never goes anywhere—let them stare, but me. I was on my own from thirteen and I've seen plenty in my time.

"There was times, you'd come back from the woods to the barrack, you could scarce drag yourself. And they, them devils, they'd done no work, they'd held naught heavier than a pen all day and there they'd be eyeing you. You'd no proper place to change and like as not they'd be dragging you off into a corner before you were through.

"Well, maybe it was one o' them sort as caught her Ma's little chick Sanya. What could she do? If she'd had her teeth grown she'd have sent him about his business with a flea in his ear, but you couldn't learn her that. I mind me before the war she came to us in Rusikha for some holiday, all blushes, she was. The goodwives couldn't take their eyes off her, an angel, she seemed, but the lads—like flies round a honeypot. Before she went her Ma'd have given her warning as they did: whatever you lose away from your home, keep your maiden honour. That's what they said in good families.

"I don't know how it all happened, I don't know. And better not ask Ma. You'd be worse to her than her worst foe."

Yevgenia listened, then continued in a hot whisper.

"She wanted to keep it hid. 'Twas said she'd let none near her girl's body. She took off the noose her own self, and washed the body and put it in the coffin. But how'll you hide a belly? Them girls as were with her, they talked. Sanya was getting all swole up, you could see it, they said. Aye, and Yefimko the ferryman, he noted it, too. 'You're looking different, Sanya,' he says. And how'd she be the same, tell me, when she was going to her judgment? Come, daughter, tell your own mother to her face how you kept your maiden honour pure.

"And so she came, poor maid, to her own home and daren't even set foot on the porch of it. She sat down on the threshold and sat there all the long night. But when it began to come light, she ran to the barn, she couldn't face the light of day, let alone her mother."

Yevgenia listened again, her eyebrows raised as she strained her ears.

"She'll be asleep, likely. Maybe she'll sleep it off." She dropped her voice to a whisper again. "I asked Ma. 'Didn't your mother's heart,' I says, 'warn you of aught ill?' 'Aye, it did,' she says. 'That night,' she says, 'I went three times to the entry and called out, asking who was there on the porch. And when it started getting light, I felt a stab in my heart. Like a knife.' She told me that, she didn't hide it. And told me how she saw the top-boots there on the porch.

"Just think, what a maid! In the hour of her death, when she put an end to her young life, she still had thought for her mother. You know yourself how it was with boots in the war. We'd be barefoot on the river floating wood, with chunks of ice on it. And there was Sanya taking her leave of life, and still she didn't forget her mother, it was her last care. She went barefoot to her death. And Ma followed her tracks to the barn. It wasn't early, it was light and you could see every mark on the snow.

"She got there but what could she do? Sanya was cold, and there by the wall was her quilted jacket all neatly folded and lying there, and her warm shawl on the top. As if she'd been saying: wear them, dear mother, and remember me dead in sorrow."

The rain was still falling. It sobbed on the old wavy glass in the window frames and I had a feeling of someone tapping and weeping softly outside.

As though reading my thoughts, she added, "I'm right feared living in this house. I can't sleep here alone. I'm not like Ma. Wintertime, when the wind howls in all the chimneys and the rings rattle on the door—I could go right crazy. At first I kept saying to Maxim, let's go live at home, what do we need in other parts? But now I've had enough. Wintertime there's no roads to the world, we go to Rusikha on skis."

9

Milentyevna lay on the stove for two days and Yevgenia and I began to be seriously alarmed and thought of calling in the doctor. In addition, we decided to let her children know.

However, to our relief it proved unnecessary. On the third day she came down. And not only came down, but got herself to the table without help.

"How do you feel, Granny? Are you all right again?"

"I don't know. Not quite, maybe, but I have to get back home today."

"Home? Today?"

"Today," she answered calmly. "My son Ivan'll be coming to fetch me."

Yevgenia and I were equally staggered by this announcement.

"And why'd Ivan be coming in this rain? Just look what it's like, outside! Are you losing your wits, Ma? And you haven't got all the mushrooms you wanted yet, too."

"The mushrooms'll wait, but school day begins tomorrow, Katerina'll be going."

"And you want to go because of Katerina?"

"I must. I gave my word."

"Your word—who to?" Yevgenia nearly choked with incredulity. "Well, Ma—that's out of all sense. Gave your word to Katerina! And your Katerina, no bigger than your fist. A squinting handful of nothing. She was here in the spring, she'd get herself off somewhere in a corner and you could call till you were hoarse."

"Let her be as she may, but if I gave my word I must go." Milentyevna turned towards me. "She's nervous, my granddaughter, and a misfortune with her eyes, too—she squints. And then a neighbour took it in her head to frighten the child with 'Why d'you let your Granny go away? She's old, she'll die somewhere on the road.' So my poor little maid cried and cried. And all night long she kept hugging her Granny."

Milentyevna spent the whole day sitting by the window in boots and woolen shawl, her bundle beside her so that there would be no delay when her son arrived. But Ivan did not come.

When at last the old clock struck five she suddenly announced that as her son hadn't come, she would go alone.

Yevgenia and I exchanged looks of horror—the rain was steady, the window-panes looked swollen with it, she was still ill, and there were few trucks along the road which could give her a lift. It was suicide, that's what it was!

Yevgenia tried every possible argument—she wept, pleaded, predicted dire things. And I of course backed her up in every way I could. But nothing helped. Milentyevna wasn't to be moved. She didn't raise her voice, she didn't argue, silently, head trembling, she put on her coat, fastened the bundle of her belongings more firmly, and cast a farewell look round her old home.

It was then that I really understood for the first time just what it was in Milentyevna which had subdued the Pizhma savages. It was not only her quiet patience, it was her firmness, her flinty determination.

I saw the old woman across the river alone. Yevgenia was in such a state she couldn't even come down from the porch.

The rain kept right on. The river had risen noticeably and carried us a couple of hundred metres below the place where we usually brought the boat up. But the most difficult part was the path through the woods. Even in dry weather the mud sucked and squelched underfoot; there is no need to describe what it was like now, after three days of rain.

I walked in front, the bog giving under my feet, clutching at the wet bushes and every moment expecting the old woman to collapse. But heaven be praised, it all ended well. Leaning on the faithful support of her light aspen stick, she came to the road. And luck was with us, she got a lift.

It certainly was quite exceptional luck. A miracle, in fact. Just as we came to the road we heard the engine. I went wild, I dashed forward with a furious shout, as though attacking.

The truck halted.

Unfortunately there was no room by the driver in the cab, the seat was occupied by a pale woman carrying a newborn infant. But Milentyevna never hesitated a second about travelling in the open body.

It was big truck with high sides and she dived inside as though it were a well. But for a long time I could see a white spot as I stood under the dark archway of firs that jostled the road.

It was Milentyevna, thrown about by the lurching of the truck, waving goodbye to me with her handkerchief.

10

After Milentyevna's departure I didn't stay another three days, because everything suddenly palled on me and seemed like child's play, not real life—my hunting in the woods, and fishing, and even the spells I wore over the old times of peasant life.

I was drawn irresistibly to the big, noisy world, I wanted to work, to be of use. To do as Vasilissa Milentyevna did and would go on doing to her last day—that peasant woman from the dense northern forests, unknown yet great in her active life.

I left Pizhma on a warm sunny day. Steam was rising from the drying log houses. It rose from old Thunderer, motionless beside a cart by the stable.

I called to him as I passed. He stretched out his old neck to me but made no sound.

Just as silently, their heads hanging despondently on the shingle roofs, the wooden horses saw me off. A whole herd of wooden horses, bred by Vasilissa Milentyevna.

I wanted desperately, painfully to hear their whinnying. Just once—in a dream if I could not hear it waking. That youthful ringing neigh with which they filled the woods in former days.

1969

Pelageya

1

In the mornings, fresh and rested, Pelageya easily covered the one-and-a-half versts to the bakery. She ran barefoot across the meadow, making a game of rinsing her feet in the dew-wet grass. The aspen boat parted the sleepy, rosy river like a flat-iron. When she came to the sandy spit she crossed it briskly, not even noticing its clinging, slippery softness.

The evenings, however, were a different matter. After a whole day working by the red-hot stove the very thought of the long road home was daunting.

The sandy spit which began just below the bakery, at the foot of the hill, was a torment. The sun had scorched the sand all day and now every grain of it gave forth a suffocating heat; gadflies attacked viciously in swarms, as though they had flown in from the whole surrounding district to this sandy bank where the sun still shone. And in addition she was burdened with a bag of bread in one hand and a pail of swill in the other.

Every time, struggling through this yellow miniature hell—the only word which fitted—Pelageya told herself it was no good, she'd have to ask for a helper. She must. How much longer could she keep it up? The extra money wasn't so much—twenty rubles for breaking her back doing the work of two—if not three.

That was how she felt until she was able to kneel down and plunge her dry lips into the river. Then, having slaked her thirst and rinsed her face, she began to have second thoughts about a helper. And once across the river and on the home side, where a hill shut off the sun and there was even a slight breeze, her sober common sense took control.

Yes, it certainly wouldn't be bad, not bad at all to have a helper, Pelageya thought as she walked along the firm, already slightly dewy damp path by the fragrant rye field.

To halve the carrying of wood and water. And kneading the dough—that wouldn't have to be done by her alone, either. But on the other hand, a helper meant eyes. And with someone watching the slops would be thinner, you'd be afraid to throw in a dollop or two of dough. And then you'd never feed the hog to seven poods' weight. You couldn't tell what sort she might be, that helper. You had to think of all that too.

Pelageya stopped to rest a bit by the plank footway over the mere—a muddy sedge-grown patch where a snorting skewbald mare and her foal paced, up to their knees in water. She had always stopped there to rest, summer and winter, ever since 'forty-seven when she went to work at the bakery. Because the village hill was steep, you couldn't tackle it without resting first.

Just to be on the safe side, she covered the bucket of slops with the white cotton headscarf she had been wearing and smoothed her hair—a thin twist of tow gathered into a short tail (the mother of a grown maid doesn't want to show herself looking unkempt) and then as usual raised her eyes to the bird-cherry on the hill beside the smoky old bath-house where Pavel waited for her every evening.

At one time—not so far distant, either—he used to meet her at the river, and on those darkest autumn nights with a lantern. Here you are, wife, step safe. You won't fall. And about the house, to be honest, she hadn't had to lift a finger. He lighted a fire in the mornings, and milked and tended the cow, and if he had a free moment he would come over to the bakery and chop enough wood for a week. But now Pavel was sick, since the spring he'd been clutching at his heart, and everything was on her shoulders, the bakery and the house, too.

Pelageya's eyes were keen—they seemed to be the only thing about her not scorched by the ovens—and she saw at once that there was nobody by the bird-cherry. No Pavel.

She caught her breath. Where was Pavel? Where was Alka? Had something happened—something bad?

With no more thought of rest, forgetting her aching weariness, she picked up the pail of slops and the bag of bread again, and splashed loudly through the water over the shaky planks crossing the mere.

2

Pavel was sitting on the edge of the bed in his white cotton under-pants, soft felt boots and a quilted sleeveless coat of hers—and she hated that frowzy old man's look! It was obvious he had only just awakened: his face was pale and damp and his hair straggled in wet strands.

"Lord ha' mercy, haven't you had enough of sleeping?" she flew out at him from the doorway. "Night and day aren't enough, you must flop down evenings, too."

"I felt poorly today," said Pavel, looking down.

"Poorly or not, the hilltop wouldn't be too far for you. And yon hay—" she jerked her head towards the window behind the nickel bed. "What'll folks think, left lying there since the morn? There's me, getting up before dawn to mow it—if you're too poorly there's our lass, or you could call your dear sister. If she's not got too grand! "

"It's a holiday today, and also Anisya's birthday."

"The better the day, the better the deed. She wouldn't wear out her arms if she helped her brother a bit."

Stamping about in her top-boots, uncomfortably tight on her swollen legs, Pelageya examined the room. It was a good room, spacious and clean, with a freshly painted floor, white lace curtains covering the whole window and a thick rubber plant rising royally in a front corner. Her glance paused on a bright red frock with a white belt tossed carelessly over a chair beside the chest of drawers where new samovars never yet used shone proudly.

"And where might she be, our heifer?"

"Gone her ways out, a young lass—"

"Aye, that's the way of it, there's you lieabed all day, naught to be seen of the girl and me nigh killing myself. It's all left for me to do."

She got her boots off at last and flung herself down on the floor. Without any mat on the bare painted floor.

For five minutes or more she lay motionless, breathing heavily. Gradually her breathing eased—a board floor does wonders, drawing out the heat from the body. Finally she turned over to face her husband and began asking about domestic matters.

The main, heaviest work was done; Alka had milked the cow and brought in grass. She was pleased, too, about the small samovar which Pavel had heated ready for her coming—apparently he hadn't only rumpled the bed, he'd got things done too.

She rose, drank off five cups of strong tea without sugar—nothing like plain tea for easing the heat inside you—then raised the curtain a little and again looked out at the kitchen garden. There lay the hay, it had been drying there all day; but it was more than she could do to rick it now, her arms and legs were ready to drop off.

"Nay, I can't do it," she said and again sank on to the floor, this time on a quilted jacket which her husband had considerately spread for her. "Did you get wine?" she asked after a little while.

"Aye, two bottles."

"Aye, well, that's right, goodman," she said, already in a different tone. "We need wine today. Mebbe someone'll look in. Were they selling much?"

"A fair bit. There's a good many not gone off yet to the far haymaking. Pyotr Ivanovich took a lot. Vodka and red wine, too."

"That he'd have to," Pelageya sighed. "He'll be having plenty of guests; they say Antonida's come, she's ended her studies. Haven't you seen her?"

"No."

"She's come, the stores manager said so a day or so agone. And he said she came from town in a launch with an officer. Wanted to look at the countryside, that's what she said. Huh—countryside. Dropping her bait, thinks to catch herself a man." Pelageya paused a moment. "He didn't say aught to you? Ask you in for a cup of tea?"

Pavel shrugged.

"Aye, that's the way of it as the days pass. Time was, Pyotr Ivanovich 'ud never think to have folks in without bidding us first of all. But now he can't hope for much from Pavel and Pelageya so they aren't wanted."

"Naught to fret on," said Pavel. "It's my sister's birthday today, she came in a bit agone to remind us."

"Nay, I'm going nowhere." Pelageya's lips tightened. "Dropping on my feet, what sort of a guest would I be?"

"She'll take it badly. Her birthday after all—" Pavel repeated hesitantly.

"That's as may be. You can't expect me to kill myself over her birthday."

At that moment there was a scraping of feet on the porch and—talk of the devil—Anisya entered.

3

Anisya was five years older than her brother, but healthy and strong, with black brows and white teeth without a single gap—nobody would think she was over fifty.

She had been married three times. Her first husband, from whom she had a child which died within months, was killed in the war. She had to part with the second in 'forty-six when she served a prison term for taking a sheaf of rye from the field. The third husband, one of a gang hired for the lumbering (and the one she loved best) drank all she had down to the last rag, beat her up as a parting caress and took himself off back to his lawful wife and family. After that she tried no more of marital bliss; she kept her freedom, was ready to go along with a man she fancied but did not let any of them become too important to her.

Her brother, however, she not merely loved—she adored him, partly because he was her only brother and in poor health, partly because with his quietness and kindliness he had never once reproached her for her loose living. As for Pavel's wife—before her she literally quailed. She went in awe of her because she recognized Pelageya's superiority in everything. She was thrifty—Anisya spent every kopek as soon as she got it, far-sighted, and in women's matters—a rock.

When she saw her husband off to the front—she was then nineteen—Pelageya told him, "You can trust me. Nobody will finger my hair but you." And she was true to her word, throughout the war she never once went to a dance.

Deeply respecting her sister-in-law, Anisya was always particularly free and easy when talking to her—let them be equal in words at least. It was like that now too.

"What are you flopping there for? Get up, the wine'll go sour."

"You and your wine. Can't get enough."

"That's as may be. You don't let a day like this pass dry." She nodded at her brother. "Come on, do. Get your goodwife up, and get dressed yourself."

Pavel dropped his eyes. Anisya familiarly reached out for his trousers hanging on the end of the bed.

"Oh, let him be, do. He's ill, can't you see?" cried Pelageya, irritated.

"Then you come, at least."

"Nay, I won't come either. I'm half dead, I didn't know how to drag my feet up from across the river. I couldn't get myself up now, not if you paid me. Nay, nay, thanking you kindly, Anisya Zakharovna. Thank you for coming. But we're nobody's guests this eve."

Anisya was dismayed. White patches appeared on her round red face.

"But lord ha' mercy, my closest kin, what'll folks say—"

"They can say what they like," answered Pelageya. "Them wi' sense'll not take it wrong, and them wi' none—I reckon naught of their chat." She turned her dry stern eyes on Anisya, raising herself on her elbow. "When did you get up the morn? Aye—but I rose, heated the stove, mowed the grass in the kitchen garden plot, milked the cow and went off beyond the river while you were still lying on your backside, not a smell of smoke coming from the chimney. Easy for you to be hale and hearty while—"

"But it's not my fault—"

"—while I went to the bakery and heated my second stove—logs two yards long, and carried in thirty pails of water, and mixed a hundred loaves of brown bread and seventy of white. And how I stood roasting in front of the stove—I don't tell of that. While you went down to the meadow and played about with a rake—I could hear how all of you was working, the glass shook with your singing the other side o' the river, and before you'd time to get up a sweat the truck comes puffing along to carry you home—" Pelageya took a deep breath, collapsed again on the quilted jacket and shut her eyes.

"Aye, yours is hard work," said Pavel peaceably, avoiding his sister's eye. "We all know that. The bakery. I've been there. I know."

"Then you won't come?" asked Anisya, her voice trembling. "Mebbe I don't invite you right?" She turned to her brother with a deep, old-style bow from the waist. "Brother Pavel Zakharovich, do me the favour—Pelageya Prokopyevna—"

Pelageya waved a hand. "No, no Anisya Zakharovna. Our heartiest thanks. We haven't asked any ourselves and we won't go a-visiting either. We can't. We're flat on our backs."

Anisya gave it up. Silently, head drooping, she left the house.

"Talking about folks," grumbled Pelageya when the

sound of footsteps had died away. " 'What'll folks say,' indeed! And her, ready to grab at every pair of trousers— does she think no one talks, and plenty, too! "

"We know all that. She's been misfortunate. But all the same we ought to do a kindness. She's my sister—"

"Now don't you stand up for her, she's only herself to blame. Folks reap what they sow."

Pavel made no reply. He lay down on the bed, wet-eyed.

4

Houses like the Amosov house are not built nowadays— and for that matter earlier on, before the war, there weren't so very many of them.

It was a big house, with two stories and a round-breasted cock on top, a big yard with an open shed and a hay-shed, and a winter room at the side.

It was with that winter room that the breakup of the house began; in 'forty-six it was taken away by the eldest daughter-in-law (Zakhar Amosov had four sons but only one of them, Pavel, returned from the war). Then the second daughter-in-law wanted her portion and dismantled the yard. The last blow came from Pelageya who decided to rebuild at the back. On her insistence the house was chopped in half. And the fine old house ceased to be. Instead, there was an ugly hulk reminiscent of a huge log lectern. In bad weather it creaked and swayed in spite of the supporting beams that braced it on two sides, and in winter it was still worse. Drifts of snow penetrated into the passage which had been closed off after a fashion with boards, and Anisya always kept a wooden snow-shovel ready.

Still, say what you would, it was very cheerful on Anisya's upper floor (the ground floor, which went to the third daughter-in-law, was boarded up), and Alka liked to spend time with her aunt.

It was high up. Free and spacious. Swallows flew past the window. And you could see everything. You could see who passed along the street and over the lowlands, and in spring when the river was in spate you could see the big white-decked steamers emerging round the spit. And then, too, there were always people in her aunt's house, it was never dull as it was at home, away at the back. If a woman had been to the shop she wanted to show someone what she had bought—and who better than Anisya? Workers who had come from over the river on their free day—where could they sit over a bottle? At Anisya's. They all came to her, the truck driver passing through, a farmer who had had a drink or wanted one, even soldiers just arrived and soon to go again—they quickly found the well-trodden path to Anisya.

On this festive evening Alka was like a rubber ball, bouncing from the house to the street and from the street to the house. She wanted to be everywhere at once, to seize a handful of pleasure now here, now there, with her aunt, and outside where the first drunks were already beginning to show up.

"You aren't a child, to be chasing fit to break your neck," said Anisya when she flew in for the twentieth time.

"Oh, let be! " She skipped across the room, climbed on a stool and leaned out of the wide-open window. That was her favourite place—the window, where she could take in everything in sight.

Suddenly she leaned right out.

"Auntie, Auntie, look! "

"What's that you've seen now?"

"Come here, quick! " Alka burst out laughing, shaking on the stool.

Anisya, who had been lighting the samovar by the stove behind the curtain, came to stand behind her niece, stretching out over her.

"Oh, that's who's there. The girl-friends."

That was the name they gave in the village to Big Masha and Little Masha, two old women, both old maids. One was like a bear, her head nearly reaching the ceiling—that was Little Masha. The other was a wisp of a thing, but with all her wits about her—so she was nicknamed Big Masha. Characteristic was the way they handled their pensions. When the great day arrived Big Masha started by buying tea, sugar, cereals and a dozen loaves, and then drank all that remained. But Little Masha had her own ways. As they said in the village, she lived one week in the month, the first after getting her pension. But that week she lived high; day and night she staggered up and down the street in her rough boots, bawling songs so the window glass cracked with it. After that, for the next three weeks Little Masha was not seen or heard. There was only a cold stove, three hungry cats and a piece of charcoal with which she crossed marks on a beam showing how many days remained until the next pension day.

The two old women stood in the middle of the dusty road where the cows had only just passed. Little Masha was calm and unruffled in her usual dark-blue kerchief, but Big Masha, her head thrown back, swaying, was urging something on her, shaking a dark finger under her nose for emphasis.

"Some idea they've got in their heads," laughed Alka. "They're people after all."

"Little Masha seems sort of down. Likely her throat's dry."

"Dry, of course. It's the driest time for her. And that sly one's getting her all muddled. Look at her, shaking her finger. She'll be talking her into selling her grass."

"What grass? That in the kitchen garden plot?" Alka turned to her aunt, animated. "I must tell Ma. To get vodka she'll sell it cheap."

"No, let be—you oughtn't to befool an old woman. It's not the time to make a bargain."

"Auntie," said Alka after a pause, "shall I call them in?"

"What for? They tramp round here often enough."

"But it's funny, you can die laughing when they start talking."

Anisya did not agree at once. It wasn't for the likes of those she had made her preparations today—in her heart she was still hoping Pelageya would think better of it and come; but on the other hand how could she refuse Alka? She wound her arms round her—January ice would have melted.

First Big Masha flitted in; she wore a man's jacket and crumpled trousers with a white stripe, women's clothing represented only by her white head-scarf and a dress of sorts over the trousers. Little Masha was still clumping up the steep stairs from the passage in her heavy boots. In the doorway she doubled up, then stepped inside and began a series of bows before a picture in the ikon corner.

"Give over, you've not come to the monastery," said Big Masha—a sly hint at far distant days when the other used to wash for the monks.

"But not to a cowshed either," said Little Masha in her deep voice.

"You blind bat—it's Lenin she's got in your corner."

Alka burst out laughing.

55

"Naught to fret about," retorted Little Masha imperturbably. "All power comes from God."

"True, true, Masha," said Anisya from behind the curtain. "Only it isn't God pays you your pension. But sit you down to table."

"That table of yours doesn't sway, does it, Anisya? Eh?" asked Big Masha, a sly hint.

"No more than your bleary eyes," laughed Alka.

Outside a motorcycle snorted and coughed and Alka was on the stool by the window in an instant. Her red-striped silk frock rucked up displaying sturdy white thighs above her stockings.

"What kind of thing do you have to keep them stockings up, Alka?" enquired Big Masha. "They're right up agin your backside."

"A belt. Haven't you seen them?" Alka's eyebrows, black like her aunt's, curved up in surprise. She jumped down from the stool and raised the hem of her dress.

"Clever, that," and Big Masha clicked her tongue approvingly.

"What's that under your frock—a belt?" Little Masha stretched out her neck, squinting short-sightedly from her narrow Mongolian eyes. "Them's panties."

"Panties! You great gawk—here's my panties, look! " Laughing, Alka pulled out the tight pink belt.

"And them's silk, an' all," rumbled Little Masha.

"I'm all silk," boasted Alka and, catching up the edges of her skirt with both hands, she twirled skittishly round on her high heels.

"Alka, Alka, you brazen hussy! " cried Anisya from behind the curtain. "That's not nice! "

"What's not nice? We won't eat her! "

"It's not the way to go on. She's still at school," and Anisya gave Big Masha a stern look.

"At school? Oh aye, and we know today's schoolgirls," said Big Masha. "Hands nim and proper on the desk, and under it feet playing footsy with the boys. Alka—who did I see yestereen with a soldier by the fence?"

Alka frowned stormily.

"That's not true, you old liar! Me with a soldier? I've never been near a soldier! "

"But them as wears gold stripes?"

To that Alka raised no objections.

"Look 'ee there, now, look 'ee there! " Big Masha

clicked her tongue again. "Her blood's running hot, aye. And the bumps on her—couldn't knock 'em off wi' a cudgel! "

"Stop, stop, Arkhipovna, I've never liked that kind of chat."

"Me neither," Little Masha put in. "She's got a mucky tongue, she has. I'm a maid, too."

Alka fell forward across the table, laughing. Big Masha's left eye shone with a greenish glow, sure sign that she had already taken on a load somewhere. So Anisya brought in the well-fried cod without waiting for the samovar, and followed it with a small bottle. The sooner she saw the backs of guests like these, the better.

"Help yourselves, dear guests."

"It's Auntie's birthday today," said Alka, composing herself.

"Nay, is it?" Big Masha's lower lip fell slackly in her astonishment. "Where's your brother and his goodwife?"

"They can't come. Pelageya's that wearied from work at the bakery, she can't stir a finger. And you know how he is—can't get off the bed nohow."

Big Masha smirked.

"Masha," she shrieked in the ear of her somewhat deaf friend, "who was it we saw a bit agone?"

"Where?"

"By Proshich's backyard."

"O-oh! Ye mean those—Pavel Zakharovich and his wife. Going a-visiting. The way Pavel's boots shone. I saw him buy them two years agone. And she wi' heels like stilts, as if she'd just come from town. Well off, they are."

For over half a year Anisya had been preparing for this day. All the money she could spare she had locked away, and hardly taken more than tea herself. She had prepared a spread—there weren't enough fingers to count all the things.

Three kinds of fish—fresh pike and grayling, a pound of each, and smoked salmon; three kinds of cereal, three kinds of jelly; fat meat and lean meat because Pavel could not eat fat; and three tins.

Her heart hot with anger, she brought everything out. Here you are, stuff yourselves! Let the meanest guests have it, since her nearest kin scorned it. At first she kept back the smoked salmon—it had cost her three days of back-breaking toil in Moneyed Ignashka's vegetable plot;

but then, when she had slaked her wretchedness with a second glass, she brought out the salmon too.

She wept unrestrainedly, like a child, caring nothing for who might be present; then she jumped up and danced wildly to the old women's uneven clapping, turned to her glass again and sobbed more miserably than ever.

Big Masha like an amorous man let her hands rove freely over Alka, who pushed her away, laughing, slapped the hands and in the end went and sat beside Little Masha who had started her favourite song, "In a garden in the valley" in a deep voice that seemed to come from her belly.

Suddenly Anisya saw a glass in Alka's hand.

"Alka, stop, don't you dare! "

"But Auntie, we're drinking to the grass. I'm buying it from Little Masha."

"Grass?" repeated Anisya in surprise, then waved it off. "Do as you like, it's no matter to me."

"I'm not deceiving her, Anisya," said Little Masha in an injured voice. "When have I ever told a lie? My grass is soft as silk."

Alka began shaking her dark heavy hand. Big Masha reached out to it.

"Let me have a shake, too, mebbe I'll get something out of it. Will I, Masha?"

"What's to do wi' ye? You'll get it out of me some way."

Big Masha, satisfied, winked and lighted a cigarette, but Little Masha started to lament again.

"It's good grass, lass. I'd ha' done better to wait till autumn. And there's my cats like it for their walking."

"But the mown ground is better for them to walk on," said Alka.

"Nay, that it isn't. They want the grass, they hide in it and stalk birds."

Little Masha shook a heavy head and dissolving in hot tears, trumpeted to raise the roof:

> *"At my lonely grave*
> *No psalms they'll ever sing.*
> *None but the nightingale*
> *I' the early days of spring."*

Big Masha set about cheering her.

"Nay, there's naught to moan for thataways. Got yourself in a rare taking.—Look at Anisya, now, her own brother's given her the go-bye on this day..."

"You let my brother alone! " Anisya sobered in an instant.

She brought her fist down on the table so sharply that the dishes rang. "I know your ways. Trying to make trouble atween us, that's what! But it won't come off! "

"Eh? Wha'? What's got into her—eh? Why's she fly out like that?"

"Oh, botheration take the pair of you! " said Alka crossly. "You're both drunk, one bellowing like a bull, the other breaking the cups—! "

Anisya recovered herself fully only somewhat later when some girls in their best frocks accompanied by soldiers burst in.

The one with gold bars on his shoulderboards swept the room with a glance, then with a wink at Big Masha whom he took for the hostess cried, "A party, eh?"

"A bit of a one, comrade—old women, pensioners—" Big Masha hiccupped as illustration. "Soviet power—strengthen our 'fences—that's right, isn't it, comrade?"

"Sure thing," the officer replied, then went round shaking hands.

"Aye, that's our way, comrade," Big Masha approved, then turned to Anisya. "And you—what are you staring at? Don't you know how to make guests welcome?"

5

It was not one of the best places they were given—at the end, by the chest of drawers, their seat a creaking plank laid across two stools instead of soft chairs.

But Pelageya was quite satisfied. Ten or twelve years ago it would have been another matter, she would have said: Nay, Pyotr Ivanovich, don't you be pushing me out into the backyard, I can sit in the backyard at home, when I come out I want to be near the window, near the light, and have good talk coming in both ears. Yes, but ten or twelve years ago there'd have been no need to say anything, their host would have given them good places himself. And she would have put on airs a bit.

But then—ten or twelve years ago Pavel was foreman, and folks made up to her, too—maybe she'd slip them an extra loaf?

Nowadays there was all the bread you wanted in the

shop. And the value of the bread decides the value of the baker. Nothing to be offended about. Better say thank-you to Pyotr Ivanovich for remembering them.

They had already gone to bed when the boy had come running over with a note. But that note had changed everything.

Pyotr Ivanovich invited folks who counted. He was not the man to pour his wine down the throats of rag-tag-and-bobtail. First of all, the men at the top—the chairmen of the rural Soviet and of the kolkhoz; then came the manager of the village general stores and his bookkeeper, then the manager of the lumber centre—he was made a big fuss of, Pyotr Ivanovich's son worked under him.

After that came the smaller fry—from the power-saw bench, the truck driver, the stableman—you couldn't get anywhere unless those rogues were kept buttered. Say you had to roof a house—you came with sweet words to Arkashka at the power-saw bench. Or if you needed a horse. You might think this was the machine age and what was the use of a stableman. But not a bit of it, the truck driver had his value, and so did the stableman. Come winter and a tight place with firewood, and you went cap in hand to Antokha.

Antonida and Sergei, Pyotr Ivanovich's children, had left before Pavel and Pelageya arrived—why should they stew in a stuffy room on a holiday?

Maria Epimakhovna, the hostess, wanted take Pelageya to see the new summer kitchen, but she begged off—later, later, Maria Epimakhovna. Let me get my breath and look round at all these good people and at the table you've laid.

The table was groaning with good things. Pyotr Ivanovich had calculated it all and seen to it all. The headmaster's wife did not drink vodka—be so kind, here's champagne to your taste, Rosa Dmitrevna. For ten years if not more the dark silver-necked bottle had gathered dust on a shelf in the shop without finding a purchaser. But now it had come in handy; Rosa Dmitrevna dipped her reddened lips in it with enjoyment.

Pyotr Ivanovich had always been a riddle to Pelageya. He had little education, only three years' schooling; his position was not a high one—all his life he had been an auditor; he checked the kolkhoz accounts, he inspected the village shop, or the general rural supplies system—but if you got down to it, he was the most important man in the village. There was no evading him. His hands were soft, they had never hefted an axe, but they had a grip of steel.

In 'forty-seven, the first year Pelageya worked in the bakery, Pyotr Ivanovich taught her a lesson. Reckoned up nearly five thousand deficit. Not five hundred—five thousand! At the time Pavel checked and calculated, and he'd some education; he reckoned and the bookkeeper reckoned, but as soon as Pyotr Ivanovich started with his abacus—five thousand missing, and that was that. At last Pelageya, who was no fool, flopped down at his feet—save me, Pyotr Ivanovich, I've done naught wrong. All my life I'll pray for you and teach my children to do the same. "All right," he said, "I'll get you out, Pelageya. You've done naught wrong, that's sure. And it wasn't on your account I did it, I was teaching that bookkeeper a lesson, so's she doesn't get above herself, she's young and cocky." And he kept his word. The five thousand was found.

That was Pyotr Ivanovich!

The main, most important guest this evening was Grigori Vassilyevich, the school headmaster. He was the one on whom his host pressed the best dishes and drinks. No need to puzzle one's head about that—the answer was Antonida. She would be teaching in his school, and things were going to go smoothly for her with nothing to trip her up, if Pyotr Ivanovich had anything to do with it.

Why he was making such a fuss of Afonka the vet, however, was more than Pelageya could understand. Afonka didn't swing any particular weight now, he was no longer Party secretary, he had been taken off that job back in the spring, and not without a good bit of scandal and items in the district paper—when would he pick himself up again after that?

However, Pelageya did not waste much thought over Afonka. Not likely, when there were so many people round who could be useful! The stableman Antokha's wife Sara beside her (those were the people she had to sit with now!) hadn't a care in the world, but she, Pelageya, had a sick husband, she had to think of everything.

So when the chairman of the rural Soviet got up and went out for a breath of fresh air she followed him. She followed him to the end of the kitchen garden to wait as he fumbled about in the outhouse, never mind if it was shameful, when he did come out nobody would intercept him first. And there were people with that idea. The stableman

Antokha—it looked like his white shirt—ran out on the porch. But he saw someone else had got there before him and went back.

She seized her chance, spoke about the hay, and slipped in a word about Alka. Much to her surprise, there was no trouble about the hay—"We'll register Pavel as an invalid since he lost his health working in the kolkhoz. And we'll allot him a section."

But about Alka, just as in the spring, he started to hedge about giving her a recommendation. "I can't promise, I can't promise, Pelageya. Let her work a year or two in the stock section. Work is the basis of everything."

"She's my only child, Vassily Ignatyevich," said Pelageya imploringly. "She needs to get some training. Her father's barely half-taught and me, I'm ignorant as that block."

"Nay, you're no block."

"A block, a block, Vasya—" (here she need not call him Vassily Ignatyevich)"—my head stuffed with moss." (The more she cried herself down the more flattering to him.)

The chairman, the old goat, slipped an arm round her and began to draw her to him. Gently, so as not to give offense, she pushed him away (heaven forbid anyone should see!) and gave him a playful slap on his fat back.

"Don't touch my bones, if they fall apart you wouldn't collect them again."

"Eh, Polka, Polka," sighed the chairman. "What hair you used to have! D'you mind that party when I dragged you from the window to the bench? Wanted to see if it 'ud take the weight. It wasn't plaits, it was gold you had."

"Don't you make things up, you devil's imp," said Pelageya, frowning. "Mebbe you dragged someone but it wasn't me, as if I'd have stood for it! "

"Nay, it was you," he insisted stubbornly.

"Well, all right, all right, then—me." Why argue with a drunk?

Suddenly she felt moisture in her eyes—not real tears, the ovens had dried them up long ago, but—something. Because once she really had had beautiful hair, oh, she had. When she had washed it she hadn't known how to comb it out, it broke the teeth of the comb. And at school the teacher had used her hair to show electricity. Tore up a heap of small bits of paper and collected them on the comb.

With a little shake she flung away memories—she had not lain in wait for this hog to join him in old memories of her hair. Resolutely she turned the talk back to business. Easy to talk to a boss when he's drunk and his heart's open.

"Very well, we'll think about it," mumbled the chairman, his thoughts seemingly still on that party long past.

Then, like the previous time, he started off with his "Wed Alka to my lad". And he kept insisting and pressing her till she regretted having mentioned her daughter. She tried to evade the issue this way and that: times are changed, Vasya, we don't tell the young folks who they'll marry nowadays. Besides, Alka's not marriageable yet anyway, she's still at school."

"Huh—and maybe she'll be there another three years."

Alka did badly at school, in two classes she had spent an extra year.

With sudden irascibility he growled, "Arrh—you think he's not good enough for you, my lad—eh?"

"Good enough, of course he is, Vassily Ignatyevich."

You don't call a man Vasya when he's losing his temper. But inwardly she was thinking—what's there so good about that thick-lipped oaf? You're not much of a catch yourself. The same fat mouth. Oh, I haven't forgotten, I mind me how you grabbed my plaits at that party.

Luckily for her, at that moment Pyotr Ivanovich appeared on the porch—as host, he had to keep an eye on things, so she seized her chance, took hold of the chairman's arm and got him back into the room.

There she was, arm-in-arm with Soviet Authority, let everyone see. It was early days yet to push her into the backyard. And Pyotr Ivanovich—let him see, too, and mark it well. He was a wise man!

Just then everybody had crowded round the open windows—a cluster of young people were passing down the street.

"Pelageya, Pelageya, look at your Alka—"

"An orange! " Afonka the vet snapped his fingers loudly.

"Look you there, now—it's an officer she's grabbed! Got her wits about her. Ha! Ha! No common soldier for her! "

"As headmaster, talk like that about a pupil—"

"Drop it, Grigori Vassilyevich, stop moralising—"

"It's immoral to take a schoolgirl walking," said Afonka loudly, "but them as is well plumped out—"

Of course all guffawed—a jest at someone else's expense is always popular—but Pelageya did not know where to look. A bitch, that girl! Barely grown and the men were round her like flies round a honey-pot. What would it be when she got older?

Thanks be to Pyotr Ivanovich, he turned the men from their bawdy neighing, filling the glasses and saying, "Let's drink to our children, friends."

"Quite right! It's them we live for! "

"As you were! "

Afonka the vet. Now what had that black Gipsy thought up? It was always his way, as soon as folks were in a pleasant humour he'd roll those black eyes and spoil things.

"As you were! " he bawled again. "To our Soviet youth! "

"Good! Right! "

"Our youth, Afanasy Platonovich! "

"As you were! Too much gab! "

There it was. That lean devil was on his feet giving orders through his teeth as though he wasn't talking friendly-like with good people but back in his veterinary sector breaking horses.

"To the World Youth Forum! To the youth of our planet! "

That's where he'd got to—they'd begun with the children and now they were God knows where.

"Bottoms up—everyone! " commanded Afonka again. He shook his black head like a raven shaking its wings. He glared round and suddenly fixed his eyes on Pavel, the only one who had not raised his glass.

"Afanasy Platonovich, he can't take more," said Pelageya, coming to her husband's defence. "He's got a bad heart."

"I in-sist! "

Pyotr Ivanovich came up—don't make difficulties, drink. And that brute bawling as if he was on a rostrum, "A matter of prin-ci-ple! "

"Just take a sip."

Pelageya nudged her husband and added in his ear, "He won't give up, sticks like pitch. Don't you know him? Drink, I tell you! " she said with sudden anger—Afonka standing there, Pyotr Ivanovich bending over Pavel. "How many times must you be asked? Don't keep everyone waiting."

With a shaking hand Pavel took the glass.

"Hurrah! " bawled Afonka.

"Hur-rah! " roared the others.

Then came the concluding glass, no host would let his guests go without one to set them along the road. And then a glass for "peace and friendship", which the host offered all who wanted it in the doorway and only then they emerged into the free air. On the porch someone started up a song but Afonka the vet (here his commanding voice was useful) quickly quieted the rowdy.

"Noise! Sing, enjoy yourselves—it's not working hours. But quietly, quiet, durn you! "

They all trooped to the chairman of the wood-chemical cooperative, a man, to be frank, of no use to Pelageya. At least, in all the years she had been working in the bakery she had never had to do with him, although—who could say what might come about? Today he's nothing in your life and tomorrow he may be blocking your road.

Yes, it wouldn't have hurt to go with the others to this chairman. But by this time Pavel was feeling pretty bad so instead she took his arm and led him home.

6

"Did you see their summer kitchen? She says it's heaven, no heat or smells in the house in summer."

Pavel said nothing.

Pelageya told her husband about her talk with the chairman of the rural Soviet about the hay and the recommendation for their daughter. She was not too greatly troubled that the chairman had hedged again about the recommendation. Alka still had a year to go at the local school, there was time enough for Pelageya to look around. She had connections in the district town. For instance, there was Ivan Fyodorovich in the district executive committee. Many's the time she had slipped him some extra bread after the war—surely he wouldn't have forgotten!

Pelageya's mind was occupied with something else—the puzzle of Pyotr Ivanovich. For three years he'd forgotten their existence, and now today he'd invited them. Why?

Clearly, she was of no use to him, Pelageya reasoned. Her day was done, who would trouble about a baker nowadays? People had stuffed their bellies with bread long ago. Maybe he had his eye on Alka?

She had heard tell that his son Sergei was making sheep's eyes at Alka and if Pyotr Ivanovich had thrown out some hint—we've lost touch with each other too soon, who knows what the future holds?—she would have known what it was about.

There had been no hint.

She had expected a whispered word at leavetaking. But there had been only a courteous "Thank you for coming." Nothing more. Go home and rack your brains.

It now struck Pelageya that there had been something queer about Pyotr Ivanovich's invitation coming when it did—actually, when all the other guests were already present. Could the idea have come not from Pyotr Ivanovich himself but from someone else?

Perhaps Fat-Mouth Vaska? (Alone, she thought of the chairman of the rural Soviet by the name used in the village).

Possible. Quite possible, thought Pelageya. His lad was of an age to marry. And he was always hanging round their house. Nay, Vaska, your eyes are bigger than your stomach, seek something you can swallow. You don't get far with an axe these days, and what else can your lad handle? A joke! Went to town, spent two years learning and came back as he went, with the same axe. Learned to be a carpenter.

The freshness of evening did nothing to make Pavel feel better. He hung on her arm like a sack.

She took off his hat, then his tie.

"Bear up a while longer. We'll soon be there. My feet burn like fire too."

These high-heeled shoes were pure hell, whoever'd thought them up? It was three years since she had bought all that finery, hat and tie and high-heeled shoes. The folks they kept company with then were educated and cultured, she had told herself, and one has to keep up with them. And all for nothing—it was the first time they had gone visiting in all those three years.

They stopped by Agrafena's cottage; Pavel was slumped on her arm with all his weight, and there, as bad luck would have it, they met Anisya. She came round the corner and bumped right into them, and not alone, either—with those no-good Mashas.

When Pavel saw his dear sister he swayed like a felled tree. And Pelageya too was stunned at first, as though she'd lost her wits. So she did something very stupid—took the bait thrown to her by Big Masha, a well-known mischief-maker.

"Well, well, Prokopyevna—come out for a breath of fresh air?"

"Aye, that's right, Masha. He got tired, lying there all the time and he says, 'Come you out into the air, wife.' "

What else could she do? They weren't at home, they were in the street, if you're asked you have to answer.

One thing she forgot, that even a log has been known to talk. And Little Masha, although as thick as a log and deaf at that, just blurted out, "What d'ye tell lies for? Ye've been at Pyotr Ivanovich's."

Then there was the devil to pay and no pitch hot. Anisya, blind drunk, shouted her opinions for the whole street to hear. "You didn't want aught to do with me—shamed of your own sister—you ruined our family house—" Whenever Anisya had had a drink she brought up that house.

Of course Pelageya was not going to let her get away with it all. If someone grabs you by the hair you don't bow and thank them. No, you give back full measure. And running over.

Then Pavel began to vomit. Long-Tooth Agrafena was leaning out of her window; this was a real treat for her, a fine morsel to get those long teeth into. Then Tolya the Sparrow flew up. No need to go to the movies to see a show. The row was enjoyed by the whole street.

There was only one thing that partially consoled Pelageya—there were none of the important people near. None at all. And since there were none, the dust raised by Agrafena's cottage would be laid by the first rain.

7

"You sat there as though clothed in a golden wave. Sparks were flying from you—it was like the sun melted and flowing over your shoulders—"

That was how Olesha of the employment commitee talked to her about the first time he saw her, by the open window combing her hair. But all she remembered of that time was the sharp pain in her head as he grabbed her hair, damn him, and his impudent, hot, squinting eyes. She never thought, never guessed that their ways would cross some day. How could they—she a plain farm woman and he a big boss in the settlement across the river? He saw a young woman in the window as he was passing by and pulled her hair, just for fun.

But their ways did cross. One evening, a week or two later, when Pelageya was rinsing clothes in the river she looked up and saw Olesha. Where he'd sprung from she couldn't say—as if he'd shot up from underground. There he stood over to the side, grinning at her.

"Why don't you take off that kerchief? It isn't cold."

"You great oaf—is it my hair you're after again? Clear off before I take the yoke to you! Even if you are a boss.' "

"All right, all right. Will it fly away somewhere if you show it?"

"Mebbe it will. When you go to the pictures you buy a ticket, here you want it all free."

"And how much does your ticket cost?"

"Get along, go your ways. I've no time to be tarrying with you."

The third time they met was by the river again, and again she was there with her washing. That was when she guessed that Olesha had lain in wait for her.

"Well, speak on—how much does your ticket cost?"

"More'n you can pay."

"I've enough."

"Not you! "

"I have. I tell you! "

"Get me a job at the bakery over the river and I'll show it you wi'out charge."

What put it into her head she didn't know, and she never expected him to take it seriously.

But he did.

"All right, I'll get you the job. Now show me."

"Nay, first money on the barrel, then reach out for the goods." And Pelageya, to her own surprise, suddenly burst out laughing and let her kerchief slip a little, a mischievous glint in her eye—the devil must have given her a nudge.

As for Olesha, he went quite crazy.

"If you let me sleep on your hair I swear to God in a week you'll work in the bakery. I'm not jesting."

"I'm not jesting either."

Within a week she was installed at the bakery. Olesha kept his word. He got her out of the stock yard, the walls that hemmed her in collapsed—he'd really lost his head over her.

Well, she too kept her word—after the first day she stayed

all night at the bakery. But when she saw Olesha to the door in the early morning she had her word to say.

"And now forget my hair. We're quits. And don't take it into your head to fire me. I can scratch, too."

How many years had passed since then, how much water had flowed down the river! Where was Olesha now? Was he still alive? Did he remember the baker with the golden hair?

She had forgotten him. She forgot him as soon as the door shut behind him.

There was nothing to remember. It wasn't for pleasure or lust she had slept with a strange man. And if this water-logged chunk of memory which had lain submerged almost a score of years had now risen to the surface it was only because when loosening her rat's-tail for the night—all that remained of her former glory—she remembered her talk with Fat-Mouth Vaska.

Pavel was already snoring. Pelageya placed the usual mug of boiled water on a stool by the bed, put pills in a glass and finally lay down on a feather-bed spread on the floor beside Pavel's bed, so as to be handy in case he needed her.

She was accustomed to Pavel's snoring, he had always snored, but tonight it sounded different, as though he were choking; fighting off sleep, she raised her heavy head to take a last look at her husband. She raised herself and—why, she did not know—again, for the second or third time that day, the past rose up.

Had Pavel guessed about Olesha that time? He had given no sign, nothing, when she returned in the morning. Not a single question, not a word of blame. Except that when he had spoken of the bath, he had seemed to avoid her eyes.

"Our bath-house is heated," he said. "When will you go? Mebbe at the beginning, with the first steam?"

"That'll do, the first."

That morning she wore out two birch besoms on herself. She baked herself and steamed herself, not only to get rid of the dirt on her body but to steam out all memory of that night. But a trace remained. And it wasn't merely that she should now ask herself again whether Pavel had guessed or not—that was nothing, who cared now for something that had happened so many years ago. The nagging worry was that now and then, looking at her daughter, she remembered Olesha and started calculating months.

Her eyes on her heavily breathing husband, Pelageya

was repeating those calculations. She had started work at the bakery in August, on the eleventh. Alka was born on the fifteenth of April. Eight months. No—she let out a relieved breath, eight-month-babies hardly ever live. Seven months, yes, but they're peaky. Alka had rolled out of her like a head of cabbage. And she had not had even one childish ailment.

However, a suspicion is not a garden weed which you can uproot, throw away and forget. Suspicion, like muddy water, makes everything unclear and unclean. And however much Pelageya reasoned that Alka could have nothing whatsoever to do with Olesha, she felt no absolute certainty.

Of course eight-month babies do not live. And what mother does not know who her child's father is; but—who did the girl get her wanton ways from? Why was she so eager to fool with boys when she was still but a child? Previously, until today, Pelageya had had no doubts; she took after her aunt Anisya, she had her hot blood and for that reason Pelageya had not liked her sister-in-law; but now she no longer felt so sure.

Pelageya lay a little longer turning her pillow under her hot head, then rose. She could not sleep, anyway. She would not be able to sleep until she had taken a look at Alka.

8

The white night of early summer was ending. Beyond the river the sky was coloured with sunrise, but the festivities were still in full swing. At the upper end of the village someone was yanking a tune of sorts on an accordion, there were shouts, and laughter from drunken women—nowadays they drank like the men—and on the street by Agrafena's house there was a really disgraceful scene—small children playing at drunks, holding on to one another, lolling their heads, babbling something, just like their fathers and mothers.

Pelageya took the field path to avoid a drunk. He'd stick like a leech. Want her to come home with him. Or maybe start a fight—you could expect anything of a drunk. However, she was not particularly worried for herself, she could give as good as she got and better. But what if they started to tumble her daughter in the dirt?

Alka was only twelve the first time Pelageya caught her necking. It was still winter, the beginning of March and that day the cow Manka had taken sick. The vet was away in town. What could they do?

Then she remembered there was a young stock expert about—he wasn't a vet, of course, but still he knew more than they did.

That was when Pelageya caught her daughter—kissing, they were. In the cowshed. She had gone to fetch mash and those few minutes had been enough. It wasn't just that the fellow was pawing the girl—Alka was only too eager. She had wound herself round him like a blade of grass, standing on tiptoe to reach his mouth better, with both arms round his neck. It was this that shocked Pelageya.

The stock expert was soon disposed of, she swung some weight in those days and got him dispatched to the most out-of-the-way hole in the district. But where can you send your own daughter?

She tried whipping her. She tried reasoning with her. No use, any of it. She was always hearing about Alka seen in dark corners and not alone. And if now, for instance, Pelageya had come upon her with a fellow in the shadow of a barn or bath-house, she would not have been at all surprised.

By the club the earth groaned with its burden, it was a long time since she had seen such a crowd. And more and more kept coming from the lower ground, from the lumber centre, from over the river, from other villages— the engines which had begun panting on the river at midday had not quietened, and there were even visitors from town.

Quietly, unnoticed, she climbed over the stake-and-rider fence, and hoped to reach the porch beside which the young folks were dancing, equally unnoticed, but her luck was out.

"Cousin, dear cousin, eh but this is a good hap! And there was me, thinking to look in on you. Where can our Prokopyevna be, I was thinking, what's happened to her?"

Pelageya would willingly have torn to bits her "dear cousin", the sister of a cousin's wife in neighbouring village, it was neither the place nor the time for such an encounter. But of course she showed nothing of her true feelings, she registered an extreme of delight, as though there was nobody on earth she cherished like this red-faced, drunken, glassy-eyed creature.

"Ah, how nice to see you, how are you, dear cousin! " she said in tones of the greatest joy and gave an old-fashioned bow—see how we cherish relatives. "I thank you for remembering me so kindly, Anna Matveyevna. Why do you never come to see us? You don't have to cross mountains nor seas to reach us, you could've surely looked in this evening."

In fact, she said all the things that it is deemed proper to say in such a case and even more, because that tipsy fool started hugging and kissing her and then pulled her to the ring of dancers.

"Look you there, now, take a look at your daughter! A sight for sore eyes! Eh, but she's a bonny lass, that she is! "

So Pelageya found herself part of the ring of young folks, standing embraced with her cousin. What could she do, you can't say "Let me alone, you drunken fool" when there are people all round. And after a minute or two she was embracing her cousin with a right good will, for never had she thought, never imagined that she thought so much of Alka.

Antonida had been away to college, and where was she? Away on the edge of things, stamping it out with her brother. And another one with town learning, the daughter of the cooperative manager, was only looking on.

But her Alka! Right in the middle, the most noticed, and who with? The secretary of the Komsomol from the lumber settlement over the river. What more can you ask? Would an important Party man lower himself to dance with any kind of girl?

And it didn't stop there. As soon as Savvateyev led Alka back to the group of girls, up came an officer, the same one they had seen through the window at Pyotr Ivanovich's. Young, tall, handsome. He walked, supple as a vine. And the shine of his shoulder-boards—like two suns.

"A star, a star's in the ring! "

Well, maybe not a star, maybe the cousin was piling it on a bit, but still, Pelageya was not the only one admiring Alka, all eyes were on her. Even the other young folks— Alka had danced round the circle three times with the officer before another two couples began to dance.

Antonida was left a wallflower, standing aside, biting

her lacquered nails. And to make Pelageya's triumph complete Pyotr Ivanovich turned up, he couldn't sit quiet at his host's table, he wanted to see how his daughter was getting along.

Take a good look at her, Pyotr Ivanovich, at your learned owl (a real owl, especially when she looked up through her thick glasses). You can't be on top all the time. And I'll look at my daughter.

So Pelageya looked and looked, her head very high. And somehow all her cares, her recent worries seemed to fall away of themselves. Her daughter! Her own daughter queening it here!

The dance soon ended, a brief joy, and Pelageya beckoned to Alka; Pyotr Ivanovich was standing by his daughter, why shouldn't she stand with hers?

Alka came skipping over—she was still too much a child to be walking sedately as a maid should, but so happy! As though she'd won something big in the lottery!

But perhaps she had, thought Pelageya, and glanced quickly round the circle—where was the officer? What was he doing?

He was coming their way. Coming without any haste, fanning his hot face easily with a white handkerchief.

"Alevtina, won't you introduce me to your mother?"

Pelageya grasped the outstretched hand but the proper words seemed to have flown from her head. She mumbled something about the heat. It was real hot. Hot working and hot dancing.

"We don't mind that," said the officer. "We'll carry out our program. Won't we, Alevtina?"

Alka tossed her head jauntily—could there be any doubt of it? Of course they would! '

Before Pelageya could collect her thoughts—how ought she to regard Alka's escapade? Ought she not to scold her for her own good? Antonida approached.

"Alka, Vyacheslav Sergeyevich, wouldn't you like some tea? We have a samovar ready."

To Pelageya this was a marvel—since when had Pyotr Ivanovich started putting the samovar on at night? But then it dawned on her—of course, he was making an effort for the sake of his daughter.

"No, no, Antonida," Pelageya swiftly answered for her own daughter. "Be so good as to favour our house. My cousin is coming for a bite (the cousin came in handy!).

Alka, why are you standing there? Invite the young folks.
That's your job."

Pelageya was smiling, but she felt the ground insecure
under her feet. What had she gone and done? Who had she
lifted her hand against? All the way to the school she did
not dare look round; she could feel Pyotr Ivanovich's angry
glare scorching the back of her neck.

9

Earlier on, before the war, the village houses had stood
like soldiers on parade, in a straight line and so close they
almost touched. As for having the well, the bath-house
and kitchen garden by the house—no thought of it. The
house had its place, so did the well, and so did the bath-
house, somewhere at the back, and a good distance away.

Pelageya Amosova was the first to upset this established
order. She it was who laid out a farmstead with the well,
bath-house, keeping-cellar and kitchen garden all together,
handy. And all fenced in. To keep out animals and unwel-
come guests.

Later, others followed her example and now there were
few houses without their fences.

But the stupid, spiteful talk there had been at first!
"Making out rich! Turning up her nose at the village!
Breaking up the family home! " They all abused her.
Pavel's relatives abused her. Strangers, too. There were
even harsh words in Moscow. Yes, there was one from the
capital who delighted in old houses. He lamented, he almost
wept—to ruin such a poem in wood! He especially lamented
the porch with its double-sloping roof. Well, the old porch
really had been beautiful, standing on its carved pillars.
Pelageya knew that herself. Yes, but it winter it was a
torment carrying wood and water up those steep steps.
And what about bad weather, blizzards? The steps were
piled with snow and so was the porch, sometimes you
couldn't get the door open.

Vladislav Sergeyevich, young as he was, thoroughly appreciated the farmstead.

"Now, this is what I call a really fine set-up! " he said
as they poured into the yard, a noisy throng.

Yes, there was something to look at. The corners of the
front were faced with boards painted yellow, there was a

74

new slate roof which had cost over two hundred rubles, the porch was town style, glassed in—you wouldn't be the last person even in town with a house like that. And the freedom, the spaciousness all round!

When Pelageya had asked for the waste ground behind the old house, they had laughed at her in the rural Soviet—the woman's crazy! Even Pyotr Ivanovich with all his wisdom had joined in the jeers—couldn't look five years ahead. But that was where she was looking, and what she saw was waste land become a meadow with fragrant hay under the windows. And now the whole village envied her!

The sun was rising beyond the river when she brought her guests to the house and, heavens, how splendid it all looked! —Shining and sparkling like something from a fairy-tale until everything was tinted crimson—the faces, the roof, the white curtains at the windows.

Whether in thoughtlessness—after all he was a townsman —or just as a joke, Vladislav Sergeyevich seized a metal spade from the porch and began to toss the hay about. The noise, the squeals were deafening. Then the cousin added her bit. She scooped up a dipper of water from the barrel by the porch and ran with it to Vladislav Sergeyevich—cool him down! Within a few minutes not a person was dry, they were all drenched. So was the hay. It was trampled as though horses had been driven over it. But at this moment she regretted nothing. She was on top of the world, laughing more loudly than any.

Laughing... But meanwhile near by, on the other side of the house wall, Pavel lay unconscious, with death breathing coldly upon him...

No, no, she admitted she was to blame. It was her fault. She ought not to have left her sick husband alone. She should not have joined the merrymaking and invited officers home when her husband was ill. But on the other hand, Pelageya asked herself later, much later, what would have become of Pavel if Vladislav Sergeyevich hadn't been there? Alka was in a useless panic and she herself seemed to have lost her wits. Their local medic was lying snoring drunk at home. But Vladislav Sergeyevich took everything in hand as though he'd been doing nothing but help people out all his life.

"Petrenko! Drag that medical fellow to the well and drench him till the son-of-a-bitch comes to his senses.

Fedorov! Take the car and drive like the devil to town for the doctor! Step on it! "

He didn't stand idle while waiting for professional medical aid, either. He opened Pavel's shirt, had them open all the windows and let in fresh air, and gave Pavel some sort of drops—would she ever have thought of all that?

No, no, although there was talk, and the women had plenty to say about the officer later on, it must be admitted: if anyone saved Pavel from death that early morning it was Vladislav Sergeyevich.

10

At first Pavel's illness seemed as though it would bring ruin, the collapse of everything.

It was impossible, unthinkable that she should cope with the domestic work as well as the bakery on her own. She would have to leave the bakery. But what would life be without it? Crawl like a snail into your shell in the backs and bury yourself alive.

But heaven be praised, she did not have to give up the bakery. Anisya came to the rescue. She and Alka took her place at the oven.

Pavel, too, got better much sooner than she had expected. At first the town doctor had stunned her with his "A stroke, paralysis. You won't see your husband on his feet again." But Pavel did get up, on the fifteenth day he sat up in bed and three days later, with Pelageya's support, he went out on to the porch. So the Amosovs got back on their feet.

For two weeks Pelageya was beside her sick husband day and night, and got through a mass of jobs at the same time. She hoed the potatoes. She mowed Big Masha's meadow. And there was the cow, and the pig. The wood and water. The washing. No compassionate neighbour was going to do all that for her. But she had a rest from the back-breaking work at the bakery, and it was like a vacation. At least, that was how she felt when she made her way there after three weeks away.

Everything seemed new to her that day. She was going to the bakery during the day, and empty-handed. Walking leisurely, enjoying the clear fine day and noticing that the fields now smelt of young grain instead of hay. Again she was her old self, energetic, light-footed, as though she had thrown off ten years.

The only thing which cast a shadow on her good mood was Anisya's complaints about Alka. Nearly every day on coming home from the bakery she would begin talking about the officer. He was always hanging about there. It wasn't right.

"What's amiss, then?" Pelageya objected. "He's a customer. Gets bread from us for his men. Why shouldn't he come?"

"He doesn't come because of the bread. It's Alka he's got his eye on."

"Nay, then, you're not the one to speak bad of your niece. Don't you be saying them things, Anisya. Leave that for strangers. What if they do fool about a bit, they're young. We did, too, in our time."

"All the same, you don't light a bonfire when there's straw around."

So at last Pelageya was going to the bakery; she was going to see for herself what Anisya was making such a fuss about.

The river seemed to smile at her affectionately, like a mother. There were no gadflies, their time was past, instead there were flocks of sand martins. They flew low, playing just above the water with gay whistling.

Pelageya paused on the beaten track at the top of a grassy dune, enjoying the sight, then trotted quickly down the slope; she was seized with a rollicking mood not at all befitting her years—she wanted to kick off her boots and wade in the warm water by the bank, to feel on the soles of her feet the sandy bottom by the gravel spit.

However, she caught sight of Antonida—or Tonechka, as she was more accustomed to think of Pyotr Ivanovich's daughter, so she approached the river at a more staid walk.

Tonechka was sunbathing. On a sheet. Reading a book. Coming closer, Pelageya saw that the "sheet" was actually a beautiful green tasseled shawl that her mother wore in winter; the book in her hand was fiery red. But Antonida herself was skinny, pale, unaffected by the sun. True, Tonechka had beautiful eyes, no one could deny that. Angel's eyes, clear as the sky. But at present they were hidden behind dark glasses.

"Well now, Antonida, seeking to beautify yourself?" said Pelageya. "Taking the sun? Take it, take it, you have to do the way science says. But why are you all alone? In pictures the young lady always has a handsome beau beside her."

She delivered her pin-prick—and at once regretted it. It was easy to hurt Pyotr Ivanovich's children, both Antonida and Sergei. Who could they have taken after? Sort of defenceless, they were.

Wishing to smooth over her bitchiness, Pelageya invited Tonechka to cross the river with her—invited her warmly, sincerely.

"Come along, do, Antonida, you won't regret it, we've got tea over there and crisp sweet buns. And that side's even better for sunbathing."

"No, no thanks, no, I've got to get home," said Tonechka in a quick patter.

Pelageya sighed, then—nothing else to do—went to the boat.

11

Everything was in its place, the bakery with the big open windows, the great spreading pine trees, the well with its windlass and the old fence falling down in places.

She climbed the path leading to that fence, met the warm fragrance of fresh bread that you can only smell by a bakery, and burst into tears. She had to stop, she could not take a step for weeping.

There were soldiers sawing wood beside the porch. They stopped their work to ask her what was the matter—and what could she say? How did she know?

She had always regarded the bakery as a millstone round her neck, as grinding toil. But it seemed that without that toil, without that millstone she couldn't breathe.

The soldiers' surprise was even greater when this woman who had just been sobbing along suddenly broke into smiles, and ran past them and up the steps on to the porch, without stopping to take breath.

Her actions in the bakery, too, were unprecedented for her; it was not the officer she greeted first but the stove, the dough and her rosy-cheeked children—as Pelageya in good moments called the loaves just out of the oven; she embraced them all with her gaze.

Only then she nodded to Vladislav Sergeyevich.

Either seriously or fooling, Vladislav Sergeyevich was standing by the stove with a wooden shovel. In his shorts. Barefoot. That wasn't so bad, Pelageya could have accepted it, he had town ways and for that matter the village men too sometimes went about without pants and thought nothing of it. But Alka, Alka—shameless baggage! She too presented her belly-button for the world to admire.

"You've lost all sense and decency too—you brazen hussy! " Pelageya flared up. "Why don't you take those off, as well! " With a jerk of the head she indicated Alka's bra and panties of flowered cotton.

"It's hot in here," Alka said defiantly.

"Hot or not, bear in mind—you're a maid! "

Her disapproval grew as she looked more closely round the bakery. At first glance, witless with joy, there were things she hadn't noticed, such as the three oven trays burned through and thrown into the corner behind the bucket of swill (more trouble with the bookkeeper), and the spatters on the wall above the flour bin (clearly, nobody had bothered to wipe the place out), and the battered besom by the door (what use was a thing like that?).

But worst of all was the bread.

One, two, three—twelve loaves, no less, wet and "sad", you couldn't say whether they'd been baked in the oven or in the sun. A few of those loaves could be borne, it wasn't machines doing the work, you couldn't help spoiling bread sometimes. But the other loaves, too, were a sorry sight.

Pelageya looked into the bowl where she kept the mixture to smear the top crusts as soon as the loaves left the oven. She always used vegetable oil mixed with sugar and didn't grudge it. Then the loaves were pleasant to see and to handle, they seemed to smile at you. Almost flew into your mouth. But these—what had they used? Pelageya cast a stern look at Alka. Plain water?!

"Is this your first time in the bakery?" she said reprovingly. "Haven't you seen how your mother did it?"

"All right, all right, they'll eat it if they're hungry."

"Today they may, tomorrow too, but the day after they'll send the baker packing! "

"Scaring me? I'm shaking as I stand! "

Try and talk to her, the baggage, she'll always find an answer or excuse.

Nay, folks said that every tree grows its own fruit, but this fruit wasn't Pelageya's kind. Would Pelageya ever have dared talk to her mother like that? She'd have got a good whipping if she had. And she'd get such a name in the village she'd never find a husband. In those times they didn't look so much at your face, it was your hands and your back that mattered.

The only occupation Alka showed any inclination for was admiring herself. She would never get tired of doing that.

Pelageya's battles with her daughter about working had started long ago, when Alka first started reaching out after pretty clothes. And now, at this moment, she was so exasperated that if a stranger had not been there she could have broken a shovel on her.

But she managed to swallow her fury.

Reluctantly, taking her time in a way designed to irritate her mother, Alka slipped on an overall.

This was where the hitherto silent officer put in a word.

"I take it you haven't been in town recently, Pelageya Prokopyevna," he said courteously. "Just now, I assure you, half the population there lies by the river in costumes like Alka's. And there is no penalty."

"That's in town, Vladislav Sergeyevich; but here—we don't favour town ways here."

He gave a slight shrug—not my place to decide the way of things here, I'm not the master—so he bowed to local prejudice and put on his trousers.

Alka sulked. She knelt on a stool, leaning out of the open window, presenting her backside to her mother. A picture to admire!

Pelageya quickly washed the wall by the flour bin, then scrubbed the floor with a new wet besom till it shone, cleared up the worktable and suddenly began to think that perhaps she might have been too hasty flying out at the girl like that. Well or badly, she had been working all these days. In the scorching heat. She felt especially embarrassed at the thought of the officer—just at that moment he came in again from outdoors. What could she blame him for? Saving Pavel's life? Or now, helping to saw and chop the wood?

Quickly Pelageya changed her tone.

"Alka, haven't you thought to make tea for your helper?" she said gently, smiling.

"When would I be making tea? I've not been sitting idle."

"Idle or busy, you should give your helper something to eat and drink. Oh Alka, Alka, fancy leaving a man with naught but beer from the well! " Pelageya smiled again—warmly, then disclosed her cards. "Put on the samovar and I'll go for some live water."

12

Pelageya loved having tea at the bakery. Her best moments there were when, after taking out the baked loaves, she could sit down with the samovar. Not a kettle, the samovar. So that in the very darkest days of winter its sparkle brightened the table like the sun, as it hummed its quiet song.

Sometimes she had visitors in the bakery. Especially earlier on. The people who had looked in then! But say what you would, she had never had one so much to her liking as today.

Handsome. Educated. And clever as they make them, could see through a brick wall.

Pelageya bought two bottles of vodka, heedless of expense. Let it be a good day for the soldiers, too. They'd earned it. The wood they'd sawn and chopped—it was piled up as high as the porch. Besides, it was a wise word: if you treat the top man, don't forget the underlings. It is through them that the path leads to their boss.

So she slipped a bottle to the crop-headed lads—slipped it as she passed so that nobody should see.

He did, though; his sharp eye missed nothing.

As soon as she entered with her purchases he was shaking a finger at her.

"Breach of discipline, mother. Don't ever give my men drink! "

He said it jokingly, with a smile, but in such a way that you'd remember and not do it again.

Soon Pelageya was quite intoxicated, not with the vodka—she had taken only a drop for company—but with the conversation.

Her greatest pleasure on earth was good talk. Although she herself had had little education, she understood the age she lived in. She had seen, for instance, how Pyotr Ivanovich had managed to get on all his life.

But beside this quick-eyed rascal, as she affectionately thought of Vladik (he had insisted on her using the familiar contraction of his name) Pyotr Ivanovich was no sounding bell but just an empty barrel. Vladik knew everything, had seen everything, been everywhere, and if he began to talk, you listened.

For instance, what was the meaning of the "mother" with which he addressed her?

An ordinary word, no better or worse than others. Commonly used in former times. Your daughter calls you "mother" because she's your daughter; if another person uses it, it is just politeness. But when he calls you "mother" your heart leaps with joy. There is respect in it, and affection, and a sort of hint. A hint of the future. A hint that all sorts of things can happen, maybe some day he will be calling you "mother" by rights.

It wouldn't be a bad thing, not bad at all to have such a son, thought Pelageya, and for her part smoothed and flattered him every way she could.

But Alka? What was the matter with Alka? What was she thinking about?

Of course, nobody expected good talk from her, that comes with the years and not to all at that, but a girl does not win a man with talk. What about her eyes? What are her lips for?

Or take clothes—Pelageya was inwardly furious about the crumpled, faded overall Alka had dragged on. The same rag in which her mother worked by the stove! Was she a pauper? Hadn't she got pretty frocks? She signalled to her daughter with eyes and fingers: change into something else, don't disgrace yourself, or take it off altogether. Why sweat now when a bit ago you wore little more than you were born with?

Alka took no notice. Stubborn as a mule. Planted her feet. That was the way she was.

But that was not all. She was plain stupid when Pelageya began talking to Vladik about his parents. Just ordinary talk. Each weaves his own weft. Pelageya expected Alka to slide into the talk. But what did she do? Began to yawn. Simply gave way to a fit of yawns. And then —worse still— jumped up, flung off the overall and ran out to the river without a word. You can talk to my boy friend, I've no time. I want to take a swim. Pelageya dared not even lift her eyes to the officer, she was so ashamed. But it appeared that she had little understanding of the young people of today. Before a minute had passed Vladik had followed Alka and not even through the door—his feet twinkled on the windowsill and he was gone, everything forgotten—

father and mother both.

Pelageya was no longer angry with Alka. Can you be angry with a young filly when she kicks her heels! You scold, you may even slap, but the next moment you are watching with loving admiration as she capers and kicks out.

Now too Pelageya looked with a quiet smile at her daughter through the open window. She had a pretty daughter. One ought to bless a daughter like that, not scold her. And if the Amosovs were to rise in the world, she thought, it would be only through Alka. Through her beauty. Through that capricious gold which the officer was now pursuing.

13

That month Pelageya was rejuvenated, body and soul.

Oh, her golden wealth of hair did not grow again, or her cheeks fill out rosily; but she felt as though youth had returned, as though it were she who had fallen in love.

Yes, Alka and Vladik embraced and kissed (how could you refuse to kiss such a splendid man when you'd already held up your lips to village hobbledehoys?), but it was she, Pelageya, who was stirred. Stirred as she had never been when she herself was being wooed. After all, there had been nothing much to be excited about. Pavel was from a good family, in former times the Amosov house was the best in the village, but he was shy. Fell into her hand like a ripe plum.

But this one—a whirlwind, a flame, mind out or you'll burn your fingers; and what he's thinking is more than you can see. "Mother, mother,"—he doesn't grudge that, and he helped carry the hay out in an army truck, but he didn't show his hand. Not a word about the future.

Of course Alka had no need to hurry, she was hardly past the age when other girls were playing with dolls. But the gossip. Who wanted a girl's name bandied about across all fences? And then, too, it would soon be the new term, what would he feel like, being boy friend to a schoolgirl?

Pelageya thought and thought, and in the end decided to give a party for the young folks. There she'd be able to winkle out what he had in mind. Parties like that were the custom in the village, they were given when a son was leaving for his army service, or when children graduated from secondary school, or for no reason at all except that you felt like giving one.

The finest parties had always been Pyotr Ivanovich's where everything was of the best—the wine, the food, the music. But for this occasion Pelageya made up her mind to go one better.

Had anyone ever yet heard of a party where there was no vodka on the table yet all were drunk? But hers would be like that. She would set out five bottles of cognac; it would cost a lot, cognac cost nearly half as much again as vodka, but why be cheese-paring? Two or three extra loaves to feed the hog and that would cover the difference, and folks would have something worth talking about.

With the food, too, Pelageya put her best foot foremost. Fish, meat, brawn—that was obvious, no table could be called spread nowadays without those. But what about berries, Pyotr Ivanovich? Did you find cloudberries, for instance, when the flowers had been nipped by frost? She did, though. She sent Little Masha forty versts to bring back a small basket, which she had begged for a sick person from her mate at the monastery who collected cloudberries for the bishop every summer.

Raspberries were Pelageya's own care. Those too had ripened badly that year, on the nearby slopes they had all dried up with heat, and she had to trudge all the way beyond the Ipatov burn. But the berries she found there! Big, juicy, and untouched, solid thickets like a green and red quilt. She quickly filled her enamel pail and then fashioned a basket of birch-bark and filled that, too. She could hardly drag herself home; it was seven versts, the weight nearly pulled her arms from their sockets and she had had only a rusk to eat all day.

"Pavel, Anisya! " she called from the entry, forcing a smile. "Scold me all you want for a flitterhead. You'd never believe where I've been."

Then she was struck by Anisya's silence, the way she was sitting idly with drooping head. She looked at her husband. Pavel was lying on the bed with closed eyes; at first she thought he was asleep but no, he was not asleep. He was breathing, deep sobbing breaths, his face was shining with sweat and he had a wet cloth over his heart. Could he have had another attack?

Pelageya quickly set down the bucket and basket of berries on the table.

"Where's Alka? Has she gone for the doctor?"

Again Anisya said nothing.

"What's wrong? Where's Alka? Hasn't she come back from the bakery?"

"Alka's gone."

"Gone?" Pelageya's knees gave way, she almost missed the chair.

So that was who had waved to her from the steamer when she emerged from the forest by the river! Her own daughter. And there she had been, thinking what a friendly daughter some parents had, waving to a woman she didn't know, a stranger.

"With yon randy-dandy?" asked Pelageya dully.

"She went alone."

"Alone? She went alone to town? Where was *that* one?"

"He went yesterday."

"Father, Father," Pelageya shrieked. "You know what our daughter's done?"

Anisya took her out into the passage for the final blow: Alka was pregnant. At least, that was what she had told her aunt and her father when she had run home from the bakery in the afternoon and suddenly started packing her things to go to town.

14

It is not trees in the wood that groan,
Not the grey doves in the field that moan,
A new-made widow that sits alone...

With those words reminiscent of childhood Pelageya longed to pour out her grief. Still more she longed to fall on her knees and wail her repentance before everyone. "Forgive me, forgive me, Pavel! It was I, I who drove you to the grave! "

But she did neither.

She stood swaying beside the coffin with Anisya, who was sobbing, her face swollen with crying, and kept back her own cries behind her teeth. Because who would believe her? Who would be moved by her tears?

Pavel was accompanied on his last journey by relatives close and distant. Those who lived in the village came as a matter of course, but in addition Pavel's cousin came from town, and aged uncle came from the lumber settlement and

Pavel's officer nephew flew in.

Only his daughter, Alka, was absent.

Pavel had died on the third day after she ran away from home, and where could they seek her? In town? Along the way there? And altogether, thought Pelageya, maybe it was just as well that Alka wasn't there by the coffin. She herself felt like a criminal, she couldn't look people in the face, what would Alka feel like? Oh, of course she hadn't wanted her father's death, but facts were facts. It was after her tumultuous departure that he died, so she, his only daughter, had helped him into the grave. Even when she was absent, every now and then commiserating whispers reached Pelageya standing by the dead man's feet: "Aye, that's what childer are like nowadays—they'll send their parents into the grave—you rear them, you care for them—" Imagine the talk if Alka had been there!

The funeral ceremonies were both old style and new.

At home everything went according to old custom, and the representatives of Authority did not interfere. While old women smoked the coffin with incense and softly sang "Holy God" these representatives stood out on the porch smoking. It's true, Afonka the vet, drunk as usual, tried to force his way in, shouting that they should stop making a mock of a man who was a communist though not in the Party, but he was quickly subdued. The representatives, Vassily Ignatyevich and Pyotr Ivanovich, quite simply pushed him out.

The new style began at the cemetery when there were speeches over the open coffin.

"He never spared himself—from the first day of the kolkhoz he was in the forefront of work—honest—an example to all—never will we forget—"

Then Pelageya began to give way. Her self-control had held firm through everything else; the laments, the looks of condemnation, the whispers had not weakened her. Until then she had stood by the coffin, a figure of stone. But when the speeches began the ground surged under her feet.

"He never spared himself—from the first day of the kolkhoz he was in the forefront of work—honest—an example to all—"

Pelageya listened, and suddenly it burst upon her: but it's all true, every word of it!

He had worked in the kolkhoz steadily and unfailingly—

like a horse, like a machine. He had collapsed, ill, while working. They brought him home from the thresher on a sledge. But who had ever valued his work while he was alive? Who had said "thank you" even once? The board? Or she, Pelageya?

No, the truth must be told: she had not valued her husband's work. But how can you value work which you got paid naught for, some years?

Now they praised him. And suddenly she felt an aching regret that he could not hear that praise.

She looked at the dead man in his coffin, at his still, waxen face and closed eyes, the big, very white hands crossed on his breast, and realisation swept over—this was *Pavel*, her husband, the man with whom, for better or worse, her life had been shared.

Then she wept, wept aloud, and now she cared nothing for what people might be saying about her or what dirt they might be slinging at Alka.

15

The rest she had so longed for had at last come.

In the morning she rose late, unhurriedly. Unhurriedly she lighted the fire, drank tea and then set out for the forest. Ever since she was small she had loved mushrooming and berrying. If there was anyone whom she had envied in those years she worked at the bakery it was those women who could do it. Now there was no longer any need for envy, she could spend the whole day in the forest.

So she did. She walked over hills and dales familiar from childhood, by old farmsteads, over old clearings; she rested beside streams and rivers, gazed into their deep autumn blue, and listened to the calls of cranes and the barking of dogs.

But how much did she, living alone, need? Three times she went for mushrooms, she filled a tub with bilberries; what did she need with more?

For some days she was occupied digging potatoes. They were good that year, large and solid, two rows filled the potato cellar and another still remained behind the bathhouse; she should have been glad and thanked heaven for its bounty, but instead she asked herself again: what was the use? What did she need all those potatoes for?

She was racked with anxiety, waiting for a letter from Alka. But none came. She had gone, and not a word did she send. As though the earth had swallowed her. And Pelageya raged at her daughter, cursed her with strong words—"Bitch! Heartless bitch! Your father's death doesn't satisfy you, you want to drive your mother into the grave too! " But when the angry mood passed she loved her daughter again and feared for her. Where was she? What was she doing? In a strange town. Without any identity papers.

One day Pelageya decided to salt a bucket of mushrooms for Alka, some day she would surely show up again. She walked a long way, five versts at least, and suddenly found herself near the Surga, by the herd of browsing cattle.

It was a dry day and bright, the sun was warm as in summer—for that matter the whole of September had been unusually fine as though God himself wanted to reward her for all the years she had spent in the bakery.

She knew every ripple of the Surga, she had been a dairy-maid there for seven years before she went to the bakery. She had not the slightest intention of leaving the wooded hillside so rich in berries and going down to the women. Why should she? There was nothing new to her there.

But suddenly an engine rattled and the cows, as though obedient to a command, walked staidly towards the long open milking shed with a double-sloping tiled roof, and she wondered what this electric milker was like. It had been in use for two years in the kolkhoz but she had never seen it.

The dairy-maids met her with jokes.

"So there's why we haven't found berries or mushrooms, there's been a thief coming over clearing our woods."

"Nay, that isn't it, it's because you sleep over long," said Oleksa Lapin, the herd, who was sitting by the light drinking tea.

"And that's a true word, we sleep plenty," the women admitted, laughing.

They laughed and it was not surprising; a machine did the milking, all they had to do was wash the udders and fix onto the teats the rubber ends of long tubes along which the milk was pumped into freezing aluminium cans. That was all milking meant nowadays.

It had been very different in Pelageya's time. Their hands were aching and numb before they finished that milking.

And the cold? And the rain? And that long trudge twice a day, from the village to the Surga and from the Surga back to the village? Mud knee-deep, and no chance of getting on the cart? If the horse managed to pull the milk-cans, you couldn't ask more of it. But now—a truck to take you home. With a canvas cover. What wonder that they laughed and joked!

Everything had changed. Even the cows looked different, somehow. Times, you had to pull a cow to the milking shed as if it was going to be slaughtered. You'd be hoarse with shouting before you finished. But now the cows went willingly, nay, eagerly, because they knew that salt licks and concentrate were waiting for them.

"Have you heard from Alka?"

If Lida Vakhromeyeva had not spoken, Pelageya would not have known her. She had turned out a beauty, with roses on her cheeks. Could that be the snivelling lump of misery who had been ready to lay hands on herself last year?

Like Alka, Lida found learning difficult; she failed the seventh form exams and was to have another chance at them before the autumn term started; but there her father, a short-tempered man, put his foot down. "She'll go to work. A dairy-maid. If she's no head for learning, let her learn about the cows! " Lida wept, pleaded with her father, her mother almost went on her knees to the chairman, wrote to her officer uncle in town imploring him to come—anything, only not the manure, not the cows. But now look at her, you couldn't see a happier girl. She was laughing, laughing whole-heartedly, with the whole of her. And how she was dressed—a picture! Those smart top-boots had certainly cost no less than fifty rubles. That was the sort of money dairy-maids earned these days.

Pelageya thought sadly of Alka; she could have been a dairy-maid. Why not? What was wrong with that job?

All their lives, from century to century, her grandmother and her mother and she herself had minded cows, and cleaned out manure, and now all of a sudden they had made up their minds that for their own children it wouldn't do, it was dirty work. Why? Why dirty, when life was based upon that dirt?

That day Pelageya wept her heart out. She wept in the forest after leaving the dairy-maids, and along the road home. But her tears were the bitterest when she reached home, when she entered the empty house.

16

Sickness crept upon Pelageya stealthily with the autumn rains and the damp, and for her it was torture. She had no patience with sickness. She took after her mother. Three days before her death her mother had asked for some work. "Give me something to do, I want to live."

Of course Pelageya was not thinking of the bakery, that was a burden too heavy for her now; but there was work which she did consider seriously. The morning after meeting the dairy-maids by the Surga, before she was up, the idea suddenly struck her: why shouldn't she herself become a dairy-maid again? Working in the open air, machines to assist her and no need to trudge all the way there on foot—surely she could manage that?

For three days she thought of nothing else. Whatever she was doing, wherever she went she was thinking of the sensation her return to the kolkhoz would cause in the village.

"Have you heard what Pelageya's taken in her head?"

"Well I'll be danged! "

"That's Pelageya. Like iron, she is."

But on the fourth morning, where was that iron? She couldn't move, neither arms nor legs. She could hardly breathe.

However, by midday it had passed off more or less and she even set about banking up the keeping cellar for the winter; but from that day on she grew steadily weaker.

She fought the sickness, by keeping herself busy about the house; she sorted and stacked wood, she cleared up and burned rubbish, she caulked the store room—every winter one corner froze—and she often walked up the hill to that vantage point from which she could see the bakery. If it was a dry day she would sit down by the bird-cherry where Pavel had waited for her and gaze across the river.

Many were the things she thought about there, in the scented quietness, and much she remembered, good and bad, but most of all her mind went back to those first days working at the bakery, to that reckless, that foolhardy boldness with which she had flung herself into the fight for a better life.

She did not see any courage in sleeping with a strange man; if need and hunger drive, you'd sleep with the devil himself. And she and Pavel had known enough of need and hunger after the war. In 'forty-six they had seen their first-born, their only son, pine away and die. Die of hunger because his mother had no milk.

Could she let the same thing happen with the second baby?

No, she saw her courage in other things, in not fearing to go against them all. Against the kolkhoz chairman who raged at losing his best dairy-maid, against the kolkhoz members ("What's Pelageya done that she's given a fat job?") and against the baker Dunka and her family.

She was victorious. She felled them all—she, alone. In a single month. And what with? With strength, or guile? With bread. With those very loaves she baked in the oven. They were her troops that went out to win people. And they did. Nobody could resist her bread—light, fragrant, tasty and filling.

17

Twice in October the village medic visited Pelageya and each time urged her to go to the hospital in town, but she only shook her head. What for? How would the doctors there help her? Didn't she know herself what her sickness was?

How many times in those years had they re-laid the stove at the bakery? And that's leaving aside the separate bricks they changed every year. They couldn't stand the heat, it cracked them.

Those were bricks, made of clay—stone, you could call them. What could you say of a woman, then? Of her, going those eighteen years with never a day's rest? So now she too had crumbled, collapsed, she could not get herself off her bed for days on end.

It was rarely that anyone looked in. Big Masha she herself had put out; she had settled accounts with Anisya directly after Pavel's funeral, it was more than she could endure to see her, the witness of her own shame; Pyotr Ivanovich did not come, that was to be expected, what did he need with her now?

The only visitor in those cool autumn days was Lida Vakhromeyeva, Alka's friend. She did come, and brought in water, and wood, and told her village news. But truth to tell, Pelageya did not urge her to come because she felt so depressed when Lida went. As though the sun had gone and a dreary night had set in.

During the day Pelageya managed to move around a bit in the house, and lying in bed then was not so dreadfully cheerless. There was life outside the window. Somebody would pass on horseback or on a tractor, or a neighbour would go to the well rattling her pails; if there was nothing else a crow would start cawing—that, too, was life. But at night it was like the grave. You could cry, scream—nobody would hear. Only sometimes drunken Afonka came by, with his headlight playing on the nickeled samovars standing on the chest of drawers.

When he had taken too much Afonka could not rest, the whole night long he would be riding round like some restless spirit on his motorcycle, from street to street, from lane to lane. How Pelageya had cursed in former times when Afonka came noisily past their window! She had called down every disaster she could think of on his head. But now, in those long autumn nights, she was glad to hear even the drunken motorcyclist in the street.

When the November holiday came round Pelageya felt neither better nor worse than the previous day. But she rose long before dawn, lighted the fire, baked meat pies, cheesecakes and currant buns, cooked fish, then scrubbed the floor, changed the tablecloth and put on a good dress.

She loved this holiday best of all.

In other times, from early morning the house seemed to ring with rejoicing. First there would be getting Pavel and Alka ready for the demonstration and trying on new clothes—there was always something new for that holiday; then round about eleven when the demonstration reached the neighbourhood, various "frozen rabbits" (as Pelageya secretly called those bosses who looked in to take a glass of something in the warmth), men like Pyotr Ivanovich, the chairman of the rural Soviet and the kolkhoz chairman slipped in unobtrusively, furtively, so there wouldn't be talk. Each would come with a joke, one would mimic the deacon, another would bleat like a goat from the threshold, "Can my frozen bones get thawed out here?"

All day Pelageya sat at the window, hidden by the curtain looking out into the village street.

This year again there was no demonstration. Three years ago a schoolgirl had died of influenza after getting her feet wet in it, and after that they had stopped walking in procession with red flags.

All day Pelageya watched tipsy men and women passing

on the way to and from Anisya's, sighed, cried a little, and when darkness came lay down again without putting on the light.

Before she had time to close her eyes, she heard footsteps on the porch, and then the ring clashed on the door. She sat up in bed—who had remembered her on this day?

It was Big Masha; her malicious little eyes gleamed in the darkness on the threshold.

Pelageya gasped, finding no words; she was thunderstruck. You'd have to think for a long time before you'd think of such an insult.

At last she got her breath back.

"Haven't you mistaken the address?" she asked acidly—she had heard that said by the people with whom she had once foregathered. Then, realizing that the sarcasm would be wasted on Masha, she drove straight from the shoulder. "Or, mebbe you've come to show off your Gifts to Christ? Something new? Is it good picking today?"

Gifts to Christ were handkerchiefs, towels, plain dresses, cotton materials, wool from the sheep and even small change—everything that believers hung on the prayer crosses or laid by them in fulfilment of vows.

These prayer crosses began to appear in the forest near the village during the war. Their construction was of the simplest. Planed crosses set in the ground were rare. The usual thing was a pine or fir tree, not too thick, cut at a height of two or three metres, roughly trimmed, crosspiece fixed on, and a few stones thrown round the base; with that the cross, rather reminiscent of some heathen image, was complete.

Of course the local atheists were not sleeping, they cut down the prayer crosses ruthlessly wherever they found them. But you can't cut down a forest.

Big Masha had got a living from these crosses for many a year. She went the rounds of those in the vicinity before every holiday, like a hunter going round his traps.

However, Pelageya got herself worked up for nothing, her anger left the old woman quite unmoved. Big Masha did not flounce out of the house, as another would have done in her place. She did not turn a hair. She seated herself on the bench by the stove, hitching the sarafan she wore over the striped trousers above her knees, crossed her legs and actually lighted a cigarette.

Strangely, Masha's impudence sobered Pelageya, other-

93

wise heaven alone knows what might have happened; decent people didn't smoke in her house without permission, let alone the sweepings of the gutter.

Nay, she's got something, thought Pelageya, she hasn't come empty-handed if she's that impudent. So cautiously, feeling her out, Pelageya asked, "What's happening these days? What's the talk going from tongue to tongue?"

"Eh, there's this and that, sort o' thing you allus have," the old woman answered evasively.

"Fratching, like?"

"Why fratching? Some do, and others are right merry."

"Aye," sighed Pelageya, "yon's a true word. Some are merry right enough."

"Nay, don't you sigh, you inna without cause for gladness."

"Me?" She raised herself in bed in her surprise.

"Aye, you."

"Hush your foolish chat... My goodman dead and me hardly living..."

Masha did not dispute that.

So it's news about Alka, Pelageya guessed and she felt suddenly light and happy as though summer had entered the house.

She rose quickly from the bed.

"Aye, you see the pass I've come to, a visitor's come and here am I lying like a log. Forgive me, ninny that I am." Suddenly she found herself speaking in her old half-forgotten voice, that warm, caressing voice which nobody, not even Pyotr Ivanovich, could resist. "Lying here the day long as I am, my wits is addled, like. Nay, nay Maria Arkhipovna, I'll put on the samovar and get me out a couple of glasses, it's a holiday, after all. And smoke, smoke, don't be shy. I used to smoke sometimes myself when my man was well and hale. And take off them boots, do, give your feet a rest, I'll get you some soft felt boots."

The news Masha had to give (after three glasses, of course, Pelageya knew she'd get nothing out of the old woman dry) exceeded all expectations: the rural Soviet had sent Alka the necessary documents for her identity papers.

"You haven't got it wrong, Masha? Not mixed things up, like?" she asked and unable to restrain herself, burst into tears. You might say she had actually shortened her life for those papers, perhaps even taken to her bed because of them; she'd gone to Fat-Mouth, pleaded with the kolkhoz

chairman, complained to Pyotr Ivanovich, and all in vain.
"Not the time," said Pyotr Ivanovich. "Young folks are
wanted on the land. Wait a bit." But how could she wait?
And a girl in town with no identity papers—worse than
getting lost in the forest.

Now that trouble had fallen away. Alka had her papers.

"But when did they send them?" she persisted, still
almost afraid to believe.

"Day afore yestiddy."

"Afore yesterday? And you had the heart to keep such
news two days from her mother?"

"Aye, but I didn't know how her mother welcome me."

"Now, now, why dig up old scores," and Pelageya flapped
her hands. "The sun can go dark, and what can you ask of
us silly women? But tell me, tell me everything, Masha."

"Eh, what more's to tell? Vassily Ignatyevich told me
yesterday in the shop. 'We've lost yon lass for good an' all,'
he says. 'The military are demanding her papers.' "

"So they sent what's needed?"

"What d'you think? It's the military."

"The military?" repeated Pelageya thoughtfully. "Then
it's have been him, Vladik, as did it.—Aye, that's it, Masha!
Heavens! " she cried, and there were tears in her eyes.
"They're together, then? Together! And there was me all
this time, couldn't rest for worrying! "

"Aye, you're her mother," said Masha meaningly.

"I wish I could but cast an eye on them," sighed Pelageya,
opening her heart. "But—nay, this illness ties me tighter'n a
rope. And that bitch, she never thinks to write. That's the
way children are nowadays. It's 'mother, mother' when
things is bad, but when it's all sunshine then they forget
their mothers."

Masha said consolingly that a letter was sure to come
now, Alka had had nothing to write about before, she'd
only have upset Pelageya more with having no papers. Then
she made a suggestion.

"If you haven't the patience to bide, I can go for you.
Right away, I can."

"You? Go to town?"

"And why not? I'll come back and tell you all of it, just
what it is."

Pelageya compressed her lips as she always did when she
had to make a decision, and reckoned what Masha's trip was
likely to cost her. Forty rubles. A lot. Nigh on a month's

wages at the bakery. But then, she thought, what did money matter? Wasn't her peace of mind worth it?

"I'll give you twenty-five rubles," she said warily.

"Go to town for twenty-five? Go yourself!" With business-like briskness Big Masha totted up the cost on her fingers. "A return ticket, seventeen-sixty. Aye? Then I've got to have summat to eat, and a bed, haven't I? My expenses? Aye, and mebbe a bit to warm my insides." Masha sniggered.

After some haggling they agreed on thirty-five rubles and buns for the journey, which of course Pelageya would bake.

18

Masha was away for nine days, three more than they had arranged and the last nights Pelageya hardly slept at all. She lay and worried, racked by her fears about Alka.

The hard frosts struck to increase her anxiety. Where was the old woman? She had gone in thin boots and not taken much with her. Had she got ill somewhere along the road?

But at last Masha arrived.

She came in, a walking scarecrow, wearing an army cap with a light peak on top of a shawl wound many times round her head and shoulders, man's gauntlets—a big man's—reaching to her elbows and a wretched apology for a sheep-skin with the wool outside. She had evidently heaped upon herself everything which compassionate people had given her.

Pelageya transformed the old woman in no time; she put felt boots warm from the stove on her feet, gave her her own knitted jacket, likewise warm from the stove, and followed that with a glass of vodka—treated her, in fact, as the most welcome and valued guest.

"Well, and how is she?" she asked impatiently when they were seated at the table. (The samovar was boiling, for the third day it had steamed from morning till night.)

"She's done right well for herself," Masha said with a loud snuffle—she had a cold—and raised a tobacco-stained thumb impressively. "She's a waitress."

"A what?"

"A waitress. Runs about wi' a tray."

The light went out of Pelageya's eyes.

"Eh, Alka, Alka, we don't have no good fortune, either of us. Where's the good o' that—running about with a tray?"

"And what's the ill of it? It isn't like here, you take aught that's thrown at you and guzzle. They gorge themselves wi' music there."

"Music?"

"Aye—stuff themselves and get up and dance so's to shake it down, like, and back to the table again."

"She'll not be in one o' them—restrongs, cabarrays—them places where men go to drink?"

Masha nodded briefly.

"Ayè—a restrong."

"How was she, herself? What did she look like?"

"All right. It isn't mucky work. And she rakes in money wi' a shovel."

"Talk sense. Who's so open-handed there?"

"There's them in town like that. And 'specially if they're tipsy and there's a lass wagging her tail at them."

"Wagging her—? My Alka? Has she gone wild or what?"

"Restrong, cabarray," Masha explained with the air of an experienced traveller. "Part of their job. So's a person gets full pleasure for his money."

"No, that's no good, no good at all," said Pelageya disapprovingly, and not so much to Masha as asking herself, she continued. "What's Vladik thinking of? Why does he let her?"

Then it all came out: Masha had not even seen Vladik. She had not been in Alka's home. And she knew nothing of how the young folks were getting along.

"What do you know, then?" asked Pelageya angrily. "What did I send you for? Mebbe you weren't even in town at all?"

No, Masha assured her, she had been there. And she had been in the "restrong" too. But if Alka hadn't invited her home she couldn't help it. "Young folks," she explained Alka's lack of hospitality. "They don't want to fash theirselves wi' an old woman."

Yes, Masha did not bring any bagful of news about Alka's doing (she hadn't even got anything clear about that pregnancy), but a mother's heart can make do with little, Pelageya was comforted and again she reached out to life.

She started off by washing and cleaning everything—the samovars, the copper hand-washbowl, the large basin (she liked to have everything in the house shining), and then set to work airing everything that could be aired. All her stock.

There were pieces of cotton and silk material to be made

up, there were summer and winter shawls, scarves, kerchiefs, dresses, skirts—Pelageya had coffers and baskets filled with these things and her greatest joy in summer, on sunny days, had been to hang up all this brilliant, colourful wealth about the garden and yard.

This past summer she had aired nothing because of Pavel's illness, so she had to do it now on overcast days, because she could not let it go until spring, the materials would be damp and could get mildewed.

The well-heated room was hot and stuffy, it smelled of stale materials and dye, but Pelageya was happy. She would take up a dress-length, shake it out, try the feel of it with her fingers, her teeth, then hang it over the rope stretched across the room just beneath the ceiling.

In the evenings Big Masha would come—another pleasure. They would sit over their tea and gossip. About everything. About all that was happening in the world, in the district and in their village. The old woman went everywhere poked her nose into everything and nothing escaped her and if she lashed out at anyone you listened.

Her angriest invective was reserved for Pyotr Ivanovich and his family, because try as she would she had never found a hole to crawl through into their house. Pelageya did not check her. Why should she? He needn't be honoured all the time, his tail could be twisted, too. The talk usually started something like this.

"Have you seen our pretty lass lately?" That would come from Pelageya.

"What lass would you be meaning?"

"What lass—there's but one, Antonida."

Then Masha's dark wrinkled face would twist as though she'd heartburn—for some reason she had a particular dislike for quiet, inoffensive Tonechka.

"Pretty lass—huh! Nor face nor colour. Like a dried fish."

"No, no, Masha," Pelageya objected insincerely. "Don't you talk that way. You're wrong. Folks all like Antonida, ask anyone."

"An' why'd I ask when I can go about and see for myself? I was in the club a bit agone. There she was, wi'a lot of fence-posts."

"With what?"

"Flat fence-posts. Bits o' girls from the school. And she's like 'em, anyways. Got naught in front, 'cept she stuffs in chunks o' cotton wool to make bumps."

"Cotton wool?" Pelageya's eyes widened. "Look you there, now, the fashions there are. Stuffing cotton wool down their fronts. Does it make her more shapely like?"

Masha exploded; she jumped up, spat, ran here and there, and as for her talk—all the venom of her heart was poured out on Pyotr Ivanovich's daughter.

Later on, when Pelageya had once more got rid of Big Masha, she often remembered and repented those disgraceful conversations with the old woman; she had a guilty feeling—was it for this spiteful talk that God had punished her? And his instrument had been that same Tonechka.

One midday not long before New Year she was hanging crepe-de-chine dress-lengths in the room—she had a special weakness for that material—when Axinya from the shop came running in.

"You was wanting a plush jack—they've just come in! " she gasped from the doorway.

Pelageya did not know how to thank her. All the married women had them, and for three years she had been unable to get one. The time had passed when the salesgirls brought her things right to the house.

It was cold out, the north wind lifted the snow and whirled it round, but she ran over lightly clad, light-footed, as she had run to the shop in former days.

She liked going to the shop, it made something special of the day. The feast of colours and scents intoxicated her. And as for the shelf with fabrics—she was ready to stand before it for hours.

The shop was empty and Axinya at once tossed a plush jacket to her—from beneath the counter. So that she should know without telling that Axinya was doing her a great favour.

The jacket was her size—maybe it made her shoulders look a little broader but one couldn't be too particular with a thing in such demand.

"Aren't you taking one for Alka, too?" asked Axinya. "I'll let you have two. The others must just wait."

Without much ado she decided to do so. Alka was a woman now, the jacket would come in useful.

"Thank you, Axinya, thank you! You won't lose by it, I promise you, I pay my debts," said Pelageya with warm gratitude. She wrapped up the jackets in a big shawl (you don't give away a person who's done you a good turn) and set off for home.

It was on her way back that she met Antonida by the club. She was wearing fashionable high boots and her face was almost hidden in a fluffy white fur collar—a hundred rubles it had cost, her mother had said. She was deep in thought and saw nothing.

Pelageya greeted her first as usual, which embarrassed Antonida, and then—some imp must have nudged her—opened up the shawl. Look, look at this, Antonida, you've no call to be stuck up, some folks still reckon with me.

Antonida liked the jacket. "It's nice," she fluted.

"Have you got one?" asked Pelageya.

"No—I don't think I have," mumbled Antonida and looked away.

I suppose she can't see anything at all in winter when her glasses freeze, she has to feel her way about, thought Pelageya and again she felt sorry for her, as she had by the river that day in summer.

In a sudden impulse of kindness she snatched a jacket from its wrapping. The black plush looked rich against the white snow, like a wolverine's fur.

"Here, take it, Antonida! I'm an old woman, I can do without a plush jacket. I don't need it, really."

"Oh no, thank you—no, why should you—"

"Don't thank me, Antonida. Don't I remember past kindness? You think I haven't any heart? The times Pyotr Ivanovich has helped me when I needed it. Nay, nay, Antonida, take it! I won't listen to a word."

Antonida was lost in embarrassment, she twisted on her heel, she sniffed, then mumbled something about plush jackets having gone out of fashion.

"Out of fashion?" said Pelageya in surprise. "All these years folks have been snatching them up—"

"That was earlier. You—excuse me, Pelageya Prokopyevna, but those jackets have been hanging in the shop since summer of last year."

Softly, hesitantly, the words emerged from the fur collar and they made Pelageya sway on her feet.

19

At the shop they finally took the jackets back; she went right up to the chairman of the general stores.

But it was a blow. A terrible one. It wasn't just that

100

she'd been tricked; she gave little thought to that, someone was always tricking someone else. The knowledge that gave her no peace was that she had made a fool of herself by falling so easily into Axinya's trap. That meant that she was out of step with the life around her. And wasn't she? The lieutenant had fooled her, that bitch Axinya had fooled her. What was she to do with her life now?

No, her day was past, it wasn't for nothing Pyotr Ivanovich had ditched her. Left behind. Gone out of fashion. Like that plush jacket she'd grabbed so eagerly today.

At home the colourful dress-lengths of crepe-de-chine, her favourite material, hung on the line, filling the room with their characteristic smell, and two more lay folded in the open basket. But she sat by the table, still in outer things in which she had hurried to the shop, without moving a finger. She didn't even glance at them.

She was thinking. Thinking of those ill-starred jackets which she had coveted for three years, thinking of those dress-lengths, the ones on the line and the ones still in the chests. She looked back over her past life. Dear God! What had she spent it on?

She had been scorched, she had sweated by the red-hot stove and carried buckets of swill across the river, she had fattened pigs, gone without sleep and driven her husband—what for? For that crepe-de-chine and cotton, the things they thought little of these days. Why deceive herself?

Pelageya burst into bitter tears. Whose fault was it that these fabrics had blinded her to life, and her husband, and everything in the world? Was it her fault that a third of her life she had gone hungry? Whose father and brother had died of hunger in 'thirty-three? And during the war? And after the war when she had had to watch her son die, her first-born? All those years there had been only one thing which you could barter for bread—fabrics. Because in those years people had worn out everything they had and could get nothing.

Who could wonder if she, having got that job in the bakery, began to collect dress-lengths. For all those years she collected them, it became an obsession, because to her it was not cotton materials or crepe-de-chine that she put in her chests, but life. A reserve of full-fed days. For her daughter, her husband, herself.

That day Pelageya took to her bed again.

20

All that winter Pelageya was ill. True, she spent little time in bed, she would rise and move about a bit, but work was beyond her. And anyway, she hadn't the heart for it.

Letters came very occasionally from Alka, very brief, a greeting and "living well", no word of affection. But how was she "living well"? Alone? With Vladik? Call to her all you would, you got no answer. Like calling in the dense forest.

One day in winter, a couple of weeks after New Year, Pyotr Ivanovich's son Sergei came—very drunk, hardly able to keep his feet.

Pelageya liked Sergei, a plain lad, without guile, and she tried, not for Pyotr Ivanovich's sake but for his own, to talk sense into him: this is no good, Sergei Petrovich, tippling this way, you're too young yet to take to the bottle.

"Too young?" Sergei burst out and struck himself on the chest with his fist—wildly, like a seasoned toper. "And if I see all black? If my heart's ready to burst?"

"What's it your heart lacks? A man as has been to college, stands out afore all, healthy, praise the Lord, and with none doing him ill—why tempt fate?"

"You don't understand, Pelageya, you don't understand."

That was true, Pelageya certainly did not understand why the young fellow was unhappy. If it were only Sergei, but the young people of today seemed all of the same mind—complaining of their black moods. And why? What for? She had had no time for moods at that age. Heaven grant that she could earn a bit of bread. Nobody fussed with your moods then.

"You're not like your father, Sergei, not at all," said Pelageya. "You haven't got his grip."

"Thank the Lord for that! " he cried, throwing up his head, the young cockerel!

What had he to be cocky about? His father with little learning had made his way and climbed high. If he had had the education he had given his son—?

"You ought to get married, Sergei," said Pelageya. "And choose a wife stronger than yourself. Without these black moods."

"I'll never marry, Pelageya. Never! " Sergei announced flatly.

"Now that isn't sense, Sergei, it's foolish talk. You need

to marry. You'll part ways with the bottle quicker."

"I won't! " he cried wildly. "My heart's broken. Shattered! "

"And who's broken it?"

"Who? Oh—! " He tossed his head drunkenly, jumped up and ran frenziedly about, and it was only when he paused for a second with a deep sigh to look at the front wall where Alka's enlarged portrait hung beside the mirror that Pelageya understood whom he meant.

Of course she did not attach too much importance to Sergei's sigh; a man can get all sorts of fancies when he's drunk. But she wrote to her daughter: that's how things are and it might be worth while coming home. Sergei Petrovich came in, he spoke very well about you.

To that came the reply: "Flip o' my hand to your Sergei Petrovich! " And what was more, she added, "I've had enough of it, with you making up to Pyotr Ivanovich all your life! "

After that it took Pelageya a long time to attain some measure of peace. What was she to do now, how was she to go on living, she asked herself. Whatever she did, it all went wrong, missed the mark.

But it wasn't Alka's letter which delivered the crushing blow. It was the bakery.

21

For a long time she had been drawn to the bakery, ever since the autumn when she had first fallen ill. She felt that if she could only see her bakery, smell the fragrance of its fresh bread, her breathing would become easier and all illness would pass off. She had never longed for anything as she did for that bakery. Not even for Alka, her own daughter.

Pelageya's first attempt to cross the river was in February, when for the first time after a long blizzard the iced-up windows were gilded by a red sun. But she got no farther than the slope by the rural Soviet, because of the drifted snow. They were terrible, those piled-up drifts. On an open place down the hill a horse would have sunk to its belly; how could she, a sick woman, hope to get through?

So she had to wait for the early thaw.

She rose before dawn. She was clean and tranquil—she

had been to the bath-house the previous day as though preparing for Mass. She left the house with a staff, like a pilgrim. And the people she met along the way seemed tranquil and happy, too.

Antokha the stableman, driving a sledge, overtook her just before the drop to the river; whenever had he stopped for her before? But he pulled the reins.

"That you, Prokopyevna?" And that wasn't all, he jumped off and held out his hand. "Get up, we'll drive together. It's slippery going down." And his smile was good.

Tears started in her eyes at Antokha's kindness. She thanked him but did not get onto the sledge.

Along the whole way she seemed to hear strange but melodious music—could it be her own heart singing?

Testing the softened path across the snow with the light aspen staff which Big Masha had got her, she caught the warm south wind gusting across the river with her lips while she tottered with small cautious steps towards the yellow log building amidst the pines on the rise.

But when she returned she was walking like one drunk, in tears, almost witless with what she'd seen. A good thing that along the river she again met a sledge, this time driven by a foreman from a neighbouring village, otherwise she might never have got home.

She was already highly disapproving as soon as she approached the bakery. A rubbish pile. Right beside the porch. Two crows were busy in it.

"What are the 'thorities thinking of?" she fumed. "What's the sanitary inspector doing—asleep? Time was, they used to come round inspecting every week, 'specially in the hungry years. Have they stopped coming to the bakery now there's bread a-plenty?"

She climbed the steps to the porch, opened the outer door and saw—a half-grown piglet. It dashed between her feet, squealing as though fleeing before the knife.

"How can they?" she asked herself again and again, bewildered. She had almost dragged her arms out carrying swill home, and fearful all the time, but here they were, feeding a pig in full view of anyone. Again she marvelled at the sanitary inspector. Dung, dirt, a stench—how could all that be allowed beside bread?

This was only the beginning; she got the whole picture when she actually entered the bakery. Heavens—where was she? In a dirty shed? An old silo tower? A byre? Everything was greasy, nothing had been washed for untold ages. A besom was thrust through the window. You certainly had no feeling of spring in here!

But worst of all was the mixer.

What hadn't she done on those days to make the bread light and fragrant! She had tested water from various wells, seen to it that the wood for the fire was not resinous—it made soot; of course she insisted on getting the best quality flour, and naturally, for the mixer she tried everything, pine and fir and heather. And now instead of a proper mixer, bast wound round a long stick and plunged into a dirty bucket of water.

Ulka, the new baker, wanted to give Pelageya tea; for the time being she had finished with oven and had just sat down; Pelageya almost threw up at the sight of her—fat and sweaty, her hair shining with grease as though she hadn't been to the bath-house for months.

So Pelageya left without sitting down. She dared not even cast a farewell glance at the dirty samovar and wash-bowl, at the stove not whitewashed once since she left. Because she felt as though all of them—the samovar, the wash-bowl and the stove—were looking reproachfully at her.

22

Outside the window spring was burgeoning.

All the winter Pelageya's view of the world had been limited to a smoky peephole she had blown on the iced-up window, but now light poured into the room. It was a time for new life, for walking barefoot on the thawed ground and filling her lungs with the warm wind blowing across the river. But she lay limply and her breathing was heavy, with a choke and a whistle—exactly like the punctured old bellows at the smithy.

Anisya ran the house as she had during Pavel's illness. She came without being asked.

Pelageya did not talk to her sister-in-law and did not conceal her dislike. Why should she like her when she had gathered within herself the health of the whole family? Pavel had died early, it might well be that she herself was not far from death but that one—nothing touched her, she was always in rude health. If only Big Masha had not been so sly at pilfering she would not have stood this robust, hearty creature for a day. But what could she do? Masha had set her sights on Pelageya's belongings even when their owner was still on her feet.

Then late one evening when the northern white nights had come, Pyotr Ivanovich paid her a visit.

How long was it since Pavel's funeral, since the last time they had met? Less than a year. But in that time he had changed almost beyond recognition; he seemed to have shrunk, he looked unkempt (who had ever seen him unshaven?) and his eyes were sunken and wretched. And he showed the effects of drinking—that was what really surprised Pelageya most of all. When had such a thing ever been known before? This had been his strength, that he never lost control over himself. He drank, of course, you can't avoid that, especially when your whole life is spent with those in a higher position whom it pays to please, but never a sign of it—he stood firm as an iron post. But now, as soon as he was inside he lurched across the room and slumped like a sack on the stove bench.

"I've come to see you. They say you're sick."

"Aye, I'm that all right."

She tried to rise, a visitor had come and no unimportant one, but Pyotr Ivanovich gestured to her—don't get up, lie still.

She attached little importance to his opening words; as usual it was by roundabout ways that he approached his real reason for coming. He talked generalities, kolkhoz affairs: nowadays you could live well in the kolkhoz, very well, people were earning good money. Take the shepherd Oska, whoever had thought anything of him before? But last year he'd raked in more than two hundred rubles in September alone.

"Aye, that's how it goes nowadays," said Pyotr Ivanovich with a sigh. "Now, you and me aren't simpletons, but have we ever seen earnings the likes of that?"

Pelageya nodded, it was all true, many a time during her illness she had thought of the big changes that had come about; meanwhile, she waited impatiently for him to come to the point. He certainly hadn't come here to discuss kolkhoz affairs.

"We was born at the wrong time," he continued. "Too hasty, that's what was wrong. Now your Alka, she's got it just right. D'you get letters from her?"

106

Pelageya's heart beat fast—what was he getting at? Had something happened to Alka? But she gave no sign, and said nothing but "Aye, she writes."

"She's not thinking of coming home? Not had enough of town yet? I don't know—but somehow I can't abide that town life. It deaves a man, the noise and the smells."

"Deaves you or not but you've got to live. It's not her alone now, there's two of them."

Pyotr Ivanovich cracked his fingers, a familiar habit of his when he was deciding something. Then he delivered the blow, like a cudgel on her head.

"I've heard she isn't living with that officer. She's alone."

Truth to tell, that was no great surprise. She had already felt that all was not well with Alka. But it is one thing to suspect and quite another when outsiders sling mud at your daughter. And in spite of her weakness she rose like a lioness to defend her child.

"And what if she is! " she said defiantly. "My daughter'll be all right. There's birches with bark torn off that are still right fair and others are dry sticks whilst they're yet maids."

The reference was cruelly plain, any dullard would have guessed what she meant. She turned cold and hardly breathed while she lay waiting for the return blow from Pyotr Ivanovich.

But he said nothing. After a minute she raised her head and was utterly flabbergasted by what she saw. There were tears in Pyotr Ivanovich's eyes.

When he spoke, his words were equally astounding. He called her Paladya, the name used by her father.

"Paladya," said Pyotr Ivanovich in a muffled voice unlike his own. "I helped you in a difficulty more than once. You haven't forgotten?"

"You did, Pyotr Ivanovich. How'd I forget?"

"And now you must help me. Please, for God's sake help me! "

Pelageya almost choked in her surprise. She did not yet know what he would ask of her. But who was asking? Pyotr Ivanovich. Asking her, Pelageya.

"My lad—he's going downhill fast," he said with an effort.

"Sergei? But how should he go down? With college education, respected—"

Pyotr Ivanovich made a hopeless gesture.

"He's drinking. Drinking hard." He rose suddenly; went

to the bed and grasped her hand. "You could write to Alka. What's she want there, in strange parts? And mebbe something 'ud come of it."

So that was it. Pelageya understood at last, he wanted Alka to save Sergei, to take him in hand. That was what he'd come for.

A dark, revengeful feeling swept over her. Her glance slid over his unshaven, shaking chin with the cleft in the middle, the piteous old-man's eyes softened by parental tears, and only now, in this moment, she realized that she hated this man, had hated him for a long time, ever since he had reckoned five thousand missing rubles against her.

Heavens, that five thousand had almost driven her out of her mind, she hadn't been able to sleep, she'd been ready to drown herself. And he, the brute, had just wanted to give a young bookkeeper a lesson. So she wouldn't be too pert. And get bread free from the bakery, too. Oh yes, that bread meant something. He had done well out of her. He'd always had white rolls with his tea. And for what, what favours? For taking her into his circle, seating her at table with important people?

Drat him and his important people, the whole lot of them!

All her life long she had run after those important people, she had been unfaithful to her husband and not spared herself, and what had she gained, what had she achieved? Alone. Sick. Her daughter gone. Her house empty.

She had a wild impulse to scream in his face: Serve you right! Learn on your own hide how others suffer!

Aloud, however, all she said was, "Very well, I'll write. Mebbe she'll take heed."

Pelageya did not remember afterwards how Pyotr Ivanovich left; she was breathless, choking with coughing. But at the same time she was happy, happy to tears, a feverish heat in her breast. With dry cracked lips she caught the air of the room but her heart sang, and her imagination conjured up hopes, those rainbow hopes Pyotr Ivanovich had roused in her.

She had no doubt that Alka would come. The lass wasn't a fool. How could she fail to understand that this was great good fortune? Of course, Sergei himself was nothing much even though he was an engineer, but his father, that was a horse worth catching. Heavens above, thought Pelageya, to walk in harness with such a man—! What couldn't they do!

For an instant she lost consciousness, and when she came to herself it seemed to her she was standing before the stove in her beloved bakery and hot flames were licking her yellowed, thin face.

She was choking. She was unbearably hot.

She must get down to the floor, lie on the floor, her old habit. A board floor draws out the heat.

That was how Anisya found her in the morning, lying on the floor. She ran to lift her—but fell back as she met the glassy, motionless eyes.

Alka was not at the funeral, with the opening of the navigation season she had got a job as barmaid on a big passenger steamer plying the Northern Dvina.

She came a week later and the first thing she did, of course, was go through the usual lamentations for her dear parents and arrange a memorial feast—an unprecedented one for these parts, with practically the whole village present.

Two days later there was a sale of the dress-lengths, samovars and other goods her mother had treasured.

On the fifth day Alka boarded up the house at the back, laid farewell wreaths of colourful paper flowers on the graves of her father and mother, and in the evening drove off in the shaky bus. She had no intention of jeopardising her enjoyable, well-paid job on the steamer.

1967-1969

Alka

1

Aunt Anisya and Big Masha had heaps of news to tell her. All kinds. Who got married, who got born, who died... How the collective farm was doing, and what went on in the district... But Alka could not have enough. After all, she had been away from home a whole year, or even two, for you could not really count the three or four days she had spent here last year, when she came for her mother's funeral.

And so as soon as her aunt or Big Masha closed their mouths, she would urge them on.

"What else, come on, tell me more! "

"Well," Aunt Anisya shrugged. "They're building a club for us. We're going to live cultured like, they say..."

"I know! You told me about the club."

"Then I don't know. Seems like that's all..."

Then Big Masha, who had been doing her best to please their guest, finally tumbled to it that she would like probably to speak about herself.

"You keep asking us about things, but how about yourself? How're you doing in that city of yours?"

Alka stretched blissfully until her bones cracked, scratched her bare heel on the knot in the floor under the table she had known since childhood, then shook her mane of red gold, which had not yet dried after the wash in the bath-house.

"I live fine! Nothing to complain of. I earn ninety every month, and at least another hundred in tips."

"A hundred and ninety?" Masha gasped.

"Sure! Why not? Where d'you think I work? In some lousy canteen in a district hole or in a city restaurant? Fillet, shish-kebab, tabaka chicken... Have you heard of such eats? Oh, you haven't? And do you know how a waitress is supposed to serve them? In your district canteen they just shove the plate with grits under your nose, and go ahead, spoon it up! But in our restaurant it's all fine and posh..."

111

Alka jumped up, moved the still purring samovar from the tray to the table, placed the cups and saucers on the tray, the tray on the outstretched fingers of one hand, and whirled about the room, weaving among imaginary tables.

"Look at her little bottom," Big Masha said admiringly. "A body would think it has no bones in it."

"That's the first thing about my job. Honey on your lips, music in your hips. Our manager Arkady Semyonovich used to say, 'Now, girls, remember that you're bringing your client joy, not just plates! ' "

Alka swept about the room once again, then, very pleased with herself, her cheeks flaming, lowered the tray with the crockery on the table (the cups giving their first tingle at this point) and poured out the remaining wine.

"Let's drink to Arkady Semyonovich! That was a man! He'd line us waitresses up in the dining hall before the public started coming in, sit down at the piano and tell us: 'Now, girls, a wag of your little bottoms, and another, and a third... And now smiling exercises...' They sacked him. For introducing alien practices into Soviet catering. Now we have a real wet blanket of a manager, a stickler for rules. Skirts strictly below the knees! I think I'll beat it soon, may go into the airplanes. Flying from one city to another..."

"And what'll Vladislav Sergeyevich say?" Masha asked.

"What about him?"

"Well, won't he be agin it? His wife flying about all over the place with young men..."

Alka glanced at her aunt, who had flushed crimson, and understood that she had kept it secret that Alka was no longer living with Vladik. To avoid gossip.

But Alka, unlike her late mother, was not one to prevaricate. So she ignored her aunt's meaningful glances and came out with the truth at once:

"I don't live with Vladik. I gave him his marching orders."

"Yourself? Why?" Masha was so astonished her lower lip sagged, which made her look like the old mare Rosie her father drove that last winter before he fell ill, carting firewood to the store.

"What else? The lousy cheat, paying alimony right and left, what do I want with the likes of him?"

"Alimony? Vladislav Sergeyevich?" Masha gasped, more surprised than ever.

"Who else? To two wives! That time he ran away on the sly I cried my eyes out, more fool me! I'm done for, I thought. So off I went to his boss in town—but all I could do was bawl—just a silly village ninny I was! But when his boss, a nice man, a colonel with a moustache, told me that Klimashin was already paying alimony to two wives, I backed out quick. Paying away half his salary for eighteen years, and me making do with the leftovers! Thank you, I said, I want none of him! "

Suddenly a powerful chorus of women's voices burst into the house. The panes in the windows rattled from the roar of a passing truck.

Alka dashed to the open window, but the truck was already gone, and all she could see was a cloud of dust in the road.

"Was that a wedding?" she asked the old women.

"No, those were dairymaids coming home from the morning milking," said her aunt. "They always come like that, singing their heads off."

"Why shouldn't they sing?" Masha snorted. "The money they get! "

"And Lida Vakhromeyeva, is she still a dairymaid?"

"Aye, that she is, but she's no longer Vakhromeyeva but Yermolina."

"What, Lida got married? Why didn't you say so?"

"But I wrote you," Anisya said. "She got married last winter. To Dmitry Vassilyevich Yermolin."

"Who? Mitya the Primitive?" Alka laughed boisterously. "What a joke! She and I used to make fun of that Mitya! "

"Well, she don't make no fun of him now. He's her husband. And they get on well. A good couple. Dmitry is a man in a thousand! "

"Ha! " Masha grunted.

"No, no, Masha, don't you 'ha' at him! " Anisya stuck up for Mitya. "He's done building over the whole kolkhoz—is that something to sneeze at? And he's nice to his wife like you don't often see these days. The other day I met them going down to the river to rinse the washing, and Mitya was carrying the basket. How many men do you see doing that? And he doesn't drink either..."

"All the same he's a rum sort, got a screw loose," Masha persisted, from which Alka concluded that the old woman had failed to get herself invited into their house—that could be the only reason for all this spite.

2

Alka had already run out into the street early in the morning, washing her feet in the morning dew, as they say, and getting a spot of the morning sun; yet she fairly hopped with joy as she went down the porch steps—so glad she was to be back home.

She wanted to go everywhere at once—to the bird-cherry bush on the hill beyond the road, where her father and she used to wait for her mother dragging her feet back from the bakery; to the meadow underneath the hill, where the mower had been chirring since early morning; and also to the river...

But the village won out.

She had not, properly speaking, seen the village yet. She had arrived late in the evening in a closed car of the District Committee (to avoid getting covered with dust) and she had got but a glimpse of it. And in the morning, when she was barely awake, Big Masha had descended on them. Nobody had let her know or invited her, but there she was, ready for a drink—she certainly had a nose for that kind of thing.

The first person Alka met in the street was Long-Tooth Agrafena, a neighbour of theirs, living in the next house but one from her aunt's. When Alka was little, the mean-tempered old woman sometimes thrashed her with nettles. But now—wasn't it hilarious!—she did not recognise Alka. She poked at her with her tin-coloured eyes, but never uttered a sound. Was that because of the pants?

Alka had first-rate pants on. Made of red silk—like flames dancing on her legs. And the rest of her outfit was super, too. A white blouse with a low neckline, smart shoes on a broad heel, a black bag with a shoulder-strap—good enough for a film star!

At the sight of Pyotr Ivanovich's house, which had sailed out from round the corner like a white steamboat, Alka straightened up. Though she had never made up to him or fawned on the crafty old fox, she had been born in Letovka and had a healthy respect for Pyotr Ivanovich.

Goodness, there was their Lampa lugging a huge basket of grass along—so big it poked into the sky, as Alka's mother would have said. There she was, as large as life, coming through the field gate, barefoot, wearing a long peasant dress, drenched with sweat. Alka's old teacher in her usual summer guise.

To think of it: Gagarin had flown round the Earth, and had even got himself killed, Americans had landed on the Moon, she, Alka had become a grown woman, but their Lampa was unchanged: she was still lumping basketfuls of grass for her cow, the same as she did fifteen years ago. To be sure, Yevlampia Nikiforovna, which was her full name, had had a hard life and she had certainly needed the cow in the hungry post-war years, so it was not quite fair to point a finger of scorn at her. But times had surely changed. Even farmers were not keen on cows these days, and she was a teacher after all, it wasn't proper that she should muck about with a cow all her born days.

Alka remembered her dark sun-glasses in a while frame, which Tomka had practically forced on her when she was leaving, took them out of her bag and put them on. Assuming a severe air, she walked towards Yevlampia Nikiforovna, who was having a breather by the fence, supporting her basket with one hand and wiping her perspiring face with her headkerchief, peasant woman fashion, with the other.

"Now, citizenness, that's a wrong thing to do! You ought to be ashamed of yourself! "

"What's a wrong thing to do, Comrade, excuse me, I don't know your name..."

"It's wrong to steal grass from the kolkhoz meadow."

"It isn't from the meadow at all. I just snipped some at the edge of the field," Yevlampia Nikiforovna whined in a piteous voice—exactly like a village woman caught in the act by the kolkhoz chairman.

Alka cleared her throat importantly and said in reproving tones, "Is that an example to set collective farmers, Comrade Kosukhina?"

"No, it isn't, you're quite right. I won't do it again."

"There you are! You're liable to a fine, you know."

At this point Yevlampia Nikiforovna became quite abject.

"Yes, I know. But I am a sick woman, my dear, and our grass plot is far away, and the cow is young and must have fresh grass if you want her to give milk..."

"Very well, Comrade Kosukhina, but see that I don't catch you at it again! "

"You won't, I assure you! I won't do it myself, and I'll explain to the others..."

At this point Alka burst into laughter. When she had

done laughing, she took off her sun-glasses and said politely, "Good morning, Yevlampia Nikiforovna."

For all of a minute Yevlampia Nikiforovna moved her thick cracked lips soundlessly. Finally she brought out:

"At your stupid tricks again, Amosova?"

Never in her life had she called Alka by her Christian name.

"It was a joke, Yevlampia Nikiforovna. Laughter is yet another vitamin, said Ho Chi Minh."

Yevlampia Nikiforovna sniffed.

"Drinking early in the morning is a joke too, I suppose?"

"Call this drinking, Yevlampia Nikiforovna? Isn't a body allowed to mark the homecoming and to remember the parents?"

"That's not the right way to remember parents, Amosova. Your parents were hard-working people, who set a good example to everybody..."

"Ain't I hard-working too? Do I sponge on anyone? Don't I earn my own living?"

Yevlampia Nikiforovna surveyed Alka with a stern look, lingering on her flaming pants.

"It's morality I'm concerned with, Amosova. The moral code of a builder of communism... Even at school you paid little heed to your maidenly honour..."

Alka bit her lip so hard tears welled up in her eyes, then nodded at two workmen from the so-called tippling unit—a building unit nicknamed so for incorrigible drunkenness, who had started putting up poles for electrical wiring when Alka was still living in the village and were obviously engaged in the same task to this day.

"So we are going to have electricity, Yevlampia Nikiforovna?"

"Yes, Amosova," the teacher said in instructive tones. "In recent years the collectivised countryside has scored great successes..."

"So we shall have electric lamps in our houses?"

"We shall, Amosova. The borderline between town and country is being eliminated..."

Alka lowered her eyes with the air of mock humility she had mastered back at school and asked, "And what will happen to paraffin lamps when we get electricity? Will they go for scrap?"

Yevlampia Nikiforovna was left gaping, very much like Long-Tooth Agrafena, and Alka, to crush her completely,

116

gave a good wriggle with her bottom—take this, you mealy-mouthed phony!

3

Alka was not one to bother about her encounter with Lampa. In the first place, Lampa deserved all she had dished out to her and more. She was a lousy teacher. When their school-leavers sat for entrance exams to college, they did well enough in mathematics, physics and geography, but invariably flunked Russian composition. Secondly, there were too many other impressions tumbling on Alka as soon as she parted ways with Lampa—the new houses (five down the street after Pyotr Ivanovich's fine place), the women, the children and the dogs.

Peka Kamenny, who dashed out from round the corner driving a tractor, struck her all of a heap, you might say. Why, only last year he had been cadging rides from drivers, and now—look at him!—perched in the cab, as cock-sure as they come. Through the glass she could see him smiling from ear to ear, his widely spaced teeth sparkling white, his round boyish face sooty all over—the hall-mark of a true machine-lover, and there was a sprig of red currant stuck over the radiator—for effect, like a carnation in the button-hole of greasy overalls.

At the sight of her Peka thrust his happy white-toothed mug out of the cab and shouted, "Hey, don't set the village on fire with those pants of yours! " And he laughed at his own joke with child-like enjoyment.

The pants, by the way, had also caught the eye of Pakha Lysokhin, who was perched on the log-frame of the house he was building for his son-in-law, a worker from the timber settlement across the river. He shouted to Alka loudly, in the manner of all people who are hard of hearing, "That a new fashion, wrapping a flag across your ass?"

Alka would've been quite happy to exchange a few cracks with Pakha Lysokhin. He was a jolly old chap. Buried his third wife not long ago, and was already, according to her aunt, setting his sights on the Ninth Dunya. Forty-five years his junior!

But no, Alka could not bother with the old man and his wisecracks when she had already caught sight, further down the street, opposite the school, of the new club building under a white slate roof. She knew about the club: her aunt had written to her about it and had mentioned it at breakfast that morning, but hearing is one thing and seeing another: she fairly gasped with delight and her heart thumped in her chest.

"Come here, Gorgeous! "

Feasting her eyes on the big log structure, which did not yet have doors or window-frames, Alka had failed to notice the builders. They were flattened out on the wooden scaffolding like so many billets, some wearing swimming trunks, others shorts. Blue cigarette smoke was floating above their black, blond and red heads.

"Sunning yourselves, boys?" she inquired, raising her arm in greeting, and walked over towards them, her red pants sewing a straight stitch across the sun-bleached bit of wasteland which separated the building from the road.

The builders jumped up and started hopping on the scaffolding, as they hastened to get into pants, shirts and plimsoles. Alka then knew what kind they were. College students, who did most of the building on their farm during summer vacations.

"Well, let's see your edifice," Alka said. She had learned quite a few long words in the two years she had lived in the city.

A swarthy student with a divine moustache, as Tomka would have said—she had a weakness for the sultry type of male, dashed up to her with devil-may-care gallantry. He had somehow found the time to put on his khaki shirt with rolled up sleeves and khaki jeans with a lot of metal buttons.

With a chivalrous bow, he offered Alka his arm, bent at the elbow, and said, "Your obedient servant! "

Alka put her arm through his and walked up the plankway into the club-house.

It was a fine club-house. There was a spacious foyer, a dancing hall and a big auditorium for various cultural undertakings (that was exactly as Moustaches, who was a kind of foreman, put it); there were also two large rooms which would house a library. It was wonderful! The only thing that was not quite clear to Alka was who was going to dance in the hall and take part in the cultural undertakings: there were no students or holiday-makers in the village in wintertime, and the indigenous youngsters could all be counted on the fingers of her two hands.

"What a pity there's no music," she said regretfully.

"Would be nice to have a spot of dancing in the new club!"

"Who said there was no music?" her escort exclaimed.

And the next minute a miracle happened: a rock'n'roll crashed out—an honest-to-God rock'n'roll—from the corner where all kinds of instruments lay in a heap.

Alka's heart blazed up—prancing about had been her favourite pastime since childhood. Well, she certainly did herself proud, bashing the floorboards in the new clubhouse, first with Moustaches, then with another chap, and yet another—ten of them altogether. The students howled in a frenzy of delight and snatched her away from each other, but Alka kept them at an arm's length—the village is not the same as town, you have to watch your step if you don't want the old women to chew you to a rag.

"Cheerio, boys, I'm off. Some other time."

She raised her arm in the same cinematic gesture of greeting, gave a broad smile for the lot of them to share out among themselves, and stitched her red way back across the rusty wasteland plot.

4

During the busy season the only place in a village where you are likely to find life stirring in the daytime is the post-office. Unlike the farm office and the village Soviet, it is not closed down for field work, so it is a kind of assembly point for the vacationers.

But Alka never reached the post-office that first day. For as soon as she climbed Strawberry Hill to the old church, there was an explosion of seagull-like shrieks:

"Alka! Alka! "

The shrieks were coming from the meadow, which seethed with multi-coloured frocks and kerchiefs. The girls were not only shouting but also waving their rakes—as much as to say, "Here! Come here! "

Unhesitatingly, Alka kicked off her shoes on the fashionable broad heel, grabbed them and galloped downhill so that pebbles went flying. What was the point of putting it off? To be quite frank, she had dreaded this meeting with her former school-mates. How would they treat her, these senior schoolgirls and college students, wouldn't they stick their learned noses up at her?

At the foot of the hill, the hay had already been raked

away, and the stiff stubble bit at her bare soles. But wasn't she the daughter of Pelageya Amosova, wasn't she a hardy village girl? She raced across the prickly patch without even wincing and burst like a bomb-shell into the midst of the maidenly bouquet.

"Alka! Alka! "

Dozens of arms hugged her until she was nearly suffocated.

"Let's see our city-girl! Make way, lasses! "

These were Vassily Ignatyevich, the village Soviet chairman, and Sweet-Tooth Kolya, the team-leader, two old rakes who had been hanging about young girls all their lives. They would have you believe it was because of their fun-loving natures, but in actual fact they were always on the lookout for a chance to paw them.

The girls scattered screaming and laughing, but Alka remained where she was. What had she to fear? Nobody would condemn her for being too free and easy—here, in the meadow, before everybody's eyes, it all passed for a joke.

Still, she didn't quite lower her guard: when Vassily Ignatyevich grabbed hold of her with a moan of joy, she began hammering his wet sweaty back with her shoes. Good and hard, too. For, if all was said and done, what was the pleasure of being pawed by a frenzied old he-goat?

The scuffle did not last long. The older women yelled: "Stop that sport, will you! Look at the sky! "

Things, indeed, looked like trouble up in the sky: swollen clouds were rolling across it, the kind that are likely to burst with rain any moment.

But clouds by themselves were not so bad. The wind was rising, its first spurts racing across the meadow.

Vassily Ignatyevich rushed to his rake he had left by the rick—this was no time for fun. They had to gather the hay into ricks before the rain started, even if it killed them.

"Come on, girls! " he shouted, "get a move on! "

There was no need to urge those village girls! They knew the danger of those clouds, and had scattered with their rakes over the meadow before the chairman gave his command.

Sweet-Tooth Kolya, wet through (the girls had doused him with two bucketfuls of water) tossed his coat to Alka on the run, as much as to say: lay it down on the hay, it'll make a more comfortable seat. But Alka never gave the coat a glance. Promptly she put on her smart shoes, seized a rake that was lying by and set to work with the others. Because if she lounged on that coat like a princess, as Sweet-Tooth Kolya suggested, they were sure to tear her to strips afterwards. The old women and the wives would pick her bones clean, and the girls would speak their minds, too.

Vassily Ignatyevich panted like a winded horse as he lugged veritable cartloads of hay at one go, but he could not cope on his own. All around him were the small fry who could do no more than rake the hay into swathes.

Katya Malkina, old Khristoforovna's granddaughter, as hard-working and conscientious as Khristoforovna herself, tried to help him, but the work was too much for her. So Alka started raking the hay at a tangent, to avoid the silent rebuke of that industrious chit: she wasn't dressed for carrying armfuls of hay, and then why should she overstrain herself? Did she have a cow in the shed waiting for that hay?

But the women—they saw right through you, those damned harpies!

"Alka, see you don't bust your guts! "

"Alka, take it easy! "

She could not stand the chaffing.

She knew they were egging her on, goading her, but she took the bait. She had always had a horror of looking cheap in people's eyes.

In a word, things began to hum. While Vassily Ignatyevich carried one forkful, she would bring two, while Vassily Ignatyevich made one step, she would make three.

Her white blouse became wet with perspiration (and it had cost quite a pretty penny!), but who cared? Sweat streamed down her hot face, her bare arms were pricked all over—who cared? The hay-dust made her itchy all over— who cared? I'll show them. I will!

And she did.

Vassily Ignatyevich, the old sinner, instead of putting his paws round her when they were done (quite a pretext, it would seem, to celebrate their feat, thanking her for the grand work) didn't give her as much as a glance and just flopped down where he stood.

Sweet-Tooth Kolya, though he was much younger than the chairman, was not up to any of his old tricks either.

They had been at it for three hours without a break—now if this wasn't shock labour, what was?

That was what the kolkhoz chairman said when he came up: it appeared that he had been helping with hay-making too—on the other end of the meadow where the old women were.

The chairman was very pleased. They had built a hundred and twenty-seven ricks, the girls counted.

"My special thanks to you, Alevtina. You flew your pants like a red banner over the meadow."

"Yes, she can work. Hasn't got soft in the city."

The women wiped their hot sweaty faces with their headkerchiefs, breathing heavily but smiling and brimming with kindness. Exactly like her mother used to when she was pleased with the work she had done.

Somebody brought a pail of water, and the chairman scooped some in a mug and offered it to Alka as a kind of prize. And nobody batted an eyelid: it was as it should be.

Hay dust was floating in the mug—the pail must have been standing in the shadow of a rick, but it never occurred to Alka to blow the dust away, as her fastidious mother would have done; she drank the mug bottoms up and even gave a grunt of enjoyment.

The chairman became maudlin with emotion.

"Come to work on the farm, Alevtina. We'll take you on gladly."

"Now wait a minute! Don't you be in a hurry to harness her to your cart. Let Soviet power have its say! "

That was Vassily Ignatyevich showing signs of life. He'd come to after his collapse. To be sure, he was still panting and his arms hung limp at his sides, but his yellow eye was already blazing, like an owl's. The man had the devil's own urge in him.

"No, no! " said Vassily Ignatyevich. "I staked my claim first. I need an assistant."

"You? To assist you in what?" the chairman asked meaningfully and guffawed.

Vassily Ignatyevich gave him a forbidding look; he knew how to pull a person up when he went too far, that's why he managed to keep his job at the village Soviet through ups and downs.

"My secretary is leaving to join her husband. That's what."

The women began to oh and ah—that was quite a job Alka was being offered.

Alka herself was puzzled. Could he mean it? She was a bad speller. Her mother had used to scold her: "With all the schooling you've had, I have to go a-begging the neighbours when I need to write a simple paper! "

Vassily Ignatyevich's sidelong glance, full of repressed lust, explained it all.

Ho-ho, she said to herself, looked like the old baboon hopes for a romp in the hay with me! Neither maid nor a married woman, he reasons, why not raid the garden?

In the meantime the women got ready to go home for lunch.

Alka's aunt came up to her—of course she had been helping with the hay, too. An old collective farmer—could she stay at home when every pair of hands counted?

"Come on home, my dear! I'll heat the bath-house. Look at the mess you've made of yourself! "

A mess she was, and no mistake. Both the blouse and the pants needed careful cleaning and maybe would have to be written off altogether. In money terms some eighty or ninety rubles had gone down the drain.

Oh, never mind, she'll get herself new rags, nothing in it. Alka was seized with a devil-may-care recklessness. "Come on down to the river, girls! "

The girls seemed to have been waiting for the command. The whole bunch raced after her, shouting and screaming.

6

The small ones pulled off their frocks at a run—children always did that to be able to dash into the water without a moment's delay. The older girls also undressed quickly as soon as they came down the high bank onto the sandy beach. But instead of stepping into the water they crowded round Alka, waiting, she guessed with a grin, to see her bathing-suit. Girls were the same the world over—rags came first with them.

Naturally she had a bathing-suit—the kind none of them had ever dreamed about. It was woolen, the colour of cherry, and it had a white belt and a little pocket with a zip fastener (she had queued for it for three hours last winter). But how could she have known she would go swimming?

All the same, she'd show them the best swim-suit of all! And in the twinkling of an eye Alka threw off all her clothes.

The girls gasped in astonishment. Nobody bathed in the nude these days—you wouldn't even drag a three-year old into the river without her panties.

Groans and grunts came from the boys' beach beyond a cluster of willows, but those soon choked to an awed silence as she carried her young supple body, head thrown back proudly, to the water's edge.

White sand creaked underfoot songfully, the hot wind laden with the tang of grasses tousled her hair, caressed her full breasts, clung to her legs like a fawning dog.

"Alka," Arkady Semyonovich had once said to her in the fullness of his feelings, "you know how I'd style you, in the lingo of the cinema?" (He was one for fancy words). "A sex-bomb."

"What is that?" Alka had asked with a frown.

"It's very high praise, Alka! It designates ... how shall I put it ... a faultless detonator of the most harsh-hearted clients. It's the sun which melts the most frigid iceberg packed into a man's suit..."

That was true enough. Whenever a client proved to be particularly irascible, Alka was assigned to straighten him out. Or suppose some catering big shot came to inspect things. And, God forbid!—in a bad mood. Who could mollify him in no time? Alka—who else?

She tried the water with her toes—it was warm; looked up into the sky—a black cloud had covered the sun; glanced back at the girls, who seemed to have panicked at the prospect of rain, and splashed her way into the depth. What was so frightening about swimming in the rain? Was it the first time?

She swam across the river at one go, walked out onto the opposite bank and flung herself down on the sand.

The girls were calling to her "Alka! Alka! " and waving their dresses on the other bank (it seemed, they had never entered the water after all), but she was lying face down on the warm sand, gripping her wet head in her hands and soundlessly swallowing tears. At school she had got herself the reputation of a tart—almost from the age of seven. As far back as she could remember her mother had been cautioning her, "I'll kill you if you bring me a bastard, you hussy, so help me God, I will! " And all the time she was a virgin—until the year before last. Of course, she had been kissed, and did not bother to pretend like some—you'd think butter would not melt in their mouths—no, she never denied she liked to have a good time. Sometimes she actually threw herself at a chap, but she never let one get his own way with her. And even that day in the bakery, when her mother swooped down on the two of them, she had stuck to her rule. And hadn't Vladik tried his damnedest? He'd all but crushed her bones.

It was none other than her own mother who had pushed her into Vladik's bed. The way she'd broken into the bakery, her eyes aflame—what are you doing here, hussy? Have I sent you here for this? And then a sudden about-turn: putting a bottle of wine on the table and asking her what she was sulking about when she should be being nice to the young man. That's been the last straw. And so she'd told herself as she jumped out of the bakery window: if he catches me now, I'll let him have his way.

Vladik did catch her, at the river, almost in the exact spot where she was now lying.

7

The rain came pouring down in a sudden gush and washed away her melancholy at once. There was no time to mope—the darkened river seethed and roared so terribly it was scary to approach it, let alone swim across.

When finally she got out of the water on the home bank, reeling, there was not a living soul in evidence: the girls and the boys were all gone. She rested a minute, grabbed her clothes—there was no time to tarry dressing—and dashed into the thundering darkness like a big white indeterminate creature.

The thunderstorm was abating by the time Alka got on the homeward Amosov path running across the field.

The rain went on pelting her back, her stomach and her legs like a half dozen besoms, and lightning went on blinding her by its flashes, but the thunder seemed to be receding into the distance. Suddenly, when she had reached the meadow, it crashed again, with so much force that the earth seemed to rumble and groan beneath her.

Alka stopped in wonder and looked around. What she saw made her gasp: the horses had broken their tethers and were galloping around the freshly mown meadow. It was their hooves that produced the thunder.

She stood poised for a second, itching to race them, but thought better of it: they would see her from the houses, a naked girl running with the horses in the meadow —imagine how the tongues would wag! But to make up for it, she ran all the way up the hill without once stopping to catch her breath—it was fun to be alive and in fine pettle! She dashed up the porch of her aunt's house without counting steps.

"Lord, look at that—not a stitch on her! "

"What's up, lass? Folks don't strip theirselves off here in the middle of the day! "

Old bags! Her aunt was forever having visitors, and today it looked as though every old crone in the district was in attendance: Afanasyevna, Lizukha, Long-Tooth Agrafena, Talia the Cherry, Ragged Domakha, and, of course, Big Masha. Six old women! No, seven!

In the corner behind the bed-head was sitting Khristoforovna.

Dropping the wet red pants and the white blouse on the bench by the stove ("not a stitch on her" was an exaggeration, she had her panties and bra on) Alka went behind the partition, changed quickly and appeared before the old women in a mini-dress, a good foot above the knees. She had put it on specially to annoy them.

But old women must have had second thoughts while she was changing, and not one passed a remark about her dress; not that she cared a damn for their disapproval, she was so hungry after her hectic day that she wolfed down the fish soup Anisya had ready for her on the table.

"Eat your fill, lass," the old women nodded approvingly, "you've deserved a good feed."

"Aye, that she has. She's driven two men into a lather. They say, Vassily Ignatyevich couldn't walk up the hill on his own two legs. They took him home in a cart."

"She comes of a good stock. Take her father, now, or her mother..."

"Aye, lass, your parents were hard-working folk! They moved mountains, they did."

Were the old women sincere in praising her and speaking well of her father and mother, or were they making up to her hoping for a treat? Anyway, Alka tossed a ten-ruble note on the table without thinking twice about it—here, have a drink to remember my parents.

Big Masha snatched the note and was off like a shot, all but dancing with joy. Long-Tooth Agrafena flushed all over her horsy face—she fancied a drink as well as the next one. Neither did Ragged Domakha or Talia the Cherry wave their arms in protest. Only Khristoforovna and Lizukha refused a glassful.

"What's the matter?" Alka asked them. "Saving money?"

"What money? Our pension don't go so far you know..."

"Them's Old Believers," Big Masha snorted disdainfully. "That stupid goose joined their crowd, too."

"Who?" Alka asked wonderingly.

"Matryokha, who else?"

"Little Masha?" Alka gasped in wonderment.

"None other! "

"And she doesn't drink, does she?"

"Not a drop. Their religion's agin it."

"They're seeking a firm shore for their souls..." Alka's aunt tried to explain in strange words, obviously not her own. It appeared that Anisya was in her thoughts somewhere near that shore as well.

"Never mind," Big Masha dismissed the matter, pouring herself a new glassful. "Let her. All the more left for us."

"You better keep your mouth shut, old witch! " Afanasyevna shouted at her angrily and even raised a hand as though to strike her. (Herself, she had just raised her glass to her lips out of politeness.) "Drink as much as you like and the devil take you! But you drag young fellows along into the pit. 'Tolya, let's drink the drought away! Vanya, let's give a chaser to these clouds...' "

A row seemed imminent, for everybody knew Afanasyevna's grandson had become an alcoholic, but Alka intervened.

"Take it easy," she said to Afanasyevna. "Who doesn't drink these days? D'you know who doesn't drink in town? Those who haven't the money, those whom nobody will stand a drink, and also Pushkin. And why Pushkin, you may ask. Because he's made of stone and his arm doesn't bend! " Alka gave a short laugh.

The old women also bared their gums, though they probably did not get the joke. Most of them had never been to town and did not know Pushkin's monument existed.

Khristoforovna, who was drinking tea, or, rather, boiled

127

water with dried bilberries, asked courteously:

"Aren't you coming home to stop, Alevtina?"

"What does she want here?" Big Masha retorted promptly.

"Well, there's her parents' house. When I go out on my porch in the morning and take a look at your poor house—I feel right sorry for it. It looks so sad, lonely like."

"Stop whining! Whole villages are shut and left these days, and here's she crying about a house... It's the epoch," Big Masha concluded with a bookish word and hiccuped in confirmation.

Alka, for her part, also hastened to reassure Khristoforovna (she was a nice old soul and had used to feed Alka up when her mother tarried at he bakery).

"I live well, Khristoforovna. The pay is good, and the work is fun. And you can have any kind of food you fancy. Except, of course, birds' milk."

Long-Tooth Agrafena said enviously:

"Aye, that's sure. Folks wouldn't be all running away to town if life was bad there."

"Not all go," Alka's aunt disagreed. "They offered a job in town to Dmitry Vassilyevich, but he refused."

"And my nephew came back," Lizukha said. "He says he likes the country better."

"Folks don't stop quiet these days," Khristoforovna contributed. She had finished her tea and, village fashion, placed the cup bottom up on the saucer. "Everybody's looking for summat. In the village it's town they want, and in town folks want country..."

"Who wants country?" Big Masha asked with a dry laugh. "I never seed such a one."

"Didn't you? Don't you mind them college girls who lodged with me a whole month?"

"Aw, them learned monkeys..."

"No, Maria Arkhipovna, you're wrong here," Khristoforovna said gently but firmly. "They don't deserve that. City folk have their fast ways, we all knows that, but those girls were all right. They were modest and respectful. They wouldn't take a drink of water from the pail without a by-your-leave, to say nothing of... 'What is it you like here?' I asks them. 'You been coming here the third summer running?' And they just laughs and says: 'We come for the living water, Granny.'"

Big Masha giggled nastily—she hated to hear anybody praised in her presence, but Alka gave her a withering look, and the old woman held her tongue.

And again Khristoforovna's unhurried speech ran on like a brook.

"No, I can't say a word against the lasses. They're respectful, and they don't scorn a chat with an old woman. They'd follow me about all day, writing down whatever I may be saying. 'Why d'you write it down, lasses,' I asks them. 'What d'you want it for? What can an ignorant old woman teach you? I haven't had e'en a day's schooling in my life. You oughter write down yerselves—you're finishing institutes, learning science.' They'd laugh and they'd kiss me, "Tell us more, Granny! ' 'What more?' I'd ask. 'About science and about institutes...' "

"Science must ha' weakened these days if they come pestering an old woman," Long-Tooth Agrafena remarked.

To this Alka retorted resolutely.

"Not at all! Ours is advanced science—who sent the first sputnik into space?" She had to have a say in a conversation like this, she had the reputation of a city-dweller to keep up. "As for students coming here and writing down tales and such like, that's the thing to do these days. Is that clear?"

"And what do they want with birch-bark baskets?" Talia the Cherry asked. "They even crawled into my garret, rummaged in the dust there and found two small baskets and a wooden spoon. The spoon's not even painted, a big one that won't fit any kind of mouth, I remember our Grandpa used to eat with it. 'What's the matter with you, girls,' I asks them,'have you gone clean out o' your minds? Are you going to eat with this ugly thing?' 'Sure, Granny,' they says. 'Course we'll eat with it! ' And laughing their heads off all the time...''

"And d'you know how much they pay for icons in town?" that was Ragged Domakha contributing her own bit with a yawn. She'd been sleeping as she walked all life long. Her man had knocked her about to make her wake up but he died before he got her out the habit.

"That's right," Afanasyevna supported her. "Last year a man with a black beard, not Russian, a foreigner of sorts, went from house to house asking for icons...''

Alka had no definite opinion as regards icons. On the one hand, it had been impressed on her at school that religion was ignorance and opium, on the other hand, the old women were right: they'd gone mad about icons in town. She once went to the regional museum with an excursion, and they were shown two big rooms taken up with icons. And their guide, a goggle-eyed little pussy on sparrow legs, the living image of Pyotr Ivanovich's Tonechka, all but sobbed when she talked about those icons, "The greatest treasure of our museum... A special temperature regimen..' "

"Go easy on the icons. They're something else again," Alka said vaguely, rose and walked up to the window. It had grown considerably lighter outside.

She swung open the old window-frame and took a gulp of the fresh ozonic air. She stood a long time looking at the sparkling puddles in the road and the black steaming roofs of the houses.

"Are there a lot of berries in the wood this year?"

She got no answer. The old women had no time for berries. They were discussing the gripping subject of pensions, and you couldn't distract them from it if you fired point-blank at them. They'd just go on wagging their tongues until they had worked themselves up into a proper temper.

Alka lay down on the bed.

She knew even less about pensions than she knew about icons. These old women had worked like cart-horses all their lives; to listen to them, they actually harnessed themselves into ploughs instead of horses during the war, and things were not much easier just after the war either, yet until recently their pension was 12 rubles. And so these former "twelve-rublers" (what a name to give a person!) were letting off steam in arguments, skinning alive those who got a bigger pension and reminiscing about their lives...

At first Alka listened to the old women with interest. They gave Big Masha a good basting because she, being of the "working class", received a pension of forty-five rubles. But when the old women reached the stage of plaints and tears, Alka became drowsy.

The last thing she remembered (or did she dream it?) were Khristoforovna's words—not about pensions but about living water:

"A person can't do without living water," Khristoforovna was saying. "So people go looking for it wherever they can. All over the wide world they look for it..."

8

First they followed the wide cart-track, well trodden and cared for, that went across the field and then through a light cheery birch-grove; then they entered Efrem's coppice —with dark age-long firs looming above and great russet ant-heaps nestling at the foot of thick resin-oozing trunks; then the track became a hunters' path weaving its way down little hollows and up moss-grown hillocks until it got bogged down in a marsh.

Aunt Anisya, who had grown suddenly subdued, took the pail off the crook of her arm, crossed herself, just as Alka's mother used to do, and started bowing right and left to the yellow amber-coloured berries which burned like candles in the green watery moss.

But Alka was in no hurry. She took a flask of mosquito repellent from her basket (the blood-sucking devils were whining all round), smeared her face and hands leisurely.

She had no intention of going berrying—she had never liked the task, and though her mother used to scold her and even thrashed her a few times, she had never succeeded in interesting Alka in berrying.

It had been the aunt who had talked Alka round during morning tea, saying they ought to visit her mother's berry haunts, in memory of the diseased, so to speak.

There were not many cloudberries in the forest. All Anisya had to show for two hours' wandering over squelching forest marsh was a couple of handfuls barely covering the bottom of her pail, while Alka had not even started gathering berries, but just kept tossing them into her mouth. Ripe cloudberries are honey sweet, and those that are not quite ripe yet (and look like a rosy-cheeked wench) are even better, sweet and crunchy.

Anisya was apologetic.

"Can't imagine what happened to the berries," she kept saying. "Your parents and I used to come here, and there was such a lot of them, you couldn't put your foot down. It was like yellow shawls spread all over the forest."

On her insistence they decided to turn right, towards the cutting. Perhaps there'd be more in light places? Cloudberry was a fickle kind of berry, growing in profusion in different places every year. Bur there were no cloudberries on the cutting or around it.

"See what a bad guide I am! " Anisya had become quite

dispirited. "I've got it all wrong. We should've gone the other way. This looks like Ekim's path. Or is it Maxim's?"

Alka did not care one way or another. She dropped her empty pail and ran to the little bridge—two birch logs thrown across a stream—to get a drink. Her mouth was parched.

But it was not easy to get a drink from the bridge, it was too flimsy. Then she decided to squat on the bank and scoop water in her hands.

"Wait," Anisya cried, "there must be a bowl hidden hereabouts."

She looked under one fir, then under another and third and suddenly hurried over beaming all over her face, a birchbark bowl in her hand.

"Whose is it?" Alka asked. "How come it's here?"

"It's your father's. He made it for your mother."

"Dad?"

"Who else? And he built this here little bridge too. You know how your mother used to roam the woods—in broad circles and at a fast trot too. She'd get all hot and want a drink bad. She always had a thirst, even before she went to work in the bakery. It was like she had a fire inside her. I never seed such a person..."

It was an easy matter to get a drink with the bowl—just you scoop and drink.

The water smelled of bog and of peat, but Alka's father knew what he was about, providing for watering at every stream. Her tiredness vanished at once.

Anisya also had a drink and even washed her face, and then she hung up the bowl by the bridge for everyone to see—let other people make use of it too. The two of them went up a hillock and sat down on a dry fir log. The wet birch-bark bowl glittered in the sunlight like a bit of mirror.

"Was Dad fond of Ma?" Alka asked pensively, looking around her and seeing everything anew, as it were.

"O' course he was! If he wasn't fond of her, if he didn't love her, he wouldn't've thrown bridges all over the forest and wouldn't've made all them bowls. Just you walk around the woods hereabouts. You'll find a bridge across each stream and a bowl beside it."

"Did he come here special for this?"

"To make the bowls, you mean? He came here when there wasn't much to do in the fields. It's a minute's job for a man to peel off some birch-bark and twist it into a bowl!"

Gleaming birch crowns swayed gently above them in the blue patches of sky, rustling and flashing iridescent sparks.

Alka wondered whose voice that rustling reminded her of until she realised it was her mother's.

Mother had not always been scolding and warning her. She had also been kind to her, especially after she'd had a good batch of bread ready at the bakery. Then she had been as soft as wax and would do whatever Alka asked for. It was at such a moment Alka had wheedled her first watch out of her—when she was barely twelve.

"Aunt," Alka said quietly, "I'd like to ask you something... Did Ma speak of me before she died?"

"O' course she did! How can it be that a mother don't speak of her daughter? It was all she thought of—that all should be well with you. She was that proud her daughter had married an officer. When the ice broke up on the river in spring, she told me to move her bed to the window and kept looking at the river. 'The steamboats will soon start running,' she'd say, 'and then we'll have guests'—meaning you and Vladik—'bringing me good health...' "

"Did she actually use these words—'bringing me good health'?"

"These very words." Anisya suddenly gave a sob and covered her face with her hands. "And you ... instead ... are neither a maid nor a wedded wife... So young... And yesterday you e'en bragged about it, letting Masha know all about you. Don't you know what a tongue she's got? She's blabbed it all over the village, she has. Yesterday, Agrafena was asking nasty questions while you were at the river: 'So she hasn't managed to harness that officer fellow? Did he kick her out?' "

"Kick me out?" Alka flared up. "But I wrote to you— I ended it all myself! "

"What's the point of ending it, if you'd opened your gate to him? You should ha' tried fitting together by and by..."

"Fitting myself to him? When he pays alimony to two wives! Am I daft to take the leavings?"

"And you shouldn't've trumpeted about that job o' yours either," Anisya went on reproving her. "Is that proper work—wagging your behind? Me now, I would never've stood for that shame—not if they heaped me with gold..."

So that was what her aunt wanted to get her away

into the woods for, Alka guessed. To wash her brains. To teach her sense. Did she have much sense herself? All her life she'd been robbed by men—and she wants her niece to follow in her footsteps!

"Let's not discuss my work! " Alka snapped. "I'd have you know that we've pledged oneselves to work communist fashion. And if that long-toothed scarecrow tried working just a day with us, she'd cry for mercy. Wagging my behind indeed! Just you try and wag it! Run about all day long, never a sit down, smiling at those drunken bastards too... And once some cadets did a bunk from one of my tables without paying—where do you think those thirty-five rubles came from? Did you pay for them? Or did Pushkin?"

"Alka, dear, I was just telling you what folks are saying," Anisya babbled apologetically.

"People! You're just like Ma—she'd tie herself into knots to have the folks' good word. As for men, Auntie..." Alka smiled. "I have only to whistle, and a regiment will come at a run! "

"A woman can't live with a regiment," Anisya said with a frown. "She needs summat firm, a home of her own..."

"I'll wait! " Alka felt on top of the world again and was in a mood to tease her aunt a little. " 'What we treasured, what we cherished has been taxed and has been blemished...' Did you hear such a jingle, Aunt? Well, let me tell you something—they don't care a tuppence for virginity in town these days. Tomka, a friend of mine, has a sailor boyfriend, and he told her about West Germany. D'you know how they go about it there? They live together openly before they get married. Making no secret of it! "

"Lord! But that's awful! "

"Why awful? Don't you think it's the same here? D'you know what Vladik had to say about my virginity? 'I thought you were a modern girl... You should've warned me at least...' It's the honest truth! "

Anisya simply refused to take in the atrocious things her niece was saying. So Alka, clowning, yelled for all the forest to hear:

"Come on, Auntie! You've given me the pep-talk, and so have I—let's go back to berrying! "

9

They spent another hour and a half wading through the marsh, diving into old brush and heady ferns, took another drink from another stream, using another of those birch-bark bowls, and then they suddenly discovered they had lost their way. They took to the right, then to the left, but every time they ended in the same point of the dark marshy wood, near an old wind-felled spruce.

The sun, as ill luck would have it, had hidden behind a heavy cloud, and they did not know how to find their bearings by wood signs, for it is not everyone that learns the forest lore. What were they to do? Yell for help? Build a fire?

They were rescued by ... a tractor.

Suddenly, as in a fairy-tale, there was a snorting and a sneezing to the left of them, and Anisya went cold with fear—these must be the woodgoblins, but Alka started running towards the woodgoblins, her arms spread out in welcome.

Before long she saw an old live fence, then ran through a copse of aspens and birches and after it there was a green field.

She fell face down into the fragrant, sun-warmed grass and burst out laughing—from joy, and from amazement. They'd been wearing themselves out tramping over marsh and brush, thinking they had got God knows where—and all the time they'd been right near this patch of field in the forest.

Anisya came up with two pails, so ashamed of herself she did not dare look Alka in the face—fancy losing her way in the woods familiar since childhood!—and started talking about the grass.

"Look how things have changed! In the old days you never seed grass standing here—they'd cut down every blade and take it home, and now the grass is getting dry and nobody's took the trouble to scythe it."

"Just a job for Ma! " Alka said.

"Yes, your mother had worn herself to a frazzle with this grass. When Khristoforovna and I washed her dead body we were struck all of a heap! Her right shoulder was one big callus, as hard as bone! "

"Really?"

"A God sees me! Khristoforovna just shook her head.

I've lived long enough, she said, but I never seed the likes of it."

"And people used to envy Ma being well off..."

"Well off? Why not? But there's not many as work their hands to the bone like your mother did. She'd come home from the bakery autumn-time, and it'd be almost dark, but she'd grab her basket and off for grass, watching out all the time, 'cos it wasn't allowed. It is easy enough to live these days. They give you hay for your work on the farm, and they let you mow more for your cow if you feel like it. But people don't want to bother with a cow these days. The Egorkovs got rid of their animals, and Pyotr Ivanovich buys milk in the shop—goes there every morning with a milk-can..."

"Not really! " Alka cried.

Hay and cow had always been prize subjects of conversation in the village, and she listened to her aunt with interest. She had not forgotten the weight of the grass basket on her bent back. But soon she felt bored, because her aunt again began to preach: don't you go away, stay at home; you've got a fine house, if you live quiet and decent, you'll get yourself a man all right.

A blue smoke was rising over the hollow sheltered from them with some brush. A hot engine was singing its iron songs there. Who was driving the tractor? How does he look, her savior?

Alka rose.

"We'll talk about life some other time, right now I'll go and have a look at the tractor."

"Go on," Anisya agreed with alacrity (she had always approved of her niece taking an interest in village affairs.) "He must be ploughing up the field for rye."

Alka washed her face diligently in a tiny spring under a birch-tree, combed fir needles out of her mane of auburn hair, and dashed out into the field nonchalantly—take care, tractor driver, see I don't swallow you whole and then spit you out!

A minute later she was all but rolling from laughter. For who d'you think was driving the tractor? Who had she intended to swallow whole and to spit out? Peka Kamenny! His smiling soot-covered mug looked out of the dusty cab.

"What're you doing here?" Peka asked, driving up. "Admiring nature?"

"That's right."

"Then, go to Kosukhin field. There's lots of bird-cherry there, I stuffed myself full yesterday. It's ever so sweet..."

"All right, I'll go there." Alka put her foot on the iron foot-board polished by tractor-drivers' feet to a sheen and looked inside the cab curiously. It was hot inside and reeked of petrol—why was the lad so happy? "What's that?" Alka cried, peering with amazement into the corner pasted with pin-ups. "Ho-ho! "

"We've pinned them up, Genka, my mate, and me ... just for fun..." Peka mumbled.

"Tell me another! For fun... When are you due for the army spell?"

"Next year."

"I bet you aren't too keen?"

"What—not keen on the army?" Peka looked at her, pityingly. "You're daft! Not to serve in the army..."

"Well, and afterwards? Will you come back here?"

"I don't know. Why bother about it now?"

"You don't know? What about the kolkhoz? What about land reclamation and raising agriculture?" Alka said didactically. Showing him she was abreast of things.

Her words, however, did not make the slightest impression on Peka. He opened his pink, spare-toothed mouth in a broad grin and even attempted a joke: "There's plenty of land... Why reclaim it? They're even bringing some from the moon..."

"You don't take it seriously, that's your trouble, Peka," Alka said reprovingly. "Ererybody knows life in the country has improved no end, and you deny it..."

"I don't deny anything."

"How much d'you earn in a month?"

"Who, me?"

"Yes."

"It'll probably come to a hundred and fifty this month..."

"There you are! " Alka jumped from the running board. "Then why the grin?"

"But this is only when there's ploughing to do," Peka explained. "In winter, when we do repairs, we only get 12 rubles."

"But you admit things have got better?" Alka persisted.

"Oh, aye. But only in summer..."

"How d'you mean 'only in summer'?"

"How do I mean? In winter the roads get snowed under, and you can't get here no how. Have you forgotten? Last

Christmas Dad had a heart attack, and we couldn't even call an ambulance. We thought he'd die..."

Alka was losing interest in the conversation.

"Well, so long," she said and went towards the road.

"Hey, listen! " Peka called out to her. "Will you be staying here long?"

"I'll stay awhile. Why?"

"Well, you know what... Teach me to jiggle, will you? They say you do it fine..."

"What d'you mean 'jiggle'?"

Peka, covered with beads of sweat, rolled his eyes.

"I mean dance... Did you see the club-house they've built us?"

"Okay," said Alka, "I'll teach you to jiggle. And will you let me drive the tractor?"

"You? Drive the tractor?" Peka waved both arms in indignation. "What are you thinking of? Tractor is a machine. You must have a licence to drive it."

But Alka was not accustomed to having her requests turned down. She climbed into the cab briskly and off they went.

They drove round the field twice. Peka was very sure in handling the levers, and she did not press him to let her drive—a tractor was not a toy, she realised that, and she was not yet tired of living. She sat beside him glancing now out the window, now at the driver: Peka looked terribly important. Never a smile or a word, he did not turn his head towards her once.

He only became his old self when they drove up to the road and she jumped out of the cab.

"You've got the idea now, eh?"

"I have. Come round in the evening and I'll teach you to jiggle. And if you wash your mug properly perhaps I'll teach you to kiss as well."

Alka laughed and made for home with a swinging step. And as long as she walked along the field, the tractor never picked up its habitual rumble.

10

To be quite frank, Arkady Semyonovich was the most important person in her life. He found her a job at the restaurant, he arranged for her and Tomka to have a room of their own, even if it was a shabby little place, he always had a present for her whenever a holiday came... What did it matter that he was bald and married—it wasn't such a lot of trouble to give a pat to his curls once or twice a month!

And yet she minded, felt cheap, unable, as Tomka put it, to get rid of her bumpkin notions.

Now again, when she climbed the hill to her aunt's house and caught sight of her own empty cottage standing so forlornly there—she had always hated loneliness—and when she remembered her aunt's words ("How long are you going to live like that, neither a maid nor a wedded woman?"), she felt sick at heart.

She was grateful for the sun, which showed from behind the cloud just then and danced and played in the windows! One couldn't feel blue when the sun was shining.

Alka jumped to her feet, pulled off her frock, poured some water into an enamelled jug and began to splash boisterously.

Then she stood a while in front of the mirror, examining with pleasure her green reckless eyes, her hot insatiable mouth full of strong teeth, her full firm bosom...

After a jug of baked milk with a white loaf, Alka was strongly tempted to dive into her aunt's bed under its white lace cover, but she suppressed the temptation. She had not yet been to the post-office, had not seen Lida with her Primitive—she simply couldn't afford having snoozes in the middle of the day.

And then she had to attend to the problem of that dashing student, Moustaches, who, if her aunt was to be believed, had hung about their house for more than an hour last night.

"Shall I have a fling with him perhaps?" Alka suddenly wondered. What was the point of making a show of lily-white purity? Who was going to believe her? There were plenty of phonies in the world besides her, and when she came back to town she would at least have an adventure to tell Tomka about.

She dressed with care (back in town she had resolved to wear a different set of clothes every day in the village), without forgetting to put on her new cherry swim-suit with a white belt and a zipped little pocket. No, she was not going to be caught napping once again!

11

She had noticed an old woman crawling on the slope by a bird-cherry bush when she looked out at the river from the window.

She had wondered who it might be and what she might be doing. Picking strawberries? But strawberries grew lower down the slope in the first place, and in the second, there weren't enough strawberries there to stay picking them in one spot a whole hour.

And so when she walked out of the house, the first thing she did was look over the fence to see whose checked kerchief was bending down there.

It was Khristoforovna, mowing grass with a sickle.

"I can't go far," explained Khristoforovna, unbending her old back with difficulty. "But I still keep a sheep. So I get what grass I can, here with a sickle, there with me hands. Where you going? Not swimming, eh? Have a swim, lass, do. The water is right warm. We been having a hot summer, a body fair drips with sweat. I had two town girls at my house, they were never out of the water. There's no water like it anywheres, Granny, they used to say. They'd run down to the river along Pelageya's path."

"You mean the Amosovs'," Alka corrected the old woman.

"No, Pelageya's," Khristoforovna said. "We used to call it the Amosovs' path, but now we call it Pelageya's. Even us old folk do."

Khristoforovna wiped her forehead—it *was* hot on the hill.

"The girls used to ask me why we'd changed the name, why Pelageya got the better of all the Amosovs. And I said it must be for her work. For twenty years, every day the woman trod that path, and not once but two or three times a day. Nobody in the village, in all the years it had stood, walked so many times along it. Then they pestered me to tell them about Pelageya."

"And did you?"

"Why not, if they wanted to know. They wrote it all down and took it to town with them."

"Why did they want to know about Ma?"

"They were interested. It was an honour, see? It 'mazed them that a path should be named after a person who lived in our own time. This is like a monument, Granny, they said. Monuments are put up to great people in towns, they said. Of stone. Did you see one?"

"Of course I did."

"So it's all right then. I thought they were making fun of an old woman. They loved a joke, them lasses. But they were respectful too."

It looked as though Khristoforovna was about to launch into another eulogy of the city girls she had liked so much, so Alka went on her way.

But she did not go into the village. She went downhill along the path named after her mother.

She walked with her head lowered, looking at the well-trodden path, seeking her mother's tracks and not finding any. They had long been washed away by rains and spring waters—it was a rare year that their river did not overflow its banks. All the same the path was now called Pelageya's. And they'd go on calling it that even when she, Alka, was no longer alive...

She wondered what Khristoforovna had told the girl students about her mother.

She did not doubt that the kind-hearted old woman had praised her mother to the skies. How hard-working she was. How she'd go across the river, rain or frost. How she drudged at the bakery, doing three men's work... But had her mother been happy? What joys had come her way? Surely baking a good batch of loaves could not be the greatest joy in a person's life?

As far as Alka remembered, her mother had never known any other joys. She only became kind and started smiling, even though she'd be dropping with fatigue, on the days the loaves were good. And not only smiled—she even harangued Alka: "Mine's the most important job on earth, if you want to know. I bake bread, I make life itself..."

Pelageya's path. Her own mother's...

It is not often that a daughter has a chance to tread a path named after her mother...

12

All the way from the village hill to the cliff across the river, where the bakery stood under some old spreading pines, Alka tried to get herself into a mood of proper reverence, but she failed.

Truth to tell, she hated the bakery. And although she breathed in the familiar bread smell with relish (it had always overwhelmed the smell of resin) and her eyes were gladdened by the large windows with white platbands, from which she had loved looking at her aunt's house on top the hill across the river, she could not forget that this bakery had driven her mother to premature death. And it had also done a lot to blight Dad's and Alka's lives. When Ma came from across the river more dead than alive, who could she vent her anger on? Of course her husband and Alka. People had gathered stores of mushrooms and berries, and they had not a mushroom or a berry in the house—whose fault was it? Of course Alka's and her dad's. And the firewood, and the water—curse them! How much scolding and weeping they had caused!

Alka did not stay under the pines besides the bakery very long—she kept fancying that a window was going to open noisily any minute and her mother would yell at her: "What're you standing there gaping for? Haven't you nothing better to do?" Mechanically, through force of habit, she pulled down her mini-skirt (she had never imagined her legs would bring her here of all places) and walked resolutely to the porch.

A padlock. A huge old padlock her mother had installed.

She had wanted to visit her mother's realm, she had specially made the trip across the river, moved by Khristoforovna's heartfelt words, and it was not her fault that the door was padlocked.

Her legs carried her promptly from the bakery to the highway and along it to the timbering settlement.

She had made hundreds of trips from the bakery to the settlement—to buy some sweets for tea (Mummy liked cheap lollipops) and just for fun. Later, in her teens, she started coming here with the village girls to dance at the club-house.

It was lunch hour when Alka entered the settlement. The lumberjacks were celebrating pay-day (the biggest holiday!), roaming the dusty street in droves, and she felt just like in the restaurant, assailed by wolf-whistles, coarse remarks and lewd glances from all sides.

She ran into Zinka the Drunk, who hugged her fondly and, shedding maudlin tears, showed her a photograph of her school-age daughter, who, she said, was living in Leningrad with her father.

Alka also caught sight of Big Masha, who must have made a special trip from across the river to cadge a few free drinks on payday. When she saw Alka, her eyes blazed with anticipation and she opened her arms wide to show how terribly fond she was of Alka.

But Alka had not yet gone out of her mind to let every drunken hag she met embrace her in the middle of the street. She flashed an angry glance at the old woman—keep off, you old pain in the neck!—and turned towards the shop.

Some young fellows, who'd been having a party under the pines near the storehouse, called out to her to join them ("Come, keep us company, Pretty!"), but she barely noticed them now that the shop was before her.

She had inherited a passion for shops from her mother, who knew no greater joy than dropping into one. In town, when Alka had a free moment, her first thought would not be to go to the pictures but to run to some shop and wallow in that kingdom of silks, woollens and cottons.

So Alka flew onto the shop porch as if on wings—and in the doorway ran plump into Sergei.

He was drunk—she could smell the alcohol on his breath—and in his hands he had another two bottles, while a third was sticking out of the pocket of his overalls.

He recognized her, of course—his eyes betrayed him, darting behind the thick lenses of his spectacles, but he pretended not to know her. And the next moment he actually started clowning, plunging down the steps as though about to land on all fours.

"Bring the dame over! " came the guffaws from under the pines.

In reply Sergei shouted some obscenity and flourished the bottles above his head. Alka looked at those bottles, gleaming in the sunlight, at his mop of blond hair, at his lanky figure in baggy, tar-stained overalls, at his dusty and down-at-heel top-boots, and her mind refused to accept the fact that this, indeed, was Sergei. The very same Sergei for whose sake she had been prepared, barely three years before, to scratch out anybody's eyes.

She was crazy about him then! And not she alone either. All girls were after him, and Anya Taborskaya, the beauty of the village, even refused to go to town to study after she finished school—and all on account of Sergei. She got herself a job as a clerk at the timber office—anything to be near Sergei, who had just been appointed chief engineer at their timbering plant, after graduating from forestry college.

And then came the day when Alka went to the dance determined to take the bull by the horns—I'm going to have him, he will see me home from the dance.

That had been three years before, three whole years, and even now the memory made her heart miss a beat. Because what was she three years before, how could she vie with the grown girls, that same Anya Taborskaya, for instance? A snot-nose, a cheeky youngster, kicking her legs out from the sheer joy of being alive and breathing. She was still wearing shoes on low heels. And, most important, Sergei simply refused to notice her. He danced all evening with one girl or another, never giving Alka so much as a glance. But she wasn't put out. She asked Genka Khaimusov, the band-leader, to announce a ladies' waltz and all but ran to Sergei before somebody got to him ahead of her.

Sergei smiled with amusement—who was this tadpole? From what nursery school? But he was a polite young man and he stood up to dance with her. In another two or three minutes he was looking down at her with curiosity.

"I offered the girls a bet that you would see me home," she was saying. "Will you? You aren't afraid, are you?"

"Did your mother let you?"

Sergei went on in this vein, playing an adult to a baby, but they did leave the club-house together—he did not like the idea of chickening out. She had played her card right.

God, but how constrained he was all the way. He never said one single word to her, and whenever they met anyone, he bent all but double not to be racognized.

Finally, when they approached Agrafena's barn (it sticks out by the road, no walker or rider can miss it) she said: "Let's get round the corner of the barn, I've got sand in my shoes."

"Okay," Sergei mumbled.

When they were behind the barn, she rose on tip-toe, gripped him round the neck and kissed him on the lips.

"This is for kicks! " she said with a laugh.

...The salesgirl, an old acquaintance, ran out from behind the corner as soon as Alka entered the shop.

"Alka, how wonderful! I look out the window thinking who might that be? Is it the engineer's wife come from the city? He's been waiting for her these last days. And it's you..." Nastya, that was the salesgirl's name, even shed a tear.

Alka did not stay in the shop long. She talked to Nastya, looked at the shelves piled with rolls of fabrics, and all the time Sergei was on her mind: what was he doing? Had he sunk so low as to drink right by the shop?

But no, neither Sergei nor his pals were under the pines when she left the shop. Only a crumpled newspaper was lying on an old box.

13

Pines, tall red-barked pines...

How many were there along the road from the settlement to the ferry? Perhaps two or three hundred—nobody had even bothered to count them. And under almost every one of them they had kissed, she and Sergei.

She had bewitched him, cast a spell on him. Every time she went to the bakery, he was waiting for her in the pine-wood.

But he was still as shy and constrained as before. He would blush as red as the pine bark at the thought that she was still a school-girl.

She was amuzed by this, found it terribly funny, and her head reeled from the consciousness of her power over him. Look at her twisting the chief engineer of the timber plant round her little finger, making Anya Taborskaya waste with jealousy and despair... Soon Sergei's shyness began to exasperate her, to drive her to tears, to a frenzy. What kind of man was he, afraid to kiss a girl under his own power? Who was the blushing maid, she or he?

Pines, tall red-barked pines... The white carpet of moss... The hot resinous smell, so familiar and so joyful, hit her in the face, caused a twitch in her nose, and tears of fury welled up in her green devil-may-care eyes.

She was sorry for the past, for her half-forgotten forest love. And her recent encounter with Sergei had shocked her deeply. God, how he had degenerated, what a sight he was!

Her aunt and her mother had written to her that Sergei had hit the bottle and was sacked from his post of chief engineer, but it had never occurred to her that he had sunk so deep in the bog. Actually, what was he about when she had run into him on the shop porch? He was buying booze for his alcoholic pals...

Three strange women with aluminium pails appeared round the bend in the road—they had gone to the village for milk and now stopped in their tracks goggling her. Who could this exotic bird be? Other people began to appear in the road—tipsy men, young fellows and adolescents, and then Sakha the ferryman's song floated on the air:

> *And under that lacy chemise*
> *A bosom rose, youthfully firm...*

Sakha never changed. Like five or ten years ago, he was still pining for beautiful love, love that was not of this world...

14

How long the days were in the country!

In the city, as you dashed about in the restaurant, you barely noticed the hours passing. But here—she had gone to the wood, she had been across the river, she had met her former swain, she had chatted with Sakha the ferryman— and it was still just after three o'clock.

Coming up the village hill, Alka made for the collective farm office, or, to be precise, for the Honour Board. It was a big board with Lenin's portrait—let's see who were the meritorious folk hereabouts?

Milkmaids. Eleven of them were on the Honour Board, and the sixth in the row was—who d'you think?—Lida! Yermolina L.V. She had totalled 376 litres of milk in June.

"Fancy that! " Alka said to herself with a shrug. "Lida a model worker—of all people! "

The house of Vassily Ignatyevich, Lida's father-in-law, was quite near the office, so Alka decided to drop in on Lida and see how she was faring with her Primitive.

Mitya the Primitive, Lida's husband, whom her aunt had been praising to the skies, had begun playing with an axe almost as soon as he got out of swaddling-clothes (you could always hear the tapping of an axe when you passed their house) and as he grew up he became quite crazy about carpentry. After he finished school, he even went to town— what a laugh!—to learn from master-carpenters. Well, it appeared he had learnt quite a few things from them. At any rate, Alka gasped at the sight of Vassily Ignatyevich's house. It had new platbands, and a new porch—with carved balusters, wooden lacework and all kinds of scrawls, a spacious attic room, and a cockerel on the roof. She just could not recognize Vassily Ignatyevich's old hovel—it was a palace, no less.

At the sight of her, Lida was struck speechless with joy.

"I thought you wouldn't come to see me, Alka. A glamour girl in red pants—what'd you want with the likes of me?"

"Rot! " said Alka. "Can you see me not dropping on a bosom friend?" Still, she evaded Lida's hug (the silly fool was actually blubbering, no less).

Their room was furnished well, you couldn't deny it. There was a nickel-plated double bed under a lace cover, a sofa, an imitation oak chest of drawers—that was nothing, you couldn't surprise anybody with ordinary pieces of furniture nowadays. But there were other things as well. For instance, there was a carpet nailed to the wall above the bed—an honest-to-goodness carpet and not just a bit of painted oil-cloth, there was a radio set with a record-player, a shelf with books, a pile of magazines...

"Mitya reads them," Lida said, and Alka heard something like pride in her voice. "He's mad on reading. Sometimes I wake up when it's almost morning, and there he is, still deep in his book."

Yes, Lida had done herself proud, Alka noted, casting her discerning eye over the room—you can't call her home a hut, not by a long chalk. But her own outfit—holy mackerel! Who would wear felt boots in summer these days, even in the country? Some dotty old man, perhaps. And Lida had felt boots on her feet, and a funny kind of house-coat of some antediluvian cut, baggy at the waist.

Then Alka tumbled to it.

"Wait a mo! You've got a bun in the oven, haven't you? Fast worker! " She came up to the sewing machine standing beside the table (Lida had been sewing when Alka had opened the door) and picked up a baby vest.

"I must've taken after Ma, Alka," Lida stammered blushing to her hair roots. "She told me she conceived on her wedding night..."

"What has your Ma to do with it? Did your Ma play bare-bellies with Mitya for you?"

At this Lida became quite incoherent and tears clouded her blue artless eyes. She was so upset that Alka regretted bringing up the subject. Lida had never been bright. Can you imagine a girl of fourteen not knowing where babies come from? And Lida didn't. She had once come running to Alka, shaking all over, pale as the sheet.

"Alka, what have I gone and done! "

"What?"

"I let Valka Teterin kiss me..."

"So what?"

"What if I get pregnant?"

It appeared her mother had been telling her she should not let fellows kiss her because that way girls got knocked up, and the silly fool still believed her at fourteen.

Lida became a little more composed when they sat down and Alka began asking her about Sergei (she just couldn't put him out of her mind), but soon Lida startled her again—by suddenly bringing up the subject of war.

"Alka, you live in the city... D'you think there'll be a war soon?"

"War? What d'you want with war?"

"I don't want war at all. I'm afraid of it more'n anything in the world. I'm terribly afraid there'll be a war..."

"Why should *you* be afraid?" Alka asked reasonably. "They don't conscript pregnant women, do they?"

At that point Lida came out with it:

"What if I have a boy, not a girl..."

Alka could see that their conversation would be about Lida's pregnancy or, at best, the milk yield of her cows— what else could you expect Lida to take an interest in? What had she seen? So Alka began to fidget and said it was time she shoved off.

"Don't go yet, Alka! Mitya will come soon, have tea with us..."

Lida was not just being polite—she begged Alka. She looked at her with admiration, with adoration ("You've become prettier still, Alka! "), and so Alka stayed. Anyway, she was curious to see her former beau.

Mitya had declared to her when she was thirteen:"Amosova, I decided to go steady with you." He made the declaration without raising his eyes from the ground, and ran away at once.

And all through the years since Mitya had been sending her coloured postcards with doves and roses for every holiday—May Day, the Revolution's anniversary, the New Year, the Women's Day... The only young fellow in the village to do it. And he had only cast her out of his mind the autumn before last, when she had gone to live in town.

Mitya began to demonstrate his oddities—and he was an odd one and no mistake—before he entered the house: he announced his arrival with a cock-crow. And when he dashed in and saw Lida, he went off his rocker altogether, picked her up in his arms and whirled round the room.

He brought with him the smell of fresh wood and resin, and Alka jeered to herself—see the carpenter hugging his wifey. But there her irony ended. Because she caught herself breathing in the strong resinous tang with pleasure. And she no longer found Mitya ridiculous. What's ridiculous about a man with the devil's own strength, his legs planted so wide apart you could drive in a cart between them, his neck as thick as a telegraph pole, red and smooth, with soft blond curls which looked like wood shavings.

Lida was hammering on Mitya's broad back to make him stop his foolishness. But she hammered with one hand and hugged his neck with the other, and it was obvious she did not mind at all.

Mitya noticed Alka at the exact moment he put his dear wife down on the floor. He jerked his head back, as though he had hit his chest onto a pole, and did not utter a word. Only his eyes glinted ferociously.

What was the matter with him? Why did he glare at her like that, Alka wondered. She was quite put out to see the kind-hearted Mitya giving her a look of undisguised hatred.

She only guessed the reason when Lida, waddling like a goose in her old felt boots, went to prepare the supper.

Why, he's ashamed of his wife, Alka thought. He's only just realized what a sorry sight she makes compared to some.

And the devil seemed to have got into Alka. In order to infuriate Mitya even more she pulled her belly in and walked across the room at her playful ass-wagging best: there, have a look! Speak about sour grapes!

She was to be disenchanted two or three minutes later, when Vassily Ignatyevich came in.

15

Vassily Ignatyevich came in coatless, in his suspenders—he wasn't expecting company—just dropped in on his daughter-in-law for tea.

Unlike his demented son, he saw Alka at once.

"So out paths have crossed again! "

And that was all. Not a joke out of him. He sat sedately, drinking tea from a glass adorned with a red flower, casting fond glances at Lida and simply dissolving with bliss every time she called him Dad. Alka could not recognize the smutty old he-goat.

Mitya began talking about Lida's work with a masterful air:

"It is my considered opinion, Dad," he said, for all the world as if he were addressing a meeting, "it's time she called it a day..."

"Perhaps it is," Vassily Ignatyevich agreed. "We have plenty of milkmaids. Why take risks?"

"It may affect your condition," Mitya said, again using an unfamiliar scientific-sounding turn of speech. This time he addressed his wife.

At this point Alka could not contain herself and gave a giggle. Look at them making a song about Lida's condition, when that condition was only a tiny bump yet.

"Don't you listen to them, Lida. Go on working to the last. Makes it all the easier to uncork..."

At these words Vassily Ignatyevich gave his daughter-in-law such a panic-stricken look as though a wild beast was attacking her, while Mitya ... Mitya glared at Alka with irrepressible rage from eyes that were piercingly light.

She got the message then—Lida was cherished here. Lida was made much of. They did not let a speck of dust set on her, they wouldn't have a bad word spoken in her presence.

Pride reared in Alka's chest until all went dark before her eyes.

You bastards! Lida was the sweet darling, Lida must be protected from life, while she, Alka, could be treated any old how, she had been through the mill...

Just you wait! She hadn't had her last say yet. She could let them have it, broadside. To this Primitive goon—look at him putting on airs, a builder, an innovator, if you please— and to Vassily Ignatyevich himself—hadn't he been grabbing at her with his old paws the day before and offering her a cushy job in his office? And she could give a lecture to her bosom friend Lida as well. Enough playing the innocent...

Before Alka could give them a piece of her mind, how- ever, a truck with dairy-maids rumbled up and hooted under the window, and Mitya and Vassily Ignatyevich rushed to help Lida get ready.

16

At home, in her aunt's house on the hill, all was very much the same—a gathering of old hags again, gossip again.

The only new face was Little Masha—a dark mountain in the middle of the house.

"I've come to have a look at the city-girl," Masha said, blunt as usual. "They say you go about in red pants."

"Why shouldn't she?" Big Masha replied, making up to Alka.

Aunt Anisya offered Alka some cloudberries—there was a whole plateful on the table, juicy and yellow like honey. So she *had* found some. Anisya's face shone with joy at her good luck.

Alka kicked off her shoes by the door, sat down at table but before she could pick up a berry from the plate Big Masha plumped herself on the chair beside her, crossed her legs and even put her arm round Alka's shoulder—bosom pal, if you please!

"Don't you paw me! That won't get you anywhere! "

"What are you on about, Alevtina?"

"Just that! Don't pretend! Think I don't know why you're sucking up to me?"

"I want us to have a good time..."

"You giving anybody a good time? Out for what you can get, that's what you are! "

Everybody became subdued all at once—the kick scored not against Big Masha alone. One of them was wearing a scarf that had belonged to Alka's mother, another a cardigan, a third a sarafan—and who paid for the funeral repast last year?

Anisya, kindly soul, to smoothe over her niece's rudeness, started talking about her beaus.

"Did you see the turnout in our street?" she asked. "Look at the lot of them. All kinds, village lads, and city fellows."

Indeed, outside the window where Anisya was pointing Alka could see Moustaches with his student pals, and further on, by the gate into the field, loomed yet another swain— young Peka. He had washed himself till he shone, donned a white shirt and come to learn "to jiggle".

"It's like this every single day," Anisya said. "They come like on sentry duty."

She said it proudly—her comely niece was praised and

appreciated. But what did her niece want with all these swains? If truth be told she felt like howling and smashing things...

As she walked from Vassily Ignatyevich's house to her aunt's, she had been racking her brains to get at the meaning of what had happened at Lida's place, but for the life of her she couldn't reason it out. Indeed, had anything happened at all? To be sure, they sat at table and drank tea, to be sure, Vassily Ignatyevich had his eyes glued to his dear daughter-in-law, coating with sugar every word addressed to her. So what? Let him! What did she care? And, why should she bother about the fuss they raised when the truck with dairy-maids drew up? What an event, by God! A cow-tender was going to a rendezvous with her horned beauties. Mitya dashed into the passage to get her boots, Vassily Ignatyevich climbed the stove-bed to get her foot-cloths... Let them! Devil may take you all! Rush about like mad, crawl over hot bricks if that's the way you like it...

But what she would never forget was what happened after Lida was gone, when the truck with the dairy-maids had disappeared round the corner. Vassily Ignatyevich— they were standing by the gate seeing Lida off—produced a three-ruble note and pushed it into Mitya's hand: "Run off to the shop and get something to wet our guest's throat. She must be parched..." Not a trace of his recent godliness left!

His eyes were darting playfully, gleaming with lust—the gay dog was back! *Now* he could be his true self. *Now* all was allowed because there was no Lida around. With her he had to act a decent elderly father-in-law, but he had no need to dissemble with Alka. Alka was of no account.

Biting her lower lip till it hurt—she always did that in the restaurant when she had difficulty with a client—Alka tossed her auburn mane to shake off the thoughts about Lida and her carpenter—they did not deserve the honour— and told her aunt to produce a bottle: let the old women have a drink.

Big Masha—she was not one to bear a grudge, you had to give her that—hopped, stamped her foot and jigged round the room like the devil himself. Then, sitting down, she started wagging her long tongue, heaping scandal on scandal.

Pyotr Ivanovich, say. Alka had meant to ask her aunt where the old fox was. Why wasn't he in evidence? Now she learnt that he had moved to a distant timbering settlement with his Tonechka. The pretext was to visit his brother-in-law, but what he was really after was a fool who would take a fancy to the learned bag of bones—that's how Masha actually referred to Tonechka—because there were no bidders in their own village.

"Have you seen your swain?" Masha suddenly asked.

"Which one?" Alka asked, and laughed. One couldn't help laughing when the old crone peered at you with her glazed eyes.

"Which one? The Primitive o'course."

Long-Tooth Agrafena broke into a guffaw that could probably be heard on the other end of the village. And Little Masha, as usual, didn't have a clue—who did she mean and what? One would think she lived in the woods—never knowing what went on around her.

"I mean Mitya Yermolin! " Big Masha shouted in her ear. "At school, when the teacher asked him something, he waved his hands about like a deaf mute. They called him Primitive. They say primitive folk used to talk that way. Is that right, Alevtina?"

Anisya, as usual, stood up for Mitya, supported by Little Masha and Afanasyevna, and there was a heated argument.

"No, no, don't you run Mitya down, Arkhipovna. Look, he's built all them houses and farm buildings—all on his lone... And he does not drink, nor smoke..."

"He's a daft one all the same," Masha stood her ground.

"Why d'you want to run down a man wi' a good head and hands?"

"Reason enough. When he was sixteen, he was put to look after the farm's radio 'cos they respected his father, and what did he go and do? Letting an old woman holler her head off on the farm's wires! "

Alka laughed. There *had* been such an incident indeed. Mitya fell asleep as he twirled the knobs of the radio set—he had to know what was going on in the world—and his granny's wails were broadcast all over the village. They did not do a thing to Mitya, of course, but Vassily Ignatyevich got it hot.

"An old story! Why bring it up?" Anisya said.

"There's newer ones," Masha persisted. "This spring Lida went to her sister's funeral in the district—did she or didn't she? She wasn't away more'n two days, but Mitya went stark raving mad in those two days. He raced to the post-office from his cow-house, axe in hand, frittening all honest folk. And when Lida came, he didn't hug her and kiss her, as other folk do, no, he grabbed her head and started twisting it this way and that. It's a wonder he didn't twist it off..."

Alka smiled. It was, indeed, very much like Mitya! But what was so funny about it? Or daft?

Big Masha, in the meantime, taking her smile for a sign of approval, really let herself go: she slung mud at Mitya, then pulled Mitya's mother to pieces (not Vassily Ignatyevich, though, she didn't dare to abuse him), and then unleashed her spite on Lida—who did she think she was, up to her knees in muck, shovelling manure, not diamonds, after all.

Alka did not interrupt the old woman, she was in no hurry to curb her tongue. Let her have her fun. After the slap in the face Vassily Ignatyevich had given her, why should she protect his precious Lida? Was Lida a princess?

But when Masha turned to Lida's belly (after picking the rest of her full of holes), Alka did try to stop her, though half-heartedly.

"That's enough. The baby's not even born yet."

"And it never will be! " Masha shouted heatedly.

"Stop blathering! " Anisya suddenly flared up. "D'you understand what you're saying?"

"Agrafena! " Masha appealed to a witness. "Didn't you see Lida packed off to the district hospital?"

"Well?"

"Aye—well! If she was well, they wouldn't take her to be mended there every month."

"That's enough! Stop it! " Alka suddenly screamed, feeling blood rush away from her face, so ashamed of herself she felt. Then she saw the old woman's baffled, obsequious face ("What's the matter, Alevtina? Wasn't I trying to please you?") and her shame became a feeling of revulsion to herself which shook her to the core. She banged her both fists on the table frenziedly:

"Go away! Get out all of you! Leave me alone! "

17

Alka was sobbing loudly, but Anisya made no attempt to comfort her. Her heart had turned to stone. She had never had guests driven out of her house! And only when Alka started bashing her head against the table, did she speak.

"What have you done now? When will you stop playing the fool?.."

"Oh, Auntie," Alka groaned, "don't ask me..."

"Why not? Who will ask if not your aunt? Who else have you in the world?"

In reply to this Alka raised her wet and swollen face from the table (Anisya had never seen her niece so unattractive) and then dropped it again. With a dull thud, as though it was the head of a dead person.

Then all locks were shattered in Anisya's heart. For who was it writhing and suffering before her eyes? Who was being torn to shreds by a tempest? Wasn't it a living twig from the Amosovs' tree?

She sat down beside her niece, gave a sob herself, and put her arm round Alka's shoulders.

"Come on, don't take on so... Tell me, you'll feel better for it."

"Auntie," Alka broke into a fresh fit of sobbing, "why doesn't anybody love me?"

"You? Now, what's got into you? Young fellows lay in wait for you ever since you were in the cradle, I'm thinking."

"I don't mean that, Aunt, I mean real love..."

And suddenly Anisya had nothing to say. This silence of hers weighed down on Alka like a hundredweight stone.

All her life she had believed that if boys were forever chasing after you, if they were eating you with their eyes, hugging you, pawing you, that meant love. But she had discovered it didn't. It wasn't love at all. Love was what Mitya and Lida, those two blessed fools, shared between themselves.

And the most terrible thing was that she, Alka, believed in that love and envied it. Yes, she did! She even knew now what true love smelled of. It smelled of fresh pine shavings and sawdust...

"Would you like a cup of tea?" Anisya finally asked. "It'll mebbe make you feel better."

Alka only gestured her away—if you have nothing to say, better keep quiet. She rose, went to the wash-stand but never reached it, collapsing on the bed instead.

Anisya snatched off the bed cover, undressed Alka and put her to bed like a child, and then lay down beside her, put her head beside hers on the wet pillow and began to comfort her with praise, knowing that Alka had a weakness for flattery, always had had, ever since she was a child. "Just take a look at yourself. Is it for you to bawl and take on with a face like yours? God must have shortchanged many a girl to make you as comely as you are..."

Alka just shook her tousled head—no, no, no! She used to think like that too—if you were beautiful you were happy. Look at Lida now—was she beautiful? But what wouldn't she give to have the thing she had seen at Lida's house today—if only for a day!

Yes, yes, yes, Lida was a sloven, Lida was a fool, Lida could never think straight.

But it was from Lida and none other that she had learnt about that other, different life. And not merely learnt about it, but saw this other life being protected by Vassily Ignatyevich as the most precious thing in the world. Protected from who? From herself, from Alka.

And Alka tossed and writhed, wriggling out of her aunt's arms, gnawing the pillow and, for the first time in her life, asking herself: what kind of person was she, Alka Amosova? And what was it about that silly fool Lida that people should set her as an example to herself?

18

"Alka, get up, Alka! "

It wasn't her aunt's voice, but one that was faint and indistinct, like the rustling of the birch leaves in the breeze; and anyway Anisya couldn't be telling her to wake up since she was snoring softly on an old quilt spread on the floor just beside the bed (so as to be nearby if Alka called to her).

"It's Ma, it's Ma calling me! " it dawned on Alka. "Why didn't I guess at once?"

She rose noiselessly, so as not to wake up her aunt, put on a dressing gown and went down the old creaky staircase to the porch.

Morning was just breaking. Her house in the back-yard, with its white slate roof, sparkled like a pink tent and a flock of swallows were wheeling above it.

The swallows were a new thing for Alka—they used to keep by Anisya's house. Generally, Alka had never liked their house in the backyard—it was no fun living so far from the street, and although her aunt and she had prized the boarding off the windows on the very first day of her arrival, she had decided to live at Anisya's and not at home.

Alka followed a narrow, grass-grown path—never used by anybody except her aunt these days—coming to a stop before a broad gateway with a metal ring, which broke into prolonged peals whenever you lifted and dropped it.

This gate had been an object of pride with her mother—nobody in the whole district, to say nothing of their village, had a gateway like that. And she had put it up, in her own words, in anticipation of Alka's wedding day—to make it possible for cars packed with guests to get inside the yard and stop right by the porch.

The little grass plot before the house her mother had loved so much had been recently mown by Anisya (they had had two crops of grass from it every year), but the clover's red and white heads were again speckling it. As soon as Alka made a few steps from the gate her feet were seared with cold dew.

She approached the porch on tiptoe, stealthily, exactly as she used to coming home at dawn from a dance. She stood listening a while (if only she could indeed hear her mother's angry voice in the passage!), then took a deep breath and, mounting the steps, peered at the heavy padlock on the door.

Not too hopefully, she felt in the hollow behind the jamb and was overjoyed to find the key in the usual place, where her mother and father had used to keep it.

She dashed across the dusky passage almost with her eyes shut because she had never been cured of her childish fear of darkness. But once across the threshold of the front-room, she heaved a sigh of relief.

Everything was the way it used to be a year or two before: the painted floor, scrubbed till it shone, the lace curtains her mother had loved so much, the huge ficus plant in the corner—her aunt had taken it back the day Alka arrived... But the house was empty somehow, you felt that nobody was living here. And it was frightening to look at the naked iron bedstead on which her mother had died.

"I've come, Ma..."

Alka raised her eyes to the whitewashed ceiling against which her voice had splashed plaintively.

No, she had not planned such a home-coming, half-dressed, shivering with morning freshness—and into a dead house. She had meant to descend on a living mother, suddenly,

157

noisily and triumphantly. Look, dear! Here's your daughter. She had gone to a strange city all alone, without a passport, her so-called husband had proved to be the lousiest of bastards—don't you think it was enough to break anybody? Yet she had not been broken. She got herself issued with a passport, found a job, and, to make it complete, taught a lesson to that bastard—had him discharged from the army.

"D'you hear, Ma, I've come..." Alka said again, and suddenly her heart jumped to her throat: a faint scratching could be heard from the passage behind the door.

She had never had any particular belief in various old wives' tales about the goblins and other fiends, but still she was only able to breathe again when a miaow came from behind the door.

"Busik! Busik! "

She flung the door open, and indeed it was Busik, their huge fluffy tom-cat.

The curtains on the windows had broken into the pink flower of willow-herb, the sun spots had started playing on the white sheet in which the samovar was wrapped, but Alka was still sitting at the table with Busik purring in her lap, stroking him and pressing him to her chest and listening keenly to his plaintive purring.

What was he singing his lament about? What was he complaining of? Loneliness? Heartache? Or was he perhaps trying to tell her in his cat language how her mother had died and what last behests she had left for her daughter in her dying hour.

Tears were rolling down Alka's flaming cheeks. God, how could that be? A cat, a wild beast, had remained faithful to its mistress and had not left her house even after her death, and she, her own daughter, had abandoned her parents' home, had exchanged it for town life...

"Ma, I shall stay. D'you hear me? I'm not going anywhere any more! "

The morning sun had flooded the room. Busik was already purring a different, more cheerful song. And, strangely, a songful joy had started welling up in Alka's breast, too.

She could not stay inside any longer. She ran out into the yard, spread her arms wide as though to embrace the sun and raced to her aunt's house straight across the dew-laden lawn, her head no longer bowed penitently, as it had been when she entered her own house.

"Aunt, Aunt, I'm staying! "

She stormed the sleepy Anisya like a whirlwind, like a tempest, and the latter did not at once grasp what her niece was saying.

"Where are you staying? Where? What new daftness did you think up?"

"At home, Aunt, at home! " Alka repeated, almost dancing with joy. "I have thought it all out, Aunt. We'll live together. And Ma's and Dad's graves are near at hand—we can always go and tend them, don't we, Aunt?"

19

The one thing Alka had never lacked was resolution—after all she was her mother's daughter—and she would have gone to town there and then to pack her things and give notice at the restaurant if it weren't for money.

She had given the money—five hundred rubles, the remains of her proceeds from the sale of her parents' belongings—to Tomka on the day she had left for the village, instructing her to send it to her village address some five days later. She had meant to impress the villagers with the enormity of the sum.

And because of that silly trick of hers she now had to stay put until the money order arrived.

But Alka did not waste time.

The first thing she did was to move into her own house. God, how happy she felt heating the stove in the morning, scrubbing the floors and putting the samovar on—all her own. And what joy it was to walk barefoot over the warm clean house!

The house was spacious and light, and she was now amazed at her own stupidity and blindness. In town Tomka and she rented a dark hovel at the outskirts, and all the time this palace had been standing empty in the village.

And anyway, Alka kept asking herself, what had she found so wonderful about the town? For the sake of what had she left her father and mother, her own hearth? Surely not for the sake of the fuddled men in the restaurant she had to please in order to get a decent tip? Was it for the sake of Arkady Semyonovich, then?

Yes, Alka said to herself, I shall live in my own house in the village. And my life will be very different from what it has been. Actually she had already started living this new life: in the daytime she worked on the haymaking with the collective farmers, and in the evenings she stayed at home sewing, as befitted a nice hard-working girl (she had never done any sewing before!) or attended to her house and garden.

Big Masha resented this "daftness" (she had no other word for Alka's new life) for, of course, not a drink came her way now, but even Anisya did not seem too happy. The drastic change in her niece caused her, it seemed, some concern and even alarm.

All this amused Alka and even touched her to tears, and ambitious plans flamed ever more brightly in her head.

She'd work in the kolkhos—she was quite firm about it. And she'd be a dairy-maid, she was quite determined about that. Like Lida. Yes, a dairy-maid and nothing else! Who ever wrote about waitresses in newspapers? And dairy-maids were written up all the time, and their photos published, too. Nowadays, the dairy-maid was the most important person in the village. And surely she, Alka, could outdo any of the others. Surely she'd push ahead of that dunderhead Lida or the Ninth Vera! As easy as pie! She was as good as wearing that little medal on her chest or perhaps even the gold star.* They called her mother Pelageya Amosova a woman of iron, and wasn't she her mother's daughter?

Alka's exuberant imagination painted the picture of her future family life. Again, on Lida's pattern. With a father-in-law as lovingly protective, and a husband as meek and devoted. To be sure, there was not another Mitya Yermolin in the world—she could do nothing about that!—but Alka was not at a loss for long.

Suddenly she had a whale of an idea—to get to work on Sergei, to set him straight and mould a model husband and citizen out of him. And why not? Hadn't Sergei gone to the dogs on account of her, Alka? Hadn't her mother written to her that Sergei was prepared to marry her, Alka, any moment, no matter what? Why, she'd had a chance to see for herself the other day, when she ran into him in the shop across the river. A chap wouldn't have cut and run like that, taking his drinking pals along, unless he still loved her!

* The Gold Star goes with the rank of Hero of Socialist Labour, the highest peacetime award in the Soviet Union.—*Tr.*

160

Days passed by, and Alka was still delighting in her new role of a blameless and virtuous young lady. She even felt sad when the money order finally arrived from Tomka.

20

Goodness, what a whopping big place the town was. There were more people on the landing stage than in the whole of their village. Alka remembered seeing this motley seething throng from the boat two years before and feeling her legs get glued to the deck—so scared was she of getting lost in this human ant-hill.

But today she took it all in her stride!

She was the first to run down the gangway and she weaved her way through the crowd like a nimble lizard. "Pardon! " "Excuse me! " "I'm in a hurry"—and a smile for everyone. And sometimes she used an elbow too, to clear the path.

Bright multi-coloured flags were fluttering on white masts to mark some holiday or other, tipsy men and hairy town-boys ogled her brazenly, and generally, the town was a wonderful place. And—there's no getting away from it—Alka heaved a sigh of regret. She was suddenly sorry to renounce all this splendour, to say good-bye to it forever.

She mounted a gay clangy tram-car decorated with red and blue bunting and it got her to her Green Street in no time, and then another five or seven minutes of tripping over dilapidated wooden walks laid past old houses, long sentenced to be pulled down, brought her home, to the hovel she shared with Tomka. They only had a tiny room with one window, and even that faced a wood-shed. In winter the room was cold as a cellar, and all the year round they were pestered by rats. Sometimes the creatures raised such a racket in the corridor that they were scared to stir in their beds, to say nothing of going out of the room. Arkady Semyonovich had sworn that Tomka and she would get an apartment in a new house in autumn, but now that he had got the sack they could whistle for that apartment.

Well, anyway, why should *I* bother? Alka said to herself complacently, as she opened the wicket. She no longer cared a brass farthing for the new apartment, and Arkady Semyonovich himself as well. She was through with it all. For good!

Tomka was home, as was evidenced by the opened window and the blaring of the record-player. Could she have a boy-friend with her? (Tomka preferred making love to music.)

But Alka had no time to stop and wonder. In the first place, she, Alka, had been missing Tomka something terrible, and, in the second, what did she care if Tomka had a boy-friend around. In the two years there had been plenty of occasions when she surprised Tomka with a boy-friend, and the other way round.

With her heart thumping against her ribs like mad, Alka flew to the rickety wooden porch beside the loo, raced along the rat-infested corridor like a whirlwind and jerked at the door with all her might—you could not open that door without applying quite a bit of an effort. And there was Tomka, her good pal Tomka, sitting on the sofa, her legs crossed (she always made a point of showing plenty of leg) and a cigarette in hand.

"I was sure you wouldn't stand more than two weeks of that wonderful village of yours! "

She spoke as she always did, in a superior and bantering sort of way—to be sure, she was five years Alka's senior. Besides, she had the resplendent job of stewardess on international lines and could jabber in English—of course she would put on airs for the benefit of a mere waitress. But at heart Tomka was as kind as Anisya, Alka's aunt, and would give you her last shirt if you asked her. So Alka disregarded the barbs and started hugging Tomka with all her might.

"Aw, get off it, I hate these sloppy ways. Let's discuss ways of raising our agriculture to a new level instead... Have you given your kolkhoz a mighty push?"

Alka sat down on the sofa beside her.

"Don't make a laughing matter of it, Tomka... I'm through... I've decided to live in the village..."

"Indeed? Has some merited tractor driver offered you his heart and his cow as well? Is that it?"

"No, Tomka, I mean it. I'll just live there, for good..."

"And may I inquire what you're going to do there? In that rural paradise of yours?"

"Oh, there's enough work on the farm..." for some reason Alka was ashamed to tell her that she had decided to become a dairy-maid.

"Well, never mind," said Tomka, rising, "we'll discuss

your agrarian plans some other time. Just now get ready for a party. I'm late as it is."

"What party?"

"One hell of a party! " Tomka cried and even snapped her fingers in delight. "It's Goshka's birthday—can you imagine the to-do? They've got hold of a launch and we'll sail down the river in the night and stop over in some meadow or other to eat and drink and smell the hay... Can you imagine it?"

Alka could. She had been in with Tomka's crowd before. Those pilots were jolly good sorts, knew masses of jokes, and could they dance! Especially that Goshka the Gypsy... But no, she'd decided to put an end to all that. She was through with parties!

"Don't you talk rot, Alevtina! " Tomka raised her voice. "By the way, I have spoken to my boss on your behalf. They'll take you on. Especially if you are nice to him at the party today. That will clinch it."

"No, Tomka," Alka said with a sigh, "there isn't a hope. How can I be a stewardess when I don't know the language?"

"Stupid cow! She doesn't know the language, if you please! Let me tell you, that men the world over know only one language—the one of the eyes and the behind. Yes, yes, yes! And you are as well qualified in this international language as anyone. And then, there's more than one stewardess on a plane. My mate Larissa, you should know, does not know a word of English, and you can't always make out what she says in Russian either, but she's nimble enough with trays, and so the sirs and misters are satisfied..."

At this point Tomka, just to make Alka smart all the more—for only recently she would have died for a chance to get a job on the airlines—began to put on her new uniform: a navy blue mini-skirt, a navy blue jacket with golden wings on the sleeve and a blue forage cap. The uniform was very becoming, softening Tomka's gaunt frame and adding femininity to it.

"Well, how about it?" asked Tomka, applying lipstick before the mirror. "Are you coming? I have to warn you that there's no food in the house."

"Never mind, I'll buy something... Off you go, Tomka."

"But why? Can't you simply go to a party? Have you joined a sect in that village of yours? No? Oh, I see. You're meeting your curly-headed Daddy tonight, is that it?" This was Tomka's way of referring to Arkady Semyonovich. "Very well, all the best then! "

She walked as far as the door and turned round.

"If you change your mind, the address is 32, Lesnaya Street. Remember, we had the New Year party there last year? At Vasilchenko's, Goshka's friend? Well, suit yourself."

Her high heels tapped angrily along the little corridor, the iron ring on the gate clanged in exactly the same way you heard them clang in the village, then Alka heard one or two muffled taps on the wooden sidewalk, and Tomka was gone, on her way to the resplendent, restive world.

Alka rose and was about to put on a new record, but the next moment flopped down on the bed and started bawling for all she was worth. What was the matter with her? Where was her resolution? Wasn't she the daughter of Pelageya Amosova? She wept and swore at herself, but all her being yearned to follow Tomka, to join her friends and their carefree merry-making...

21

For two years running, coloured picture postcards rained on Anisya—blue, red, yellow, and green, bearing wondrous foreign pictures and short notes in Alka's handwriting: "Hi, Aunt! " "Greetings, Aunt! " "Life is fun, Aunt! "

"Why can't she stay in one place?" Anisya complained. "Who has she taken after, I can't understand! "

"Let her! " Big Masha used to answer. "Her mother never set foot beyond the district in all her life, her grandmother ended her days on the stove-bed, you've been stuck here all these years... Mebbe she wants to do the flying for all her kin."

"What about settling down? What about making a nest of her own? Isn't she just the right age for that? Or is she waiting for her house to topple down?"

The house in the backyard *was* getting old and rickety before Anisya's eyes. It had suddenly sunk down into the ground and gone all askew, and in wet weather the sight of its tear-stained windows made her want to cry herself.

And still, all of Anisya's anxieties and alarms proved to be as nothing compared to the storm that broke over her head one autumn.

A letter came from Alka. In a few lines, without offer-

164

ing any explanation, she asked her aunt to sell the house in the backyard and send her the money at once. In all her life Anisya had never contradicted either Alka's mother or her niece. She did whatever they bade her, even tried to forestall their wishes. But at this point she jibbed: as long as she was alive, no strangers will own that house. It was not for that that your father and mother slaved and toiled...

In short, she stood her ground. She put all her thoughts on paper, mailed the letter, and then took to her bed.

Autumn rain scratched at the window, as softly, as a mouse, the iron ring clanged faintly on the front door.

Anisya knew it was the wind clanging the ring, not Alka. And all the same she listened fearfully to every rustle, expecting a light-hearted and smiling Alka to appear in the door any minute and announce:

"I've found a buyer for the house, Aunt. Now, set the table and let's have a drink to the deal..."

1971

Mamonikha

1

The arrival of visitors had clearly caught Aunt Grunya unprepared. She came running out onto the porch barefoot, bareheaded, in an ancient gingham sarafan which she had once probably worn for big church festivals.

"Oh, for mercy's sake, look who's come! " she cried in that familiar homelike singsong. "And there was me thinking you'd all changed your minds! "

His face wet with the old woman's kisses and tears, Stepan Ivanovich stepped into the grateful coolness of the cottage (it was already thirty degrees at eleven in the morning!) and everything was explained: his brother and sister were indeed not coming, Aunt Grunya handed him telegrams. Nikodim, it seemed, had suddenly had to make an important business trip, and Tatiana's son had just as suddenly fallen ill.

Stepan Ivanovich's disappointment was keen. They had exchanged letters, it had been definitely settled that they would all meet this summer in their old family home—after all, it was ten years since they had been together. And besides, they had to decide what was to be done about the house itself; with every letter Aunt Grunya had been lamenting that the hunters and shepherds were pulling the place to pieces, there were only the walls left and soon they'd be gone too.

However, Stepan Ivanovich was not one to nurse a disappointment for long. If they weren't coming—well, it couldn't be helped. Things happen. But what on earth should he say to his wife?

For the last three months she had been preparing to meet these fine Moscow in-laws, making new frocks and collecting feminine fal-lals because she didn't want them to think she was just a hick. The money she'd spent on them, too! And all for nothing.

So at first the atmosphere round the table was funereal.

Everybody, Aunt Grunya, her corpulent neighbour Fedotovna who had just dropped in to take a look at these visitors from distant parts and, of course, Stepan Ivanovich, all were damped by Polina's gloom. It was only after the second glass that she thawed a little.

Stepan Ivanovich let out a sigh of relief and removed his shoes, followed them with his sweaty socks, and began to walk barefoot up and down the unpainted floor; it was many years since his foot-soles had felt the gentle give of wooden boards.

"That's right, walk," and his aunt nodded approvingly. "The spit of your dad, his feet always wanted out. No matter what house he came to, his own or a neighbour's, first thing off came his boots or he couldn't be easy."

"Aye, it weren't for naught they called him Barefoot," Fedotovna remarked bitchily.

Grunya, however, wasn't going to let pass any implied slur on her dead brother. Didn't they all have nicknames those days? Maybe they did call him Barefoot, but he didn't live barefoot. Who else had a house like his? Who gave so much to the kolkhoz? A cow and a bullock, and a mare in foal, and a broken stallion, and three sledges, and two carts...

"No, no," she concluded, "it wasn't by that nickname they spoke of Ivan Artemevich but by his family name, and our name, Ustinya Fedotovna, speaks for itself—Sytin* Then all of a sudden she burst into bitter weeping. "Gone, all gone, Stepan, there's no more Mamonikha now, there's naught but the bears and Hunchback-Sokha living younder."

"Hunchback-Sokha? Is she still alive?"

"Aye, she drags along somehow. All winter long the poor soul never puts nose out of that hut of hers, like a bear in its den."

"You've no call to waste your tears," remarked Fedotovna sourly. "She needs none o' them. She's got her own helpers a-plenty."

"What helpers?"

"Her own kind; aye, all her life she's had wood goblins and imps serving her, all them ill things and unclean powers doing her will."

"Don't ill-speak her. Wagging tongues can blacken a body till you won't know them."

"Where've you been living all these years, have you

* From *syt*—fed to repletion.—*Tr.*

168

just dropped from the clouds?"

The talk took an acrimonious turn, voices were raised; it had always been like that with these two old women, neither would give way. Stepan Ivanovich began looking uneasily at the door leading into the other room where Polina and the boy had gone to rest not long before.

Aunt Grunya wagged her head a little—was her nephew henpecked?—and Fedotovna put two and two together in her big rather masculine head and looked pityingly at him. But Stepan Ivanovich did not react. Let them think what they liked. What did they know about the journey and how hard it had been on Polina and Victor? The day and night of sweltering heat in the train, then most of another day waiting at the local airport, and then the local bus with its heat and stuffiness and crowding and dust—enough to choke you.

The awkward moment was relieved by a runny-nosed little girl who suddenly called out under the open window.

"Fedotovna, what are you doing, slumped there like a barge, when there's your goat bleating fit to bust, she's all tangled up round the peg."

"Manka? How's she got that way?" The old woman was on her feet with amazing speed. "I was by her only a moment agone." And before many seconds had passed her heavy steps and heavy breathing passed outside the window.

"Now there'll be gossip all over Rezanovo," said Aunt Grunya with a sigh when Fedotovna had puffed herself away. "She'll spin a yarn—a mile long."

"What's there to spin a yarn about?"

She pressed her lips together—why pretend? Don't you know Fedotovna? She changed the subject, started to talk about the house.

"You'd do better to sell that house of yours before the shepherds and hunters burn it down. I was there last spring and they'd been making a fire in the front room. A sort of fireplace of bricks on the floor, and burned-out embers in it."

"Isn't there a stove?" asked Stepan Ivanovich, outraged.

"They won't fash themselves lighting the stove. Stick a bottle in their gob and toast themselves at the fire. Like hikers. Rogues they are these days, scurvy villains, no decency." Again she urged the sale of the house.

"But would anyone buy it?" asked Stepan Ivanovich. "On my way here I saw empty houses in every village."

"Them's old ones, only good for firewood. But houses as are still sturdy, they'll find buyers, folks who'll take them down and put them up again somewhere else. Our Gennady Matveyevich rakes in big money on it, moving houses to sell in town. He was here, the other day. Write to your clever lad, he says—meaning you, how long is he going to shilly-shally about that house of his? Is he waiting for it to crudle till he has to let it go for naught? Aye—Gennady'll take it for naught himself without blinking. You know the sort he comes from."

"I don't understand, Aunt, who d'you mean?" he shrugged.

"Naught to understand as I can see," said the old woman. "MAZ-Gena, Bullock-Matvei's son."

"What? Bullock-Gena here?" Stepan Ivanovich's eyes moistened and he felt no shame. They had lived in the same street, grown up together, gone to school together, been called up for their military service the same day—shared more than you could reckon.

"Aye, he's here all right, but they don't call him Bullock these days, he's earned his own name, drives a truck, a MAZ it's called, a huge big thing. When it goes past you can feel the house shake. So now he's not got his father's name any more, he's MAZ—there's none even remembers Bullock nowadays."

Eyes slightly narrowed, she stretched her pale old neck towards the open window.

"Did you see yon fine brick house as you came into the village—where the forest warden's house used to be? That's MAZ-Gena's, now Gennady Matveyevich. There's never been any in Rezanovo had a house of brick, nor in other villages our way neither, not so long's I can mind, but he took and built one. Even the warden hadn't the like, I don't speak of the rich farmers in the old days, they was paupers alongside him. Oh, he's a good 'un for raking it in. Wood and people and all. A man wi' machines—that's the sort gets everything that's going."

"I'll have to look in on him sometime," said Stepan Ivanovich.

"Not sometime but now if you're wanting to get home quick. Or he'll be off to the mowing or somewhere—you'll never find him."

2

To Stepan Ivanovich Rezanovo was a second home. As far back as he could remember he had been taken to visit Aunt Grunya. So once outside the house he could not refrain from taking a look round—at least, in the upper end of the village.

Rezanovo was not much better than those villages he had seen on his way there. There wasn't a house to be seen that could be called new, and the old ones seemed ready to tumble down. One sagged drunkenly forward, another leaned over sideways, a third had a tired dip in the roof—like a camel, while a fourth gaped with windows and doorways—just a shed. And where were the kitchen gardens all the houses had had? Where were the sheep which on hot days lay like black or grey boulders under the windows and in the shade of old bath-houses?

But Stepan Ivanovich felt particularly bad when he turned into the back-yards where the livestock sheds had been, most of them had been pulled down now and sawn up for firewood. In 'forty-seven he had been herd-boy in Rezanovo; the families living at this end had had forty-three cows—how many were there now? Wasn't there even one left?

The cloud weighing his mood was partially dispersed by Aunt Grunya. No change in her! How long had he been walking round the upper end of the village? Ten minutes or fifteen—twenty at most, and there she was already, busy with her scythe round the kitchen garden at the back.

"Does it need setting?" called Stepan Ivanovich gaily.

She made no reply, she was absorbed in her work. Like a truly pious believer at prayers, nothing else existed for her.

Stepan Ivanovich followed an old, familiar path that skirted the former stables, trotted past the threshing barn and—there it was, the house of white brick set a little back which he had taken for a hospital when he saw it from the bus.

The place was one he remembered well. Here was what used to be the warden's garden, a thicket of bird-cherry and rowan; in the autumn the schoolboys had run there during break—he could taste those sour-sweet berries still. Now only a few spreading old birches remained from that garden, and those only at the back; in front of the house there was not a single tree left and the bare windows looked like searchlights from the sun's reflection.

Stepan Ivanovich shaded his eyes with his hand, then dropped them to the truck and tractor standing conspicuously before the windows, and gasped at the sight of the entrance gate, high, iron-bound, painted green and with a peaked top.

Had Gena really done all this with his own hands? Where had he learned how to?

Gena's father, Bullock-Matvei, was a prize layabout. Can you imagine, for instance, that in a village where the forest was jostling you on all sides, anyone could lack wood for the fire? But Bullock's family did. Stepan Ivanovich had been only small before the war but he could remember Berry-Masha, Gena's mother, coming to them one morning in tears, begging for a bundle of wood, she'd nothing to make a fire with and the children were cold.

As far as laziness was concerned Gena wasn't far behind his father, and in sheer bull-headed obstinacy he far surpassed him. After the war, when he was old enough to work if he took a grudge against the foreman, he'd dig his heels in and not turn up to work for a day or two or three, and there was no moving him, neither persuasion nor force had any effect. And speaking of force, he was the strongest of all the young colts. As soon as he'd got his growth he began bullying the other boys—bring me a bun, bring me an egg if you want to stay in one piece. As time went on, his insolence increased, he even blackmailed old women. He would march into a cottage in broad daylight and seat himself at the table. "Ekimovna, how are your carrots coming up?" "Nicely, nicely, praise be." "Well, tonight the lads are coming to trample them all down." "Nay, what should they be doing that for? What scathe ha' I done them?" "Dunno, I'm sure. But I heard talk. If you don't want your carrots trampled bring me a pitcher of milk. I'll watch over 'em." So Ekimovna would bring it—what could she do?

Gena emerged from the house before Stepan Ivanovich came near, when the dog started barking. He came out, shouted "Kennel! " at the black-and-white beast, almost as big as a calf, and advanced to meet the visitor, arms outstretched.

"Stepan, man, is it really you? I happened to glance out of this barn o' mine—" with a languid, contemptuous

172

jerk of the head at the house—"now, who might that be, I thinks. Coming along staring pop-eyed at my shed. And then I saw—It's me own old pal, from Mamonikha—red ears and each one wi' a hole."

He burst out laughing, baring two rows of strong, nicotine-stained teeth.

"Well, Grunya told me a while agone she was expecting guests."

For a moment Stepan Ivanovich's breath was stopped as the extended arms went round him in a bear's hug, lifting him from the ground.

"Well, now, so you've come at last. How many years is it since you've been home? Got no feeling, that you haven't. Now me, it's my weakness, I don't want any of your towns. Home! To my own swamps and wood-cocks. I suppose you're living there in the south like at some resort, one long holiday, eh? Eating pears and grapes and every sort o' fruit and berry? Eh?"

"Grapes don't grow where I live and for that matter—" Stepan Ivanovich shrugged. "You don't see much holiday resort when you're bang up against cement works. It's all you can do to grow a few vegetables."

"You don't say," Gena marvelled and smiled in great self-satisfaction. "In that case, if you've naught agin it, come and take a look at my poor lot."

The metal latch rasped and Gena stood aside for his guest. The same instant another dog resembling the first in coat and size made a leap at Stepan Ivanovich. Gena kicked him aside.

"Get out, you brute! Showing off—can't you see your master's here?"

"How many have you got?" Stepan Ivanovich asked when he got his breath.

"What—dogs? Three. There's another for hunting, I fool around with a gun, times. But this one's only for noise."

Stepan Ivanovich nodded towards a battered aluminium bowl containing the remains of the dog's food—two weary-looking potatoes in their skins, without any addition.

"He flies at folks because he's hungry. Are old potatoes all you give him?"

"Blockhead! If you don't keep him hungry he'll just lie and sleep. I want him like a hungry wolf. Make sure there's no thief pushes his snout in here. Get me?" And Gena made a sweeping gesture round him—the proud

173

gesture of an owner.

Following his gesture, Stepan Ivanovich gasped. An orchard—and what an orchard! Apple-trees, pears, plums, and every kind of berry patch.

"Aye, we're coming along a bit," said Gena. "Shows what we've done since the war, eh? That fine gentleman, the warden—what did he have here? Rubbish, that's what. Right? And the climate's good enough. I was by the Baltic with the army, and I wouldn't say they've got much better climate and soil than ours. Winter's milder, that's all. Right. We wear thick coats in winter, why shouldn't we give our apple-trees something warm, too? We aren't short of straw, or rags either."

Gena leisurely led him from tree to tree, showed him gooseberry, raspberry and currant bushes, strawberry beds, tomatoes and cucumbers, and Stepan Ivanovich could not hide his admiration. Everything in exemplary order, every bit of ground made use of and as for weeds, not one dared to show its face. Everything in place, everything tidied up with hands, rakes, the sun, lime—a picture.

But the pride of its master's heart was the apiary, fifteen beehives like tiny multi-coloured huts standing at the back of the orchard along the tall fence.

"Sing fine, don't they?" said Gena, listening to the humming with a contented grin. "A lot of work, though, 'specially winters. But it's worth it. Honey fetches good prices."

Stepan Ivanovich, who with head thrown back had been looking at the richly flowering limes along the fence, hazarded a guess.

"Have you planted limes specially for the bees?"

"What d'you think? I'm no fine gentleman to be setting out bird-cherry or rowan—what's the use of them? All right, they smell, and they make a mess. But if I want to keep that flying livestock contented I've got to have feed for them at hand. And mind, feed's all right as far as it goes," Gena went on with a wink, "but I've found another job for the limes. Like putting two collars on a horse."

"Two collars?"

"Aye. That's the trick of it. What they call rationalisation, first class." Gena drew him to the nearest lime. "Feeds the bees, you've seen that, eh? And what holds the fence in place?"

174

Sure enough, the tall fence of sharply pointed palings wound about with barbed wire was supported by the trunks of limes and poplars. It was the first time in his life Stepan Ivanovich had seen a living fence like that and he could only wag his head in amazement.

"So you approve of my rationalisation? Ha-ha! Remember Hoof-Oska who wanted to mate a cow with a bear so's it would live through the winter without fodder? Well, I'm following in his footsteps."

How pleasant it was in that orchard, stippled with shade and sunshine; and the air—you couldn't get enough of it. However, it was time to talk business. But a fine chance there was of that—Gena wouldn't hear of any business, all these years they hadn't seen one another, what did Stepan take him for, a heathen, to let an old pal off without a drink.

So they went inside, and there was more showing round. A spacious verandah with a painted floor, a roomy entrance and pantry, lobby, kitchen, front rooms...

The gentleman's mansion which had stood there had been burned down by local snot-nosed "revolutionaries", back in the Civil War, long before Stepan Ivanovich was born, but whether it had been richer than Gena's house was a question. Stepan Ivanovich was far from sure of it.

"I made up my mind I'd had enough of wood," said Gena. "And you needn't look surprised. Them Germans' houses are all stone or brick, while we, who won the war, crawl into wooden kennels. No, it's time to make an end of wooden Russia. Am I right?"

"That you are," said Stepan Ivanovich. "Only bricks—they cost a lot. Where can you find the bricks hereabouts?"

"Aha, for that you've got to look sharp. If you do, then you'll find your bricks. And the cash'll come rolling into your pocket, not out."

All this time the goodwife, who unlike her husband was thin, silent and sour-faced, was busy putting out refreshments on the table, and as soon as they had downed a glass or two Stepan Ivanovich again spoke of his own matters—a lift in the truck. This time Gena heard him out.

"No." He shook his head decisively. "I can't today. Some big men from the town promised to come, and maybe there'll be someone from the regional centre, too. I've got to take them fishing. Tomorrow, now, or the day after, whenever you like. And anyway, what do you want to stick your nose into that hole for? Stop here. If you get tired of your aunt's, come to me. I guess I've space enough, eh?"

"I want to spend my first night in my father's house."

Gena smiled condescendingly.

"You're daft. Life hasn't taught you anything, I see. Well, go along, then. The mosquitoes are getting impatient."

3

Stepan Ivanovich decided to make his own way to Mamonikha on foot. He found an old two-wheeled handcart in his aunt's shed, big enough for their luggage, the sort which in former times the farmers had used for wood, hay and every kind of thing; for the rest—what was wrong with walking? The road would be dry, it would be a pleasure, going through the woods!

As soon as he mentioned it, however, Polina flew out at him. What, hadn't they stood enough these past few days, without tramping goodness' knows where through forests and swamps! Drat your Mamonikha and everything to do with it!

But Aunt Grunya quickly quelled her.

"Of course I wouldn't know, Polina," she said with staid dignity, "maybe in your parts it's thought proper to trample your men like doormats, but here we've different ways. Among us Sytins the man is always the head. So if you can't curb your tongue in respect for your husband, at least don't disgrace him in front of others. You've come all this way already and now you're making a fuss about the last seven kilometres to his family home. Whatever will folks think! "

So they started out, Polina and Victor of course carrying nothing and Stepan Ivanovich pushing the handcart. He had harnessed himself easily, he had even found it pleasantly reminiscent of old days. Sometimes you couldn't get a horse for months on end, so you'd take its place between the shafts.

To Polina, however, that handcart was the last straw. What respectable man harnessed himself to a cart these days! If Nikodim had been there they would have had a car, and respect, too, driving with the state farm manager or maybe someone bigger.

Stepan Ivanovich tried every way to put his wife in a

better humour. He jerked his head at the pine woods they were passing, "Just look, you wouldn't see anything prettier at the cinema," and talked about how he had run along this road when he was at the Rezanovo school. He tempted the two of them with wild strawberries—"Go a bit left, can't you smell them?" But nothing helped. Polina marched ahead without vouchsafing a word or a look, handsome, full-bodied, her auburn hair hanging loose over her broad hollowed back. But Victor only trailed along flabbily. A boy of ten ought to be running about like a dog, pushing his nose into everything, instead of puffing and panting like a little old man. All because of Mum's buns. How many times Stepan Ivanovich had protested against stuffing the boy. He ate at school, he ate at home, and then he'd run to the kindergarten where his mother worked and eat some more there; and now here was the result.

The first birches and firs appeared, the first mosquitoes whined overhead—they were approaching the marsh.

"The road's going to be a bit soft here," Stepan Ivanovich warned his family. "It oughtn't to be bad though, it's a dry year."

Silent as automatons they topped Toshka's Hill, where one winter, it was told, a drunk from Mamonikha had frozen to death, and came up against a dark, thick fir wood.

Polina and Victor stopped dead.

"What's the matter, seen a bear or what?" Stepan Ivano-vich called cheerfully from behind them. He let go the handles of the cart with relief and went up to his wife and son, smoothing back his damp hair with sore hands.

Mud. Thick and black as pitch, stretching across the whole road.

"Now maybe you realise why your brother had to take an urgent journey, and your sister's child was urgently sick."

"There usen't to be mud here at this time of year," mumbled Stepan Ivanovich, avoiding his wife's angry eyes. "It must be the tractors have broken it up."

"Thanks, that's a very comforting thought today! " snorted Polina and began removing her shoes.

"Mum—do we have to go through that?" whined Victor.

"Now then, my fine bold lad, the mud's only ankle deep and if you keep to the verge it's as dry as asphalt. Look."

Of course all that was said more for his wife's benefit

than for his son's, but when had she ever heeded him? Off came her shoes and straight into the mud she went, holding them in her hand.

"Mu-u-um! " screamed Victor.

But Mum, ignoring everything, went on splashing through the middle of it, like a laden horse. She was sturdily built.

Finally Stepan Ivanovich picked up his frightened, screaming son, carried him along the verge at the edge of the mud—it was as dry as he expected, he didn't even wet his shoes, then went back for the luggage and finally the cart.

After that the road became—thank heaven!—more or less decent again; the scent of the Voronikha ferns came to them, then the stream was heard—a merry babble, chuckling as though it recognised him.

He flung himself down on the soft green bank to rest; everyone coming from Rezanovo had always rested there. They drank, and washed their faces and feet. Polina and Victor unpacked the food. But Stepan Ivanovich was not interested. He listened to the song of the stream, so familiar from childhood, and had room for only one thought.

"Come home, come home," sang the stream, and in the end he could hold out no longer and jumped up.

"Don't hurry, take your time. Mamonikha's quite close now. I'll just go ahead and scout round a bit."

So—just imagine it!—he left his wife and son in a strange forest and hurried on, forward. Like a kid, or an arrant fool. He came to himself, brought up with a jerk, when he reached the first Mamonikha fields—or rather, the aspens.

Yes. The remains of big entrance gates lay on the ground; a hawk, wings outspread, hung in the sky just as one always had—but where were the fields, the soil which he had once ploughed and harrowed?

There were no fields. A thick growth of aspens rustled over them.

4

It had been a Sytin custom to plant a tree beneath the window when a child was born. So at various times a cedar had been planted for Nikodim, a birch for Tatiana, a rowan for Maria, a bird-cherry for Anna (the last two had died in childhood) and only the runt, Stepan Ivanovich, had been left without a green marker in the soil; he was born in 'thirty-three when people were dying of hunger and there had been neither time nor thought to spare for things like trees.

However, his mother had made the omission good when he was already doing his military service. Shortly before her death she had written him that now he too had his tree in front of the family home—a poplar. And that poplar was the first thing he saw as he approached the house. It had grown, spread, and excelled all the others—the cedar, the birch, the rowan, the bird-cherry. The green giant leaning over the house met him with its rustling poplar song.

But the house itself was almost unrecognisable. The annex where they had lived in winter when they froze out the beetles from the main part was gone, so were the shed and barn, and the roof had been ripped off the porch. As for the inside! He had thought his aunt was letting her tongue run away with her when she had spoken of the shepherds, the previous evening. But she had been telling the simple truth. In the middle of the room was a pile of ash. They had brought in bricks from somewhere outside and made a fire on the floor. After all, any fool can make a fire in a stove, but it takes originality to heat the place with a bonfire.

Even in the hardest times, when they were starving, his mother had had a thorough spring cleaning before Easter. She had scraped and scrubbed the pinewood ceiling and walls, and in the dreariest weather the front room had been bright. Now it was black with soot.

The other room was just a little better. The nickel bedstead on which Grandad Artemy had slept was still intact, so was the table, and Stepan Ivanovich's eye was caught by the iron ring in the ceiling; his cradle had been suspended from it.

"That's how your dad started, Victor—swinging in a wooden cradle hanging from the ceiling—" Stepan Ivanovich began to tell his son and choked. Polina broke in practically,

"We'd better start by getting this place halfways decent, we can talk about cradles later."

"Yes, yes," Stepan Ivanovich caught himself up. Better get busy, it was four o'clock already and endless things to be done.

The first thing was to shovel all the dirt out and light

the stove, even on a hot day a stove made things pleasantly homely. Then Stepan Ivanovich came with a great armful of hay from the stack just behind the house for bedding. It was fragrant, fresh from this year's mowing. They would sleep well on it!

"Don't bring it in yet," said his wife, meeting him in the porch with skirt tucked up and carrying a bucket (where on earth had she found it?)

"You're surely not going to wash the floor?"

"You don't want to sleep on all this filth, do you?"

The well had a sweep, unknown in Polina's steppeland, and Stepan Ivanovich called after her, "Wait, I'll help you! "

But Polina wasn't waiting for anyone; she quickly grasped the wooden pole and the wooden bucket descended.

"And what shall I do?" shouted her husband gaily. He wanted to restore harmony in the family as quickly as he could.

"You can mow the grass," said Polina amicably.

"Right! "

He picked up the old scythe that stood ready by the porch—he had found it in a shed and sharpened it—and set to work on the yard with rhythmic sweeps right and left. He did not look at the grass (peasant work was in his very bones) and took no notice of Victor whining somewhere behind. He wasn't going to be outdone by his wife!

5

At work Stepan Ivanovich often heard talk about being tired of the same old gal all the time, about having a try at a bit of young meat. And they had their try. On Mondays first one, then another would hint or boast of Sunday conquests.

Stepan Ivanovich simply did not understand it. There was nothing gave him greater pleasure than to look at his wife, to watch her dealing with domestic chores—cooking, washing, sewing; when he was held up at work and she was already in bed rosy and warm, her auburn hair spread over the pillow, he wanted nothing more this side of paradise.

The first time he saw Polina was during his military service. One of his mates, Boris Ogarov, took him along and when he saw her room, bright and clean, with geraniums on the windowsills and a white bed like a snowdrift, a mat embroidered with a deer and fawn over it, he gasped—he felt that he had never seen anything so lovely. He did not venture then to cherish any hopes with regard to its occupant—a wonderful girl like that! Besides, Boris obviously had an eye on her, and what was he compared to Boris? A sack of potatoes. A duck beside an eagle.

No, he was quite content to be able to visit that house, that paradise, instead of being at a loose end when he was given a pass. True, he did not spend very much time inside it. Boris would warn him, "Leave me a clear field," in other words don't stick around all the time. And anyway, he himself felt uncomfortable, sitting idle. Polina's mother was ill, her brother and sister were little, and Polina worked her fingers to the bone to earn a little extra, sewing or knitting on top of the endless domestic jobs—the kitchen garden, the pig she was rearing, the poultry, the firewood. So he and Boris tacitly divided their spheres. Boris stayed inside to amuse Polina, while he would chop wood, or dig the garden, or mend the pigsty—a dozen jobs. All he saw of Polina was when he said goodbye or when she came out to look at his work.

One day, about a month before they were due to be demobilised, Boris announced, "You smarten yourself up today. I'm going to storm the fortress."

Well, after all, it was to be expected, thought Stepan Ivanovich. Only an arrant fool would let a girl like that slip out of his hands.

They went along together, taking two bottles of wine (one was even champagne), and a cake, and flowers.

Boris started right off, almost before they were inside: this is the way of it, Polina dearest. I'll soon be free of one set of ties and I'm looking for another—will you marry me?

Polina first laughed, then turned serious and shook her head.

"No, Boris, I won't marry you. Now, if Stepan here asked me I might think of it."

The wedding celebration was quiet and modest. Nikodim and Tatiana did not come, and Polina's family did not think much of Stepan Ivanovich. He could understand it—in his badly fitting tunic he looked puny and insignificant compared with the bride, who was like a flowering apple-tree in her rich beauty.

Towards the finish Polina herself apparently had second

thoughts, and when they were left alone she burst out sobbing. That had been the most dreadful moment in his life, in all the almost forty years of it.

6

Within some three hours they had brought the house into a semblance of order. At least it provided a place to lay their heads for the present, and shelter against rain and the mosquitoes. That was the main thing, the rest could follow gradually.

Satisfied and happy (even Victor had stopped whining) the Sytins sat down to their first supper in Mamonikha.

"Well now, Victor," said Stepan Ivanovich gaily, "work gives you a good appetite, doesn't it?"

"Uhuh," Victor agreed through a huge mouthful of fresh cucumber, one of those Aunt Grunya had given them.

Stepan Ivanovich too was eating with a fine appetite, but his thoughts were in the village. Just think, all these hours he had been on Mamonikha land but hadn't seen anything of Mamonikha itself! And finally he jumped up, leaving half his tea in the glass.

"You do as you like, but I can't wait any longer. I'm off to take a walk round the village."

Much to his surprise Victor wanted to go with him.

The Sytin house stood somewhat apart from the others, and in the old days a smooth well-travelled road had led from it to the village proper. But now? Stepan Ivanovich sought here and there—no road. Everywhere there was a scanty growth of meagre rye mingled with sturdy over-ripe couchgrass. Must have been a field here once and this is self-seeded, thought Stepan Ivanovich and marched in a straight line to the end house.

The end house had belonged to Pavel Vassilyevich, Lida's father; as soon as Stepan Ivanovich saw that old two-storey house with its white lacy window-carving warmed by the evening sun it plunged him into a sea of memories. It all came back clearly, how he and Lida used to run across to each other's houses—barefoot, in winter!—and how later he had been in love with Lida and she had mocked him cruelly in ditties.

After the war the lads were called up for army service, some to the infantry, and some to labour battalions on the railways, or in construction sites; but him they turned down. Too small. And Lida was the first to sing:

> *Oh you fine tall cockerels*
> *Move aside a crack,*
> *Let me see my bantam,*
> *He's hid behind your back.*

How she laughed at him and mocked him when he was sent to the special "centre". That was something they had then for recruits who were small and undernourished because of the war. It was reminiscent of the way kolkhozes would fatten calves for sale to the state.

But all that was in the past—the humiliation, the disgrace, it no longer mattered. What had happened to Lida, though? Where was she? How had things turned out for her? Because when he was nearing the end of his army service and was already engaged to Polina, this same Lida had written to him.

"Stepan, I have been tied down here in this Mamonikha till I cannot stand any more of it, I hate everything about it. You know other places now, for God's sake take me away from here, as your wife or however you like, I agree to anything."

Pavel Vassilyevich's house was still sturdy, quite fit for habitation. But the windows had not been boarded up and the glass was smashed. He had a vivid picture of how Lida must have left. It had all become so hateful, so sickening, that she had not waited even to board up the windows.

"Dad," said Victor softly, almost timidly (even he had probably been given cold shivers by the empty gaping eyes of the house), "what's that growing there?" He pointed at the nettles which made a thick wall round the porch.

"Nettles."

"But the ones at home aren't like that."

"They're smaller, you mean? But d'you know what those nettles do? They stop bad people coming in."

"Oh!" Victor looked at his father and slid a hand into his.

From then on, father and son walked hand in hand through dead Mamonikha. Walked past the houses through tall, dry, slightly trampled grass.

They were silent. It is not seemly to chatter in a cemetery —even Victor evidently felt the same. And this Mamonikha was a cemetery.

Even the poplars above the roofs, many for some reason dried up on top, seemed to rustle mournfully, not a bit like the way those vital, cheerful trees should.

7

It would have been hard to find a cottage in Mamonikha in worse repair than Hunchback-Sokha's. It faced the backyard, it was propped up on all sides, the windows were small and crooked; but with everything round about so neglected and wild, even Sokha's tumbledown place was a home.

It was pleasant to approach her cottage. Both sides of the path were mown and so was the lane, and the clipped grass beside her rickety but clean porch was so full of small birds that they made quite a wind when they rose in a cloud.

Stepan Ivanovich had no great belief in all the tales about Hunchback-Sokha, but nevertheless when he reached for the latch he stiffened his spirits with a joke.

"Now, Victor, chin up, you're going to see Baba Yaga* herself."

One door scraped on the worn floorboards, the second scraped, and then the fairy-tale came true—a hunchbacked old woman was there with a cat, a speckled hen and a cheeping brood of yellow chicks.

"Well now, thank ye kindly for coming to see me, I looked out a while agone and there was Ivan Artemyevich's chimney smoking, now who might that be, I thinks."

Stepan Ivanovich embraced the old woman and his eyes were moist. But Victor suddenly blurted out, "Good evening, Grandma Yaga! "

Stepan Ivanovich flushed crimson, but Granny Sokha, as he had mentally renamed the old woman, was not in the least offended.

"Yaga, that's right, Yaga, my dear. Limping and hunchbacked, overgrown with moss. Aye, that's how it is, my dear."

"And can you weave spells, Granny?" asked Victor, with growing courage.

"Nay, with spells I'm a poor sort of Baba Yaga, childie.

* Baba Yaga—Grandma Yaga, a witch from Russian fairy-tales.—*Tr.*

184

If I knew spells and charms, you know what I'd do first of all? I'd charm myself a new leg and a new back. But you see how it is, all my life long I've hobbled on one leg and given folk the grues."

Granny Sokha followed the old ways, so the first thing she did was to offer her guests something to eat, putting on the table all she had: freshly salted mushrooms—the tiny ones for which Mamonikha was famed, a whole pitcher of ripe, red wild strawberries, and honey-sweet cloudberries.

At the sight of all this fresh, fragrant forest wealth Victor's nostrils twitched, and Stepan Ivanovich certainly had no thought of refusing; these were things he had not tasted for a very long time.

"Now then," said Granny Sokha, well pleased as she saw how it had all disappeared, down to the last mushroom, the last berry. "Now I can ask ye how you're doing."

"Sure you can, Granny Sokha. We've come here to take a look at my old home."

"And how do you find it, your father's home, did you know Mamonikha?"

"Well—what can I say? There's naught left of what was but the hawk in the sky. It's all overgrown, all gone back."

"Aye, all on it," the old woman nodded. "Birches and aspens ha' come on it like bandits, they even clamber on to the roofs. It's as Uncle Prokopy said when the village was built again after a fire. He kept saying, 'You're wasting your strength, men. Mamonikha hasn't long to live. If fire doesn't kill it, the scrub will.' "

"He said that?"

"Aye."

"And there's something else I've seen, the poplars by some of the houses are drying up."

"Aye, they're dying." The old woman nodded.

"What's killing them?"

"The poplars? Who knows? Mebbe they're pining for their own folks as planted them."

"The trees are pining?"

A shout came from outside; probably Victor chasing the birds. Stepan Ivanovich did not even glance out of the window. Let the boy amuse himself, why should he sit here in a stuffy room? Carefully moving his legs—the cheeping chicks were trying to peck them and it tickled—he looked at Granny Sokha again.

"How are you managing here, all alone?"

"And what can I do, Stepan Ivanovich? It's the fate I was born with. It's hard, aye, it's hard in winter. The snow drifts up agin the windows, I don't know what's doing outside, whether it's day or night. Times, I can't go out for weeks. There was one year the snow was that deep, when they brought me my pension, twenty rubles they give me, they couldn't get here and had to take it back again. Well, and how's things wi' you, Stepan Ivanovich? They say you're living in warm parts, ye won't be having to worrit about firewood any more, I'm thinking?"

"We don't use it, we heat with coal."

"Ah, so that's the place ye've found. In a town. Aye, everything's gone topsy-turvy these days. You canna tell where the duck is and where the drake. Now, I mind me in the old days, my brother—he's dead these many years agone, poor soul—well, he lived in Yaroslavl and was doing well there. Head salesman he was with some merchants, the Krasulins. But no, he left gold and silver and a fine brick house. I'm going home to Mamonikha, he says, to my forests. Aye. But today it's all the other way, they go off to the towns; they want to live richer and more free, like. And haven't you ever seen Lidia Pavlovna in them towns?"

"You mean Pavel Vassilyevich's Lida?" he asked quickly.

"Lida, aye. Your neighbour. She went off as well, seeking fortune and ease. But I dunno if she found it, no."

"Why shouldn't she? Others do."

"Aye, but d'you know who she went with? Kotya Kura."

"Kotya? The stove-builder?"

"Him, and no other. A drunken sot, and nigh twice her age."

"Was she crazy?"

"The life she'd had of it was enough to craze a body. First her mother was paralysed and then her aunt. She brought the aunt to look after her mother and think of it, before half a year was gone there she was too, lying like a log. Lida was ready to howl, there they was, all going to other parts and she was tied hand and foot. And she had the kolkhoz calves to look after, a whole barnful, and at home one and the other, both like logs. And I see she's beginning to look into the bottle, and smoke, and talk bad. Oh, I don't blame her," the old woman sighed. "Nine years of it, what sort of life for her, and at her age? Nine years, cleaning out manure from under two old women. She was real desperate, poor thing, life wasn't worth living.

She came running to me before she went and 'Granny,' she says, 'I'm going to town with Kotya Kura.' 'Well,' I says, 'now ye've buried mother and aunt, you can choose how ye'll live.' Why should I try to stop her? Twenty-nine, she was, and what could she do here? Wait for a prince to come riding? So Lida left us. 'I just need to get out of here,' she says, 'then I'll find something.' I don't know what her fortune's been in new parts."

8

Stepan Ivanovich left Granny Sokha with the last light of the day. A burning red sun was settling into the dark firs behind his house.

Stepan Ivanovich staggered a little. He had asked Granny Sokha for a drink because of the depression that had overcome him; he felt so sorry for Lida that he could have wept.

Lida Mamonova had been the prettiest girl in the village and the best pupil in the school. When the old maths teacher, Yevstolia Vassilyevna, had given bad marks she had sighed, "What's to be done, potatoes aren't as clever as bread," in other words, I don't blame you, children, I understand why your brains won't work, it's because you get only potatoes and wild greens to eat. But how happy she was, how she seemed to cast off her years when she picked up Lida's paper. "No, no, children, the best bread in my class was never as good as this potato. Mark my words, this potato will do well for herself." Do well. She had married Kotya Kura.

Stepan Ivanovich was not to blame, what could he do when he was engaged to Polina, as he had been when that dreadful letter came from Lida. But all the same—all the same—perhaps he was to blame, too.

Emerging from the lane into the village street he broke into song.

> *Times when you plough the furrow*
> *You give the horse a rest*
> *And to a smiling cottage*
> *You go, a welcome guest.*

He wanted to shake off his sombre mood, to cheer himself with his father's favourite song before meeting his wife whom, after all, he had abandoned in a strange house.

"Polina, Victor, you won't scold me, will you? I've just had a snifter—you understand, ha-ha! "

He lurched across the threshold, went into the far room and saw his wife and boy sitting embraced on the bed. He was so touched that tears welled up in his eyes.

"I've brought you a light from Granny Sokha, it'll be more cheerful with a light, eh?" He dived into his pocket for the candle he had begged of her.

"Dad-dy-y-y! " Victor's voice was fretfully tearful, and Stepan Ivanovich assumed a stern tone.

"Now then, son, be a proper man! "

"Oh, for heavens' sake shut up with your proper man!" Polina suddenly burst into tears. "Can't you see how he is?" As though in confirmation of his mother's words Victor broke into choked coughing, barely able to catch his breath.

Stepan Ivanovich sobered on the instant. Lord, could it be the same thing that had happened three years before? They had been on holiday in the country not far from home. Everything had been fine, they had swum, lain on the sand or the fresh grass and sunbathed, then all of a sudden one evening, two days before they were due to leave, Victor had fallen ill—choking before their eyes. He and Polina had been in a panic, afraid they would not get him to the hospital in time. It was a near thing but they did, and the choking passed off. What the sickness was, what had caused it they never properly understood.

"What are you standing there for? Are you going to wait for the child to choke to death? You go wandering about, visiting witches—maybe she's poisoned him?"

"Don't talk rubbish, Polina, why on earth should Granny Sokha poison us? She sent a candle for him."

Stepan Ivanovich lighted it and fixed it in a glass jar which had held bottled fruit.

"Here we are, kid. It's cheerier with a light, eh? You'll be all right now, won't you?"

"Dad-dy-y-y! "

Stepan Ivanovich put the jar and candle on the table and rushed outside. At first he had hoped it was nothing much, it would pass off, but that cry was so hoarse, so imploring, that there was no longer any room for doubt; it was the same illness he had had three years before.

It was darker now. He started out for the Rezanovo road

but then thought better of it. It would take a long time to get there and what would he find when he did? At best a nurse. So he decided to make for the station, it was farther, ten kilometres, but there would certainly be a doctor there.

The sun had set some time ago and mist was drifting over the fields. Stepan Ivanovich crossed a hollow, tangling his feet in the long grass, came out by Pavel Vassilyevich's house and began struggling through the river of grass which had once been the village street. It was waist high, the soil was rich in these parts; he could still distinguish the silhouettes of the houses but beyond the village the darkness stifled him like a sack. Which way should he go? How could he find the station?

9

He knocked at the outer door; he kicked it and banged on it with a log; then he felt his way through the darkness to the window.

"Granny Sokha, open the door, please open the door."

Only the spoken plea brought a response.

"Granny Sokha, please! Granny Sokha, please help us. It's my boy, he's ill, he's bad."

"What troubles the little lad?"

"We don't know. It's the second time it's happened. He can't breathe. He's choking. Come, quick." And Stepan Ivanovich impatiently caught hold of the old woman in the darkness.

"Nay, I'm no help to you. You need a doctor."

Stepan Ivanovich almost sobbed.

"But where can I find one? I'd have to go to the station, and he's choking, choking, I tell you!"

"There's naught I can do."

"Why not? In the old days you helped, I remember it well."

"That was the old days. When I had the strength."

"But don't you understand, Granny Sokha?" His voice rose. "The boy's choking. Choking!"

Without listening to another word from the old woman he dragged her with him.

Along the path as far as the street the going was easy but after that they fumbled it the darkness like blind kittens. Stepan Ivanovich could feel certain of his whereabouts only when he heard his poplar, its leaves rustling in the faint wind like a flock of fluttering birds.

Polina was horrified when she saw the hunchbacked old woman in the doorway.

"No, no, I won't let her touch him, I sent you for a doctor and who've you brought?"

But then Granny Sokha spoke—with authority.

"Be still! You'll affright the child."

She went up to Victor, who in the first moment had been thoroughly seared, and now her voice was kind and gentle as a summer brook.

"Don't be afraid, don't ye fear aught, childie. Granny's come to make you all right agin. Where does it hurt you? Your throat. And you've no breath. Now don't ye fret, your breath'll come back agin, dearie."

Faintly like a distant sigh, like the morning breeze in the leaves, came the familiar whispered words: "I stand the slave of God—" and Stepan Ivanovich wondered if perhaps the old woman had been right when she refused to come with him, perhaps the power really had left her? But he stifled the thought because who else could help Victor now if she could not?

Surprisingly, the old woman's voice gradually grew stronger and words came, words that brought a chill, a shiver to him.

"Ye powers of ill, ye spawn of Beelzebub, overlookers, cutters down... Avaunt ye into the stumps, into the roots, into the bogs, into the foul water... Seethe there, boil there, 'neath the aspens, 'neath the stones, 'neath the earth, and let the moss and grass grow over ye..."

Stepan Ivanovich looked at his wife—was it only his imagination? Was it only the distant fears of childhood which had come to life around him? No, Polina too was under the sway of those words, of the old woman's voice which filled the room, she sat gazing, wide-eyed, barely breathing, spellbound.

Three times Granny Sokha repeated the incantation against the pain and sickness, softly passing her dark hand over Victor's throat and chest, and he seemed easier, he no longer choked and his breath did not rasp.

Suddenly he spoke in a weak voice.

"Give me a drink."

Stepan Ivanovich made a dash to the other room, but Polina had water ready.

Victor took a drink.

"And now," said Granny Sokha, "you, the father, go out, cut an aspen stick the length of your axe and drive it into the ground, taking the sickness with it. And let none ever pull it out."

Stepan Ivanovich had an eerie feeling; it was uncanny, all this, but a man will do anything to save his child. And could he argue with Granny Sokha? Just a fragile, helpless old woman she had been, but now she had grown until she seemed to fill the room with her power, like a cloud during a storm.

He thought he would never find his way in the darkness to the thicket behind the house, but he found it. And in that thicket he even managed to distinguish an aspen by its bitter smell and the trembling leaves. In fact, he did everything as the old woman had said.

He had his reward; when he returned, wet with dew, Victor was out of danger. He knew it before he even saw him, his wife's face told him, happy and loving as he had seen it only once, when he came to the maternity hospital to rejoice in the arrival of the long-awaited son.

10

The old woman struggled weakly back to her cottage, leaning on a stick and helped by Stepan Ivanovich; but she could not climb the steps to the porch; she sat down on them, her slight strength utterly drained.

"You saved us, Granny Sokha, thank you, thank you."

Stepan Ivanovich had thanked her already, time and again, but gratitude kept bursting out. "I was desperate. Victor was choking, there was no doctor, and you woudn't come, I didn't know how to move you."

"I don't do any of that now."

"A pity. Three years ago we had the same thing happen and the doctors worked with Victor the whole night, but you—you just passed your hand over him and spoke some words and he was well at once."

Following the old custom, Stepan Ivanovich spat over his left shoulder to avert further disaster and, deeply moved, continued half humorously, "Now come on, Granny Sokha, give me your diagnosis. What was that sickness? How can we avoid it? All those learned men can only shrug, maybe some allergy, metabolism or something—a man can't make head or tail of it."

The old woman sighed but said nothing.

"Why won't you answer? I'm not trying to get at your secrets, I want to know for the boy's sake."

"What can I tell you, Stepan Ivanovich? I haven't got learning. Prayers and herbs and words wi' power in them—that's all I can do."

She was evading a direct answer, that was clear, so he too became evasive, approaching the subject by roundabout ways.

"But tell me, I can't help wondering where you learned it all? All that—well, exorcizing ill powers, taking away evil, all that. Well, for instance, we have all sorts of courses and technical schools for truck drivers and medical assistants, that sort of thing. But what about you, where did you learn all the things you know?"

"It was need, lad, bitter need as made me. I was thrust into life lame and hunchbacked, my dad was drunk and dropped me when I was but a mite; and how could I keep from starving, aye, and defend myself? Folks have no love for one as is ugly and crippled. Childer, some of 'em, would throw stones at me out of daftness. But there was one good old man was pitiful of me, an ugly one nobody loved, they called him Old Vasya."

"You mean the sorcerer?" Stepan Ivanovich felt a shiver run through him. Old Vasya had died before he was born but as a child they used to frighten him with that name when he was naughty.

"I myself was desprit fritten of him," said Granny Sokha with increased animation. "Well, once I was in the forest getting berries, that was the only place I was happy, trees and shrubs didn't mind me being ugly, and all of a sudden an old man comes out from behind the firs. Aye, Old Vasya. He was shaggy and white, wi' a stick in his hand and I nigh fell down from fright. But he came up to me and laid his hand on my head, like as if I was a child, and he says, 'Why are you feared, foolish one? If you want folks to stop girding at you, then they must fear you, and not you them.' Folks' fear, he says, will feed you and protect you."

"What did he mean?"

The old woman seemed not to hear.

"So Old Vassily taught me a bit, the words of power he taught me, and the herbs. He knew a lot. But now it's nigh gone. The strength drained away from Mamonikha and it drained away from me."

"What's that? What's that you said? Strength left Mamonikha and it left you too?"

"Aye. While Mamonikha had its strength, I had the power. But when Mamonikha began to bleed, I got weak."

"So that's how it is! I thought it was age you meant, age had made you weaker."

"Age brings no joy, we all know it, but God forbid that you see your own village dying before your eyes. First one house stands empty, then another, and a third... But it isn't just the houses, either. Times the house dies because its master died. You mind Vassily Yegorovich?"

"The one as lived at the upper end?"

"The same. He's gone to his rest. A year agone he comes with his wife, like you, about the same time. 'We live well, fine and prosperous. Our childer all have learning and earn good money! In Mamonikha,' he says, 'I never knew what life could be, it's only now in my old age I know.' Well, two weeks passed and they began getting ready to leave, they lived in distant parts. They got as far as the field·gate and Vassily Yegorovich says to his wife, 'Maria,' he says, 'I've forgot to shut the damper in the stove.' 'Oh, leave it,' she says, 'the house is falling to pieces and you worrit about a damper.' 'No,' he says, 'the damper ought to be shut.' So he went back. Half an hour, an hour and still he didn't come and Maria didn't know what to think. So at last she went back to see what had happened to him. And there he was, hanging from the ceiling hook."

"Hanged himself?"

"Aye."

"H'm," said Stepan Ivanovich. "Cheerful stories, you have to tell."

"Ye go somewhere else for cheerful stories, lad. Them's the kind we've got in a village as is dying. It's when they're building folks can laugh and sing and tell merry tales."

11

It was the happiest morning in his life. He wakened, opened his eyes, and the first thing they lighted on was the iron ring in the ceiling from which his cradle had hung. And when he rose and went out on to the porch he saw his wife, prettier than a picture, stretched out on a red quilt in the middle of the yard like a white fish in the sunshine. Above her a hawk was circling slowly in the sky as though it, too, were admiring the picture she made.

"Where's Victor?" he cried gaily, running down the steps.

"Oh, somewhere about." Reluctantly Polina raised her auburn head and dark glasses from the pillow and turned it right and left. "Victor! Victor! "

"I'm here, Mum, in the raspberries."

Victor's voice came from the shrubs at the back; Stepan Ivanovich made for it, pushing through the thick growth of weeds in what had been a cabbage patch. The soil was rich here, it had been manured every year.

"Well, how do you feel, lad? All right? It doesn't hurt anywhere?"

Victor only said "m-m-m"—he had no time for talk; like a bear cub that has found sweet berries, he was clearing branch after branch.

Stepan Ivanovich was delighted to see his son so full of life and displaying his usual excellent appetite. But how could one get used to those raspberries, that thicket of alders and aspens behind their house? There had been none of that twenty years ago. And looking from the shrubs to the house, he thought glumly that the house was as good as lost. Even if the people spared it, the forest would smother it, that forest which was advancing on Mamonikha from all sides.

"Dad! Dad! " Victor's voice came from somewhere by the Vertushikha.

"Yes, what is it?"

"Come quick! I've found a little house."

"What house?"

Stepan Ivanovich parted the raspberry canes, still wet with dew, came out by the stream and saw his son by their old bath-house—black, smoky, with a tiny window, and a wooden bar on the door in place of a latch.

"Why, Victor, what do you think it is? It's a bath-house."

"A *bath*-house?"

"Gosh, boy, you're like a foreigner in your father's village."

But after all, was it so surprising? How could Victor know about old country bath-houses when he had never seen one?

Stepan Ivanovich opened the sagging door—ah, such familiar music, like landrakes calling; he looked into the entry, then into the steam-room—it still held the old bitter smell of wet besoms—and was suddenly struck with an idea.

"I tell you what, Victor! Let's stoke the old place up a bit, eh?"

In a moment, it seemed—like the old "table spread yourself" fairy-tale—there was wood in the stove and water bubbling merrily in the cauldron—the stream was handily near.

"Victor, you look after everything here while I run to the forest to break fresh twigs for a besom."

"I want to go with you, Dad."

"No, I'll go alone, but I'll take you another time, sure thing I will."

Stepan Ivanovich went down the recently trodden path to the stream and crossed it over stepping stones—it was not much of a stream, a crow could walk over it when it was low—and plunged into the thicket of alders and aspens, the first forest of his childhood, which in those far distant times had been full of goblins and pixies and other shivery things, and where he had set his first snares.

In those days the birch grove had been a long way off, they had had a good verst to go for their besoms, but now as soon as he emerged from the riverside thickets he found himself in the middle of a young growth of birches covering what had been meadowland. Stepan Ivanovich bound two besoms in a matter of minutes and then where did he go? Back home? No, forward.

It was only a step to Pakhomka's Burn, gay hillocks and hollows with a growth of springy heather where in long-past days a fire had raged, where as a boy he had gathered berries and mushrooms. How could he resist taking a look at it, seeing what it was like now?

Since he had already climbed Pakhomka's Rise (the name it was given in Mamonikha), once he had got so far then of course he had to go down to Ma's Cradle, that lovely mattress of green moss in a hollow—could a man resist it? And beyond Ma's Cradle there was Antokha's Digging—fine grain used to grow there. And then came the Vyrvei, a singing woodland brook, and after crossing that there was a choice of three paths, as in old fairy-tales. Which should he choose?

Thus imperceptibly, sometimes following a path seething

with industrious ants like in the old days, sometimes through rough grass, sometimes over moss, Stepan Ivanovich plunged ever deeper into Mamonikha land.

Everything was wild, the land had all gone back to scrub, sometimes it seemed only the names were left of the old places. But those names! The old folks had a name for every hummock, every bit of woodland, every path. They loved their land, the soil on which they had been born. Pakhomka's Burn, Ma's Cradle, Riverside, Antokha's Digging—names that slid pleasantly off the tongue.

But nowadays? Take the settlement where he lived. It was quite a good-sized place, they said it would soon achieve the status of a town. But the people living there seemed to have no language. There were three lakes in the vicinity where people actually went fishing and presumably caught something, and what did they call them? Quarry No. 1, Quarry No. 2 and Quarry No. 3—dating back to the time when they got sand and stones from there for the cement works. And it was the same with the roads, they were asphalt, and apple-trees were set out along them, in spring they were white with blossom like a bride—but they had no names, only numbers.

However, it was time to come to his senses, to make for home, Victor would be tired of waiting. Stepan Ivanovich turned right, to Mikhei's Whisker, it was the same distance but he would be taking a different route. And it was just this eagerness that let him down.

Mikhei's Whisker was a tangle of new growth. In some places he could see the path or feel for it with his feet, but in others it was completely covered with moss or scrub. And then came further trouble—Gena's tracks, broad cuttings torn up by tractors in the midst of the forest.

Stepan Ivanovich jumped like a goat from rut to rut, went this way and that and ended up completely lost.

12

Mamonikha was close by, he knew that all right—he could not have wandered off heaven knows where in some twenty or thirty minutes. And the surroundings looked familiar. But he could not find the path, it was all moss, swamp, and coarse grasses, while the firs were so tall and thick that there was a permanent twilight beneath them.

He had to laugh—really, it was absurd, losing his way in three firs, as the saying goes—but on the other hand he gradually began to worry. What about Victor? Would Polina think to see what he was doing?

At last he felt firmer ground beneath his feet and then spotted a gap in the trees. He made for it and there was Riverside. He'd wandered about lost, got tangled in grasses, sweated and all the time just as he'd thought, he was right up against Riverside and Mamonikha. In the old days they'd have said woodgoblins had turned him about, and maybe whispered something about Granny Sokha. But whom could he blame now?

A rumbling came from the village—it sounded like a lorry engine. Must be someone from Rezanovo, thought Stepan Ivanovich, and cut straight across the grass to a familiar dead birch, which he knew stood near the Vertushikha just opposite his house.

He had barely taken a dozen steps when a great crash seemed to shake the ground.

Frightened out of his wits (where was Polina, where was Victor?) Stepan Ivanovich with one bound cleared the stream, pounded up the bank and gasped: the poplar, his poplar lay on the ground.

"Stop! Stop! " he shouted at the man with the mechanical saw in the front garden.

Too late, the cedar crashed down.

Wiping his forehead (he was wet with sweat from head to foot) he went up to the house, and whom did he see? MAZ-Gena. All the trees in his front garden—the poplar, the bird-cherry, the rowan, the cedar—all were laid low, but Gena stood—stood like a tree suddenly grown up there, in rubber boots reaching to the groin, grinning.

"What d'you think you're doing? Who said you could?"

"What am I doing? Letting in a little light. I went in and it was like a tomb."

"None of your business. Play the master in your own house. Victor—" Only now Stepan Ivanovich saw his despondent son. "What were you about, to allow it? I told you all about those trees—Uncle Nikodim, Aunt Tania."

Victor burst into tears.

"That's right, weep on each other's shoulders. The poor dear trees! " Gena guffawed.

"What are you braying about? You know who planted those trees? My father, back before the war."

"And who gives the orders about them now? You don't know?"

"All right, that's enough, you two fighting cocks." That was Polina approaching. "What do trees matter since we're selling the house, anyway? You can't take them with you even if they were pure gold, that's one thing certain."

"Now, there's good sense." With a smirk Gena picked up the saw, then threw a merry look at Polina. "Maybe there is summat else I can do for you? Lay out Nevsky Avenue by the Vertushikha so's you won't hurt your bonnie little feet when you go for a morning dip? Just say the word while my heart's hot. I'll take all Mamonikha apart if you say the word."

"No, we'll let it stand." But her eyes sparkled with enjoyment at this badinage.

"As you like. I can saddle this horse of mine—" he jerked his head towards the powerful caterpillar tractor, muddy half way up the cab, "and have it done in a jiffy."

13

Gena put out two bottles of good quality vodka left over from his conference, as he put it, with the big fellows—in other words, from the fishing expedition; he had come straight from that without even going home first, he said; but Polina wasn't being left behind, she, too, produced a bottle. Where she had bought it, and when—at the airport, or in town when he had run off to see some old friends, Stepan Ivanovich did not know, and what did it matter? The main thing was that she took Gena down a peg. Stopped him swaggering with his bottles, as though they were paupers.

She was dressed to impress, too. Everything was very classy—red pants pulled tight, a white blouse with a soft gilt belt, white high-heeled shoes—an actress prepared to make her appearance.

Actually, Stepan Ivanovich was not particularly keen about drinking with Gena, but how could he refuse when Gena had been the first to put out bottles? After all, he was a guest. And Polina, of course, had been all enthusiasm, she must show off her finery at least once!

They settled down outside, on freshly mown glade behind the well, under a young rowan.

"Well, here's health to one and all," said Gena, and emptied his glass like water. He spat, took no chaser and plunged into bargaining without more ado.

"Look here, I can offer you three hundred for that lot of old firewood," and he jerked his head contemptuously at the house without vouchsafing it a glance.

Polina, a bookkeeper and at home in financial matters, responded with a calm smile.

"Yes? Suppose we drop joking and talk seriously?"

"Isn't that serious? Don't you know how much old wood you can get for nothing in the villages?"

"Of rotting wood there's plenty. But houses like ours—no. If you cart it away to the station how much will you get for it?"

"Well—how much?"

"Two-and-a-half thousand at least."

Gena whistled. "The woman's daft."

"All right, all right, save your breath to cool your porridge. We've met smarter than you."

"But not a smarter woman than you," and he clapped Stepan Ivanovich on the shoulder. "Some folks have all the luck—where did you dig up one like her, eh?"

Stepan Ivanovich only wagged his head, smiling proudly. He had not much respect for Gena, never had had, but nevertheless these words were unction to his heart.

"All right," said Gena decidedly and brought his massive fist down like a sledge-hammer on the fragile table (a plywood confectionery box). "Bleed me, then. I'll add another hundred—just for the sake of your pretty eyes."

"Nine hundred," said Polina.

That was when the hard passionate bargaining began. Gena, acting the plain rough-hewn fellow, grew heated and even used some pretty strong language, and although Polina kept her smile the red patches on her face showed that she, too, was coming to the boil.

Finally she exploded—at Stepan Ivanovich.

"And what are you sitting there for, like a dumb fish?"

Stepan Ivanovich assumed a business-like expression, "I was just thinking—we really must—"

"What must we? What?" she cried hotly.

Gena laughed loudly, his wide cavernous mouth full of teeth gleaming in the sun; but Victor let out a glad cry.

"Granny Yaga! Granny Yaga! "

Stepan Ivanovich looked towards the village, and there

she was, Granny Sokha, coming towards them from behind Pavel Vassilyevich's house, nodding like an old horse. Her head-scarf shone white above the wild rye. Evidently she had dressed specially to pay a visit in the old style.

But—what on earth? Suddenly the old woman turned and went back.

Stepan Ivanovich called to her. "Granny Sokha, why are you going away?"

"Don't fret, she won't be coming here," said Gena and spat.

"Why not?"

"Because there's no way for her when I'm here with the tractor. Ill powers can't abide iron and petrol."

"Oh, rubbish."

"Rubbish, is it? Where were you born—America? Don't you know how much scathe that old bitch has caused folks? Gave one a rupture, made another break his leg, and made a third one's cow go dry. And now there's no folk nigh, you know what she does? Plays her tricks on the birds and beasts. You listen to the hunters, them as lives by it, they're groaning, there's not a feather round Mamonikha, driven them all away, she has, so's none can have them."

"I'd say that's more like your work. I walked along Mikhei's Whisker just now, the whole place is ploughed up and the forest stinks of petrol. Why would birds stop around there? Even the trees are shrivelled up, the leaves hang on them like bits of rags."

"Eh dear, weeping for the trees again, you can't think of naught else. There was a book I happened to get hold of, poetry, it was, and every poem wailing about them trees. 'Specially birches. Oh you lovely birch, ah you sweet slender birch, joy of my eyes—and we cuss them birches coming up everywhere, durn 'em. They're in all the fields soon's you turn your back; leave 'em a bit and they're full of that birch scrub. And you—! "

"I'm not talking about trees or scrub but about Mamonikha. What they've brought it to. Just look! "

"And who brought it to this—who?" Gena challenged him sharply.

"Who, who—I guess it doesn't need any explanation."

"All the same, you just explain. Nothing to say? Then I'll say it. You did! "

"I? I've brought Mamonikha to this? I haven't been here for twenty years! "

"Exactly, you haven't been here twenty years, and another hasn't, and a third—how's the place going to stay alive, eh? Oh, you know how to criticise. Your sort, you come every summer and it's 'Eh, how bad, oh, how sad—MAZ-Gena's spoiled it all.' If you want to know, it's only thanks to that MAZ-Gena that there's any life left. Take your aunt, and Fedotovna—if I didn't bring them wood they'd freeze like beetles."

"Oh, let it go," Polina said pacifically. "Can't you be satisfied, just sitting here under the rowan?"

"No, if we're going to have it out, let's have it all out," said Gena with unabated heat. "It isn't the first time I hear: Gena's living in paradise. And every day I get onto the tractor, it's like getting into a tank. Like going out to battle. My wife crosses me, she doesn't know whether she'll see me back or not. Last year Oparin from Zhitovo drove into them beautiful white birches and there was a hole, a bog hid under the turf, and there he lies. You get what I'm talking about?"

"Sure, sure," said Polina angrily—her patience was at an end. "You two—you grew up together, and all you do is snarl at each other."

"You're right, too, we've got off the track." Gena gave in at once and reached out a dark hand. "Well, how about it—shake hands on it? Or I may change my mind."

"Change your mind about what?"

"Why, about that pile of firewood of yours."

"Daddy, Dad, don't sell it! "

It was as though it took his son's cry to stiffen Stepan Ivanovich; he spoke up with a decisiveness unexpected even to himself.

"I'm not going to. That pile of firewood, as you call it, may have been the last thing my father thought of when he lay dying at the front; am I a Judas?"

In the ensuing silence the leaves of the poplar rustled in the breeze and fell silent again.

"Sound the retreat—is that it?" asked Gena, turning to Polina.

She looked a question at her husband, but he, conscious of the newly-found support of his son who had grabbed his hand and was squeezing it, was adamant.

"Well, that's that," said Gena. "You wouldn't take rubles, you'll be glad to get kopeks later on."

14

Polina retaliated with a boycott, as she usually did when things did not go her way; eyes cast down, tongue mute: I don't want to see or hear anybody.

Stepan Ivanovich tried every way to win her round. He heated the bath-house, he tramped to the station to buy fresh cucumbers and tomatoes, he even managed to get two chickens in a neighbouring village, not to mention mushrooms and berries from the forest. But it was all received with cold silence.

Such character she showed; she did not spare even her petted son, and it was pitiful to see poor bewildered Victor. His mother would have nothing to do with him, and he could not make up his mind to go over to his father's side.

As for Stepan Ivanovich himself, he found a refuge with Granny Sokha.

In the morning he would leave the house and turn towards the forest as though to gather the provisions it offered, but then he would cross the Vertushikha and make for the old woman's cottage by back ways, along a newly trodden path.

With Granny Sokha he could unwind, right to the end; she always understood and never condemned. He told her everything, left nothing out; about his daily life with Polina, about Lida, about Gena.

But the surprising thing was that as soon as he spoke of his old family home—and after all, the house was the cause of all this upset, all this family conflict—Granny Sokha looked away.

"I just can't understand you, Granny Sokha," he said heatedly. "Surely you don't want me to pull down Father's house with my own hands? Why, maybe I'll be coming back to live in Mamonikha some day! You told me how your brother came home to live when he got old."

"Aye, but that was in them old days."

"Makes no difference. The world's come now to revive what's been neglected, fields which have been abandoned and gone back are to be sown again. Some clever folk have maybe said Mamonikha's finished, Mamonikha's not worth saving. But now the command is: stop! Back a bit, think again. You could make out all Russia's not worth saving, at this rate. Isn't that a true word?"

"Nay, I dunno, I dunno, Stepan Ivanovich," sighed the

old woman. "But I wouldn't counsel ye to leave the place where ye've put down roots."

"Why?"

"It's hard, living in the country nowadays."

"Hard? But was it any easier for our grandads? They'd but spades and axes and clumsy ploughs to till the fields, look at all the machines they've got now! "

"Aye, there's machines a-plenty," the old woman agreed. "But the folks is different nowadays. Spoilt, they are, wanting easy living."

"Doesn't matter." Stepan Ivanovich was not to be moved. "Folks are all kinds today, too. Take us, you and me, we've gone through war and hunger and cold, the lot. Have you forgotten the muck we ate after the war, buns made of potatoes we gathered on the fields in the spring? And what we wore—you remember?"

On one of these days Stepan Ivanovich, who had been secretly fretting about Lida's fate, confessed as much to the old woman.

"I still can't understand, Granny Sokha, how on earth she came to take up with Kura. When I think of it my head goes round."

"What could she do? You didn't come back after the army."

"I? What had I to do with it?"

"She was waiting for you."

"Lida? Lida was waiting for me?" His breath left him.

"True and faithful. She allus said, 'When Stepan comes back we'll get wed.' She told that to Gena when he bid for her."

"Gena bid for Lida?"

"Aye. He was after her day and night. He thought it was me turned her against him, that's why he plagues me, but I didn't say a word to turn her. It was herself. Herself. Wouldn't have him any way. 'I've got Stepan,' she says, 'I'm waiting for him.' "

Stepan Ivanovich went away dazed.

Lida, Lida had been waiting for him! Their princess, the best pupil at school, the girl whom he'd run with from house to house in winter trying to see who'd be faster. And he pictured to himself what it must have cost the proud, wilful Lida to write him that desperate, humiliating letter offering herself.

That day, surrendering to memory, he wandered for a

long time through the unmown water-meadows by the streams, through the weed-grown fields, through the berry-patches, along brooks and over hillocks—all the places where he had been with Lida. He recalled how in their teens they had gone with the other lads and girls to games and dancing in the nearby villages; no hunger, no hard work, nothing could crush their youth, their burgeoning life. Towards evening he made his way to the neighbouring farms, hamlets and villages.

They were many of those in that forest region, their forebears had raised the soil from beneath the roots and whether it had repaid them with abundance or not, they had given their homes names that spoke of good bread—Rzhanovo, Ovsyanniki, Kalachi.*

Even in the old days Kalachi hadn't been much of a place, you could count the houses on your fingers, so Stepan Ivanovich was not particularly surprised to find only one boarded-up house to show where it had been. It had evidently been boarded up a long time ago, probably in the 'fifties, because not only the roof had rotted, even the planks which had been nailed over the windows had been rained on and shone on until they were crumbling. But Rzhanovo did surprise him. It had been a big village by their standards, twenty-five or thirty houses, and well-to-do. In even the hungriest years after the war it had been possible to barter clothes there for bread. And people did. Stepan Ivanovich's mother had carried all his father's old clothes there.

Now there was no sign of life in Rzhanovo, in fact, you could say Rzhanovo itself hardly existed. Two cottages at the upper end, one in the middle and three below—could you call that Rzhanovo? And those houses were not particularly good ones, either. It was obvious that the sturdy ones had been dismantled and carted away, either to the main centre of the state farm or to the district town where the station was. And it didn't take a very shrewd guess to know that Gena had had more than one finger in that pie.

But no, there was life in Rzhanovo. Stepan Ivanovich heard the sound of an axe—the sweetest music in this silence of abandonment. Then, as he walked through the dead village, he saw a man. He was at the side of the familiar dirt road which led out and away; a thick pinkish cloud of

* Taken from the Russian words for "rye", "oats", "white roll".—Tr.

dust hung over it, a truck must have just gone down.

With his axe the man was squaring off a thick tree-trunk, probably from a dead tree and resinous, because the axe rang sharply and the chips that flew out were small.

"I don't understand what in the world you are sweating over that for," Stepan Ivanovich said in place of a greeting.

The man straightened up. He was elderly, probably pension age, but sturdy, he breathed evenly, and his eyes spoke of goodness and kindliness.

"You think I understand myself?" He stuck the axe in the wood and looked at the village, or rather, what remained of it. "I've got a sort of idea—to put up something to remind folks of Rzhanovo."

"You mean you want to put up a sort of monument?"

"A monument, you can maybe call it that, something so's folks'll know it was here. I want to fix a board on this post, cover it with aluminium, and put on it everything about Rzhanovo: when it was founded and who by, how many people lived here, and how many were killed in the war."

Roman Vassilyevich—that was the man's name—kicked the beam lightly with the metal-capped toe of his boot.

"What d'you think, will it last a score of years?"

The log was of larch, the strongest wood, and Stepan Ivanovich, giving it a kick in his turn, answered with certainty, "Sure, it will. Larch. It'll stand for fifty."

"No need of fifty. I just want it to stand until all this business of first centralising everything into big villages and then backing down and getting the old ones going again is finally worked out. Without it, the new folks as comes here won't know who used to live hereabouts. History of the place'll be gone."

"You think Rzhanovo'll live again?" asked Stepan Ivanovich, his breath coming faster.

"I'm sure it will. Sure thing. How else? The scientists reckon that by the year two thousand the population of the world will double, d'you think they could afford to be growing scrub here?"

Roman Vassilyevich turned out to be a thoughtful, knowledgeable man who had worked for thirty years on big important construction jobs, and Stepan Ivanovich, always drawn to educated people, thoroughly enjoyed talking to him, the more so that he was plain and unaffected, making no parade of superior education.

205

It was dark when he got home. Victor was already asleep in his corner, as for Polina, she was either asleep, or still sulking. Anyhow, she did not react in any way to his return.

He had eaten nothing all day but berries and felt decidedly hungry, but did not venture to help himself. He undressed quickly, rubbed himself briskly with his hands so as not to chill his wife, and lay down on the edge of the bed. At once he was enveloped by the oven-like heat emanating from Polina, and from force of habit he had an impulse to fling himself into that heat. But he held back, his wife did not like boyish fooling. And soon he forgot about her and began to turn over in his mind the events of the preceding day.

Seven days he had been in Mamonikha and what had he done? Walked about the village. Wandered through its surroundings. No, no, that was no good. Take Roman Vassilyevich, he had thought of something. Making the name of Rzhanovo eternal. Why hadn't he thought of something of the kind himself? Wasn't Mamonikha a village, too? Hadn't it got its own history, its own past?

How had he put it?—Stepan Ivanovich tried to recall exactly those wise words of Roman Vassilyevich. See to it what with all our new construction Russian history is not lost. And the Russian landscape. Yes, Roman Vassilyevich had said there would be new fields. Mamonikha, and Rzhanovo, and Kalachi would grow grain again. But I want those new fields to have Russian names.

After some time when his thoughts began to tangle in the mists of approaching sleep, he remembered Lida. It was the first time in all the seventeen years of his married life that he had thought with regret of another woman.

15

Victor was the first to be wakened by the rain.

"Mum, what's that dripping on me?"

Stepan Ivanovich quickly lighted the lamp and saw water streaming down from the ceiling. He ran out onto the porch and found such a downpour that it was impossible to take a step outside.

There was no more sleep for anybody that night, and with the first light he climbed up on to the roof.

He clambered about, patched here and patched there under the pouring rain, and much good it did, he returned to find a flood.

"Well, now do you understand why you must sell the house?! "

For three days it rained, for three days they couldn't set foot out of doors. Victor whined, and Polina's nostrils flared.

But that was only the start. The real trouble began when their bread gave out. That meant going to the station or to Rezanovo, but how could they go through the thick, deep liquid mud in thin shoes? And they had not had the sense (Stepan Ivanovich was to blame there) to bring rubber boots.

Granny Sokha saved the day. She hobbled over through the pouring rain with a whole bundle of bread warm from the oven, wrapped in sacking.

But man does not live by bread alone—at least, not a modern man, and most especially not a spoiled individual like Victor. One day passed, but by the next he was grumbling, he wanted butter, he wanted meat. And Stepan Ivanovich was hard put to it to explain to a ten-year-old why they could buy butter and meat at home, but not here.

Stepan Ivanovich began thinking seriously about evacuation. What could they do? The rain did not stop, the cottage was damp even though they kept both stoves red hot all day, and in general things were miserable; Victor was coughing and Polina was beginning to develop sniffles.

So Stepan Ivanovich decided to take the only course left him—go cap in hand to Gena in Rezanovo. Nothing else to be done.

But Gena came himself.

In the morning after breakfast, when Stepan Ivanovich was just going to take off his trousers because after such rain, he'd be wading in mud above his knees half the way, they heard a metallic clattering and clanking under the window.

Victor and Polina shot out, and never mind about rain. Very soon Gena appeared in the house.

"Well, well, tourists? How d'you like it on your fields gone back to scrub?" He guffawed loudly.

He was well able to laugh with his rubber boots, rainproof canvas coat nearly to his heels and quilted jacket on top, and spirits to warm him within.

But Victor and Polina did not mind his mockery. They saw him as an angel bringing salvation and were ready to kiss him.

"Uncle, have you come to fetch us?" Victor asked again and again, hardly believing in their good fortune.

"Aye, I've come for you all right," Gena laughed good-naturedly. "It's only him as thinks Gena's a brute," he added with a jerk of his head towards Stepan Ivanovich.

The departure was more like flight.

After flinging their things into the body of the truck Polina and Victor took their places in the cab and Stepan Ivanovich climbed up into the uncovered body.

"Want a raincoat, or are you going to harden yourself?"

"Harden myself! " Stepan Ivanovich snapped. He could not quite keep his feelings in although he exerted every effort.

"All right, have it your own way," said Gena with the same good humour which held a touch of mockery, and climbed into the cab.

Suddenly Stepan Ivanovich remembered Granny Sokha.

He threw off the cold, stiff raincoat (Gena had tossed it over at the last moment), and drummed on the wet, bulging metal of the cab.

"Wait a half hour, I must say goodbye to Granny Sokha!"

"Settle that with your goodwife, I'm only the driver," said Gena, thrusting his head out of the window.

"Are you crazy? I'm frozen, my teeth are chattering; at least think of your son! "

Stepan Ivanovich did not insist, Granny Sokha would understand and would not blame him.

The engine roared, they slithered right, slithered left, the wheels gripped and they were on the road. His father's big house appeared once more through the dull curtain of rain and then melted into it; on the right, above the wet, despondent aspens, which seemed to have grown still thicker in these days, Mamonikha appeared, a dark and formless cloud across the fields.

His wet eyes became hot.

It was little, very little joy that Mamonikha had vouchsafed him—it had been more like a harsh stepmother most of the time, but it was his birthplace. And he knew that whatever life might bring him in the future, wherever it might fling him, the dearest, most sacred spot on earth, nay, in the whole universe, would be this Mamonikha in its forest region gone wild.

Laughter came from the cab—probably Gena was out to amuse Polina.

Stepan Ivanovich felt chilled and shivery. Could he be getting ill? Again and again thoughts ranged through his heavy head—about Mamonikha, about Lida and Granny Sokha, about Roman Vassilyevich.

He did not know when he would be able to visit his native parts again, whether he would stay long, whether it would be with Victor and Polina or alone, but he felt that much, very much would change after this trip. Meanwhile, he told himself, he must gather his strength because they would soon come to Rezanovo and the battle for his father's house would start all over again. They would all attack him—Polina, his aunt, Gena, and Victor, too. And he must hold out, at all costs he must defend his father's house.

1972-1980, 1981

There Once Lived a Salmon

A Northern Tale

1

Her name was Pretty.

She was a small speckled fish, pale gold with red spots who was almost as fancy as the redfins, the smartest-looking little fishes of Russia's northern rivers. But, unlike the redfins, Pretty had a very large head, and so the family of redfins who lived in the backwater by the bank never ventured into the runnel which Pretty considered her home.

This runnel was a small side-branch which veered off at the rapids and was divided from the mainstream of the river, the habitat of the big fish, by a huge porous boulder. The boulder was all spotted with the white droppings of the wagtails, who were always hopping about on the boulder, and beneath the boulder there were deep holes with cold spring water. Those holes gave Pretty relief from the heat, and if a storm broke out she found shelter in their depths. But, most important, they provided refuge from her enemies.

And she had enemies galore. They were the toothy pikes scouring the sedge by the bank, those orange-finned predators the perches, the burbots, who pretended they were grey sticks lying on the bottom, and even the ruffs, who were as cheeky as they come. They'd swim over in a bunch, line up, as though for attack, and goggle at her with their huge blue eyes, their prickly spines all bristled up.

So Pretty never left her runnel. In the morning she would hunt various water bugs and spiders, and then, if it was a sunny day, she played, butting the sparkly pebbles with her nose or leaping at the emerald dragon-flies as they swooped down to the water, and sometimes even pouncing, just for fun, on some absent-minded minnow.

But what she liked best was observing the big fish. She could spend hours watching the dance of the frisky graylings in the noisy rapids, or following the handsome white-fish with her eyes as they streaked like silver lightning through the darkness of the deep pool on the other side of the boulder.

On the whole, Pretty was quite content with her life in the cheery runnel.

But then the days grew dark and sombre, with rains and fogs, and Pretty began to mope.

The sun appeared seldom now, fallen leaves, shaggy and soaked, cluttered the runnel and it became a depressing place. Moreover, a marauding burbot began prowling near the boulder at night. Ugly, naked and slimy, he poked his whiskered mug underneath the boulder, snorting and sniffing. Pretty would squeeze into the deepest hole and tremble there with fear until daybreak. This went on one night after another.

What was she to do? There did not seem to be any escape.

And then one morning, as she was once again wondering dismally what was in store for her, she suddenly saw on the other side of the boulder, in the mainstream, a huge handsome fish she had never seen before. The fish was swimming slowly downstream, and when it struck out with its tail, waves ran to all sides. How handsome that fish was! Its long strong body was covered with pink and golden spots, and its large fins had an orange border...

The big fish was followed by a shoal of little speckled fishes, who were very like Pretty, but a bit bigger. The amazing thing was that they swam along gayly and fearlessly, as though they were under the protection of the big fish.

Pretty swam across towards them.

"Will you please tell me," she asked politely, "who is that big fish that swam past just now?"

"Don't you know the salmon, your own kin?" the specklies retorted.

"My kin?" Pretty gasped. "You don't mean to say that I shall grow up to be as big and strong as them?"

"Of course you will! What a ninny! " the specklies answered and burst out laughing. "Where did you come from?"

"I live in that runnel over there."

"Oh, she's only a baby samlet," said the specklies disappointedly. "She hasn't seen anything yet. Would you like to come with us to the rapids?"

"What will you do there?"

"Isn't she silly? What do you think everybody does when salmon are spawning?"

Pretty did not like the supercilious tone of the speck-lies. On the other hand, why not join them?

Odd things were happening on the gravel bar above the roaring rapids. The big salmon was ploughing into the gravel, jerking its body and working its fins, and beside it jerked a smaller salmon, pink in colour, with a long bony head and an ugly gristly growth on the end of its lower jaw. Pretty was told that the big fish was a female and the smaller one a male named Hook.

"What are they doing?" Pretty asked in an undertone watching the two big fishes with curiosity.

"They are digging a trough for the spawn."

The specklies gave the big salmon a wide birth and approached the rapids.

"Oh-oh-oh, I'm afraid! It's pulling me down! " Pretty cried, working her tail frantically.

"Don't be afraid, silly! Call this rapids! "

Actually Pretty was afraid not so much of the rapids as of what she saw below it. Under the caps of foam was a throng of large fish: dark-backed graylings with orange fins and big-headed slimy burbots. What was the point of hurtling down into their big mouths?

Pretty stayed with a group of specklies who lingered by a small boulder away from the current and waited to see what would happen next.

The sun was a dull leaden disc above. Pebbles disturbed by the salmon's fins rattled down the chute.

Suddenly, when the two big fish had half disappeared into the trough, the water around them began to churn. The salmon were beating their tails furiously, squirming and rubbing their bellies against the gravel.

The specklies watched them alertly.

"And what are they doing now?"

"Dimwit! They're mating! "

"What for?"

"You'll see..."

Pretty orange peas slithered from under the tail of the female salmon, and immediately a milky cloud was ejected from the male's belly.

Some of the peas floated downstream, and the specklies rushed to catch and swallow them. Pretty also caught several.

"Well, do you like the taste of salmon spawn?" a speckly asked Pretty.

"It's delicious! I've never tasted anything like it! " Pretty replied, wagging her tail with enjoyment.

"Quite right! "

Meanwhile, the peas kept rolling from under the big fish's tail, and floated downstream in an amber chain. Specklies caught them, burbots swallowed them, graylings rushed after them. And so it went on for a whole day and night.

Soon Pretty was so full she could hardly wiggle her fins.

She was very grateful to the big salmon and decided to thank her.

"You have delicious spawn," she said, approaching her cautiously from the side.

"You cannibal! " the big fish wheezed. Her eyes were dull and she was obviously dead tired.

"What do you mean?"

"Every one of the eggs I spawn could grow into a little samlet. You've been gobbling up your own brothers and sisters."

"Have I? Oh, how awful! Please excuse me—I had no idea..."

For a minute Pretty stared around in confusion, then she rushed to admonish the specklies:

"Stop! You mustn't! D'you know what you're doing? You're eating your own brothers and sisters! "

The specklies just laughed.

"Look at her, holier than thou! She's had her fill, but she doesn't want the others to do the same... Who are you to preach?"

Pretty came back saddened and said to the big fish: "They won't listen to me."

The salmon said nothing. She was crawling out of the trough. Hook had disappeared.

Overcome by curiosity, Pretty swam over to the edge of the trough and looked inside. A pile of gay orange eggs lay on the gravel bottom which sparkled with silver scales. The eggs seemed to smile, happy to have come into the world. Would little fish really hatch from these tiny blobs?

Suddenly pebbles and sand came flying into the hole. Pretty darted back in fear. The big fish, working with her fins and tail, was filling in the trough.

"But listen! " Pretty shouted in dismay. "What are you doing? The eggs will die under the gravel! "

"No, they won't," answered the salmon. "They will die

214

if I don't cover them up. The other fish will eat them. But now they will lie there until spring. The flood tide will wash this heap of gravel away, and by then the little fish will have hatched. Do you see?"

"But why did you let the fish eat the eggs?" Pretty persisted. "Why didn't you chase them off? You're so big and strong."

"You're a silly baby yet. When your turn to be a mother comes, you will understand what a hard job it is. I'm exhausted, I have no strength left. I can barely move my fins. And now I have to go back to the sea."

"The sea? What is the sea?"

"The sea..." A sparkle flashed in the salmon's dull eyes. "The sea is very far away. You will know all about it when your time comes."

The big salmon arched her tail to turn round. She was a sorry sight. Her body had become terribly thin, as flat as a board.

Bleeding wounds and bruises covered her belly.

The current caught her up and carried toward the chute.

"Have a happy journey! " Pretty shouted after her.

There was no answer. The rapids were roaring. A little hillock rose over the spawning trough. The specklies, heavy with all the eggs they had eaten, started swimming lazily upstream.

"How strange and puzzling life is," Pretty thought. "Why did the salmon go to the sea? And what *is* the sea?"

2

Pretty asked this question of many fish. But none of them, neither the whitefish, nor the graylings, to say nothing of the silly cheeky ruffs, had ever heard of the sea. Perhaps the pikes or the perches knew? But how could she approach such cutthroats? They struck fear into the hearts of all the other fish, and it was a deadly risk to come near them.

The nights had become even longer and more dismal. White flakes fell from the sky for days on end. Shaggy islands of frosted snow floated down the river. What had happened to the sun?

Pretty heard talk that this happened every year after the salmon left the river. Had the big fish taken the sun along?

Oh no, that would be too cruel!

The fish had become sluggish. Many had moved nearer the rapids where it was easier to breathe.

But finally the rapids, too, became bound with ice. There was now unending night on the river.

"What is happening?" Pretty asked the other fish fearfully.

"The season of Great Stuffiness has come, the hardest time of all."

There was a terrible crush in the hole which was the wintering place for the fishes. River-dwellers, large and small, had moved into it. It was dark and difficult to breathe. In the lower layers the burbots were on the rampage. It was whispered that this was the time of burbot courting, and the screams of the victims sacrificed for their feasts often rose from below.

Pretty, who had taken up position near a stone on the approaches to the rapids, was more dead than alive. She was suffocating. She did not mind the hunger and the lack of movement, but what wouldn't she have given for a gulp of fresh water. Just one gulp! Gradually she fell into a long tedious slumber.

Relief came, oddly enough, from the pike, or at least that was what the other fish said. The pike got good and mad one day and struck out with its tail at the ice crust. And it broke up.

What happiness to be able to breethe freely again, to swim, to catch larvae, to eat her fill!

All over the river the fish celebrated the release from their icy prison and played nuptial games. The pikes set the water boiling near the banks, the perches ran amuck in the creeks, spreading about a grey muslin of roe, shoals of graylings sped along merrily through the turbid water, and even the blue-eyed ruffs, their spines truculently erect, were having a ball in the quiet pools. Then the rapids spoke up, the underwater meadows, the summer-time pastures of all the fish, turned green, and then ... then the sun pierced the water with its rays and scattered golden sparks on the pebbly bottom.

Hurray, the salmon would be coming soon!

Pretty could not sleep for excitement. She listened to the sounds around her, to every splash, ventured often into the mainstream and furtively peered at her reflection against the bright pebbles. She so longed to be bigger and prettier. Well, she had grown quite a bit, and her coat had become even more colourful. At last, no longer able to stand the suspense, she went to live closer to the rapids. It was from there, from that seething chasm, that the big salmon would come. And she, Pretty, was determined to be the first to welcome her.

It was near daybreak. The fish were only awakening. Suddenly a thunderous crash reverberated all over the river. Great waves rolled one after another. The Queen-Fish was announcing her return to her subjects.

There she was! A silver wedge streaked out of the depths. A furious lash with the tail and her body flew up over the water among spray and foam.

The river lay subdued when the salmon finished her dance. All the fish, large and small, cowered in their hiding places.

Pretty bravely swam up to the big salmon. What had she to fear? They had met before.

"Good morning! Do you recognise me?"

The big salmon gave the speckled mite a morose look and made no answer.

"But you must! " Pretty went on excitedly. "Remember last autumn and the spawning trough. I saw you off to the sea! "

"No, dear, you're confusing things. I didn't come here last year."

"How strange! Then it must've been another salmon, but she was exactly like you. Only her coat was different, it was pinkish with yellow spangles. And she promised to tell me about the sea."

"The sea?" The salmon's eyes lit up. "The sea is a wonderful place. There's a lot of sun there just now. And what storms, what huge waves! "

"How I'd like to go there! " Pretty exclaimed.

"It's too early for you yet. In another year," the salmon continued, giving Pretty a more amiable glance, "you will see the sea. But now move over so I can take a run along the mainstream."

She swung her tail, and a merry bubbling trail sparkling with white and yellow ran into the dark depths of the river.

Life became very interesting. The pikes no longer dared to poke their noses out of the sedge growths, the burbots, made languorous by the heat, spent their days hiding under snags. And the small fry were terribly envious of Pretty! Imagine, being friends with the salmon herself! No fish dared to take a stroll along the salmon's pathways, but Pretty went there everyday. Who would venture to approach the salmon when she was taking a rest in a growth of weeds and start a conversation about the sea?

But what Pretty liked best of all was to watch the salmon's morning and evening dances. Boom! Boom! resounded over the river, as the enormous fish beat the water with her tail, and somewhere to the side, nearer the bank, small circles spread out as if from rain-drops. That was Pretty learning salmon dances.

Yes, she learnt a lot from the big salmon. But there were many things in the life of the adult fish that Pretty could not comprehend at all. For instance, Pretty never saw the salmon eat anything.

"We salmon," came the answer to her question, "do not eat anything while in fresh water. The time will come when you, too, will learn to do without food."

And there was another puzzle. The salmon's silver coat suddenly grew dull and acquired a rosy sheen.

"You've got a suntan," Pretty once said to the big fish, hoping she would take it as a compliment.

The salmon merely smiled.

"It's not a suntan. The spawning time is approaching, the time of nuptial games, and for that we salmon don new colourful dresses."

"Tell me more! "

"You're too little. It's too early for you to know about such things."

Then the salmon stopped her morning and evening dances. Most of the time she lay dozing.

"Are you bored with me?" Pretty asked. "Have I done something wrong?"

The salmon usually gave no answer to such questions, but once she flared up angrily:

"Leave me alone! I'm sick and tired of your questions!"

Perhaps this would have been the end of Pretty's friendship with the big salmon—after all one cannot force one's friendship on others—if not for the great misfortune that befell the fish in that river.

People—the fishes' most terrible enemies, as Pretty was told—came. They looked like the trees which grew by the bank, but they could move and they issued a terrible noise.

They lowered long poles into the river and spread a deadly cobweb across it.

The fish dashed about the pool like mad.

When all became quiet towards evening, Pretty went in search of her kinswoman. Goodness, how the river had changed. No more merry graylings splashing about in the rapids, the home of the fat dace was empty, and so was the camp of the good-natured whitefish.

Pretty found the salmon—the Great Salmon—hiding in the most unlikely place of all—a deep dark hole under a moss-grown snag near the bank.

"Have they gone?" the salmon asked.

"Yes."

"They will come again," the salmon said with grim conviction. "They won't rest until they get me."

And indeed, on the subsequent days people came again, again lowered their poles and smothered the river with their cobweb.

The salmon never left her shelter any more. The ruffs gloated brazenly and jeered when they met Pretty:

"Yellow, is she, your auntie? And we don't care a hoot. Nobody can touch us! "

The pikes now went marauding with impunity.

"Go away! " Pretty implored the big salmon. "I shall miss you terribly, but you can't stay here. They will catch you! "

"No, I cannot leave here," the salmon answered. "You're too little to understand."

There followed a stretch of grey monotonous days and constant rain. Dawn broke with difficulty. Pretty was quite exhausted, what with dodging her enemies, procuring her sustenance and paying visits to the big salmon.

But one day the big salmon was not in her hiding place when Pretty came to visit her.

For two days Pretty dashed about the river looking for her. It was raining. There were great waves. The fishes clung disconsolately to snags and boulders. And not one of them knew what had happened to the big salmon.

In the end Pretty found her by the rapids lower down the river. It was much as it had been the year before. There was the big trough in which the salmon lay thrashing heavily while Hook executed his magic dance above her, twisting in abandonment and spreading a cloudy trail of milt above her, while downstream a throng of burbots, graylings, and speckled samlets were stuffing themselves with salmon eggs.

"Oh, how happy I am to find you at last," Pretty said, approaching the big salmon. "I was terribly worried. Why did you leave without telling me?"

The salmon gave no answer, and Pretty moved aside tactfully so as not to be in the way. Later, when the salmon crawled out of the trough and began filling it in, Pretty swam up to her again.

"Are you going to the sea?" she asked. "Please, take me with you."

"You're too young. You have not the strength. It's a very long journey. I am afraid of it myself."

"Then stay here. I'll run all your errands for you."

"Don't talk nonsense. I'll suffocate in this paltry little river."

The big salmon swung round, said "Farewell! " in a tired voice and, caught up by the current, her head and sides knocking against the stones, hurtled down the rapids.

Pretty's heart was gripped by anguish. She stared into the frothy chute of the rapids, where the big fish had disappeared, thinking with horror of another winter under ice. The lack of air, the darkness, the ever-pressing fear of the pike and the burbot... And there, far away, was the wide expanse of the sea. And lots of sunshine.

No, she wasn't going to stay in the river any more! She just wouldn't!

Pretty tensed her muscles and, shutting her eyes tight threw herself into the seething maw of the rapids.

3

Noisy boiling rapids, broad pools, bottomless pits. And there did not seem to be any end to them.

The old salmon, emaciated, bruised, her fins all shredded, seemed to be approaching the end of her tether. Going down the waterfalls, she was whirled about like a chip of wood, and knocked breathless against the stones. But she kept on swimming.

The hardest thing for Pretty was to get enough to eat. While they were in the little river, it had not been so bad: she managed to catch a bug or a worm now and again and swallow them hastily.

But when they entered the big river, Pretty lost heart.

She was racked by hunger. True, there were occasional opportunities to turn into a shallow spot and do a bit of hunting. But a bug or two could not sustain her.

One day, as they were swimming along a dark sombre mainstream, the old salmon turned round and asked her:

"So you're tagging along, are you?"

Pretty was embarrassed: she thought the old fish had not noticed her.

"You're a brave girl," the salmon said. "But I'd advise you to turn back. We shall soon enter an even bigger river, and there you'll not be able to find any food at all. Turn back. There is still time to make it before the Big Stuffiness sets in."

Pretty listened in dejected silence.

"Listen to me, you silly samlet! " the old salmon shouted sternly. "Do you know how many of us perish on this great journey? Your time has not yet come. Young salmon, smolts, go to the sea in springtime, with the floodwaters. Is that clear?"

The old salmon's words thoroughly disheartened Pretty. She now understood how rashly she had acted in setting out on this journey. But what was she to do now?

Soon they entered a larger river. My, how black was the water! How dark it was all around, how deep! Not a single shoal anywhere along the way! Pretty felt dizzy from hunger, her fins became limp and did not obey her. She cried, envying the old salmon, who could do without food for so long.

Once, completely fagged out, she begged for mercy:

"Please, let's make a halt. I can't do without food any longer. Wait for me here while I swim over to the bank."

"I can't stop! " the old salmon croaked. "I'm starved. I've dried up until I'm nothing but skin and bones."

"Then let's swim over to the bank together! "

"You're forgetting that I cannot eat in fresh water. There's no food for me there."

"But surely you can wait for me a few minutes! " she cried and, counting on the salmon's sense of decency, Pretty made for the bank. The water's edge was bound in ice. Nevertheless Pretty managed to find several worms, and, greatly encouraged, hurried back. But the old salmon was not where she had left her. Pretty swam around and called frantically, but finally realising that the old fish had swum on, hurried to catch up with her. She swam a long time but there was no salmon in sight. Pretty was gripped by horror and despair. What would happen to her now?

But luck was with her. After a while a group of salmon who were also swimming downstream caught up with her. Pretty was overjoyed to see them.

"Where are you going?" she asked them. "To the sea?"

"Yes, we are going to the sea."

"I'm so glad! I'm going to the sea, too."

"You? Going to the sea?" the salmon laughed wearily. "Listen to her! What are you doing here anyway?"

"I've come from very far away. The old salmon and I first swam along a small river, then along a bigger one and finally reached this one..."

"Ah, so you're from the clan that goes into the upper reaches of the Yula every summer."

"Yes, I've heard it said that our river flows into the Yula. And where are you from?"

"We? We're not so silly as your clan. Our birthplace is much nearer to the sea. We don't get so tired. Still, how did you manage to get this far? It's unheard of! Silly girl!"

"I suppose I *am* silly," Pretty confirmed sadly. "The old salmon said the same thing."

"She is silly too! Sillier than you. How could she take a samlet like you along? Look, you're still wearing your baby coat! Look at her! Going to the sea! "

Let them laugh! As long as they didn't drive her away. And again she was swimming. Again she was hungry. Again there was the endless gloomy river—without banks, without bottom...

Then one morning at daybreak the salmon reached a sandy bank. Ahead something was thundering and crashing. The turbid green water which rolled over in waves had a salty taste.

Listening to the crashing ahead, Pretty asked timidly: "What's that noise?"

"That's the sea, silly! The sea! How wonderful! "

The salmon were lying on the sandy bank as if on a feather bed, terribly tired and wasted, swaying gently on the greenish waves. Their toothy mouths were wide open and they swallowed with enjoyment the bitterish salty water, which made Pretty's head swim.

"Feeling sick, are you?" the nearest salmon asked her. "That's sea sickness. Don't worry, it will pass soon. You're a lucky little fish. I don't suppose any other salmon has

222

ever reached the sea at your age."

The salmon lolled about a while longer, then suddenly gave powerful lashes with their tails and plunged ahead. Pretty hastened to follow, but the waves threw her back.

"Wait for me! " she called. "Don't leave me alone! "

"Don't be afraid, little one! " an encouraging voice came from the depths. "Just try and get over the bar: all is quiet on the other side."

The surf was roaring, churning up the sand on the bottom. For a long time Pretty was tossed back and forth like a chip of wood until at last she got across to the deep place where the salmon had paused motionless.

It was dark and gloomy. Above she could see huge white ice-floes rocking on the waves.

So this was the sea, the sea she had dreamed of! No, she had not pictured it like this! She imagined it as a vast light river flooded with eternal sunshine. Or had they lied about the sun, which the salmon were supposed to take from the rivers and carry into the sea? Where was it, this sun? She had never seen it once along the way.

There was another disappointment in store for her. A shoal of silvery fish like minnows appeared in the green thickness of the water. Yelling, "Herring! " the salmon attacked them. A terrible slaughter followed. One shuddering fish after another disappeared into the toothy mouths.

Pretty watched the feast with horror. So that was what the salmon went in the sea for!

When no more herrings were left, the salmon said, burping contentedly: "The great fast is over. Now we are going to eat our fill! "

"Why did you just stare? Aren't you hungry?" one of the salmon asked Pretty.

"I only eat worms and shrimps."

"No," the salmon said, "worms and shrimps are not proper salmon food."

"I can't understand how you can swallow live fish. Don't you feel sorry for them?"

The salmon burst out laughing.

"Remember this, little one. In the sea it's either you eat or you get eaten. With nothing but a worm in your belly, you won't get far in the sea. The sea loves the strong! "

"And remember another thing," another salmon added.

"Keep away from your own kind, too. We may not always look whom we eat. Is that clear?"

And the salmon sped forward, arching their tails.

4

They were gone. Pretty was alone in the whole vast sea. What was going to happen to her now? Should she try to follow them? But she remembered the salmon's warning, and her heart shrank with fear. They were all enemies, even her own kind.

She could see some dark fearsome shadows flitting by. Below was a black bottomless abyss. Hunger was tearing at her insides.

Pretty swam towards the shore. There must be a bottom there, and on the bottom she was sure to find a worm or two.

But she wasn't fated to find any food that day. No sooner had she caught sight of the golden sandy bottom than a huge fish with red fins appeared and darted at her. Pretty rushed aside, working with her tired fins desperately.

That night things were very much as they had been in the river. She was lying by a big rock, pressing her shivering body into the sand. She was hungry and lonely. Why, oh why had she come to this sea?

The night was long and dark. Odd red and blue lights were crawling around. The rock shook as ice-floes knocked against it. Distant stars, their rays prickly and cold, peered through the gaps between the ice-floes. All through the night the hungry little salmon never closed her eyes and never dared to leave her shelter by the rock.

By morning the water froze around the rock. Pink dawn glimmered weakly through the ice. Gradually, the yellow sandy bottom, bare and uninviting, became visible. Where were the worms? Where were the little shrimps? Was she destined to starve to death?

Suddenly she saw a tiny sandy hump stir. A sharp nose pecked its way through, followed by a tiny wiggly fish. It was a sand-eel that digs itself into the sand for the night. Without thinking, Pretty made a dash for it. She wept as she swallowed the sand-eel, because she discovered she was a predatory fish too—just like all the other salmon.

But now she knew she would not starve to death.

In early spring huge shoals of herring gather by the Norwegian shores to spawn. The bays and sand-banks packed with herrings look like huge boiling cauldrons. The air is torn to shreds by the screeching of the insatiable seagulls. Trawlers grind their winches uninterruptedly. And from the sea side the helpless herrings are attacked by salmon.

Our little Pretty was having a feast in one such bay that spring. But you would hardly recognise her. In a matter of eighteen months a speckled samlet the size of an ordinary gudgeon had grown into a two-foot-long fish sparkling with silver. Of course, she was still undersized as compared to the adult fish, but her strength and agility could be envied by many an older salmon.

She never experienced enfeebling weariness now. She had no fear of storms. She could spend a whole day following the grey shadows sliding along the sea's surface, for seagulls are the salmon's chief guides at sea. Sooner or later they lead them to a shoal of herring.

She had a voracious appetite whetted by the salt water. Besides, she had learnt her lesson well—"the sea loves the strong! " So she ate for all she was worth to gain in size and strength.

Unlike the smolts, who come to the sea in spring, she had not had the long summer to adapt to the new conditions. She had had to learn her lessons in a hurry, in late autumn. And she passed the test with flying colours. She had spent nearly a month near the mouth of the Northern Dvina. And all through that month she had eaten almost without interruption. So she would grow up and be as strong as the other salmon!

And finally the day came when she felt strong enough to join the last shoal of salmon going out into the open sea.

The novelty of everything took her breath away. Fantastic underwater meadows of red and brown sea weeds, new, unfamiliar fish, jellyfish, huge fearsome sharks, seals who popped out of the dark depths like logs...

There were many enemies in the sea. She had to be on the alert every second. But what freedom there was, what vastness! It made her dizzy.

The salmon of the White Sea travel hundreds and thousands of miles to reach the shores of Norway, their traditional feeding grounds. There they feast day and night.

Pretty would pounce on a helpless herring with the speed of lightning. While the older salmon were still picking out their victims, she would be already tearing at her pray with her young teeth. A minute of crunching, and she would speed after the next victim. She could not afford to tarry, for the older salmon would not stop to wonder if she was a herring or their own kin.

Weeks and months passed. The sun never set over the stormy Barents Sea. It was the favourite season of the fish. But what was the matter with the salmon? They were swimming ahead more and more slowly, stopping every so often to smell the water, and finally the day came when they got into a shoal and turned back.

Pretty was nonplussed.

"Excuse me," she asked the salmon swimming at the tail end of the shoal. "Why have you turned back? Isn't there enough food for you here?"

"Why, don't you know that this is the time for us to go back to our homeland?"

"What is our homeland? Another sea?"

The old salmon stared, then burst out laughing so loudly that the others stopped to see what it was all about.

"Just you listen to her! She doesn't know what homeland is. She thinks she was born in the sea."

The salmon surrounded Pretty and berated her indignantly:

"You ought to be ashamed! How could you forget your homeland?"

"Don't you feel its pull, you miserable creature?"

"Have you forgotten where you were before you came into the sea?"

Pretty thought hard, trying to remember what her birthplace was, where she had come into the sea from, but all she could remember was a sensation of stuffiness, and a long, weary journey.

"You are the most miserable of salmon!" the biggest salmon said in tones of condemnation. "To forget our homeland, to forget the great law of our ancestors!"

"Please excuse me," said Pretty. "Why are you speaking to me so harshly? Perhaps I am at fault. I really have a very weak recollection of what you call my birthplace. But, you see, I came to the sea when I was a tiny samlet, and I have never heard of the great law of our ancestors."

226

"This is the limit! " cried another salmon indignantly. "What are young people coming to? She has never heard about the great law of our ancestors! What *have* you heard of then?"

At this point Pretty lost her temper.

"Why don't you tell me, instead of bawling my head off? What's wrong with frankly admitting a fault? Do you want me to lie?"

There was one sensible fish in the shoal who started speaking to Pretty calmly and reasonably:

"Now, you're telling us that you've never heard about the great law of our ancestors. But haven't you obeyed this law? Have you never been back home yet?"

"No, never. I came to the sea from somewhere as a tiny samlet."

"That's amazing," the salmon said to one another. "We must tell her about the great law of our ancestors."

"Now, listen," the sensible salmon began, "and make sure you remember it till your dying day.

"It was a very long time ago. Our ancestors lived in the rivers then and were little different from the other fish, especially from our kin, the whitefish and the graylings. Like the whitefish and the graylings, they were content to travel up and down the river from its source to its mouth, eating what food came their way. There was not enough of it, and our ancestors often went hungry. So they were undersized and weak and had white flesh like the other fresh-water fish. Then winter came, and matters got even worse. They suffocated under the armour of ice and perished. Pikes and burbots harassed them. It went on like this until an extraordinary young male was born to the salmon tribe. His name was Lokh. He was a remarkable fish. Nature itself marked him out. On his lower jaw he had a hook—that is why all our males have since been called Hooks. He was so brave legends were composed about him. He feared neither the burbot, nor the perch, and he did not even make way for the vicious pike. And once, when the time of Great Stuffiness began to approach, Lokh collected a gang of young brave salmon and urged them:

" 'We cannot go on living in the old way. Our tribe is dying out, killed by vicious pikes, overcome by the stuffiness. Let us go in search of vaster waters! '

"The old salmon ordered Lokh to appear before their council. There were many heated arguments there and even some fighting. But in the end the wise old fish decided that there was a lot of truth in what Lokh said: the salmon tribe *had* been growing weaker from year to year.

" 'Take the youngest and the strongest,' they said to Lokh, 'and go seek new rivers. But before you start on your way, you must give an oath, Lokh, that you will never forget your mother river, the birthplace of your forefathers, that you will bear it always in your heart, and that you will come back. Otherwise luck will be against you.'

"So Lokh and his gang of braves gave the oath and left.

"For a long time nothing was heard of them. Everybody thought they had perished, and the burbots and the perches taunted the salmon, while the pikes became so brazen that they attacked salmon shoals in broad daylight. But once, after the time of Great Stuffiness was over and the sun was back, unusual fish appeared in our rivers. They were few, but how splendid they were! They were huge and strong, their bodies seemed to be cast of silver. They swam along the mainstream and all the fish scattered out of their way, and when they jumped out of the water in play even the pikes trembled with fear.

"Our ancestors were frightened of them too and started swimming away with the other fishes, but suddenly a thunderous voice rumbled over the river:

" 'Why are you fleeing from us? We are your sons and brothers. Have you forgotten your Lokh?'

"Yes, it was Lokh, Great Lokh, speaking in our salmon tongue. And then our ancestors turned back and swam to meet those splendid salmon. There was great rejoicing in the salmon tribe.

" 'Where have you been, Lokh? How did you manage to grow so big, while we here barely survived the stuffiness?'

"And Lokh told them how long he had travelled with his friends, many of whom had perished on the way, and then he started praising the sea, the sea that begat great powerful fishes. The sea was endlessly vast, said Lokh, there was such a lot of food that he and his comrades would not need to eat all through the summer. 'Come nearer and feel my muscles,' Lokh said, 'feel my tail. All this has been given me by the sea. I've been salted through by seawater, and my flesh has become pink as the sunset.'

"And then our ancestors, inflamed by his speeches, cried:

" 'Lead us to the sea, Lokh! We want to become as big and strong as you and your friends! '

" 'Very well,' said Lokh, 'I'll take you to the sea. But not before the time of Great Stuffiness sets in. In the meantime I want to enjoy the fresh water, to play my fill in my native river, for it was only the thought of our birthplace that sustained us in our struggle with the elements out at sea.'

"And ever since then," the sensible salmon concluded, "we have been living by the law laid by Great Lokh. When the time of Great Stuffiness comes, we go out to sea, but when it ends, we return to our birthplace."

Pretty had been listening spellbound. So that was the mystery which surrounded her salmon tribe! So that was why the salmon went to sea! And she had stupidly been thinking only of food to stuff herself and other pleasures. She became terribly ashamed that she had been leading so petty and selfish a life.

"Tell me," she said, "what happened to Great Lokh?"

"Nature has bestowed immortality up on him for his great exploit."

"So he is still alive?" Pretty cried in surprise.

"Yes, he lives among us."

"Oh, shall I see Great Lokh, then?"

"No," said the salmon. "You will never see him. The law of Great Lokh does not live in your heart. You have forgotten your homeland. And Great Lokh takes for his mate only such as..."

"So one can even be Great Lokh's mate! " Pretty cried, interrupting her. "How I would like that! "

"No," said the salmon, "you will never be Lokh's mate. He chooses the one who is most deserving, the bravest and the most abiding to his law."

Pretty became sad. What a pity she would never see Great Lokh and be his mate! But wasn't she brave? Didn't the old salmon tell her that in their whole clan there had never been a samlet who dared to go to sea at her age?

Pretty took heart. She wanted to ask where and how Great Lokh chose his mate—why not try her luck?—but the salmon were already on their way. They seemed to have forgotten all about her.

Pretty hurried to catch up with them. Yes, she would abide by the law of Great Lokh. She would go to her native river and perhaps one day, on hearing about her, Great Lokh would himself come to claim her.

Long was the salmon's journey through the turbulent

229

sea. They passed rocky reefs, they went down to great depths, they passed over sandy shallows.

Pretty often forged ahead. One never knew, Great Lokh might be watching them from somewhere, and she wanted him to notice her.

Once, near a sandy spit, they met another large shoal of big salmon. Pretty's heart throbbed in sweet anticipation. This, she thought, must be the place where salmon converged from all over the sea, and where Great Lokh inspected them. But the old salmon she turned to for an explanation just curled her lips in disdain.

"These are sea salmon. Great Lokh has no respect for them."

"Why?"

"Because they don't observe his law properly. They only go to their native rivers in autumn, and they come back the very same autumn."

Pretty would have nothing to do with such heretics since they had half-betrayed Great Lokh. She swam ahead easily, plunging bravely into a roaring roller—Lokh liked valiant ones!

Then came the unforgettable moment when she tasted fresh water. The old salmon floated on the ripples limply, weeping unashamedly.

"Oh, how sweet is my homeland," they whispered prayer-like.

"I can smell my native river! " came a joyous shout.

"So can I! And I! " other salmon shouted.

Pretty was terribly excited. She, too, fancied she could taste a trickle of water that set her heart fluttering. Then the impossible happened: it all came back to her, the memory of the distant river and the songful rapids.

"How wonderful, how wonderful! " Pretty whispered to herself. No, they were wrong to say that the law of Great Lokh did not live in her heart. It did. She now knew the road to the land of her ancestors. That little trickle would lead her there like a guiding thread.

The road was not easy. There was a strong head-on current, there was ice blocking the way, there were jammed logs. But what did she care for all these obstacles when her life had a new meaning now?

"Well, we have arrived," some salmon said one day, stopping amid a broad pool. "Can you hear our river greeting us?"

A roar of water was coming from afar.

"Those are our rapids," the salmon Pretty had often swam next to explained. "You have no idea how beautiful they are. And we have pure spring water. Come with us," she said to Pretty. "You're a fine friend. We shall have lovely time in our river. We shall teach you our dances. And what fine Hooks we have! "

"No, no," said Pretty. "I must go to my own river. Don't you know the law of Great Lokh?"

Some time later another family separated from the shoal and stayed behind, then another, but Pretty swam on with a much depleted shoal. It was a pity, of course, that her native river was so far away, but one does not choose one's birthplace.

Only a few fish were left when finally they entered their native river at dawn. But how happy they were! Water was gurgling at the mouth as it leaped from one rock to another. Mists were floating above and a young rosy sun was peering curiously at the big silver fishes who were splashing in the rapids.

"What lovely water! " the salmon said blissfully as their native stream caressed their bodies. "There is none to match it in the whole world! "

Having rested after the journey, they proceeded to the nearest large pool and began their first dance—the traditional greeting to their native river established by their ancestors.

Everyone admitted that Pretty leaped higher than any of the others, and she liked being praised by her more experienced friends.

Then followed the incomparable experience of travelling along her own river. The pebbles sparkled on the bottom, the sand was like gold, the rapids sang their song. There was the languid silence of crimson dawns... Small fry scattered in a panic. Dace, ruffs, and graylings—all made way for them. The silly things! What had they to fear? The pikes were a different matter—she would not mind teaching *them* a lesson. They had done enough marauding. But where were they? Were those prickly lights that flashed in the sedge by the banks their eyes? Afraid for your skins, are you, brigands?

Gradually the river became more shallow. One after another the salmon stopped in the pools where they had grown up. Each offered to share her home with Pretty, but each time she refused. She could not break the law of Great Lokh. No, she would not stop until she reached her own pool.

So, quite alone, she travelled for another few days up the river. At times she was overcome by despair. The river was becoming ever more narrow and shallow. Often Pretty had to leap over rapids, falling on sharp stones and getting badly bruised. And when she finally reached her home, she did not know whether to rejoice or to grieve. Everything was so small, so unprepossessing. Burdocks grew on the banks of the somnolent pool. The rapids she had feared so in her childhood lisped like toothless old men. And her own runnel, in which she had known so much joy and fear, proved to be just a sluggish brook clinging to a grey boulder. A tiny speckled fish dived into a growth of water-weeds at the sight of her. Could she have been as tiny once?

Not a single fish came out to welcome her. The sea put a barrier between her and the river-dwellers. She was just a guest who had come for a short time. Still, she was glad to be home. The salmon lived by the law of Great Lokh, and she was going to abide by it.

6

It was a scorcher of a summer. The white nights, brief and light as a single breath, did not refresh the water which had become green with slime. It was difficult to breathe. To make matters worse, Pretty was infested with parasites, which ate into her skin, and in the shallow rapids she was unable to wash them away.

Still, she bore the trials with courage. In the morning she danced and chased the pikes if they dared to enter her pool. Let them starve in their slimy sedge. After all, protection of the weak was also among the laws laid down by Great Lokh. Great Lokh could not be unjust...

The white nights dimmed and darkened. Thick mists wove over the river. Then the long-awaited rain at last came, strong and beneficent. The river at once filled out. The rapids began to rumble. That was good. The river was clearing the way for Great Lokh.

Pretty dreamed of him day and night. On the dark autumn nights, she hardly ever slept. When a star fell, she fancied it was Great Lokh coming to her in a starry aura. And what was that noise near the rapids?

Leaves were floating down the river whirling round and round. The sun was now a rare guest in the pool. Yet Lokh did not come.

One morning a dark-pink little hook came to the pool, panting in his eagerness.

"Come along, let's dig a spawn-trough! I have been looking for a mate for many a day."

"With you?" Pretty nearly burst out laughing, so funny and impudent was this undersized young hopeful. "The idea! "

"Why, don't you want to spawn? All the salmon are digging troughs at this time of the year..."

"No, I don't. I'm waiting for Great Lokh."

"Great Lokh, Great Lokh..." the hook said offendedly. "Don't be so stuck-up, smartie! I'll be big too one day."

The poor little fool had not even understood to whom she was referring.

Other hooks came after him, all small and ugly, with long bony heads. They implored her to join them in digging the trough.

"How heartless you are! " they wailed. "Why must you torment us?"

She did not wish to torment them. But what could she do if she had no desire to mate with them? She had not come all this way to play with such milksops!

Snow began to fall, and in the morning a crust of ice rimmed the banks. Great Lokh was still not in evidence. Had he forgotten about her? Or had she been too sure of herself in believing that the royal Lokh would want her for his mate and not some other salmon?

Once, as she lay on the bottom of the pool listening to the river noises, she felt a strange unwonted languor in her body. The gravel bar by the rapids now drew her irresistibly.

"Oh Great Lokh! " she implored. "I have tried to live by your law. I have been waiting for you so long. Why don't you come?"

Not a sound came in answer to her cry.

"Have I done something wrong?" it suddenly occurred to Pretty. "Have I angered Great Lokh by my refusal to mate with his sons? Is he punishing me for my pride? Where are those hooks? There doesn't seem to be a single one about."

She swam up and down the pool and even went below the rapids. There were no hooks.

At last, utterly exhausted and burning with desire, she lay down on the gravel bar above the rapids.

It was a pitch dark night. Shaggy ice-floes were floating down the river colliding with one another. The pebbles rustled as they were carried down the chute.

Pretty was digging a trough. Digging it frenziedly and senselessly, obedient to the all-powerful instinct of procreation. When the trough was ready, she tumbled into it, her strength spent and—for the hundredth time—called to Lokh in hot whispers:

"Oh, Great Lokh! Why are you punishing me so? I may be not worthy of you. You may have forgotten about me. But you have many sons. Why don't you send one of them along? Any miserable puny hook?"

No sooner had she uttered those words than there came a clanging and crashing from the rapids, and then a blinding light burst out like the sun itself illumining the night.

She had never seen anything like it. Surely that was Lokh, Great Lokh coming to her! Who else would arrive in such thunder and brilliance? There was her happiness, there was her reward for all the sufferings she had borne in this river.

Sweet languor suffused her entire being. She lay on her nuptial bed, subdued, spell-bound, waiting...

The blow was sure and ruthless. The steel prongs of the fish-spear pierced her head. She was still thrashing about when they pulled her into the boat.

"A salmon! " a big hefty fellow who was holding the boat in place with a pole shouted jubilantly from the stern.

"Shut up, you scum! " a bearded man said hoarsely, glancing around in fear. "Wanna get fined?"

The boat was rocking on the water. The flames of the torches set up in the bow of the boat were swinging back and forth. Sparks were flying into the dark black sky.

The bearded man stepped on the fish with his heavy boot, pulled the spear out of her still shuddering body, put a finger under her gills, lifted her and spat.

"A young one, dang her! First time in me life I see a little squirt like her get herself a spawning trough."

Still, when he slit the belly of the young salmon, he found a lot of roe. He squeezed the roe out into a pot, looked at the now scrawny fish and suddenly tossed it into the river.

"Why'd ya do that?" the young fellow asked in wonder.

"No point in keeping her. She was all roe, the rest's just skin and bones."

For a while Pretty's light, disembowelled body floated on the surface of the water that reflected the red flames. Then the current carried her to the rapids and further on down the river, along the road she had travelled two years before, when she had set out so bravely for the sea.

1962

To Petersburg for a Sarafan

Again the forests were burning somewhere, again the sun was shrouded in smoke as if spellbound and the white-hot sandy street of the village, criss-crossed with black shadows cast by the sheds, fences and stacks of firewood, shone with some strange unearthly light. At times I fancied that the land beyond the window was either the kingdom of Kashchei the Deathless from a half-forgotten tale I had heard in childhood, or some fantastic planet.

But inside the house, where Pavel Antonovich and I were sitting at the table, there was nothing fantastic. It was an old peasant cottage, with windows closed against the smoke and soot outside, with an old-fashioned mud-brick stove from the top of which came the pungent smell of aspen leaves (the old man kept a goat), and we were engaged in the most ordinary of pursuits—conversation.

Pavel Antonovich held a towel in his hands and kept wiping the sweat away—it was stifling hot in the house—but he still looked quite vigorous. He sat straight, and the look in his shrewd eyes was resolute under his bushy brows. Human memory is a strange thing. Pavel Antonovich remembered in detail the hoary legends about the Chud, the tow-headed people who once lived up here on the Pinega, before Russians arrived from Novgorod and Moscow. He could tell lively stories about the strange ways of the military governor in Kevrol, who had his drinking water brought from a cold spring fifteen versts away. He knew about the hermitages in the depths of the forest where schismatics and deserters hid. But when it came to the Civil War in the North, in which he himself had fought, his memory often failed him.

And so from time to time we had to turn for help to his wife, Marya Petrovna, a plump old woman with surprisingly young eyes.

English translation © Progress Publishers 1982

"You got it all wrong agin," she corrected him with a slight smile, giving me an encouraging wink. "Here, write it down," she said to me as I bent over my notebook. "Life is all on paper these days."

After a while, looking with compassion at me and her husband, Marya Petrovna said:

"Look at you, all steamed up. Maybe I ought to go ask Filippyevna for some kvass. She always has some down in her cellar. She keeps to the old ways still." Suddenly she exclaimed: "Why, look! Here comes Filippyenva herself."

The twig broom on the porch rustled. The outer door creaked. An old woman came into the cottage. She crossed herself solemnly, made a low bow, and muttered, "May you be well one and all," or some such greeting.

What a tiny, ancient thing she was!

Again I thought of an old folk-tale in which there was a kindly and pious old Homey Granny. However, she was dressed in present-day peasant wear—a brown quilted jacket without sleeves, a grey apron and men's top-boots; her faded purple sarafan*, hand-woven sash and a dark-blue kerchief worn low on her forehead under a warm shawl were the only remnants of the past.

"Have you come visiting, Filippyevna?" asked my hostess, offering her a stool.

"Visiting, she asks," grumbled the old woman. "Visiting, in broad daylight. They don't pay Filippyevna a pension. That's for you young people to go visiting. I came to find out about my birthday."

"Oh goodness," cried Marya Petrovna. "I forgot to tell you. Your birthday is tomorrow."

"Tomorrow, is it? That's why I just couldn't sit still. I been spinning tow. The chairman says to me, 'Give us a hand, Filippyevna, we haven't a rope left between us—no one wants to do the spinning.' And I says to him, 'And when there's no Filippyevna, what will you do then?' "

"Granny," I spoke up, "how old are you?"

"Who is it you have visiting? I can't see plain, everything's in a cloud." Filippyevna lifted a dry little hand to her brow and peered at me, squinting weak-sightedly. "A young fellow, looks like. Where from?"

"From far off, Granny," I raised my voice to suit her years.

* *Sarafan*—a long sleeveless, collarless garment, part of the national costume formerly worn by women in Russia.—*Tr.*

"I can tell that. Our way of speaking is softer like."

"I'm from Leningrad, Granny. Have you heard of it?"

"She's more than heard. She's been there," said Marya Petrovna pleased to be able to surprise me.

"How do you mean, I've been?" asked the old woman in mock petulance. "It was Petersburg where I was."

"They're the same, you know, Granny," I laughed.

"The same, and not the same. People ride to Leningrad in cars, and fly there on airplanes. I went to Petersburg on foot."

"On foot?"

"On foot."

"From here? From Vaymusha?" The village is about four kilometres from the Pinega district centre.

"From a little farther off. Add another ten versts. From Shardomen."

I looked at Marya Petrovna, then back at the old woman. Were they, perhaps, fooling me? After all, that was ... how far? From Pinega to the Dvina, from the Dvina to Vologda... More than a thousand and five hundred kilometres! And this tiny little creature had measured out that whole distance with her own two legs. But I was still more surprised to hear what she had gone to Petersburg for—what do you think?—a sarafan!

"Oh yes, it's the truth," Marya Petrovna assured me eagerly, and looked proudly at the old woman. "Our Filippyevna made the trip on foot. For a sarafan. Tell him how it was, Granny, you haven't forgot, have you?"

"How could I forget," said the old woman pensively. "They warned me that I'd remember Petersburg my whole life long. And they were right. Soon as it gets evening, my bones start aching. All night long I lay stiff as a board, 'fraid to move with the pain."

"That's the years catching up with you, Filippyevna," said Marya Petrovna sadly.

"I'm not that old yet, you know. I'll be eighty-three. My mother still went picking cloudberries when she was ninety."

Pavel Antonovich, who had tumbled onto the bed when Filippyevna came, and till now had kept silent, lifted his large bald head:

"He's not interested in your mother. Tell him how you walked to Petersburg. Used to be that was all you talked about. They called you the Petersburg lady."

"That they did. And I liked to tell the story. But now the whole thing is hazy. Time was, soon as I started to recollect I could see every bush and hollow."

But finally she gave in to our pleas.

"You see, my father was a soldier, a poor man," she began unhurriedly, "and there was five of us, all girls. I was already fourteen, but still going around in my old blue home-spun. Once I dropped in at the neighbours', and they'd got a parcel from their son—he lived in Petersburg. He sent his sister such a fine sarafan, it took my breath away. Bright red, with sky-blue flowers. I can still see it plain as plain... Well, soon a church holiday came along, the Feast of the Virgin. Maryushka—that's the daughter of the neighbour that got the parcel—she and I went to our first grown-up dance. She had on her new sarafan, and I was in my old blue home-spun, only I put a new sash on it. Made it myself. Well, I saw that the sarafan caught the boys' eyes. I was small and slight—you might say I lived out my life without getting my growth—but my face wasn't bad, comely it was. Maryushka, she was nothing but a lump and her mouth would hang open like she was asleep on her feet. But now all the boys were after her, in her new sarafan. I felt miserable. If only I had a sarafan like that! Because supposing I was left an old maid? But where would I get a sarafan like that? My parents weren't rich. I didn't have any brothers. It looked like I'd have to find a way myself. But how? How could a young girl make money? They wouldn't take me to work in the woods, or hire me as a hand. And I couldn't get that Petersburg sarafan out of my head. Other girls had sarafans too, but not from Petersburg, and the boys didn't pay them the same kind of mind. Well, so I decided to go to Petersburg for a sarafan. And go I did."

"Oh, come on now," said Marya Petrovna, a little impatiently. "Tell how it was you went! "

Filippyevna wiped her eyes with her dark hand.

"When my mother heard that I'd decided to go she started crying. 'Olyushka,' she said, 'what's got into you? You've lost your mind! ' But my father, God bless his soul, had been a soldier, and what he said went. He took the icon down from the nail and said: 'That's my girl. Go, Olga. Other people go, why not you?' Well, Mother wasn't one to cross him—those times weren't like now. Next day I got up early, baked some loaves, and Father hitched up the horse. Mother cried so loud the neighbours came running: Where

240

are you sending the girl off to? But Father doesn't say a word. He picked me up like a feather, sat me in the sleigh, and off we went. It wasn't so easy for him either... He took me thirty versts, to Marya's Hill. There he said goodbye, and gave me a ruble in coppers."

"Just think, a ruble to go all the way to Petersburg," sobbed Marya Petrovna.

"Well, money doesn't grow on trees. There were four more mouths back home. So, Dad gave me the money, and made the sign of the cross over me. 'Go now, Olga,' he says, 'go and find your happiness.' Soon as I saw him getting into the sleigh I started to bawl. 'Oh Daddy, Daddy, don't go,' I cried. 'I don't need any sarafan.' But he says, 'No, Olga, you go. They'll never stop teasing you in the village, calling you the Petersburg lady.'"

Again Filippyevna wiped her eyes.

"Well, I went to Petersburg, but I still got the name. They'll call me that to the day I die."

"Tell how you were in the woods alone," said Marya Petrovna tearfully.

I felt my eyes smart too.

"Well, there I was. Fir trees all around, like bears on their hind legs, and me all alone in the middle of the road. I was afraid to go on, and there was no going back. Our Dad didn't like to repeat his orders... People were good to me. They took me all the way to Petersburg, just like they led me by the hand. I'd knock at a cottage, begging shelter for the night, and when I told the people where I was going, they shook their heads, ohing and ahing. 'Get onto that stove bed, child,' they would say, 'warm yourself up.' Sometimes I got a ride, and sometimes, when I saw carts on the road I ran after them. Only once I met someone mean enough to show me the wrong road for a laugh. Did people in the next village cuss him for that! 'For shame,' they said. 'Tricking a child! He'll pay for your tears.' But that was nothing, really. They welcomed me in every village, gave me milk to drink and baked potatoes for the road. There wasn't much bread, true. That was a hungry year."

"Come, come," corrected Marya Petrovna, "not everybody made you welcome. Have you forgotten how that man made you work for the patches on the boots he gave you?"

"Well yes, but that was farther on. I was already getting near Vologda."

"That's right, that's right. Before the patches you had walked to summer."

"Not to summer. To spring. That's what comes after winter, right?"

"Well, go on and tell us about that," said Marya Petrovna. "Don't forget about the cranes."

"Look, she even remembers about the cranes," Filippyevna nodded towards me, and a smile lit her dark, wrinkled face. You could see that this memory was precious to her. "Yes, there were cranes," she sighed. "It was wintertime when I started out from home, and by the time I got to the Dvina the pike had broken the ice with its tail. 'Go right towards the spring,' they told me. And so I headed towards the sun. It was warm. The grass started to peep out, and then the cranes were flying. I got terribly homesick: they were flying back towards home. So I'd stand and throw back my head. 'Oh cranes, dear birds,' I'd shout, 'tell them back home that you saw me on the road. Alive.' When Dad was getting ready to pass on, he remembered: 'Olga,' he says, 'all that spring I kept asking the cranes if they hadn't seen my little girl somewheres.' "

"Write it down, write it down," said Marya Petrovna. She leaned over towards me, all in a flutter, sweating from the heat and from emotion.

"What does he want with fairy-tales? He wants to hear about the Civil War and the Revolution," came Pavel Antonovich's voice from the bed. So he was listening too, not sleeping.

"Of course he should write it down," said Marya Petrovna angrily. "People ought to know about this too. People came from Leningrad last year and took down fairy-tales and songs from the old days. And I told them, 'You listen to our Granny: she's better than any fairy-tale.' Well, Filippyevna, how was it that you got those patches?" And Marya Petrovna winked merrily at me, anticipating the story to come.

"That was near Vologda, you know. My clothes were all worn out and raggedy. The road was wet and muddy, there were puddles now, and me still in felt boots. In one of the villages a man says to me, 'What do you mean, silly girl, scaring the summer like that? I have a pair of boots I'll give you for nothing,' he says. 'All they need is a few patches.' Well, was I glad! 'Just one condition,' he says. 'For every patch I put on, you spend one day looking after my kids.' "

Filippyevna chewed at her lips a bit, and smiled a crooked smile.

"He put quite a lot of patches on for me. I was at his place for about three weeks."

After this the old woman, not without help from Marya Petrovna, recalled several more amusing incidents from her long, hard journey, and then, guided still by the tireless Marya Petrovna, came at last to Petersburg.

"The houses were so big, and made of stone, and each of them had so many windows—we don't have as many in the whole village as one house has there. And Lord, the people flowed by like a river. And the horses galloping. There I was with a white sack over my shoulder, with my stick in my hand, barefoot, right on Nevsky, their main street. That's where my legs quit on me. They went fine along the road, but then they quit. I was afraid to dive into that ant-hill. I thought to myself: I can get in all right, but how will I get out? I had to find my neighbour, Maryushka's brother. Then I remembered: hold on, I have a paper where it's all written down. So I got out that paper, and stood holding it in my hands. Dad had told me, he said, 'You ask the poor people, Olga, they'll be more ready to help you.' But you try and tell who's poor there. Wherever you look, nothing but gentlemen and ladies. Well, finally a gentleman did help me out. He read the paper. 'You have to get over to Vassilyevsky Island, girl,' he says to me. 'Keep going along Nevsky, you'll see the Tsar's palace! '" Filippyevna looked up. "I saw it, too. The Tsar's palace, and that stone column. Is it still there?" she asked me, and for a moment her dim eyes lit up with curiosity. "So it is, is it?" she nodded. "Well, of course it is. It's stone—what could happen to it?"

Frowning, Filippyevna tried to straighten up, and rubbed the small of her back with her hand.

"You see, that's what I have to remember Petersburg by. I never did get my growth. All my life people laughed at me. 'You wore yourself down on the road,' they said to me."

"You tell him about Petersburg," said Marya Petrovna, once more nudging her back to the story.

The old woman pursed her lips, and looked reproachfully at her.

"What is there to tell? I wasn't in Petersburg to have a good time. The babies there soil their nappies the same as here in the village."

"She was a nanny there," explained Marya Petrovna. "She worked a year for a German."

Meanwhile Filippyevna had got to her feet. Marya Petrovna started to fuss about; she opened her antique sideboard and got out a parcel.

"Here's a treat for you. For your birthday," she said, thrusting the parcel wrapped in newspaper into Filippyevna's hands.

"But you never told the main thing," Pavel Antonovich suddenly boomed from the bed. "What about the sarafan?"

"I bought it, all right," answered the old woman pettishly. "I went all up and down Nevsky, and bought one just like Maryushka's."

"Well, and did it do the trick with the boys?" Pavel Antonovich laughed: he obviously knew the answer already.

"It did. I never got married till I was fifty."

Marya Petrovna, genuinely angry, waved at her husband to be silent: Why do you want to open old wounds? But Pavel Antonovich spoke up again:

"You probably didn't buy the right one."

Filippyevna did not answer immediately, but when she did speak you couldn't tell what there was more of in her words: lasting bitterness or belated self-ridicule.

"People explained it to me afterwards. It wasn't the sarafan, they said, made Maryushka so popular. It was the cows. Her father had five; and that summer my father didn't have a one."

As she went out onto the porch Filippyevna looked up at the sky, shielding her eyes with a dry, brown palm.

"She's looking at the sun," said Marya Petrovna with a sigh. "Figuring how much time she wasted sitting here. Never an idle moment for her, she's used to the old ways."

I leaned at the window, watching that little figure on the sandy village street which was deserted at that hour. She walked with small strides, her short, unbending legs in top-boots far apart, and swung her arms gravely. She came to an old house, and disappeared around the corner.

Now the street was completely deserted. There was a smell of smoke, and a desert heat came from the sandy road. Only a barely noticeable chain of footprints showed that someone had passed this way not long ago.

And I thought: once a little girl from Pinega, whose name nobody ever remembered, left footprints just like that, all the way to Petersburg. Those tracks were long ago washed away by rain, and by time. Soon time would wash Filippyevna herself away. But her journey, like some fairy-tale, would remain in people's memories.

Yes, that's a good thing: to leave behind something, if only a tiny little story that will help people along.

1961

The Heart of a Mother

Not one is left, they're all gone. Like a grove of fine upstanding trees they were—Petya, Vanya, Pavel, Yegor, Stepa. Five men to till the soil. When the time came to birth each one I wasn't thinking of how I'd feed and clothe them all, but how I'd squeeze them in round the table. It wasn't a big table my man's father had, he'd made it for himself and his goodwife and his son, but when I came to live there was soon a flock of childer.

I'm not talking of the older ones, the war swallowed them. I got three death notices in one year, that's how the war smashed down on me. And Yegor got caught in it, too, he was taken prisoner by the Germans. But Stepa, my little one! He lies heavy on my conscience, I let him slip away and I can't get over it, it's twenty-seven years agone and still I torment myself. I keep on thinking: if I'd but taken thought quicker, I wouldn't have been left lonely in my old age. I lie down with it nights and rise with the same in the morn.

When did you leave home? Before the war? In 'thirty-eight? Aye, then you won't mind Stepa. I had him in 'thirty-four. All my childer were good childer, I can't say bad about any of them but there was none like him. You couldn't wish better. Long as he lived—he wasn't nine when he died—my girl and me, we never knew what it was to get in wood or water. He did it all. He'd stand behind the bench, you couldn't see him, only hear the saw rasping. And bringing in mushrooms and wild berries—I didn't have to send him, he'd run off himself.

He was allus busy and I didn't see beyond it. It was only when I saw that blood I knew summat was badly wrong. I went to the outhouse in the morn, I don't know why I was still home when it was light, I allus went to work in the woods, felling, in the dark and came home in the dark, too. I'd never see the children weeks at a time, that's how we worked in wartime. But that day I was late, I don't know why. I looked down and there, dear Lord, the snow by the outhouse was all blood, and blood frozen on the logs.

I got me back to the house.

"Childer, who's been at the outhouse just now?"

Both of 'em stopped quiet, both lad and lass.

"Dinna hide it," I says, "summat's wrong, ye need the doctor."

Then Stepa says, "It was me, Ma."

But I'd guessed already. Right from the autumn he'd been peaky, he'd be one day at school and three lying up. And there was that time I come home, I'd been off carting hay.

"Ma," he says, "a bird flew here to me today, I was lying on the bench and it perched on the edge of the window-frame and tapped and tapped at the glass, and all the time it looked at me. What did it want with me?"

"It was just frozen-cold," I says. "It wanted to come in to the warm. It's that cold out—the very logs crack."

But it wasn't an ordinary bird, it was the death bird. Come with a warning: prepare, soon I'm coming for your soul.

When Stepa told me about the bird, though, I didn't think of that, I was tired and cold, I'd no thought for birds. But when I saw that blood by the outhouse in plain daylight—then I minded me of yon bird.

I ran to the foreman, and told him the way of it—"My lad's sick, Pavel Yegorovich, he's real bad, let me have a horse to take him to the doctor."

But the foreman, God rest him—you'll mind him. Ugly Mug we used to call him, a brute and every second word a foul one. Well, and all his answer was "Get off to the forest, you this-and-that, don't let me see you round here any more! "

"Nay, Pavel Yegorovich," I said, "shout all you like, but I'll take my lad to the hospital. You've no right to hinder me."

Pavel Yegorovich stamped about and talked of the war. "Was it me as started the war?" he says, but when he saw the war didn't move me down he flops on his knees. "Think on, what it'll be. Your lad can stand it for a week or two, but me, if I take a horse from work they'll murder me."

So I went home and cried.

"Childer, what'll I do? The foreman's making me go to the forest."

But the childer—what could they say? What's the good of asking little 'uns?

"Go, go, Ma, we must help our brothers."

They was all alive then, Petya and Vanya and Pasha and Yegor. Well, so I went, naught else to do. Them times, we didn't work in the woods just to make money, it was our own way to help fight the enemy. That's what they told us, grown-ups and childer alike. Hold on, they says, it's to help your sons and brothers at the front.

Eh dear, what we went through! When you talk of it there's some just don't believe you. How could you live through the winter without bread, they say. But we didn't see any bread that winter, all the grain, to the very last of it, went for the war. Aye, and not so much potatoes either. It was only cabbage leaves we'd plenty of. And it was because of them cabbage leaves Stepa took cold, it was them as made him ill. Round about the Virgin's Day he came running home from school. There'd been a thaw and the fields were all snow and water. And he says "They're all on the cabbage field gathering leaves. We need them, too."

"That we do, lad," I says, "but your Ma can't get out of harness nohow."

Well, in the eve I came home from work and the house was full of cabbage leaves. My lass Anka was sitting there with a wood splinter for light, washing them in a trough. No need to ask who'd got them—Stepa. He was on the stove-bed shivering so his teeth rattled, chilled through he was. You know yourself what it's like, going about on a cabbage field in that water and mud. And with the sort of boots we had.

Look at the sense I had then. Working in the woods, they gave us two rusks a day, take them and be glad. All right, I thought, there's a good side to all. I can feed Stepa up a bit. Mebbe he's peaked because he never sees bread. So back I came home and Stepa was real bad. I tipped the rusks out on the table with "Stepa, dear lad, here's summat to eat, eat them all if you want. All at once." And Stepa took a rusk with both hands and held it in his mouth but he hadn't the strength to bite it. "I'll have it some other time," he says.

Well, the horse was still outside, and I didn't take it to the stable, they could do what they liked with me, shoot me on the spot if they wanted, but I was getting my child to the hospital.

But I didn't get him there. I had only one verst to go—you know that hill just before you come to town? There's a big larch, with the lower part scorched. And it was by that larch Stepa died.

It was bitter cold, a hard frost, and I'd covered him with all we had in the house, and there, by that larch, I opened up the covers a mite.

"Stepa," I says, "we're coming to the town, mebbe you'd like to look a bit?" He'd asked me, "Ma, tell me when we come close to the town." He was just a child and he'd never been anywhere, he wanted to see the new places.

Now Stepa, my Stepa lifted his head and said, "Ma, how light it is. And how fine our town is..."

And with that he died. Gave up his soul in his mother's arms.

I don't know what would have happened to me then, I'd have wept and cried there beside the larch and mebbe frozen to death because it was cruel cold. But by good fortune or bad, Taissia Tikhonovna happened along, the chairwoman of our rural soviet. She was on her way home from town. Walking. They all had to walk those days. There were only three or four horses kept on the main farm, the rest were off in the woods, for the whole winter.

We'd a good chairwoman. No softness about her when she sent you off to work in the woods or some other place, but when there was sorrow in the house, a man killed at the front or aught else like that, she was always there to mourn and comfort. Times, she'd say, "I've naught to make it easier for you, our Soviet power has naught these days but tears and pity." And she'd weep with you and not spare herself. But another time she'd have no tears or pity for you, only scolding and harsh words. And there was many a day she scolded me, too.

"How long are you going to keep up with your crying? You've got sons at the front, mebbe hungry, mebbe cold—what good's all your crying to them? Don't forget," she says, "you're a mother but there's one above you too, your motherland, the mother of all mothers."

Eh, Taissia, Taissia Tikhonovna! The years have passed, it'll soon be twenty since she died. It was soon after the war she laid her down, broke her heart with our griefs, and

I still talk to her—aloud, nights. Then Anna, my daughter, wakes up.

"At it again? You've outlived your wits! I've told you—it was the war killed Stepa."

"And mebbe not. I couldn't watch over the older ones, but the child was right by me, and I didn't watch over him."

"How could you watch over him? You were in the forest."

"And what would have happened," I says, "if I'd gone to the forest two days later?"

Anna couldn't answer that and anyway she had to get up early, she's a dairy-maid, so she shouted, "Will you give me some peace? When are you going to stop?"

I say naught, folks are all nerves nowadays, shouting and snapping, but I think to myself: never will it stop. Not to the end of my life. As long as my heart of a mother beats.

1969

The Swans Flew By

When people first began to notice Avdotya Malakhova's protruding belly, it seemed there would be no end to the gossip. What! Pregnant at forty-three? Had she lost her mind? Not a tooth in her mouth, arms and legs crippled with rheumatism—it was time for her to start thinking about entering a home for invalids, not giving birth... And the main thing—how had she gotten herself into this predicament? Maybe Vasily had wanted to leave a little something of himself behind before departing for the next world?

To tell the truth, Avdotya herself didn't pay much mind to the gossip. Let them chatter, that's what women's tongues were for. But would she be able to have the baby? Hadn't this happiness, a life-long dream, come to her too late?

After examining her, Dina, the local doctor's assistant, was adamant:

"Not on your life. Go to the district hospital. It might not be too late..."

And in the troubled days that followed there was only one person in the village who stood by Avdotya—Manefa, the village wench, three years younger than her.

"Have the baby, Dunya. Don't listen to anyone. What business is it of theirs?" She was referring to the other village women. "They've all got more kids than they can handle... And I would go through any torture, even death..." And without finishing, she burst into tears.

Shortly after that Manefa paid Avdotya another visit, this time with a gift she had bought at the market in the district centre.

"Here, I've brought you something that'll perk you up," she said cheerfully, and unfolded a shiny, lacquered tapestry.

Lavishly depicted on the tapestry was a full-figured, rosy-cheeked beauty with flowing red hair and large breasts which swelled up above her partially lowered slip. The beauty sat leaning on her elbow by an open window of some sort of spire-roofed tower, reminiscent of an old neglected silo, and looked languishingly down below. And below there was a lake, where two yellow-beaked swans were kissing.

"Not a bad picture? Something worth looking at?" Manefa said with an admiring click of her tongue.

"Yes indeed. Very nice," Avdotya agreed.

"Since you think so, it's yours."

Manefa herself hung the tapestry up on the wall over the bed, and it seemed to grow brighter in the gloomy, low hut.

Before leaving, she said:

"Keep on looking at this picture and you'll give birth to pretty lasses like these."

"Twins?" choked Avdotya. "My god! I'd be better off with no picture at all! "

But the tapestry remained in place. And later, when Avdotya was no longer able to get around and spent hours lying in bed, she would gaze for long periods of time at the two yellow-beaked kissing swans.

But what else was there for her to do? She couldn't hold a needle and thread, she had terrible headaches, and all the other women were at work. She hadn't seen Manefa in a while either—run off to town again, they said, after some new beau, and anyway she enjoyed looking at the picture.

In the end everything turned out the way the wayward Manefa had predicted: Avdotya, to everyone's amazement, gave birth to twins—a boy and girl.

The girl was given the promising name Nadezhda.* She would be of much help to her mother: robust, loud-voiced—you could hear her bawling from outside. And there was no need to ponder over a name for the boy: frail and puny at birth, he wouldn't survive no matter what name he was given. This was the general consensus of all the neighbors who gathered together at the christening ceremony. And therefore, when they noticed the familiar tattered, rabbit-fur cap of Panka, the brawny, half-wit shepherd bobbing beneath the window, someone said:

"There goes Panka. What about that name?" (After all, the child had to be given some name, even if only to write it down in the registry.)

And so the boy was named after the half-wit shepherd Panka.

* *Nadezhda*—hope.—*Tr.*

2

Within four years' time Avdotya had become an old woman. She had worn herself out completely; and all, of course, because of Panka, because her heart bled every time she looked at him. With a huge head, lop ears, and a puny little body, each rib protruding, he did nothing but lay—couldn't raise his head from the pillow.

"Panka, darling, tell me what's ailing you?"

Little Panka would start, open his toothless mouth, and a minute later he would roll his eyes once again—it was as if he were always listening to something. Only his ears seemed to be alive.

"It doesn't look as if our Panka is going to make it," Avdotya said once to her daughter.

Nadka cried and carried on so that her mother barely managed to calm her down.

"No, no, your Panka is not going to die—just take good care of him."

And sure enough, from that day on you couldn't separate Nadka from her brother. She would talk to him for hours, tug and pull on him: get up, Panka, get up. And putting her to bed at night was a bother: she had to be together with Panka, with her arms wrapped around him so as not to lose her treasure while she slept.

And what do you think? Maybe it was due to Nadka's efforts, and maybe not, but the child began to come to life: he started to move his little arms and legs, raised his head up from the pillow, and then the day came when he stood on his own.

Oh, how well Avdotya remembered that day!

It was on Whitsunday, just at the time when they began cutting birch twigs for brooms. And Avdotya, not wanting to lag behind the others, went to the woods in the morning to cut twigs, and in the afternoon, after taking care of work in the farmyard, she sat down and began binding them together.

It was a warm day. The sun shone so gloriously that the sparrows got carried away and flitted right beneath your nose. And at the lake there was such a ruckus! (Avdotya's house was next to a small lake, and the children played in the water from early spring until late autumn.)

Avdotya sat on the porch—daydreaming, buried up to her knees in fragrant birch leaves—she was sitting there binding twigs—and suddenly there were shouts:

"Look, look! Here comes the hippo! "

She turned around quickly and—my god! Panka, her Panka was on his feet! His white head swaying, his whole body swaying, like a dandelion in the wind, and with his arms outstretched, he toddled towards the green bank of the lake.

The children jumped up out of the water—even for them this was no small miracle (everyone loved Panka):

"Come on, hippo, come on! "

But here Nadka burst forward—she too had been swimming in the lake—grabbed her brother in her arms and turned to the others like a lioness defending her cub:

"You can't have him! I won't let you have him! He's mine, Panka's mine! "

"Nadka, Nadka, don't be silly!" Avdotya yelled. "They're not going to hurt your Panka. Let him play with the others."

"I don't care! " Nadka exploded. "He's mine, mine! Everyone keep away! " And that was all there was to it.

What a character the girl had, Avdotya marvelled. And from whom had she inherited this possessive streak? Her father was always ready to give the shirt off his back, and she herself shared everything with the other women... But then, after reflecting, she calmed down. Perhaps it was all for the better that Nadka was so attached to her brother. Who knows? If something were to happen to her, to Panka's mother, to whom would he turn in life?

3

At six, Nadka was a lovely child. Rosy-cheeked, a mouthful of teeth, she bounced around as if on springs—never still for a minute.

And how bright, and industrious! She knew everything, kept an eye on everything that went on: who had just been born to what family, who went where, and what was currently for sale in the stores. And at home she swept the floor, washed the dishes, and even covered up the samovar in a storm—not every adult would think to do that.

And very often, admiring her daughter, Avdotya would turn with a sigh to her son. No, she wasn't worried that the boy had grown up puny and weak. After all, she reasoned, nowadays things are different than they used to be. People use their heads to earn their livelihood, not their hands. But what went on in this child's head? Why was everything inside out with him?

Once Avdotya bought a box of crayons and paper. "Here, kids, draw something. You've got to start your lessons while you're still young."

Nadka's eyes blazed—in a flash she was at the table. "What should I draw, Mama?"

"Anything. Draw whatever you see. Look, there's Matryona's cow—see, she's running around the garden with her tail up in the air."

Nadka glanced out the window, and in no time she had drawn a house with a chimney; there was smoke pouring out of the chimney, and by the house there was a cow—with horns and a tail, just as you would expect.

"Like this, Mama?"

"Yes, I suppose so," Avdotya said compliantly. "Your mama doesn't know all that much—never made it further than third grade."

Then she turned to her son: well, Panka, you've been working away, sitting here puffing and drooling over your pencil. Let's see what you have?

She looked, and didn't know whether to laugh or cry: it was more like a beetle than a cow, with six legs sticking out.

"Dummy! How many legs does a cow have? Six?"

"It's because she's running," Panka said.

"Running, yes," Nadka teased her brother. "But cows don't grow legs while they're running, do they, Mama?"

Another time Avdotya sent her son out to pick some grass for fodder. Nadka, as ill luck would have it, had cut her foot on a nail, and the hungry ewe had set up a fearful howl in the shed—she had just lambed. And she herself was tied up with the wash.

"Come on, Panka, give your mother and sister a hand. You've got to learn to do your own share of the work."

So Panka went out to pick grass. One hour passed, then another—where had the boy got to? Avdotya dropped everything and ran off to look for him. And it seems that Panka had made it to the first bush, where he had seen some sort of bird, and that was it—all thoughts of the grass, of home, had vanished from his head. He had forgotten why he had gone out.

And Avdotya could remember many such instances. But she kept silent, of course. What kind of mother would put her own child to shame? There would be time enough later on for people to have a good laugh at him.

Spring came early that year, and the snow thawed quickly—in just one week it was gone. At the lake the water rose higher by the hour. This in itself didn't worry anyone. After all, it was only a lake, not a river. But what if the river were suddenly to come to the aid of the lake? What then? It was behind the lake, in the low-lying land, that the main wealth of the kolkhoz—the livestock—was kept. And without waiting for the river to begin acting up, they decided to put up a dam.

Quite a crowd showed up. It was great fun to work when everyone joined in together. Wagons and wheelbarrows. The children, like tiny ants, trekked along the fresh sand. And towards evening, when the embankment was already finished, someone shouted:

"Look, the swans are flying! "

Where, what swans? It was only in times long past that swans would fly overhead; nowadays you only saw such a sight in pictures. Maybe that was why almost every household had one of those tapestries with the swans.

But the swans were actually flying across the evening sky. They soared high, high up in the sky, like two little white boats rocking in the blue expanse. And as they approached the woods they gave out a cry: accept us, earth. All day long we've been flapping our wings, it's time we rested too. And they began to descend towards the dense fir forest, towards the Swan lakes, where the sunset had spread like red calico across the sky.

"So, rare guests have arrived. They've brought us an omen," people began to say, after the swans were hidden from view behind the woods.

"Probably a cold spell," said old man Zosima. "Snow used to fall down from their wings."

The words of the old man were taken seriously—and the whole way home they tried to guess when the snow would come. How much longer would they have to keep the livestock penned in?

While this unpleasant conversation was going on—who didn't run low of fodder in the spring?—Avdotya forgot about Panka. She always kept him within eyesight, but as they drew near the porch she realised that she was holding only Nadka by the hand. This one would rather starve than miss what the grown-ups were talking about.

"Fool-headed girl, where's your brother?"

"Panka, Panka! " Nadka yelled.

She howled and sobbed: something like this had never happened before; Panka had never left her side—they were always together. At the first moment, however, Avdotya was beyond feeling sorry for Nadka—she was ready to give the little scatterbrain a good whipping. What if something had happened to the little fellow? Water from the spring thaw was everywhere—something terrible could happen any moment.

Distracted, Avdotya ran back towards the embankment. "Panka, Panka..."

And thank the good lord, this time misfortune had passed them by! Panka was standing on the embankment, just like Ivan the Fool in Russian fairy tales. Darkness was gathering around, the sun had already set, the water was raging below (the river *had* overflowed its banks!)—it was enough to make a grown person feel scared. And he just stood there, as if rooted to the ground. His cap had slipped down over his ears, and he stood, like a little tree-stump, only his pale face visible in the darkness.

What had entranced him so? What sort of spell had this red scrap of sunset over the black fir grove cast over him, so that he couldn't tear his eyes away from it? After all, this wasn't the first sunset he had ever seen.

Good god in heaven, Avdotya realised all at once that he was pining after the swans. He was watching out for them. She should have guessed it at once. The boy had always been crazy about birds ("Nadka, look, a bird just landed! ", "Mama, wait, there's a bird over there"), and now—just think!—he had seen real live swans.

"Panka, dear," Avdotya began to coax, "let's go, honey. The swans have flown off, and you're still standing here. This is no way to carry on."

His little hands were frozen, his pants soaked, his nose running, and how much longer would he have stood there on the embankment, if she hadn't come to fetch him?

5

That evening they ate supper, drank tea—everything just as usual—then they went to bed. They slept on the floor. The bed wasn't large enough for all three, and the children didn't want to sleep separately, and Avdotya herself felt better when they were both at her side.

So they went to bed. Nadka was totally played out and went right off to sleep. You could've dragged her onto the street by the feet and she still wouldn't have wakened. But Panka was wide awake. He lay, tucked in like a little mouse between his mother and sister, but he wasn't sleeping—Avdotya could tell by his breathing.

"Panka, are you warm enough? Go lie on the stove-bed."

Silence.

"Well, if you're not cold, then go to sleep. Tomorrow we have to get up early and go to the farmyard."

"Mama," he suddenly breathed into her ear, "where did they go?"

"Oh, god, he still has those swans on his mind." Avdotya let out a big yawn (she had been half-asleep), and turned to her son.

He was lying with his eyes wide open. Maybe the moon was keeping him awake?

She got up and draped a shawl over the window.

"Sleep. Nighttime is for sleeping, not for conversations. Close your eyes, and I'll close mine—we'll be asleep in no time."

"Mama, but where do they build their nests?"

No, it was clear, he wouldn't give up until he found out everything.

"On the lakes. They say they used to nest here on the Swan lakes. But now they'll probably only rest here over-night and then fly further on."

"Further? But why?"

"Why? They would probably be glad to stay—their wings aren't made of iron, they get tired flapping their wings for days on end, but nesting places have gotten awfully scarce. The woods have been cut down, people are all around."

"Don't they like people?"

"You're an odd one, Panka! Even a dumb sparrow—whish!—and he's gone, and these are swans we're talking about. Alright, now go to sleep."

"Mama, have you ever seen them on the lakes?"

"The swans?" Avdotya thought for a second, then sighed. "Once I saw them. I was just a little girl. My dad—your grandfather—took me to pick cranberries. We left home early. I'm walking along, my eyes still glued together, just like I'm walking around in the dark. And Grandfather stopped suddenly and tugged on my arm: 'Dunya, Dunya, look, look over there.' Still half-asleep, at first I thought it was a white ice-floe floating on the lake. I had seen plenty of white patches along the road. It was thaw time, and there was snow here and there under the firs. But as soon as they saw us the swans cried and beat their wings on the water, and then they took off right towards the sun. And the sun, like me, had just awoken, and was peeking out from behind the pines. It was a grand sight—real pretty," Avdotya concluded in a sing-song voice, and again she yawned.

Panka sighed.

"Okay, don't sigh. When you get big you'll see it for yourself. Nikifor the hunter says he sees them every spring."

"Mama," Panka asked a bit later, "are the lakes where you and Grandfather saw them far away?"

"No, not far. You know the old barn behind the farmyard? They're only a few miles from that barn. The road goes through the woods, over hills and hollows. There are plenty of mushrooms and berries around. As soon as summer comes, we'll go there, I'll take both you and Nadka."

Avdotya pulled the covers up over her chest, adjusted the cotton scarf on her head—she caught cold easily, and always slept with a scarf over her head.

"Are you asleep, Panka? Okay, then sleep," she said, not waiting for a reply.

Then carefully, so as not to disturb her son she stretched out her legs—they were aching that night, probably from a change in the weather.

Well thank god, he had quieted down.

And that was the last that she was able to remember later, when trying to recall that evening.

6

They noticed that Panka was missing in the morning, but they did not find him until evening. And between morning and evening was a long, nerve-racking day, which reverberated with the sobs of Avdotya and Nadka.

They both called Panka:

"Panka, Panka, come home," Nadka wailed from the porch.

And at the same time with the same heart-rending cry Avdotya rushed back and forth along the paths which ran through the woods.

It had turned sharply colder overnight; a cold, damp

wind blew out of the north, and the trees in the forest creaked and moaned. She cried: "Panka, Pa-a-n-ka." And in response only: "O-oo ... o-oo-oo..."

And not a single trace on the paths. The earth has turned as rigid as a stone.

Avdotya ran down to the Swan lakes—covered half of Old Swamp (more than one road started behind the old barn)—he was not there either. And once again, for the umpteenth time, she came out by the old barn.

No, it was clear that she would have to call in the others—she wouldn't find him by herself, she thought, and suddenly she saw the shepherd Panka.

He was chopping the remains of the old barn into firewood.

Avdotya wept bitterly. This poor tongue-tied soul was terribly attached to her Panka. When he discovered that a second Panka had appeared in the village he rejoiced like a small child, and devoted all his free time to the boy. He would catch him live hares in the woods, bring him the first berries, make him various toys... Not a day passed, it seemed, that the shepherd, on his way home from the pasture, wouldn't bring the boy some sort of handmade fife, birchbark whistle or box.

"What are you doing, Panka, waving around that axe?" Avdotya said, swallowing back her tears. "Where's your name-sake?"

Panka goggled his round light eyes and gave an idiotic grin.

"Good-for-nothing lout!" Avdotya stormed angrily. "Why are you smiling? I said, where's Panka? Panka's gone, run off to the woods during the night. He's probably sitting beneath some tree right now freezing to death, and you're standing there grinning."

And thank god for the shepherd. He found Panka after all. How many times had she run past the pond between Old Swamp and Big Lake, and had never thought to look there, and as it turned out, the boy was sitting there, under a fir tree, just a mile or so from the barn.

Panka was delirious. They undressed him, rubbed him down with alcohol, covered him with all the blankets in the house. And he lay beneath the blankets, breathing heavily through his mouth, burning red with fever.

"Panka, Panka, don't die," Nadka pleaded hoarsely.

Once it seemed as if Panka had come to.

"Nadka, Nadka, I saw them..."

And then once again he began gasping for air. His eyes, dulled and burning with fever, began to roll back in his head.

Avdotya fell on her knees and stretched out her arms towards the sorrowful image of the Virgin Mother which glimmered dully in the front corner of the house.

"Heavenly Mother, perform a miracle. I'm the one who led the child into the woods. I showed him the way myself."

But no miracle happened. Towards morning, at dawn, Panka died.

7

The life of little Panka, like a spring brook, rustled through the village street. How much of a trace does a spring brook leave behind? How many will remember it? And Panka was forgotten, almost overnight.

They remembered Panka once again, three months later, when Nadka died...

No, no one was surprised by the fact that death had paid Avdotya's house another visit so soon—there was no stopping that old woman from visiting whom she chose. It was something else—the child's mysterious, incomprehensible illness. A healthy girl, rosy-cheeked and glib-tongued, if anyone was made out for life, it was her! But as soon as her little brother was buried (God rest his soul, the little runt), she began to wither, and neither the doctors (they brought them in from the district), nor the knowledgeable older women—no one was able to help. She dried up like a blade of grass alongside the road.

This was what most of the conversation was about on the day of the funeral. What kind of illness did the child die of? What sickness had eaten away at the girl? Pining for her brother? It was true, they noticed, and Avdotya complained: the girl was pining away. She would sit every day by the window staring out at the street, and towards the end she began to fancy things: "Panka, Panka, come home," she would call.

Yes, maybe she did pine away—this sort of thing happened often enough. But all the same it was hard to believe that someone so young could just pine away and die.

1963-1964

Pine Children

1

We drove along in silence. The driver, teeth clenched, spun the wheel furiously. The road, churned up by a bulldozer until it was nothing but all ruts and holes, passed through a patch of forest recently destroyed by a fire. The charred pine trunks were still smoldering, and the air in the cab of the log-truck was hot and smoke-laden.

That summer had been unusually droughty, with dry thunderstorms, and there had been innumerable forest fires on the Pinega. The logging stations couldn't keep up with the felling plan; their workers, sooty and dropping on their feet from exhaustion, went without sleep for many nights on end, fighting the fires. My driver was just back from yet another outbreak. He talked to me without ceremony now. "So you must get to Shusha, must you? Couldn't you wait till I'd had a few hours' sleep? Very well, then get knocked about, what do I care! "

I was being tossed as if I were on a swing, and crashed into the door of the cab every other minute. But at last the burnt-out wood ended. The truck reached the Shusha, a merry gushing river with tall reddish banks covered with green larches. The driver, in a sudden fit of sympathy for me, or feeling relieved himself after the terrible pitching, said,

"Call this a road?"

I responded readily: really, the logging station could have taken better care of a road that was right next door to it.

But no! The driver made a mental about-turn. "Why the hell should they," he retorted. "When did they last do any logging on the Shusha? Even the roads in use hereabouts are paved with nothing but curses. See?"

The burnt forest had now receded, and it was easier to breathe. Tall pines overshadowed the road. But the next moment we found ourselves driving in the blazing sun again.

Not a tree, not a bush around, only stumps. An endless scattering of fresh massive stumps. The relentless sun danced on their yellow, resin-flooded tops, and you felt as though thousands of searchlights were hitting your eyes.

To see the forest mowed down right next to the river was so staggering, it was such a monstrous thing to have done, that I gave the driver an involuntary questioning glance, seeking sympathy and understanding.

But the driver did not bat an eyelid.

"Who had that bright idea?" I could not keep from asking.

"Who?" The driver gave a wry grin, his metal-crowned tooth glinting. "Who d'you think? We have to fulfill the plan, haven't we? Last year winter came late—the frost never hit us till January—the roads were a river of slush, and then the blizzards set in... Just you try carting timber from twenty kilometres away in a blizzard! And what about the men? They still want to eat and drink, don't they? And if there's no felling, there's no money in the pay-packet. That's how it is... Of course they fined Drobyshev, our manager. But when our station overfulfilled the plan, they changed their tune. The very same administration which fined him gave him a bonus. You overfulfill the plan—you get the bonus. That's how it is..."

The logs that formed a bridge over a dry stream bed danced underneath our wheels. The truck ground its way up a rise. On top of it stood a pole with a sign: "Shusholskoye Forestry". Further along the road I saw a slogan inlaid in white limestone: "Peace to the World! "

"Goshka Charnasov's little joke," the driver said curving his chapped lips in a humourless smile. "A fool! Nothing else to do, that's why. A forester sure has a soft job. He sleeps the whole winter through, and he doesn't sweat in summer either. Just takes a stroll in the forest once a week and spends the rest of his time fishing on the river..."

He paused, then came out with an unexpected conclusion:

"He's a bastard, that one! "

"Why so?" I asked after a startled pause.

"Why? I suppose because he got his training in them prison camps. The swine will feed an elk to the wolves but won't help a man out."

"But shooting elks is against the law."

The driver's jaw clenched and he ground his teeth. "The law, you say... And what about never having any meat in the shops—is there some law about it too? Some crooked frauds up there on top have come up with a lot of eyewash, and the working men have to pay for it with their empty bellies, is that it? Just try slaving in the forest every day without proper grub! The law... Did they ever count the number of elks killed by the wolves? You walk through the forest, and there are elk bones all over the place. But no, let the wolves have their feast, and you men keep away! Is that right?"

I said nothing. Then the driver threw me a quick suspicious glance and asked:

"Who are you anyway? Goshka's boss? Or some kin of his?"

I did not know what to say. Should I admit that Igor—Goshka to him—was a childhood friend of mine and that I had come to see him? But were we really friends? We had not seen each other for twenty-five years. A quarter of a century... Could this visit be a silly idea? Would we manage to span the stream of time that lay between us?

At the age of fifteen Igor stole his father's revolver and ran away from home. The story was told that he robbed a savings bank in some village or other. Then somebody allegedly saw him in Arkhangelsk. Then the rumour spread that he was already in the Caucasus. In a word, the boy was on the loose.

Nobody was sorry for Igor himself—it was generally held that he had been a ruffian since childhood and deserved whatever he had coming to him, but people *were* sorry for his father.

He was an extraordinary person. As a child, when I saw him out in the street, tall and gaunt, striding along in his long cavalry greatcoat and tall black astrakhan hat reaching up almost to the eaves, I'd go numb with awe and admiration. His high boots would squeak in the frost (Anton Isaakovich wore leather boots even in the fiercest frosts), and I felt as though a windstorm was bearing down on me. With a trembling hand I'd give the Young Pioneer salute to the Red partisan. But Anton Isaakovich never noticed me. His eyes, which blazed with a fire out of this world, were always fastened on some point far in the distance...

His greatest passion was revolutionary holidays. Not one building in the village, neither the village Soviet, nor the school or the community centre were so colourfully adorned for the occasion as his post office. Nobody could vie with him. Long before May Day or the Revolution's anniversary, Anton Isaakovich started laying in a store of paraffin (it was rationed in those years) and dyed bed-sheets and other pieces of linen red. Then he'd cover ply-wood boxes with red cloth. The women in the village lost their sleep and peace of mind: "He'll burn the village down, he will for a fact. He thinks of nothing but fire all the time."

At last the long awaited evening would come. Fiery slogans blazed out on the former priest's house which had been converted into a post office. Their reflections, like the Northern Lights, lit up the sky. We boys would stand in front of the post office for hours, hypnotised by the passionate appeals that clutched our hearts: "Long Live the October World Conflagration! " "Death to the Bourgeois Hydra! "

The truck braked abruptly. I had not noticed that we had left the forest behind.

"Look here, mate," said the driver, avoiding my glance. "It's a five minute walk to Charnasov's place. See that mansion with a garden? That's where you should steer for. I have to gather me some logs."

The huge, dust-laden log-truck backed and turned round and began to recede with a rumble.

I was left alone on the road.

2

Shusha is an old abandoned logging settlement. You see a lot of them in the northern forests. There were five or six sunken barracks, sitting glumly askew in the sun's glare by the river. In the dark holes of their former windows, grass was sprouting. Across the river rose a red cliff with a birch grove shimmering in the hot haze on top, and where I stood all was open space dotted with stumps. For all of two kilometres there was nothing but dog-rose brush and clumps of willow-herb. And not a single tree worth the name!

In the midst of this forest desert the sight of a lived-in house with the green mane of young poplars gaily glittering in the sun was all the more gladdening to the eye. The house, standing apart from the barracks, was squat and clumsy in shape, made of crudely hewn logs knocked together any old how, like the barracks, but it presented a pleasant contrast to them in its vigorous vitality: the walls had been repaired with new logs here and there, the window-frames were painted white and the little covered porch by the side-wall still smelt of resin.

The doors from the porch into the passage and further into the living-room were wide open.

I went up the steps and through the spacious passage ... and stopped in wonderment. What was that? Before me was a vast barn-like room—or was it hall-like?—and it was full of birch boughs. They lined the walls, stretching all the way to the ceiling, they were propped between the windows, and the leaves on the boughs stirred the way they do out in the open.

However, on taking a closer look, I also discerned signs of human habitation. To the right of the door, by the only window in that particular wall, stood a table with three unpainted stools. Opposite the table a massive stove loomed white through the birch boughs. By the farthest wall, submerged in green twilight, I glimpsed a chintz curtain—the bed was probably behind it...

A flaxen-haired woman, barefoot and wearing a white dress, ran in from outside. It could only be Igor's wife Natasha.

"A fine way to welcome our guest! In he comes and there's nobody at home! Well, it's your own fault—why didn't you come when you promised? We waited and waited a whole week, and this morning I lost my patience and sent Igor to the forest in the morning. How long can we keep waiting, I said. There are fires all around..."

Natasha blurted this tirade out in a single breath as though we were old friends who had known each other a long time, and then, walked barefoot over the birch twigs scattered on the floor towards the windows and pushed the birch boughs aside. Sunlight came pouring into the room.

"We've made this burrow to hide from the heat. We've been living in the bushes like this all summer. Look how big these windows are—like a gateway. This house used to be a bakery."

Suddenly, behind the birch boughs which concealed the

chintz curtain, something stirred and flopped onto the floor. I started in surprise. A hare! A grey hare with big ears and a twitching upper lip.

Natasha stamped her foot at it in mock anger:

"Shameless creature! So you've been lolling on the bed again?"

The hare plunged into the bushes.

Natasha laughed and turned her round comely and open face to me.

"We've had him since last year," she said, her big dark eyes scrutinising me. "Igor found him in the forest. A tiny thing, limping across a glade—the fox must have taken a snap at him, or a badger perhaps. And the silly thing has got so used to us we can't chase him away. In winter it turns white as snow..."

Natasha offered me the choice of having tea of a wash a in the bath-house after the road. They had a fine bath-house, she said, light and clean. But I said I'd rather wait for Igor, since she said he would be back any moment now.

We sat down at the table. Shading her eyes from the sun and still studying me, Natasha asked, "Why didn't I hear you driving up? There I was, doing my washing down by the river and suddenly I see a stranger standing by the porch. Of course I knew at once it must be you! "

I told her how I had reached Shusha.

"I see," Natasha said with a frown. "It was that shameless Pronka Silin. So he didn't dare come up here, did he? I'd have told him a thing or two... Poacher No 1 at the logging station. He killed a prize elk this winter—look: there are his antlers," she pointed to the wall. "He's had it in for us ever since. Whenever he's had a few drinks, he starts hollering for all to hear: 'I paid a fine because of Goshka, but I'll make Goshka pay me back with his life...' "

Natasha looked through the window.

"I don't know why he's so late. He left early this morning and didn't take a crust of bread with him... Would you like to lie down to rest for a while after your trip? Or perhaps you'd like some raspberries? We have the early variety and there are lots of ripe berries."

But the heat had not yet begun to abate. Taut hot air shimmered over the kitchen garden, where I could see a white goat dosing among the potato plants. The smell of black currants was wafted from the river, and the small window of the bath-house blazed among the bushes like an owl's eye.

The garden, full of the somnolent babbling of poplar leaves, adjoined the blank wall of the house from the south side. As distinct from the kitchen garden, it was surrounded by a wattle fence, with a wicket made of smoothly planed narrow boards. In short, the owners of the house thought a lot of their garden. I went in through the wicket and gasped in surprise. Young russet maples, yellow acacia, several varieties of lilac, jasmine, barberries, hawthorn, elderberry... And what were those? Young apple-trees, cherries—here, on the Pinega—right next to the Arctic Circle!

Natasha did not seem to share my enthusiasm.

"Nothing to it," she said with a note of defiance. "Anybody can plant a bush. Come over here and I'll show you something really special..."

Moving aside the raspberry canes covered with plentiful berries, she took me into the distant corner of the garden.

"Know what these are?"

At first I did not notice anything except slim poplars glittering in the sun, then I caught a resinous aroma and looked to the left. Young cedars! Blue-black, with long needles, morose and bristly like so many bears.

Natasha stroked the squat sapling nearest her.

"There's a choosy tree! How we babied them! And they grow so slowly, not at all like the pine, even though they're as prickly."

She thought a moment, and then suddenly said with a shy smile, her pale cheeks flushing pink:

"These cedars won him my heart."

"Who?" I asked, puzzled.

"Igor, who else? Why else would I marry an ex-con like him? Just out of prison, twice my age and scary to look at. No woman would have him, and I was just a slip of a girl then. Not yet eighteen. But these devil's own sperm did the job..." Natasha again stroked the cedar's top with a smile. "Honest. I was coming home by steamboat that autumn. There was a crowd of people on it. And he was there, too, my intended. I didn't give him so much as a look, of course. I'd never given him a thought. There are many of his kind, ex-cons, wandering about our parts. Then I noticed that he kept glancing into a huge basket covered with a cloth that stood at his feet. Did he have some animal cubs in there,

I wondered. After all he was a forester. That got me curious. So when he walked away for a moment I went and looked inside the basket. And nearly spat in disgust. Little pines, nothing else. The man must be daft, I thought. Haven't we got enough pines in our forest that he should be bringing more from some place else? But our teacher Nyura Kanasheva, who was with me, took a look too and said: 'No, Natasha, these are not pines, they're cedars.' And I began dreaming of those cedars at night. Honest! All through the winter I dreamed of them. And in the spring, when the snow melted, I made a special trip all the way to Shusha—to take a look at the cedars. Thirty kilometres! That's how silly I was." Natasha shook her head. "What a to-do we had at home! When Mother found out I'd taken up with an ex-con, she just wept and wept. My brother came here to take me back home. The tongue-wagging at the settlement—you can't imagine it... Well," she broke off, "enough history. Have some raspberries. I have to hang up the washing and see to that goat."

3

Natasha had hung out the washing, milked the goat and even put on a new dress. And I had been down to the river for a swim, but there was still no sign of Igor.

"Shall I give a shot from the gun, perhaps?" Natasha kept asking with a worried look.

We were sitting on the steps of the porch looking at the river and the path that went up the tall bank on the other side. It climbed over red, now darkening clay, passed over the top of the hill and disappeared in the young birchwood. According to Natasha, Igor was to appear from there.

The sun was setting. A soft golden light poured over the porch. The air had at last cooled a little. Nature, numb and exhausted by the day's heat, began to come back to life before our very eyes. Plovers were whistling in the gully by the river, a flight of swallows had appeared from somewhere, and, of course, the scourge of the North, mosquitoes came in swarms...

Natasha's keen ear was the first to catch the distant crunching of dry twigs beyond the river. A considerable time passed, however, before the figure of a man in a white shirt tinted pink by the sunset came looming onto the hill. On seeing us, he shouted something, then waved his arms and dashed down the steep cliff at a run. Stones rolled down and a red cloud of dust spurted up on the path.

"The crazy devil!" Natasha said with a sigh and rose. "One day he'll dash himself to death. It's always like this with him. He can't walk the earth like normal people do."

Bushes stirred and began to crash beyond the bath-house, shrouded in a pink cloud of mites: Igor was taking a short cut through the brushwood. The next moment he was hugging me, his face feverish red, all of him smelling of resin...

I had expected him to look different. Bigger, with broader shoulders and younger-looking perhaps. I had not expected those unnaturally white eyebrows on a thin face that seemed to have been desiccated by heat, or that receding hairline. Only his eyes seemed unchanged—piercingly light and, like his father's, with a wild, crazy glint.

"Where've you been tarrying? We looked and looked till our eyes hurt..."

Igor let go of my hands with an embarrassed smile and nodded at his wife, who was coming down the porch steps with a pail of water:

"Look at my own private NKVD! Up for questioning the minute I'm back..." He wiped his sweaty face with the sleeve of his shirt. "I met the foreman from the logging office in the forest. Looking for another lot of pinewood near the river." Igor winced and turned to me. "I'm up against the lot of them, Alexei. They keep looking for loopholes to get into the preserve's zone. Did you see what they've done to our Pinega? Boats used to sail up and down it all summer long. And now they've stripped the poor river naked."

"Come on, Alexei doesn't need your pep-talk. He knows about things. Take off your shirt."

Igor obediently pulled his sweaty, resin-stained shirt over his head. His lean body was tatooed all over. On his chest was an eagle with outspread wings, on his brown arms, among the light hairs, anchors and full-breasted mermaids.

He was obviously feeling awkward in front of me, but nonetheless poked his finger at his chest defiantly and pronounced: "Life's little mementoes!"

Natasha poured the pail of water over him.

When we sat down to supper, the sun was nestling on the top of the hill like on a feather-bed, tired and limp after the day's labours, its gentle slanting rays shedding their lustre meekly on the windowsill. Both hungry, Igor and I were bolting down our food in the matter-of-fact, silent fashion of working men. Not far off cranes called, and Igor remarked after listening a while:

"Out foraging. In this heat birds are only active at night. You can't hear a twitter as you walk through the forest in the day-time."

He paused, then added:

"That's the way we live, Alexei—going to bed when the cranes start calling and rising in the morning when they come back from their feeding."

"Not much of a life," Natasha said. "Cooped up in the woods. We never even get to see a film."

"Never mind the films," Igor retorted. "We have plenty of our own kind of cinema. In winter there's snow up to the windows. And the elks come to the river. They'll stand still, and the dawn will light up their fur... They bring that dawn as a gift to us... I even make hay to feed them up in winter, Alexei. See that rick by the river? We owe a big debt to that animal. How many were killed out of hand..."

Natasha shook her head.

"You're like a child. Have you forgotten all those winter evenings? You know what he once said? 'I'd give anything for a visitor, even if he was the woodgoblin himself! ' "

Igor grunted in embarrassment.

"You used to paint," I said. "Have you dropped it?"

"Dropped it?" Igor gave an enigmatic smile, and his eyes suddenly blazed up. "Why, I want to paint up the whole earth. Did you see my nursery? My cedars? Just you wait, I'll carry out a green revolution. Down the length of the Pinega..."

"There he goes all Anton Isaakovich again," Natasha said indulgently.

Indeed, at that moment Igor was amazingly like his father.

"Why not, Alexei?" he cried, blazing up again, "Look at all this sloth around here! Why can't we plant a cedar forest? Would it hurt us to have cedar nuts? And did you see a garden near any of the houses? Our peasants hate the forest, they do! They have nothing but bread and potatoes, but they can't be bothered to plant raspberries or currants under their windows... They fear any shrub like the fiend. Take logging camps, now. First they cut down every blessed tree, and then they start to build houses. And they sneeze from the dust all summer long. Take Shuiga, for instance. There's just one bush near the school-house for the whole settlement. No, I want to prove by my own example that any kind of berry bush can grow on the Pinega. And even apple- and cherry-trees. The only thing is I live so far away from everybody. I ought to move nearer to other people. To have my nursery in everyone's eye."

"It looks like it, doesn't it?" Natasha said discouragingly. "At loggerheads with all your bosses."

Igor looked at his wife with a guilty smile and wagged his head self-deprecatingly.

"She's right, too, Alexei. I did have a row... Did you see fresh stumps along the road? There was a real invasion last winter. And they tried to break into my territory as well, crossed the stream. Did I kick up a shindy! I grabbed my gun and yelled, 'Stop right now or I'll start shooting! ' I lived in a hut in the woods a whole week, but I didn't let them touch that stretch of forest. Ever since then, Drobyshev's had it in for me. He's a heavy-handed chap. 'So I gave you a job,' he said, 'and now you go putting spikes in my wheels.' And on top of that I had a misunderstanding with the head manager of the Timber Enterprise. But that was a different matter altogether. On account of salmon..."

"That was something you could've let pass," Natasha said, giving her husband a stern look.

Igor said nothing, surprising me with this meekness, so out of character for the Charnasov tribe.

"Just imagine! " Natasha addressed me in indignant tones, soliciting my support. "In autumn they go to war about salmon. They even took a pot shot at him once. They even poisoned Baldy and now we don't have a dog. But no, he won't give in."

"Never mind," Igor said. "I'll get myself another dog. You can't do without a dog in the forest."

The white night was peering into the room. Mosquitoes droned overhead, and I could hear the hare nibbling at a twig behind the stove.

Natasha closed the windows, then opened the door and, waving a scarf, started chasing the mosquitoes out.

Igor and I took a pillow and a sheet and went to get some hay. They decided to make a bed for me in the bath-house where there would be no mosquitoes whining and the hare-boy, as Igor put it, wouldn't bother me.

The hay was stored in the lean-to behind the bath-house. Earlier in the day, when I had gone for a swim, I had noticed some odd iron things lying under that overhang. One of them was a tractor's track some four metres long with spikes welded onto it. Another was a massive pivot with brackets, which looked like a hedgehog. Now, seeing these odd objects again, I asked Igor what they were for.

"Can't you guess?" he said with a dry smile, dropping the pillow and the sheet on the hay. "It's my equipment for planting trees. This," he pointed at the caterpillar, "is for scraping off the moss layer, and that hedgehog is for heavier moss. Not much to boast of, is it?"

I thought of the machinery at the disposal of logging stations. Trailer tractors, bulldozers, powerful log-trucks, winches. And the petrol saws they had these days! Mowing the forest down like grass with a scythe!

"Hmm, you can't do much planting with this technology," said I, looking sadly at the clumsy primitive implements made at the local smithy out of scrap iron.

But Igor would have none of my pity.

"Yes, I can, Alexei, I can plant trees with these tools, too. All you need is the will. You can even do it with your grandfather's hoe. Tomorrow I'll show you a young pine-wood not far across the Shusha that was planted with a hoe."

He threw a wary glance at the porch, where Natasha's dress loomed white.

"Or would you like to see it now?" he asked in hot whispers. "What the hell! Did you come here to sleep?"

Truth to tell, I was pretty tired after my long day, which began with an interminable wait for the plane at the airfield, then there was the flight to the logging station in a jerky, antediluvian one-engine plane, such as are still in use in the provinces, then the bumpy road to Shusha... And, anyway, hadn't I seen enough pinewoods in my life, having grown up in forest country? On the other hand, I was loth to dampen Igor's enthusiasm by refusal. So I only asked:

"Won't Natasha scold us?"

"Natasha?" Igor smiled a broad happy smile. "I have a jewel of a wife. It's only for your benefit that she's playing at being strict with me. We get on just fine..." Igor lowered his voice to a whisper. "You know, Alexei, sometimes I feel afraid... Have I dreamed it all? Why should I deserve this happiness? She's young you know, fourteen years my junior. Imagine being cooped up with me in this wilderness! Sometimes I pack her off to the settlement to visit her mother and brother. Go and stay with your mother for a while, Natasha, I say. At least you can take in a picture or two. But no, she'll be back the next day."

Silence reigned around. Only the water in the Shusha murmured, splashing. Light wisps of fog clung to the brush in the gully. The smell of black currants was strong and pungent.

The door creaked on the porch. Natasha had finished her chores and gone in. Igor, who seemed to have been waiting for that sound, perked up.

"Come on! We are free men now, Alexei! "

4

Wasn't it the height of stupidity to wade across a river in the middle of the night, even if that night was as light as day, take our boots off and then pull them on again, climb uphill—and all for the sake of seeing some pines—a familiar sight since childhood!

Up on the top, in the sweet-smelling birchwood, Igor broke off two twigs and handed me one to keep off the mosquitoes.

The sunset was not yet completely over. On the horizon, I could see the jagged line of treetops. Above that line, here and there towered purple pines—shaggy as fairy-tale bears standing erect on their hind legs.

Dry twigs crunched underfoot. Restless, sleepless aspens babbled incessantly brushing my hot face with their cool leaves. Igor, in a white shirt, wrapped in a grey cloud of mites, swung along through the bushes like a stag. An old experienced stag, making his way surely and effortlessly.

We had not yet entered the forest, but the hot sharp smell of pine resin had already assailed my nostrils. And then the plantation was before us.

We had just emerged from the aspen wood, and before us stretched a vast plain bristling with young pines. In the distance, to the west, the plain crawled up a gently sloping hill, and it seemed that a broad sea-wave was rolling down from up there towards us. The young pines themselves— some bluish-black, others whitish grey, still others golden-brown, with amber drops of resin—made me think of the sea sporting a smart dappled coat.

"Well, isn't this worth seeing?" Igor asked.

And suddenly he put his arms round the nearest growth of little pines—they were planted in clumps—and pushed his face into their prickly manes.

"They're my children! "

"You mean you did all this with a hoe?" I asked, my eye roving over the plain.

"Yes, Alexei, with a hoe—and with this pair of hands! " Igor tossed forward his rather small dark hands clenched into fists. "I came here in winter. Reforestation—they didn't know the word! But I thought—no, brother, you won't catch me twiddling my thumbs. I hadn't come here to watch the forest being destroyed. If they put me in charge of the forest, then I had to take charge of it. The hardest problem was the seeds. But I found a way. I asked the schoolchildren to help—launched a cone-collecting campaign, so to speak. It was fun for them to climb the pines, and it was useful for my purpose..."

Suddenly Igor fell to thinking and gave a heavy sigh.

"Natasha toiled like a navvy, poor girl. That was later, of course, when these little shavers had risen on tip-toe. It was a hot summer, and they started withering—like kittens which get no milk. Well, I grabbed my hoe and started swinging it. And Natasha was with child then. I shouldn't have let her work with a hoe. I should've known better, Alexei. It was courting trouble. The doctors say we aren't going to have any children now..."

The white night was looming above us. Mosquitoes were droning annoyingly in my ears. Igor, white as a ghost, stood with his head bowed, submerged in the prickly dark wave of young pines up to his waist.

"Never mind," he finally brought out in a strangled whisper. "Never mind! " And again embraced the young pines with the same sweeping gesture, broad and generous, like a father's hug. "These are my children. Natasha cried a lot after that, but I told her: don't you cry—some bear children with arms and legs, but we shall bear pine kiddies with roots. They are hardier, the pine children. They'll live for ages. Am I not right, Alexei?" Without waiting

278

for my answer, which he seemed to know beforehand, he gave a loud, rolling guffaw, which sent an echo bouncing over the subdued pine plantation.

It was time to go home. But I felt reluctant to part with the young pinewood. Was it because these adolescent pines were no longer just young trees, but Igor's children?

"Did you ever see a pine sprout?" Igor suddenly asked me.

I smiled. It was a naive question to ask a man who had grown up in forest country.

"No, you didn't! We're all like that. We wander about the forest, stamping down all that grows at its edge, breaking off bird-cherry branches when they're in blossom, but we have no idea how a working tree shoots up from the soil. Would you like to see?" Igor's voice had that tempting and mysterious ring I knew so well from childhood. "It's jolly interesting. Two-week-old pines. What about it?"

5

And again, like two night-birds, we were trudging through the nocturnal twilight. Overhead was the obscure hazy sky, and below were the pines. They were still giving off the heat of the day. The pines caught at our clothes with their resinous needles, bit at our hands.

"Got sharp teeth, haven't they," Igor remarked contentedly. "Like puppies with a temper. They'll grow into sturdy trees, they will."

The white night was working wonders. Time had disappeared. Again we were ten-year-old boys. And again, as in those long past years, Igor was the leader.

A whistle, thin and fragile as a ray of the setting sun, came and went out at once.

"That's a hazel-grouse, Alexei," Igor said, stopping. "A funny time for one to be about."

He speculated for a while about the grouse's strange behaviour, then went on to say:

"I have lots of birds here, Alexei. They like these forests. There are even eagles on Sysolsky Lakes, imagine that! But on the whole, the birds have gotten jittery. And how can they help being jittery when iron thunder roars all over the north country? Take the crane, for instance. It flies here all the way from the south in spring, flapping its wings day and night and thinking it will soon be home and have a good rest. But what does it find—people everywhere, not a nook left to build its nest in peace."

Holding onto the branches of birch-trees, we went down an incline. The ferns were growing thick and tall here, up to the waist, the grass was slightly dewy and there was even a breath of damp coolness coming from below. But the drought had reached here, too, for there was no water in the stream. The pebbly bottom had sprouted fluffy cushions of green moss that felt springy underfoot. Suddenly—it always happens suddenly—a hazel-grouse flushed up to the right of us and flew low over the ground, its wings purring like a propeller, towards a thick growth of firs. We heard it alight on a fir-branch. Igor smiled.

"Watch me have a parley with him." He pursed his dry cracked lips and gave a whistle.

The grouse responded rather half-heartedly.

Igor smiled again.

"Know what he told me? 'I'm not coming, come yourself if you like.' "

"How can you tell what he meant?"

"Honest to God, Alexei. Grouse have only three calls for their friends: 'I'm flying over', 'I'm coming on foot', and 'Come yourself'. Don't you believe me? How else would they find each other, especially during the mating season? The hunters know their language and tune the whistle to give different signals. If he says, 'I'm flying over', don't you move, he'll come. If he gives the signal 'I'm coming on foot', you can wait too. He'll come. It'll take him time, to be sure. How big is the grouse's stride, after all! But if he says 'Come yourself', there's no point in waiting. He won't come however hard you call him. He's got character that bird, for all that he's so small."

Beyond the stream we came into a clear patch again—rotten stumps surrounded by little bushes of wrinkled, dried up strawberries, sparse plants of herb-willow with bumble-bees crawling sleepily over the clusters of flowers, then another stream with alders and birches growing along, and then we were climbing a hill.

Underfoot was the veritable tundra, a carpet of pure-white reindeer moss, and overhead—I raised my eyes—were the crowns of pine-trees.

I gazed at those shaggy-headed giants with trunks so big

you could not get your arms around them and their dark crowns streaked with grey and dishevelled by endless winds, and they seemed to me like the dauntless warriors of the Russian tales, who, by some miracle, had blundered into our own day and age. Or else it seemed to me—white nights put you into a mood for fantasizing—that I had stumbled into an enchanted kingdom and was wandering among those drowsing warriors. Could the tale perhaps have been suggested to our ancestors by white night and the magnificent pines.

Igor's sigh brought me back to reality.

"These pines remember Peter the Great. That's what the whole forest used to be like—magnificent, aren't they? And now this is the only little island of old pines left hereabouts. And the only reason they survived was because they used horses to haul the timber. They couldn't cart it from up here. Today they'd have made short work of it. A tractor can pull the devil himself along..."

Igor gave another sigh.

"I used to feel sort of timid when I entered the forest. I'd see a woodgoblin under every tree. And now the woodgoblins have been crowded into the bogs where they cower, the poor creatures, afraid to poke their noses out... Well, come on. Not much left—less than a mile."

But Igor's mile must have been measured by the proverbial staff of his forefathers which knew no count or reckoning. We walked over cleared patches, in places quite dry, in places covered with lush grass and foamy-white luxurious umbels of caraway plants that looked like small clouds which had settled on the ground. Then we skirted a small lake with water as brown as strong tea, steaming slightly—"The devils are heating their bath," Igor remarked jocularly. We crossed corridors cut into the massif of the forest, trampled the creaking reindeer moss and got entangled in sturdy juniper bushes. And Igor kept up a running commentary all the while—talking about everything that met our gaze, now in subdued whispers (and then, in his loose white shirt, with his dark, sun-burned face with the unnaturally white eyebrows, he looked like an old forest wizard), now in a voice modulating like a gurgling stream.

He told me about firs and their amazing vulnerability ("You can kill a ten-metre tree with a blow of an axe"), about the carpet of needles underfoot ("Things are arranged very wisely in the forest, Alexei. First it provides itself with a supply of nutrients and only then does it go to sleep for the winter"). He complained of the cheeky birches—and I was quite surprised to discover he had an axe to grind with the birch ("A weed, that's what it is; the birch and the aspen are the first to settle on cleared patches"), and then, when we flushed a wood-grouse, he told me a kind of yarn about that ancient bird.

I watched Igor, recalled his 'prison-camp universities", and it occurred to me that I knew nothing about this man.

He was strong and indefatigable in the true Charnasov tradition, and he was as wild and expansive a dreamer as his father had been ("I'll carry out a green revolution!"), but whence this amazing love and compassion, that Russian compassion for all living things? No, his father, ruthlessly unbending, thinking in terms of world revolution, did not have this vulnerability. Was it a mark of Igor's job as a forester?

The morning dawn was stealing over the crowns of pine-trees like a red fox. A light breeze fluttered like a sigh. Or was it the rustle of the white night, as it retreated into the depth of the thickets?

6

"We're here," Igor said.

I peered ahead, but could see nothing but an endless stretch of burnt forest cluttered chaotically with snags and branches. Red gleams of dawn were playing on their charred cracked bark, and it made you feel the fire was still smoldering.

Another puzzle?

Igor laughed contentedly. His lean sunburnt face with white eyebrows gleamed pink, like a pine trunk.

"Don't look ahead! Look down in the furrows."

Indeed, the earth was cut with sandy furrows. There were a lot of them. Like yellow snakes they were crawling all over the charred earth.

I bent to the nearest furrow. There were torn roots poking out of the edges, tracks of a tractor, then I discerned a tiny bunch of smoky-grey grass, then another and a third... They were no more than an inch in height. The tiny bunches merged and flowed in a scanty trickle glistening with a spark here and there, flowing timidly down the sandy bottom of the furrow.

It was an unusual little trickle. It smelled of resin. Was this the way a pinewood started?

Igor told me to pull out a shoot—they grew too densely anyway, he'd have to thin them out.

Oho! The grass was prickly and stuck to the fingers, while its long root had the pine's strength and tenacity.

What a strange feeling it was—to hold a tree in the cup of your hand, root and all.

I stood bent over this baby-forest, breathing in its primordial smell and fancied I was witnessing the birth of the world at dawn...

Igor laid a hand on my shoulder gently.

"This was done by a tractor. Sanka Ryakhin and I sowed them here exactly a month ago. That lad did an honest job of work. But the other day I asked him when we met in the settlement: 'Well, Sanya, shall we do some more of that work to atone for old sins?" 'No, Igor,' he said. 'I like sowing forest. It's fine work, but I won't do it any more.' You see, Alexei, it's all a question of pay. He has a family, kids, and they pay him for this work at the standard rate—and not a kopeck more. There's no getting round it. Why is that so? Those who fell trees get all kinds of premiums and bonuses, but those who sow the forest must do it out of a sense of duty alone. Why is that so?"

We were walking along a narrow, well-trodden path. The forest resounded with chirping, warbling and whistling—the birds were in a hurry to get the day's work done before heat set in.

"They're my helpers," Igor said, when we heard the tap-tapping of wood-peckers. "But there aren't enough of them these days. I should try and do something to increase the wood-pecker population. You haven't read anything about it by any chance, have you?"

Then he started complaining about the forester's lot. Not about his personal troubles. They didn't need much, Natasha and he. He wouldn't leave the forest if they promised him heaps of gold. But how could a forester with a large family live off the meagre wages? So only invalids and all kind of riff-raff would take the job. And even if the man was a sound one, he still couldn't accomplish much because his main concern in summer would be to lay in a stock of hay for his cow. And the amount of work a forester is expected to do! Guard the forest, remove the rot, clear up the cuttings... And what about seed purveyance? The devil's own work. You have to pull every cone to pieces with your fingers. And what about digging ditches along the roads to prevent forest fires?

Igor shook his head.

"I just can't understand it. We have forest fires every year. And this summer all of Northern Russia is blazing away. They say you can't breathe for the smoke in Arkhangelsk. Are we out to heat outer space or what? How much do these fires cost the state? The lumberjacks remain idle for weeks. The collective farmers have to drop their own work to fight the fires! And for some reason it doesn't occur to the higher-ups to do the very simplest thing—increase the number of forest-rangers. Do you know how large the area I'm responsible for is? Two hundred and forty thousand hectares! Why, I can't hope to make the rounds of this kingdom of mine in a year. A year! I'll die before I've been to every division. We foresters have been crying and pleading for an increase in the number of forest-rangers! There'll be fewer fires! But no, nothing doing. We toss billions of rubles into fighting fires, but we begrudge the wages for a few extra forest-rangers. Why is that so, Alexei? I've written to the district, and to the region, and to Moscow, too. Where else can I write?"

7

The road back proved to be straight and short. It then dawned on me that Igor had been deliberately meandering to show me the forest. Nor did he deny it.

"Now you've completed your pinewood education," he said with a grin when we emerged from the forest and sighted Shusha.

It was a wonder. The man had spent the entire day on his feet and followed it up with that nocturnal ramble. He had had no sleep, but he did not look any worse for it. He was as fresh and brisk as the forest itself in the morning. The only sign of fatigue I could discern was the more pronounced wrinkles on his narrow face and on his sinewy neck sunburnt almost to the colour of charcoal.

We met the sunrise sitting under a spreading branchy

pine-tree—a huge monster that had grown unimpeded in an open place. Old cones that were lying in heaps in the hollows between the stone-hard roots, glowed purple in the crimson light.

"I owe my life to the pine, Alexei, in a manner of speaking," Igor began. "The forest made a man of me. I'm not going to tell you about how I got into the clink. I was young and foolish... You're an educated man, Alexei, you write books. But can you explain what was the matter with me, how my mind became all twisted? Why wouldn't I stay at home? All my pals were doing something useful—you were studying, the others were working. But I just felt the pull of the open spaces. Like the crane is drawn into the sky. Why was that? And what d'you think—I regarded myself as a hero—no less. But when the war began, it knocked the foolishness out of me. I wept blood. My brothers were fighting, my father was dying of cancer, and I was behind barbed wire. I worked, of course, I declared war on the hardened layabouts, but still I was in a prison camp. I, the son of Anton Charnasov, fighting the war from prison! "

Igor cracked his interlocked fingers.

"Today, when a man is released from prison, everybody wants to help him, they'll give him a job, anything. They beg him to work honestly. But when I was let out after the war, I was up against the wall. I honestly wanted to work, to live—I had not lived at all, I was put behind bars when I was only seventeen—but everybody shied away from me as if I were a leper. I worked like hell, setting records in my navvy job—we were building a road then, my shirt was never dry and all of me was salty grey, but whenever anything happened in the settlement—if something was stolen or just got lost, it was all laid at my door. Everybody gave me queer looks. Igor was the convict. Can a man bear it, Alexei?

"It was only in the forest that I felt as good as the others. Nobody asked me about my past. A bird will perch on a branch nearby. The hard-working pine pumps resin day and night. It has no time for foolishness. It is the prop of our whole planet..."

I could not refrain from smiling at Igor's unexpected and sweeping generalisation, though I knew my smile was out of place and might offend him.

"But it is, Alexei! Of course, it is. Just you stay and live here until winter-time, and then you'll see for yourself. The icy winds will start blowing—from the Arctic, from the Pole itself—and who stands in their way, who protects the country? The pine. If it weren't for the pine, those winds would reach all the way to the Black Sea, and there'd be a draft sweeping all across Russia. And in summer when there's a drought and everything around dries up? Even the birches go weak with the heat. But look at the pine—it's a wonder. It gasps, it pours its resinous sweat, but it goes on with the job in hand. It's so unfair! We sing songs about the birch, we recall the bird-cherry at every step. But what are they compared to the pine? Mere hangers-on! They can only exist because there are pine-trees in the world..."

"Aren't you being a bit unfair?" I objected, taking offence on account of all the other trees.

"Oh, I love them all, Alexei! After a stretch in prison, I've gotten soft. I pity all living things. But still, compared to the pine... They're no match for it. They haven't its character! Take the fir, for instance. It's a useful tree, there's no denying it. But why must it be so sly? It's a sly one, that tree. I can see right through it. It only lives in marshland. Try and get at it! You have to lay a railway across those marshes, or pave the way with logs. 'I'd rather rot than let Man get at me! ' That's the kind of tree it is! And when the weather is wet, I just can't bear to look at it. Life is dull enough as it is, and there's the fir weeping its eyes out... And the aspen gets on my nerves. Why the hell does it have to tremble all the time? It's too concerned with itself..."

A cone from last year dropped at our feet. We both raised our eyes. Above was a tangle of mighty interlaced branches, and in a gap between them, like in a well, we could see a patch of blue sky lit by the sun.

"There's strength for you, Alexei! You can't bend it! " Igor whispered with admiration. "I like to listen to the humming of the pines. It is quite different from the fir. That one in bad weather wails like a dog when somebody has died in the house. But the pine... Its roots are deep in the earth, its head is way up in outer space, and when it starts a song, the earth trembles. That's the kind of tree a pine is, Alexei. We must honour it. For its faithful service. For always being in the front ranks. For never stopping to dodges. For never expecting a reward! "

The sun was blazing hot when we returned to Shusha. There was the acrid smell of smoke in the air—there were fires about Shusha.

Igor decided not to waken Natasha and went with me to the bath-house. He fell asleep the moment his cheek touched the pillow. His was the sound sleep of a working man. But I lay awake for a long time, my eyes open, thinking about my childhood pal, and his father, and about the pines...

1962

Why the Horses Weep

Each time I came down the village hill to the meadow, it was like falling back again and again into distant childhood—into a world of scented grass, dragon-flies and butterflies and, of course, horses which would graze each tethered to its own stake.

I often took bread with me to feed the horses, but even if I had no bread, I would stop by them, patting them affectionately on the back and neck, encouraging them with a kind word; I would rub their velvety lips and for a long time afterwards, if not for the whole day, I would feel on my palm the strong, unmistakable smell of horse.

The horses aroused in me the most complex, contradictory feelings.

They stirred and delighted my peasant heart, adding a particular—equine—beauty to the empty meadow with its sparse hummocks and clumps of osiers. I could watch these kind, intelligent animals for hours, listening to their monotonous munching interrupted from time to time by a snort of displeasure or short hiccup—as they came upon a dusty or indigestible blade of grass.

But most often it was pity I felt for the horses and even a sort of unaccountable guilt.

Mikolka, the stable-man, was perpetually drunk; sometimes he wouldn't show up for a whole day and night and the turf—let alone grass—round the stake would be chewed down and trodden into mud. They were constantly thirsty, aching for water, eaten alive by midges—and in the peace of evening a grey cloud, swarms of mosquitoes and gnats, would hover over them.

There is no denying it—they had a tough life, poor devils. I therefore did what I could to lighten their load. And I was not the only one. Rare was the woman, of whatever age who, finding herself in the meadow, would walk past them unmoved.

But this time I didn't walk—I ran to the horses, for whom should I see among them but my beloved Klara or just plain Ginger, as I used to call her in the good old days, when there were none of them Thunders, Ideas, Victories, Stars, and we had Darkies and Blackies and Toffees and Gingers—ordinary horses with ordinary horses' names.

Ginger had the same points and blood as the rest of the mares and geldings. She came of the Mezen breed, horses of medium-size, not much to look at, but hardy and even-tempered, well suited to the tough conditions of the North. And Ginger had had just as rough a time of it as her friends. At four her back was covered with saddle sores, she had a dropped belly and even the veins in her groin had begun to swell.

For all that Ginger stood out from among her fellow horses.

Some of them were unbearable to look at. Broken, unkempt, with matted, moth-eaten coats that were beyond moulting, suppurating eyes and a sort of dull submissiveness and doom in their gaze and in the whole of their bent, dejected figures.

But not Ginger. Ginger was a clean mare and what is more she had managed to retain the high spirits and strong-headedness of her youth.

Usually when she saw me coming down the hill, she would straighten up, poised to attention, neighing sonorously and sometimes, in so far as rope allowed, she would trot round the stake i.e., she would perform what I called her welcoming circle of joy.

Today Ginger showed not the slightest sign of life at my approach. She stood by her stake, as only horses can stand, motionless, dead to the world, and in no way did she differ from the rest of the mares and geldings.

"What's up with her?" I wondered with alarm. "Is she ill? Has she forgotten me?" (Ginger had spent the past two weeks in a distant hayfield.)

Still on the move, I began to break off a big chunk of bread—it was thus, by feeding her, that our friendship had started, but now Ginger totally disconcerted me: she turned away her head.

"Ginger, Ginger... It is me ... me..."

Grabbing her thick, grey-flecked forelock, which three weeks ago I had clipped myself—it completely blocked her eyes—I pulled her head towards me. And what should I see, but tears. Big, horse's tears, the size of a broad bean.

"Ginger, Ginger, what's the matter?"

Ginger continued to weep in silence.

"OK, OK, I can see you're in trouble. Tell me what's wrong?"

"We had an argument..."

"Who's we?"

"Us, the horses."

"You had an argument?" I was startled. "What about?"

"About the life of horses. I told them that there had been times when we horses were loved and cared for above all else on earth, but they made fun of me, mocked me..." here Ginger again burst into tears.

I had a hard time calming her down. And this is what she eventually told me.

In the distant hayfield, from which she had only just returned, Ginger had made the acquaintance of a certain old mare. The two of them had been harnessed to the hay-mower. When they had had just about as much as they could take (and the work there was back-breaking) the old mare would cheer Ginger up by singing to her.

"In all my life I never heard anything like it," said Ginger. "From those songs I learnt that there were times when we horses were known as bread-winners: we were cared for, cherished, decked out in ribbons. As I listened to the songs I forgot about the heat, the gad-flies and the blows of the strap with which the evil-tempered driver continually flogged us. And I found it easier, much easier—I really did—to pull the heavy mower. I asked Joy—for that was the old mare's name—whether perhaps she hadn't invented these glorious songs about the carefree life of the horse? But she assured me that all this was the absolute truth, that these songs had been sung to her by her own mother, when she was a foal. And her mother had heard them from Ginger's grandmother. And thus these songs about the happy days of the horse had been handed down in their family from generation to generation.

"And so," said Ginger, finishing her story, "this morning as soon as we were turned out into the meadow, I began to sing the old mare's songs to my mates, but with one voice they all shouted at me: That is all lies, damn lies! Shut up! Stop torturing us. It is bad enough as it is."

Hopefully, imploringly, Ginger lifted towards me her huge, sad eyes, still damp with tears. In their violent depths

I suddenly saw myself—a small, diminutive man.

"Tell me... You are a man, you know everything, you belong to those who spend all their life ordering us about... Tell me, were there such times when we horses lived well? The old mare wasn't lying to me, was she? She wasn't deceiving me?"

Unable to bear Ginger's direct, inquiring gaze, I turned away. And now it seemed to me that from all sides I was being watched by the big, probing eyes of the horses. Could it be that what Ginger had asked me was of interest to them too? In any case, the usual sound of munching that was always to be heard in the meadow had stopped.

I have no idea how long this silent ordeal in the pasture under the hill lasted—perhaps one minute, perhaps ten, perhaps an hour. I broke out in sweat from head to foot.

It was all true, absolutely true, what the old mare had told them—she hadn't been lying. There had been such times, and not so very long ago, within my memory, when one lived and breathed for one's horse, when one fed her the tastiest morsel, or even the last chunk of bread: we would make do somehow to last out on an empty belly till morning. We were used to it. And in the evenings, when the old girl, exhausted after a day's work, turned into the home lane, the whole family, young and old, would run out to meet her: they would unharness and tend to her, lead her to the watertrough, comb her, rub her down! And many was the time during the night that the master would get up to visit his treasure!

Yes, treasure—no more, no less. The main support and hope of peasant life, for without a horse a peasant was stuck: he could go neither to the field, nor to the forest. Nor could he live it up in the proper way.

In the fifty years that I've trodden the wide world, I've seen more than a few miracles, both at home and overseas, but mark my words, there is nothing to touch the Russian Shrove-tide sleigh-rides.

Everything was transformed as in a fairy-tale. The menfolk: young and middle-aged were transformed—cutting a dashing figure as they drove light painted sleighs with iron runners. So were the horses. Gee-up my beauties, faster my dearies! Don't let us down! Give a bit of fun to a stalwart heart. Send a blizzard and of snow-sparks flying down the street!

And the horses did just this. The bright-coloured patterns on the shaft-bows danced rainbows in the crisp winter air, the burnished copper harnesses shimmered with a July heat, and the bells, oh the bells—balm to a Russian soul...

A peasant lad's first toy was a wooden horse. A horse would gaze down at the child from the roof of his father's home. His mother would sing and tell him stories about Sivka-Burka, and as a grown man he would carve a horse on a distaff for his beloved. The horse was worshipped—I don't remember a single iconcase in our village without an icon of St. George on his horse. And a horse-shoe—symbolizing for the peasant long-sought-after happiness—would greet one from nearly every porch. The horse was all, all came from the horse: the whole of peasant life from birth to death...

It is hardly surprising, therefore, that it was on account of the horse that passions flared most turbulently in the first of collectivization years!

Matters were thrashed out at the stables which hummed with activity, meetings from morning to night. The black horse's withers were covered with sores, the bay hadn't been watered in time, the chestnut had been overloaded, the roan driven too fast ... and fists and tempers would fly.

Not to talk of the owners of the horses, the muzhiks, who had lived all their life off their horse!

On the eve of the war, even I, severed from my roots, a student at university, was unable to walk calmly past my Karko. At one time like the sun, he had brought light into the life of our family of many children, orphaned at a tender age. Nor did the war erase the memory of my childhood horse.

I remember coming back to my village in forty-seven. Hunger, destruction, desolation, every home sobbing for someone who had failed to return. The very first horse I saw brought Karko to my mind.

"Your Karko is no more," said the old stable-man. "He gave up the ghost on the forest front. Did you think only human beings fought in the war? Not a bit of it. Horses also played their part in forging victory, and how..."

Karko, as I was later to learn, lost his life on Victory Day itself. Such an occasion had to be celebrated. But how? With what? It was decided to sacrifice the oldest, most emaciated horse around. To cut it short, when Karko returned from the forest pulling his usual load, they threw down on him some of the heaviest loop from the top of the wood pile. Pushkin's Prince Oleg, it would seem, lives on in each of us, and about three years ago, when I happened to be in Rosokhi, where timber was procured during the war, I tried to find the remains of my horse.

The timber station had long since disappeared. The sheds, roughly put together by old men and boys, had fallen down and were overgrown with nettles and on the sawing-floor where the ground had been well manured by rotting wood chips and bark, thick clumps of pink willow-herb had grown up.

I wandered round the willow-herb, in one or two places I even cut a path through it, but I found no trace of bones...

...Ginger was still watching me. And so were the other horses. It seemed as if every inch of space in the meadow under the hill was filled with horses' eyes. All of them, those that were alive and tethered and those long gone—the whole horse kingdom, both the living and the dead, was questioning me.

Suddenly affecting an air of reckless boldness, I exclaimed:

"Come on now, that's enough moping! Stop cramming your heads with old wives' tales. You had better chew bread while it is there for the chewing."

After which, avoiding Ginger's gaze, I hurriedly threw onto the grass, close to her extended muzzle, the piece of bread I had long prepared for her; quickly distributing bread among the other horses, and with the same air of bold recklessness, I raised my hand in a theatrical gesture:

"So long! Either way we won't be able to get to the root of all this without a glass or two." ...And thrusting my hands deep into the pockets of my stylish jeans, with a quick, nonchalant walk I made off towards the river.

What answer, after all, could I have given those poor wretches?

Tell them that the old mare hadn't invented a thing, that horses had known happy days?

I crossed the dried-up lake and came out onto the old boundary strip, a relic of pre-kolkhoz days, which always delighted me by its lush, chaotic growth of grasses.

But now I saw nothing.

My whole being, all my powers of hearing, were concentrated on the horses. I waited with every single nerve in my body for them to start chewing the bread, for the usual champing as they clipped the grass in the meadow.

Not the slightest sound was to be heard.

I suddenly realised I had done something terrible, irreparable: I had deceived Ginger, I had deceived all those unhappy nags and between Ginger and myself there would never be the same degree of sincerity and trust that had existed up to now.

Anguish, heavy equine anguish overcame me, bowed me to the ground. And it wasn't long before I, too, felt myself to be some sort of absurd, obsolete being belonging to the same equine breed...

1973

Very Russian

Oh those bear hunts! Abybody with sense would know beforehand that it would simply end all over again with empty hands and tired legs. Yet—yet—once you hear about a bear, where are all your sensible resolutions?

It began this way. I found myself in the district club, and there in the manager's office a shaggy skin was proudly displayed on the floor before his table. Who had killed the bear? Where? Why, he himself, Kapshin. In a field of oats.

In the oats? In a field? I knew how hunters surround a bear in its den, I knew how they set traps of various kinds, and twice I had waited by the torn carcase of a cow on dark autumn nights. But oats? No, although I'd grown up around the Arctic Circle that was a new variety of bear hunt for me.

We got a ride from town and soon our two became three, when we were joined by Zakhar Vodennikov, chairman of a manufacturing cooperative. Plenty of such executives leave town at the weekend, on bicycles, motorcycles and lorries, carrying baskets and buckets, all of them making for the forests to lay in free provisions for the winter. Then when we came to Shiryayevo (after that we would journey on "shanks' ponies"), one more wished to join our company, a retired teacher called Yevlampy Yegorovich with whom we stopped overnight, and Kapshin, good soul, welcomed him in, too. The more the merrier.

So off we set for the Kornei clearing, the whole troop of us—a troop of invalids to be exact, because Yevlampy Yegorovich had his old man's stick, Zakhar Vodennikov was short-winded and his meaty neck was soon hot enough to light a match, while I had my own troubles, an old wound spoke up and I kept slipping in the mud. Only Kapshin was robust, but he, as I soon discovered, was no real hunter. His voice rang through the forest as he displayed his talents, imitating now a hare, now a fox or owl, and if a hazel-grouse rose or a jay slipped under a fir he grabbed his gun and banged away with both barrels.

But I became still more depressed when we came to the clearing itself. I had visualised a tiny little field of oats, a kind of yellow patch jostled on all sides by the thick firs. Instead, I saw a great field stretching out into the distance. A fence with a sturdy gate. Hawks floating in the sky. And what was that in the distance, behind those bushes? It looked uncommonly like a roof. Could it possibly be a house?

"Yes, it's a house," said Kapshin calmly. "There were nineteen here once."

I stared. Were we going on a bear hunt in a village?

"Why, don't you believe there can. be bears here?"

Kapshin, striding purposefully ahead, led us along the edge of the oat field, thickly overgrown with birch saplings.

"Well? What would you say that is?"

The oats were certainly crushed and trampled at the edge, that was a fact. But why did it have to be a bear? There were no clear tracks on the sandy soil.

"All right. Let's go on."

We went a little farther by the forest edge and then Kapshin halted, pointing silently downwards.

A huge pile of black dung!

Yes, there could no longer be any doubt, a bear had been here and fairly recently, not more than two or three days ago, to judge by the tiny flies covering the dung.

The atmosphere changed at once. This was serious. We held a brief council, right there by the dung heap. The best thing, of course, would be to take up our position in the far corner where the oat field sloped down to damp fir woods. That was where the beast was most likely to emerge and on our side it was dry, with enough birch scrub for cover. But time was short, the sun was reaching out for the tree tops. Besides, in the damp corner, according to Kapshin, there would certainly be other hunters. There had been some last Saturday, he had heard in Shiryayevo. So we decided to stop where we were.

Without loss of time we loaded up and anointed ourselves with mosquito repellent; heaven forbid that you stir a finger while waiting in a blind.

2

A hunter without faith is no hunter; perhaps that is why all hunters intoxicate themselves with "hunter's yarns". I, too, wanted to believe in success.

Here I was, perched in a birch on a bit of board fastened to a broken-off branch with rusty wire, a "blind" fixed up by some previous carefree hunter—sitting there with my double-bore, cocked, on my knee; beneath me lay the oats, so appetising for a bear, gilded by the evening sunshine; around me was primeval silence, mosquitoes, and wisps of mist hanging round the birch thicket. And why shouldn't a bear, I thought, emerge quietly under the excellent cover of those wisps of mist? One had come last year to meet Kapshin's slug. And when I returned to Leningrad there would be a shaggy skin for my study, just like Kapshin's.

But then I looked at the distant scrub, at the shingled roof stained rosy by the sunset, and a sense of strangeness came over me; everything seemed slightly unreal, dream-like—that oat field, the wisps of pinkish mist, Yevlampy Yegorovich half concealed like an old owl in dark spreading fir, and myself a forest goblin, surrounded by a cloud of mosquitoes.

A magpie scolded somewhere nearby on my left, some small bird sent down a few dry leaves as it flew away, and again there was silence.

The mist was rolling up. The roof lost its glow and mist gathered round it, thick and white—as though people in the village were heating their bath-houses.

A fancy came to me; in a moment some goodman over there, seeing me, would shout raucously over the field, "Come down, you loon, before you set us all a-laughing! "

But nobody shouted. Everything was silent. Dead. The mist hung over the chilly field and from the evening sky the first solitary star looked down.

3

I don't know whether any bear came seeking oats that night; in any case we could not have shot him. The mist thickened into a fog so dense and high that we nearly lost our way seeking the house. We found it only thanks to Yevlampy Yegorovich; he knew these parts from childhood and seemed to smell out the way. Foresighted Zakhar Vodennikov had some dry birch bark (each contributed something!) and we felt around in the darkness until we discovered some firewood.

When the fire blazed up the first thing I saw was a wet rowan with the lower branches broken off and pendant bunches of red berries; the flames became brighter and log walls appeared behind the rowan. There were no window frames, only gaping black holes.

On our left beyond the grassy lane was another house, likewise with gaping holes for windows and likewise swathed in thick fog.

Kapshin, thoughtfully crunching rusks, looked at the black August sky.

"Yes, only two houses now—what's left of them. There used to be a whole village here, nineteen families. Soon these'll be gone, too. Last spring hunters burned a house. Wanted to warm themselves from it, the bastards."

"But the owners?"

"Them? Scattered, all over the place. Some went to the lumbering, it's not far from here, about six kilometres, others wanted to try somewhere farther, and some came to Shiryayevo. Yevlampy Yegorovich, how many came your way?"

The old teacher thought a moment.

"Five."

"There you are! They didn't want to move over to a big village. And why? Well, what did they have here? No club. No cinema. And the children had to go nine kilometres to school." Kapshin held out his damp quilted jacket to the fire (we were all doing the same) and shook his head. "And you know, though they lived here in the forest, sort of isolated, they were a decent set of folks, and understood when things had to be done. I was working in the district committee then. Say, it was time for the fixed-price grain deliveries—no trouble with them at all. If it was necessary, all right. Anyway, they were well off. Bathed in cream, as the saying goes."

"Folks used to call them creamers," Yevlampy Yegorovich added. "If they were short of waggon grease they'd use soured cream. Better for the axles. Grandad Kornei was good at thinking up things. He put up the first cottage here, made in his own style. The windows were small, right under the roof."

"Is that so?" Kapshin marvelled. "So you can remember the first house, Yevlampy Yegorovich? I thought this hamlet was a hundred years old, at the very least."

"No, less," said the old teacher. "It's all happened in my time. I remember Kornei's first house, I remember it very well. Mother and I had gone berrying, but she wasn't very good at finding her way about in the forest and we got lost. We kept on walking and walking, I was crying, I was just a child, and Mother was crying, we'd been walking a long time. And then suddenly we saw a house. A new one. And smoke coming from the chimney. 'Thank God,' said Mother. 'Now we shall be all right, this is Kornei's place, I can see it now.' " Yevlampy Yegorovich'a old eyes looked slowly round as though searching for the spot where Kornei's house had stood. He was silent for a moment. "Yes, it was an original sort of house. The logs were very thick, you'd hardly get your arms round them, and the windows tiny, like in a bath-house. I remember how I asked Mother why they were so small. 'It's because they need less glass,' she told me. 'Kornei's just starting, every kopek counts. And besides, there'll be less mosquitoes getting in.' It was terrible, the misquitoes here. A goblin kingdom. And a few minutes later, not far from the house, we could see Kornei with his sons grubbing out tree-stumps."

"Was he a strong old man?"

"Very. He wasn't so tall, about medium height. Less, if anything. But strong as a bear. He got all this done with his own hands." Yevlampy Yegorovich swept his hand round in a semi-circle. "There were no bulldozers in those days. Though it's true, he had the right kind of family. Seven children and all boys. Kornei himself was dark but the boys took after their mother, every one of them fair-headed and tall."

"That's right," said Kapshin, smiling. "Everyone in the place was fair-haired. I remember, I used to come here."

"Not quite everyone," Yevlampy Yegorovich amended. "After Kornei brought in two men from neighbouring villages they got another strain. Quite different."

"Well, all right," Kapshin quickly interrupted, afraid that the old man with his usual love of detail would diverge onto the topic of these two men. "What about Kornei, how did he welcome you?"

"He did little welcoming, busy as he was grubbing out stumps with his sons—what time had he for us? He just came up, greeted Mother and got down straight away to business. 'Now look, Agrafena,' he said, 'I want your Tonya for my Pyotr's wife.' And Tonya, that's my sister, was barely fifteen, what age was she to wed? 'That's all right,' he said, 'I can wait a year.' 'Nay,' said Mother, 'you need a good worker and my Tonya's weakly. I won't give you my daughter to torment. She's my only girl.' 'You're right there, Agrafena, it isn't for an easy life I'm taking your Tonya. You can see how much work there is here. I need one who's a woman in front and a horse behind.' Well I remember those words of his. 'And one that'll bear us a son every year. Now, I've seen your Tonya at work. She'll do. So get ready. Come autumn, we'll be there to fetch her.' "

"What a gritty devil! " cried Kapshin in unfeigned admiration. "He actually said that, right out?"

"Yes, his very words. But that summer my uncle took Tonya off to Vologda, got her a job as servant girl and saved her that way. If it hadn't been for uncle I'd have found myself related to Kornei Ivanovich, because he always stood by his word. Once he'd said a girl would do for his family it was settled. He'd come to the village and make his proposals all in due form. If the girl was willing —good. If not, he'd just take her, unwilling. He'd swoop down on the village with his woodsy gang, snatch the girl, into the sledge or cart with her and that would be that. The main thing for him was to get a good look round and pick a girl to suit him. He'd go thirty or forty versts if necessary. There was one time the men nearly killed him for these goings-on."

"No—really?" cried Kapshin.

"Sure thing. It was a church holiday and we kids were running about the street when there was a terrific hullabaloo—the forest men had carried off Prokhor Kuzmich's Manka. And you know how folks were on a holiday. They'd all been drinking and were ready for trouble. So they grabbed up axes and stakes and off they trooped to the hamlet. But the men there weren't asleep, either, they stood like a wall, grim and bearded, with their own axes. Well, Kornei Ivanovich found a way of settling. He fired his gun and then went to the villagers wearing his medal. The one he'd been given for clearing the forest. 'Are you out of your wits?' he said. 'Come to your senses. I'm making Russia,' he said, 'making forest into good land. And you come to war with

302

me. Go back for the love of God, and keep from death and killing.' Well, Prokhor Kuzmich, Manka's father, snuffled a bit and had second thoughts. The girls's good name would be blown upon in any case. Too late to mend things now, he should have acted sooner. Kornei had given him warning."

"M'yes," said Kapshin thoughtfully. "That was a character. 'Making Russia.' And there was a good deal in what he said. Russia didn't plough itself up. Somebody cleared away the forests and thickets. They say in the old days it wasn't only here in the North, round Kiev way too there was thick forest. It was there Ilya Muromets caught Bandit Nightingale. Isn't that right, Yevlampy Yegorovich?"

Yevlampy Yegorovich nodded silently, rubbing his old man's hands with a dry sound before the fire. Zakhar Vodennikov, who had been listening with mouth half-open (he was rather hard of hearing), gave a deep sigh, got out a pack of cigarettes but then changed his mind.

Kapshin put a fresh piece of wood on the fire, a door post with a metal hasp. Beside the hasp was a small hollow made by the pressure of fingers over the years.

I looked at the house with the rowan. There was no roof. No outer door, no entry passage. A block of wood lay before the threshold to serve as a step.

Suddenly I heard, "But in 'thirty I dispossessed Kornei as a kulak."

Kapshin, sitting beside me on a log, started and stared at Zakhar Vodennikov.

"Yes, we had a good bit of bother at that time with that family," he continued. "The great sticking point was what paragraph of law to sling at him. The old man kept harping on that. 'First prove that I've exploited anyone,' he said. He was a shrewd old chap."

Yevlampy Yegorovich began getting to his feet.

"Isn't it time we turned in? What do you say, fellows?"

We too rose.

Before leaving the fire Zakhar Vodennikov took out some plugs of cotton wool and plugged his ears.

"It's from constantly being on the move," he explained, catching my eye. "It's undermined my health. Ever since then, since 'thirty, I've been in command posts, in the front line so to speak."

303

4

However, it was a long time before we slept that night. No sooner had we settled down on the floor near the entry than voices sounded outside under the window aperture.

"Hunters," said Kapshin. "They're the ones who were in that damp corner. I told you, remember?"

There was a loud tramping of boots in the entry and again the door which we had hardly managed to close rasped open.

"Ah, here are the bastards who spoiled our hunting," cried one merrily, shining the light of a match on us.

"Did a bear come?" asked Kapshin.

"Sure did. Quite close to me. But there was no way of getting at him. The brute came from the back."

"Oh, drop it, Pashka. Nobody believes you, anyway."

"Don't then. But I'll get him. Starve him out. He didn't have a feed today, he didn't have one yesterday, tomorrow he'll come out."

"You're a blockhead, Pashka. A bear starving in the forest! "

"Well, you'll see! "

Feeling their way about, the hunters stood their guns in the corner by the stove and found places to lie down beside us on the floor with a great rustling of hey.

"Wouldn't hurt to block the windows with something. At least, by our heads. It'll blow in cold in the early morning," cannily remarked one, the one who had cut Pasha short, judging by the voice.

"Let Ivan do it, I can't feel my way round."

Somebody, probably the Ivan referred to, went out; floorboards creaked outside the door and then all was silent.

"Easy for him, in his own house," said Pashka. "No need for any flashlight, he sees in the dark like a bat."

Kapshin sat up, jostling me.

"Who's that Ivan of yours? Not one of Kornei's lot?"

"Yes, Kornei's grandson."

"So that's it. Ivan Martemyanovich?"

"Something like that. But who are you? How d'you come to know of him?"

"Sure I do," said Kapshin, excited. "I used to visit him here collecting for the state loan. And he shoed my horse."

"He still works a smithy."

"Where? At the lumber camp?"

"Yes. He'll just sleep here and then go to work."

"So that's it," said Kapshin thoughtfully. "The lumber camp. And his brothers Miron and Mikhei—they're alive?"

"No. Both dead."

Ivan returned, having closed both side windows with shutters. I very much wanted to get a look at this man but felt awkward about lighting a match. Hay rustled in the dark corner. Heavy boots thudded on the floor. There was a sigh. Then silence. Ivan had lain down.

"Well, how does it feel on your parents' feather bed? Is it soft?"

"Shut up, Pashka! At your old game again. Badgering a fellow. I'd like to see how you'd feel in his place. If it was your house."

Pashka laughed, carefree. "I've never had a house of my own. And never will. Think I'm a fool? I've my two hands and my feet, I'll always find a place to live."

"You're an ass, Pashka! A fool! At thirty it's time to use your wits a bit."

"And don't I use them? There he lies, sighing. Who forced him to make off to the lumber camp? Me? He didn't move over to Shiryayevo. Well? And why the devil didn't he?"

"But just reckon up what it would mean," said a husky voice. I realised this was Ivan. "Nine versts there and nine back. You can't take the fields with you."

"Reckoning, calculation. It's all calculation with you. Can't you live without calculating?"

Then an argument started, the real Russian style without beginning or end. Of course they forgot all about Ivan. It was a large-scale argument, the scale of all Russia.

Kapshin argued with unexpected heat that remote little villages like this one of old Kornei's were doomed by history. As on the previous evening, he stressed cultural amenities. What was there in such a village for a person in the cosmic age? And what about the young folks? Would the youth of today consent to a primitive life such as old Kornei and his sons lived?

Ivan's sober-minded pal disagreed. Of course you had to have culture. That was essential. But what about the land? How many tiny villages like this one were being abandoned over all of Russia?

They went on for a long time. They suggested this and that but without untangling the knot.

Pashka, bored with the talk, began to get at Ivan again, but he did not answer. Then Pashka turned his attack on Zakhar Vodennikov, who had long irritated us with his snoring which was like the bubbling and gurgling of frogs in the spring mating season. But he was well protected by his cotton wool ear-plugs.

Soon Pashka himself was snoring too. Kapshin kicked around a bit and then he too began blowing into the back of my neck. But I lay wakeful. Sleep obstinately fled me.

Outside, the fire crackled as it burned down. Red flickers trembled in the cracks of the shutters. But what was that, in the front corner? What kept on rustling and scratching? Was it mice? Or was it Ivan, unsleeping?

5

I was wakened by the cold.

It was already light. An open stove yawned at me. But there was no housewife rattling fire-irons as she cooked breakfast. There was no sound of beasts in the yard. And the men were not hurrying out to the fields; they lay snoring, scattered over the whole floor.

I rose quietly and went out. Heavens, what a fog! It smothered everything, there was neither sky nor earth.

I cut across the lane through the grey, wet grass and stopped in front of the house opposite.

The corners of this house were sheathed with boards which bore traces of old paint and the foundation was of thick pitched posts; the house had been built strongly, to last.

I looked up and saw a round-chested wooden horse looking down at me from the fog. A piece of string with the remnants of dry, blackened rowan berries hung from it; such bunches were hung on all the northern houses in the old days. Frozen rowan berries were sweet and tasty, and the first cure for anyone affected by charcoal fumes.

Suddenly I became conscious of somebody walking about inside. What the devil? A house-spirit wandering about in the deserted house? But the footsteps became clearer, closer, scraping heavily. A floorboard creaked, then something fell—in the passage, judging by the sound.

I went round the corner and stood expectantly by the porch.

A man emerged, tall and fair-haired, in a quilted jacket and thigh-boots with the tops turned down.

This must be Ivan, I thought, and when he approached me I asked, "Can't you sleep?"

"It's habit. We always used to get up early."

So that was the last shoot of the Kornei tree! I remembered the previous night's talk.

"Which house is yours, then?"

"Both of them. The one where we slept was my father's, and this one belonged to my wife Maria's father."

"Interesting."

"What's interesting? That they're both empty?"

"No, of course not." His penetrating gaze confused me. "I mean, it's unusual for such close neighbours to marry."

"It was our way. They handfasted us when they were still building these houses. We were just kids, really. We'll join fortune to fortune, they said."

"Was that long ago?"

"Eh, what's the good of remembering." He waved it away and again looked hard at me. Then he went over to the other house and took down a zinc bucket from the wall.

"If you want to wash, come along."

The fog still lay thick on the ground but here and there the tops of shrubs were already visible. Walking was wet and unpleasant. Old limp grass stroked our knees and the shafts of my boots were short.

"Don't they mow here any more?"

"They don't have the time," said Ivan without turning. "They only reap a few fields. And can you call that grain? Times, we had crops of rye—if it was flattened it was a nightmare for the women."

He stopped, so suddenly that I almost collided with him. He was glaring at an alder which had loomed up out of the fog before his nose. Then he looked around.

"You see. That bitch! Crawled out on to the stubble now."

His cheeks were white. His hand went to his belt, apparently seeking an axe out of old peasant habit, but there was none, and he gave the alder a kick: it snapped off. Ivan jerked it out and threw it away, then turned from me and wiped his hands on his jacket.

I could hear a brook gurgling down below in the fog.

I was going to make straight for it but Ivan stopped me.

"The water higher up is for drinking. Down there we used to water the horses."

The slope down to the water was cobbled, with a birch handrail at the side, still firm. Down below among the willows and currant bushes was a kind of cup. Big dark stones with green trails of weed formed the circumference, and in the middle a pure, transparent spring bubbled up from sand and gravel.

Ivan scooped up a palmful of water and drank.

"Chills your teeth. Wherever I went during the war I never tasted water like it."

"The old home pulls, does it?"

"Me? It's all right for me. I've settled down. But my wife—"

He filled the bucket with water and set the lid on firmly.

"This is for her, for Maria. She's bed-ridden, her legs are paralysed. But when she can drink some of our own water she seems a bit better, a bit livelier, like."

On the way back, musing over this man and his wife, I asked him why he didn't do like so many others, move the house over to the lumber camp. It was just going to rack and ruin. And Maria would feel better in her own house.

"I wanted to, but my wife didn't. She wants to die here, in the hamlet—somehow." He was silent, then looking narrow-eyed at a crow flapping awkwardly away from an old drying pole, he added, "He's likely got the same idea. People leave their homes, so do crows. But this one's stayed."

The fog was clearing, the sun was a red patch behind the houses.

When we got back all were up and the fire was crackling. Ivan's friends had their guns. One of them, the oldest, handed Ivan his and the other, Pashka, shook hands with us, with a parting joke.

"Don't kill my bear. You'll know him by his ears—he's got two of them."

The water splashed in the bucket. Ivan, hunching his shoulders peasant fashion, went through the back-yard.

"Ugh, the witless loon, leading us by a new path again!" cried Pashka and ran to overtake him.

Rubber boots scraped and splashed in the fog but nobody

could be seen; only once Ivan's fair head, lit up by sunshine, flashed for an instant on a rise and then was extinguished again.

We stood for some time looking after the hunters, and all the time I seemed to hear a strange sound like water splashing in a zinc bucket. Drops falling from the roof? Or was it the spring calling to us from below?

1963-1964

The Last Ancient

I know all in our village, young and old, even the children, by sight if not by name. But here was an ancient man ploughing his way through the dust, coming from the post office. Who was it? His high boots were huge and his dried-up legs stuck out of them like sticks, and he'd a staff glistening in the sun.

I got closer and didn't believe my eyes: Pavel Vassilye-vich Savin.

He had become gaunt, dried up, and his eyes were sunk deep, as if he was looking back from the next world. And his beard? What had happened to his beard? Only a year or so ago it had been long, thick, bushy—a whole sheaf on his chest.

What a man he had been when he was young! Strength and boldness striding the earth! In the spring when all the rivers are full and they float timber down the Pinega, the boldest of the young fellows would cross with a boathook over the logs from bank to bank, showing off. And he did that too.

When he went to fetch his bride—I was quite little then —it was a sight to behold! Never in all my life have I seen such wild galloping on spirited horses with festival harness that blazed in the sunshine. Frost, sunshine, a painted sleigh and there he was, standing on it in a crimson shirt, bare-headed, all furious impatience.

"Pavel Vassilyevich," I said. "is it really you! "

"Me, lad, me. I'm right sick, got my orders for the next world."

I did my best to find words of comfort.

"Nay, don't ye try to talk me round, the feast's ended for me. I've just been to the post office, taken out money for my funeral. I'd six hunner saved and I took it all out. I don't want my childer to ruin theirselves for me. But I want to take leave of my neighbours all right and proper, with summat for all that comes, so they'll mind how the last ancient in the village went to his rest."

His words didn't surprise me. There were three or four very old men in the village, but he was the one they called the last ancient. He was one of that fast disappearing generation of Russian muzhiks who could do things on a grand scale, who worked with zest, and did things their eccentric way.

Pavel Vassilyevich died that day, towards evening as the sun set.

All through the spring and summer he had lain on his old wooden bed by the door, but now suddenly he asked to be put on the floor. His children—sons and daughters had all gathered—did as he wished, they spread a feather mattress on the floor where the table usually stood and carried him to it.

"And let Matrena lie beside me."

Sons and daughters exchanged looks; what had he got in his head now?

"Put your mother here beside me, I tell you."

Matrena was sitting with her back to the warm stove, in an old quilted jacket. Time was when she had been beautiful and Pavel Vassilyevich had had many a desperate fight about her with his rivals; and when they were getting on in years he had still worshipped her.

"Matrena's going too ... my Matrena ... Matrena and me..." You heard that from him all the time, drunk or sober.

But now Matrena seemed not even to hear when her husband spoke about her. For three years she had been witless.

"But, Dad," said one daughter cautiously (Pavel Vassilyevich had always been strict with his children), "why mother? It's not right."

"Lay her down. I tell you, beside me."

Sons and daughters exchanged looks again. What should they do, how could they go against their dying father's wish?

"Matrena," said the old man when the old woman was lying beside him, "put your arms round me for the last time."

Matrena, whose wits had returned by some miracle for that moment, awkwardly embraced her husband with her gnarled arms.

"There, that's all right," Pavel Vassilyevich had tears in his eyes. "Now leave me alone. I am going to die."

And soon he did die.

The whole village went to his funeral. Young and old followed his coffin, accompanying their last ancient on his last journey.

1980

Jobbely

It was Yevstolia who dragged me along to that merry-making. Actually, she tricked me, sly as any fox. Came to me with "I heard yon iron horse of yours is tired wi' standing, you wouldn't have aught against taking me to Yurmola, now? There's an old woman I've got to see, she bid me come for a sheep."

Now, how could I refuse, come out with a "no"?—A neighbour you run over to whenever you need something—milk, or potatoes or onions. Or maybe it's a rake or pitchfork or scythe you need—who else could you borrow it from?

Off we went on the Niemen motor boat (so new it was not yet run in), with its twelve iron horses which soon ate up seven kilometres; we pushed the boat up the sloping river bank and there we were, right by the village.

That was when Yevstolia came clean, as we emerged by the bath-house on to a green meadow and heard music.

"Get you ready for a randy. It isn't any sheep we've come for, it's a jobbely."

"A what?"

"Oh, you know—the kind of thing they have when a body retires with a penshun."

"A jubilee?"

"Aye, mebbe that's what they call it, them with learning. But us, we grow up with the tree-stumps and we're like 'em."

I made a brisk about turn; I'd only just come from town and there was work waiting at home, jobs of all kinds—I hadn't even mowed the grass growing rankly about the house, and she'd taken it into her head to drag me off to some "jobbely".

Yevstolia, however, grabbed my arm and gave it a good tug—she might be on the fat side but she had some muscle—and smilingly set to work talking me round.

"Didn't you guess at once what I was going for? Katerina's my cousin on my ma's side and she's just retired. Turned fifty this week. And she says to me, she says, 'If you don't come I'll never speak to you again! ' "

And she finally disarmed me when, red with embarrassment, she turned herself round before me, shifting awkwardly from foot to foot with "Take a look, here's me prinked out in all my best, does a body get herself up like this for sheep?! "

We turned into the Yushkovs' lane and plumped right into the middle of it, everybody dancing to the accordion, the whole company: girls, married women and some goodwives quite on in years but brisk enough, and men not yet drunk who had tumbled out into the street for what was probably the first time since the celebration started. All danced as they pleased. Some, sweating and limp from the stuffy heat inside, just shuffled on the spot, turning and waving handkerchiefs to fan themselves in the fresh air, others were stamping enthusiastically as though they meant to wear out the grass in the lane and then drive holes into the ground, while some of the lads and younger men were hoofing it like stallions round a young blue-eyed beauty with smoothly combed hair; it took no wits to guess that she was the belle of this particular ball.

It was this lively goodwife who was the first to see us. She came running up to embrace Yevstolia and then myself all in one movement.

"Come to table! To table! " she cried, and taking our arms led us into the cottage.

"Here, sit here, the place of honour! "

The tables, arranged in an open-ended oblong, looked as though they could barely stand up under the weight of good things baked and roasted, and as for the cloudberries, I'd never in my life seen such a quantity of big, ripe ones, whole platefuls and large bowls that spilled over.

According to custom we had to take a "penalty" drink to make up for what we'd missed, the whole company insisting "bottoms up", and the blue-eyed young woman who had seated herself opposite us adding for good measure, "So's a fly couldn't wet its feet in the leavings! "

I turned to Yevstolia. "Where's our hostess?" I whispered.

"What? What's that?"

"Where's the queen of the jubilee, and Gordei, too?"

316

Yevstolia threw back her head and laughed till the rafters rang.

"He didn't know you, Katerina! " she said to the pretty young woman. "He wants to know where you are! "

"Let be! " A massive broad-faced old woman in an old-style head-dress with a gold brocade top flapped a hand. "I'm her neighbour and I didn't know her, and him—naught to be 'mazed at, he hasna seen so much of her."

I had seen Katerina, though, and more than once; I had even, I remembered, drunk tea with them a few times, but you don't feast your eyes for long on a countrywoman crushed under the quadruple burden of work on the kolkhoz and at home, of children—and husband. And Gordei most certainly didn't make life easy. A fly wouldn't dare buzz when he was at home. He was a drunkard and at work he had never risen above watchman at the stores; he was a victim of daftness, as he sometimes jokingly said (he had lost the left arm through some stupid prank in his schooldays) but he had managed to make people afraid of him—both his family and his neighbours, who preferred to keep out of his way.

"See how the penshun's put a bloom on her," said Yevstolia, moved. "Good enough to get married all over again."

"Aye, that penshun isna the bit we get," said Malanya, the garrulous old woman in the head-dress. "Not twenty rubles but a hunner-twenty. Summat worth having, that."

"And she's earned it! " Vitaly the foreman brought his fist down on the table (he was already far gone and hadn't recognised me).

"Aye, that she has, Vitaly Ivanovich! " people hastened to agree (the foreman had a nasty temper when he was drunk). "Of course she earned it, all her life long working with them calves."

"But where's the goodman?"

Whether Yevstolia really wanted to know, or whether she wanted to divert attention from Vitaly I couldn't say, but her question brought general grins.

"He's in the shed! " Katerina answered gaily.

"The shed? What's he doing there? Earning money while his wife celebrates?"

"Let be! " Malanya flapped her hands. "We filled him up with drink from the morn so's he wouldn't be blustering here, you know what he's like, he'd spoil it for us all."

"So that's why she's so nim and pert, she's taken a day off from Gordei."

"Aye, that's right, Yevstolia. You couldn't see Katerina for that devil crushing her."

"You let Gordei alone! " bawled Vitaly and burst into drunken weeping.

"We won't touch him, Vitaly Ivanovich," said Malanya appeasingly. "It was all her cares took the life out of her. How many did you have, Katerina?"

"Childer, you mean? There was a dozen born but only seven lived."

"Oooh, Lord ha' mercy! " There was a concerted groan. "They don't want to be plagued with one these days, and she going down with a dozen! "

"I never seemed to see Katerina empty, she'd always got a full belly."

"And right! A tub oughter be full! " This time Yevstolia shut Vitaly up.

"Go to the devil! I didn't come seven versts to listen to you bellowing! "

Probably to distract attention and prevent a quarrel from developing, Katerina's voice rang out boisterously.

"Hi, girls, bring in the meat! "

"Hark to her! A real commander today! Got a voice like one, too! "

"The chairman, make her chairman! " When Malanya had sufficient drinks inside her she was neither to hold nor to bind. "What do we want with all them fancy folks from way off?"

"Aye, right! Ri-i-ight! "

Two of Katerina's daughters—nothing to look at compared with their mother, like dry crusts beside a luscious cake, in spite of their perms and gold rings (lived in town, they did!)—brought in meat cut fine and laid out delicately on small plates. Katerina had been smiling, showing surprisingly youthful white teeth, but now her smile vanished,

"What d'you think you're bringing us?" she snapped angrily. "Is it for the cats or decent folks?"

One daughter shook her head reproachfully.

"You're sozzled, just lovely?"

"And if I am it's not on your money, it's my own! "

"Mum, you're crazy! " Now it was the other daughter trying to repress her angry mother.

Katerina jumped up and stamped.

"It's my day today, mine. Don't you try to boss your ma! Do as I say and quick about it! I want all the meat on the table in one second, every bit of it! " Utterly flabbergasted—they weren't used to such an imperative tone from their mother—the daughters flew to obey her, while at the table (where Vitaly slept with his face in a plate of fish ramnants) there was an awkward silence.

Suddenly Katerina burst into tears.

"Don't be 'mazed, girls. Underneath, I'm real desprit! "

"You—you desprit?"

"Gospel truth! I nigh raped Gordei to get him! "

"What's that you're telling? You're just trying to whiten that whoremaster of a man of yours, and him with childer in every village! "

"Nay, girls, I'm not making it up. You mind the war, how many lads left and how many of 'em came back? We was ready to queue up for them, they were goods in short supply. And whether you fancied them goods or not, you couldn't pick and choose. So long's it was a pair of pants. It was them times. Well, I lost my knicks while the war was still on."

"Mother—! "

"Hush up with your 'mother'! " Malanya spoke up for Katerina. "Mealy-mouthed and namby-pamby, can't stand a straight word! Isn't your ma human like all of us? What d'you do yourself in bed with your husband? Hunt fleas?" Suddenly she burst out laughing. "You needn't hide aught, Katerina. Me, I opened my gate while I was still a maid, too. As God sees me."

"And you can count me in," said Yevstolia. "My fortress didn't hold out, either."

"I was sixteen when I first began to hanker after Gordei. Aye, just turned sixteen. I was sent out collecting resin and sap and he was foreman there. Well, I saw all of 'em grabbing for him, girls and wives, too, and thinks I, am I any worse than them? I knew the diff'rence atween trousers and a skirt all right. One day I met him in the woods, and I says right out, 'Why d'you go for all the others and never a look at me?' But he says, 'You? You're only a kid,' and so I was by him, he was twenty-seven. But it was too late to back out and I was mad, too, and I says, 'You try and see if I'm a kid.' But he, he only laughed and said, 'Fly away, little pigeon.' "

"Decent, was he?"

Katerina laughed mirthlessly.

"Aye, decent. He hadn't gone fifty paces when he was back again. And in four months I was having to make new holes in my belt."

"Mother—" The expostulatory voice of a daughter again.

"Why d'you keep on trying to stop my mouth? It was you, you that was swelling my belly! Yes, see what a gaby I was, girls! And after, when I understood, I was right sorry! There was Sergei, we'd been together at school and he writes from the front to send him my picture, and another lad the same, and me with a belly and nobody wanting me now. But there was good folks took my part, 'What are you about,' they says, 'you shameless blackguard, got a maid with child and now you turn your back!' So Gordei took me—took me for his second woman."

Tears welled up again in Katerina's troubled eyes and her face was flushed with emotion.

"Devil take him, he was living with a shop assistant, with that one's mother." She jerked her head at the accordion player, a sturdy flaxen-headed fellow in a white nylon shirt and black tie. "Five years I shared him with her. She could bait her hook with wine, and me, what had I got, what rope to hold him with? Oh, enough of that," Katerina cut herself short. "Let be wi' moaning. It's a holiday I've got today, not a wake." She jumped up and took a few dance steps. "Give us some music!"

The accordion player refused mulishly, "Not after that talk about my mother."

"Wha-a-at? You won't? You won't play?"

"Valery, you scum!" Yevstolia, good-natured Yevstolia was so furious that she grabbed up a wooden beer mug with both hands. "Who are you blaming? Who's been your real mother?"

"It's not right, not fitten, Valery Gordeyevich," Malanya backed her up. "It isn't the one as bore you that's your mother but the one as fed and tended you. And you were running to Katerina soon's you could set one foot afore the other."

"Talking of his mother! That mother o' yours hadna a thought in her head beyond running after a pair of trousers. And plenty families she broke up, too."

"That's right. A bit o' dirt, that's what she was. Aye, if you're so hot to defend her—why've you forgotten the road to her door?"

"Who is it you go to? Who do you come to for your holidays every mortal summer?"

"And brings his childer, too! "

The women had certainly made mincemeat of him, and Valery with shamefaced reluctance played a note or two.

"It isn't a burying we've come for, play, you devil! " cried Yevstolia as imperatively as before.

She pulled off her head-scarf and wiped her face and her plump white neck; it was hot in the house in spite of all the open windows.

"Takes it into his fool head to stick up for his mother. We know that dove wi' crow's feathers. If I was Katerina I wouldn't let one of Gordei's bastids in the door," declared Yevstolia and without troubling to lower her voice went on, "But you can see them all, here round the table." She made a sweeping gesture. "D'you think they're all village grease-monkeys? Nay, not one belongs in Yurmola. They'll soon be closing down the whole village, that lot's all from town. Gordei's work over thirty years. From five mothers, or seven, or mebbe more. A good kind pa. Take 'em in, Katerina, for the summer, feed 'em well and dinna forget the vodka, they'll be hungered and athirst, frying their selves all day on the river bank. When the sun shines you can see the hollows they've made. Or they'll take a fancy to go after berries or mushrooms, lay in a stock for winter. Come autumn, they go back to town all hung about wi' baskets and bags like Santa Claus."

What with one thing and another the women had defeated Valery's stubbornness and he played—at first any kind of way, but then he got carried away. Katerina did the trick.

I have seen plenty of dancers in my life, professional and amateur, and Katerina, to be quite frank, wasn't a dancer at all—just a hop and a skip and a stamp or two. But there was such youthful verve, such energy, such tirelessness in her legs and her whole body, her figure was so neat, girdled by a black belt no longer fashionable—you'd never say she was a mother of twelve—and there was such happiness, such mirth in her blue eyes that the talk died away and all eyes were bent on her.

"Just look at her, now," Yevstolia whispered to me, "like as if she's changed places with her daughters. They oughter be the ones going off on penshun, not her."

It was quite true. Compared with their mother, the daughters looked like stale buns. It was only Katerina's hands that betrayed her age: big heavy peasant hands, with swollen veins and broken nails, hands which had got through an incredible amount of the hardest work.

For some time Katerina pranced alone, but then one stepson jumped up to join her, a second, a third. The floor creaked and groaned. And soon everyone began to notice that Gordei's sons were devouring her with their eyes, crowding her and grabbing at her; the men's blood was dancing in their veins.

At last the daughters couldn't stand any more.

"For goodness' sake, Mother—take shame for yourself! Don't set all the folks laughing at you! "

Katerina stamped with a force more masculine than feminine.

"Hold your tongues! This is my party, mine! You dance all you want but me, it's mebbe the first time in my life! "

"Dance your fill, dinna fret for them! " cried Malanya.

Excited by all this, Katerina herself added fuel to the fire.

"Let be, or I'll be taking your men off you! "

Laughter exploded and filled the cottage. Vitaly the foreman wakened and bawled wildly, "I protest! You've no right! "

Nobody had any attention to spare for him. Wild merriment gripped them all, even my own feet were tapping under the table and when we poured out into the street (the room was as hot and steamy as a bath-house) it was like Bedlam. Even Malanya, that old hen Malanya, joined in the dancing.

"Hi you with the accordion, don't go to sleep! We'll all freeze! "

Katerina still danced without taking a moment for breath. The player gave place to a second and then a third (all Gordei's sons could tweedle a bit), the huskiest men left the circle, but that slender woman in a blue frock drawn in by a shining black belt still twirled and stamped, and the cheap silver ring flashed on her heavy dark hand.

The dancing was interrupted by the lowing of a cow in the back yard, the herd had come home.

"Eh, Malka, Malka, you don't let me dance my fill," sighed Katerina. "You folks go on, I'll soon get through wi' the milking."

"What daft idea's she got now?" said Malanya. "You've your lasses here, two of 'em, can't they do the milking for

322

their ma on a day like this?"

So the daughters went to the cow and Katerina remained.

"Play up, there!—Till you turn it inside out! " she commanded and the accordion player began again, but the other women begged for mercy.

"Enough, we've danced enough, Katerina! We can't beat a hole right through if we dance all night! "

"Then we'll have a song! Walk through the village singing like in the old days."

The sun was setting in heavy clouds beyond the river; and from there came its own metallic song, from a dozen boats with outboard motors racing at varying speeds.

Arms round one another, we strolled in two rows along the grass-grown street (tractors and carts were few in Yurmola) singing Katerina's favourite song, "The Soldier Will Return".

Yurmola offered no treat to the eye. There was not one new building (construction had been prohibited for five years now), and well-kept houses could have been counted on your fingers; the general effect was one of dilapidation, a dying village: boarded-up windows, piles of rubbish lying about, waste plots where life had once seethed but now thick with weeds, and ancient cottages with roofs fallen in, the home of birds.

Old Malanya was the first to give way; she burst into tears.

"Nay, he won't return, the soldier won't come back to Yurmola, our village is wasting away."

Then all of them, old and young, those who only a moment before had been all carefree merriment, began to cry, to wail as if they were at a funeral.

I seized my chance in the general confusion, to dive into a lane leading to a familiar house.

In the morning Yevstolia shook me awake.

"Get up, deserter! Yesterday the girls began to look round—where's our writer got to? And seems the writer'd crawled into the hay, he wanted his sleep, poor lad! "

I got myself up with a great effort, because it had been dawn before I actually got to sleep. The mosquitoes had given me hell, I must have fought them for all of three hours; the shed was dilapidated and full of holes.

Overhead, above the old besoms left over from the previous summer, came a sound reminiscent of sobbing, piteous, childish sobbing; as I put on my jacket I looked at Yevstolia, puzzled.

"That's rain, thank goodness some rain's come," she said.

"Rain?" My first thought was how we were to get home. Yevstolia divined my worry.

"We aren't sugar or salt, we shan't melt. And rain's wanted. It'll bring the potatoes on and there'll be mushrooms for the picking."

We soon came to the Yushkovs', only slightly damp from the light drizzle. Yevstolia wouldn't hear of our going on home without looking in to say goodbye.

"What are you thinking of? She'd be right offended. And I need summat for my head, it's splitting, I'd never make it home."

At the Yushkovs' they were drinking tea, five burly men, six strapping lads (men too, really, only with fluff on their upper lips and empty fish-like eyes), two daughters, three daughters-in-law and the master himself at the head of the table—morose, with a shaggy grey head, in a shirt open the whole way down, an empty sleeve dangling, limp as a rag.

Katerina was serving at table; I recognised her by the silver ring on her heavy dark hand, but apart from that—what was left of yesterday's beauty? This was an old woman. A faded frock sagging at the sides and with a ragged hem, trodden-down felt boots cut short on bare feet, and a grey head-scarf in small checks pulled down over her eyes and fastened at the back of the neck.

This sharp change in Katerina startled not only me but Yevstolia too; she quite forgot her usual polite greeting on entering and it was only when Gordei turned a lowering visage to her that she said, not very affably, "Good day to you all."

"Good day it is," barked Gordei in a voice hoarse with drink and then turned hopeful eyes on me. And Yevstolia exploded.

"What are you goggling at him for? D'you think a writer's got casks of gold? You oughter be treating him, not waiting for him to treat you! And you needn't think you can fritten me wi' your glaring eyes! " she raged, brandishing her arms menacingly. "Takes more'n you to scare me! I've seen plenty worse snakes in my time! Come on," she turned furiously to me. "The jobbely's finished." Without a word of leavetaking or even a glance at Katerina she stormed out of the house.

She did not speak again until we had crossed the street and walked down as far as the bath-house with its ancient bath-house smell brought out by the rain.

"Eh, if I but had the strength I dunno what I wouldn't do to that lump o'muck. You know why he was goggling at you? Thought you'd brought a bottle. That's the sort of scum he is, I can see through him like he was glass. And I havena much praise for his fool of a wife, either. Look what she was yestereen, a picture, you couldn't find prettier. And today? A rag, down again under the heel of Gordei and his bastids. Why d'you think she's got that shawl wrapped all round her head and over her eyes? Gordei's beaten her black and blue! "

"Not really?"

"And why 'not really'? Don't I know? He wakes up in the morn, yesterday there was a crate of wine or mebbe two and today there isn't enough to fill a thimble. His tribe swilled it all, take after Gordei, they do. Don't stop while there's a drop left, and who gets the flame? Katerina, of course. Oh, the so-and-so, this-that-and-the-other! "

The rain was coming down now in good earnest. Yevstolia's old cotton raincoat of indeterminate hue rapidly darkened and the hem of her skirt flapped wetly against her unhealthily swollen legs, but she had no attention to spare for such trifles.

"I don't know what's wrong with us," she said with growing heat. "All our lives we've let brassy-faced spongers and no-goods like him ride us. Why? What right have they? Why can't we stand up, as people? Yestereen Katerina got away from them cows, got off her knees and stood up tall, and all nature seemed to be taking joy in her. You mind what a day it was? The sun shone and every leaf danced, every bird sang. Aye, it 'ud be like heaven come down, if we could be proper people. But she stood up, a real person, only once, once in fifty years. And why? Isn't she as good as Gordei and his bastids? Them—they're not worth Katerina's finger-nail. And look—nature's turned its back on us, weeping. And the sun's hidden behind black clouds. It's shamed to look at us so it's hidden, it's as if it said: I try my best for you all but you—you won't move a finger for yourselves, I'm sick of you, go to hell! Oh, how wonderful life would be, beautiful, if only Katerina plucked up courage and spat in the ugle mugs of all that bunch and Gordei with them! Make an end! Finished! You've trampled me enough, now I'm going to give the orders since you're no good! "

By this time we had reached the boat with the rain drumming on its metal surface, and Yevstolia was wound up to the limit.

"Well, why d'you stand there mum?" Now it was my turn. "Call yourself a writer! I'm not telling fairy-tales or singing ditties. And you see yourself what Yurmola's come to, slipping into the grave. The women came to me, May day it was, even back then they was saying, 'We ought to ask that writer man, mebbe he could help, for it looks like we're sentenced to death, they don't give us 'lectricity and they've driven the calves away, soon they'll be driving us away an' all.' But the writer, he just sits and drinks and then he's gone, off to sleep on the sweet-smelling hay in grandma's shed. Tired, poor man. Would it have killed you if you'd talked to the folks a mite? They kept asking: where's the writer? I was right shamed, I wished the earth would open and swallow me."

It took some hard pushing to get the boat afloat, the bows had sunk deeply in the rain-softened sand. But when it was on the water, Yevstolia, soaking wet (as I was myself), sat down, presenting her broad back to me, and didn't speak another word until we grounded on the home bank.

1976-1980

A Disciple of Avvakum

1

It was a very raw, inexperienced driver I had got hold of, still wet behind the ears, and full of self-assurance into the bargain; if I wanted to go round some bad place he drove straight on, if I advised going straight he'd plough his way round. Well, so we finally got bogged down in soft mud to the axles. And where, of all places? On the highway by the Pinega, just opposite Koida, where nobody has been stuck in a hundred years.

If we'd had an axe with us, chains, a spade, getting out would have been simple: put logs or any rubbish under the wheels, dig out the worst of the mud and step on the accelerator. But that snot-nose not only lacked those tools, he hadn't so much as a rusty knife with him.

For about an hour-and-a-half we tried this and that, but what can you do with your bare hands? So finally, tired, sweaty, muddy to the eyes, we sat down under a birch by the roadside to wait, hoping that someone would come along; after all, this wasn't some out-of-the-way cart track, it was the main Pinega road.

But time dragged on, I smoked a cigarette and then a second, the driver went down to the river to bathe (the young folks of today don't lose time) but no help appeared and nothing could be heard on the road but the rustle of burch leaves in the wind.

"Hi, wait a bit—what day is it today?" Something had dawned on the driver. "Not Sunday, is it?"

"That's right, Sunday."

"Then we can sit here sunbathing till nightfall, no one'll come by. We'll have to go to Koida," he said decidedly.

Koida was on the opposite bank and it ought not to be difficult to get there. But I was in no haste to jump up and go. For ages past that village has had a bad reputation.

In the north, to be more exact along the Pinega and the Mezen, there has for a long time been an illness rampant among the women; they called it hiccupping. It's lessened somewhat recently but quite a short time ago there were few working women who hadn't known that gasping fever. It would attack some unfortunate; she would be sick, aching, choking with it till she screamed and cried—like a cat, like a dog, and sometimes even foul curses would burst out.

It is only in very recent years that medical science has paid any attention to that sickness, you won't find a word about it even in the Great Soviet Encyclopedia; so it has always been believed in our parts that the hiccupping sickness was called down by the spells of certain wicked people, referred to as hiccuppers, and Koida, a small old village shut off by the river, is considered a nest of these hiccuppers.

Of course, it's a long time since I credited these stories, but still—! And when we got to the other side in a leaky, antediluvian aspen dugout and neared the village, I didn't exactly shiver, but something like pins and needles ran through me.

The driver had some distant relatives living at the upper end of the village and he suggested that we both go there ("We'll get a glass of tea even if there's nothing stronger"); but I decided to take a stroll through the village; who could say if I'd ever visit it again?

It was somewhere round ten years since I had been in Koida, and it hadn't improved in the meantime. After all, why should it when it was destined to be pulled down? There wasn't a single new structure and the old half-tumble-down cottages with sagging roofs were like old horses put out to pasture, silent and still, sunk in a kind of torpor.

They were pitiful, pitiful to the point of tears, these dying houses, yet at the same time I felt comfortable among them. They smelled of sun-warmed wood, the lush grass grew up to the very porches, and overhead was the sky, that wide village sky. Not like my own village, everything there is wound round with wire and torn up by tractors and bulldozers.

2

An old woman—ancient, rather—was sitting on a log beside the road, her chin supported on a staff, barefoot, in an old-style dark blue sarafan; she seemed to be unaware of anything round her, but when I approached she suddenly turned her wrinkled face to me and examined me with lively black eyes that belied her years.

"Well, Grandma, so you've come out to warm your bones in the sunshine?"

"Aye, that's right. I'm waiting for my daughter. She went off the morn for bread and not back yet. We go five versts to Rovda now for our bread."

"That's a long way. Isn't your shop working?"

"Nay, it's nigh on three years since they shut the shop, and folks say they'll soon be shutting the village, too. It's some sort of new-fangled ways they've brought in, burying alive the good soil. But why d'you ask? You aren't from these parts, seemingly?"

I said I was passing through, sat down by the old woman and next moment almost jumped up again when I heard her name.

Solomida! The greatest hiccupper in Koida!

I calmed down a bit as a young, freshly shorn sheep, breathing fast (it was a hot, sunny day), came trotting up to the old woman and trustingly pushed its head between her knees.

"Eh, then, and what d'ye keep rubbing against me for like a cat? Get along with you, crop grass. Go now, wi' God's blessing."

The old woman pushed the sheep away, crossed it with a dark hand that trembled with age, then crossed herself. I saw that she did it with two fingers.

"Do you hold to the Old Belief, Grandma?"

"Aye, that I do; I've gone through all my trials, all my sufferings with the two-fingered cross."

"Have you had much trials and suffering?"

The old woman suddenly sobbed, tears welled up in her eyes but dried at once as a small child's do.

"The Lord has not begrudged me. I've been starving time and again, I lost the use of my legs, my man was beaten nigh to death, and evil folks have dragged me to lockups and jails. And here in my own village, the sorrow and grief I seen. Like living in a desert. Nobody came to me, and there was none wished to wed wi' my daughters, all five of them withered on the stalk."

I knew well enough the cause of the old woman's trouble, but the question came out involuntarily.

"But why did they treat you like that, Grandma?"

"Because of folks bad-naming me. All my life I've been called a hiccupper. Whenever one was sick or the cattle died, it was all Solomida's doing, it was Solomida sent the hiccups, or put a spell on the beasts. And God is my witness," the old woman again crossed herself devoutly, "I was not to blame in word or deed. All my life I've followed God's word, and held to the Old Belief like to a saving rope. Right from that time I made a pilgrimage to Pustozerye."

"Pustozerye? What Pustozerye?"

"There's but one in the world," and her voice took on a stern note. "In them cold parts by the Pechora River where evildoers burned that great and righteous man, the herald of the true faith. Arch-Priest Avvakum."

I had no cause to disbelieve the old woman, but all the same I couldn't take it in. Pustozerye—it must be four or five hundred versts from Pinega, and there had been no way of getting there in former times—in summer because there were no roads across the woods and marshland and the mosquitoes would eat you alive, and in winter because of the cold and the snow.

"I walked there," sighed the old woman. "A bit of a lass I was and I walked all the way there. As a pilgrim. I'd made a vow. One day I came home from the mowing, it was a main long ways off, forty versts or more, and all the way firs and wet underfoot, and when I got home I found Ma had visitors, Ivan Martynovich from Zaozerye with his wife, and relatives from our village. And they asks me, 'Aren't you tired, lass?' 'And what for should I be tired?' I tells them, 'Nay, not a mite. I'm going to join the games and dancing.' And off I went. I'd red and black wheels turning in front of my eyes but I went all the same. Aye, a lass would. I wanted folks to think I was spry. I thought I'd find me a man quicker. But the next morn Ma called me when the buns were ready, and I couldna stand up. My legs felt as if they weren't mine, when I tried to stand they bent like they hadn't any bones. See how the Lord God punished me for my boasting! Well, me and Ma we cried and took on, right in harvest time it was, and here was a pair of hands without any feet. What could we do? It pleased God to chastise me, it was his holy will. They sat me in a steaming hay sweatbox, they rubbed my legs with ant oil, they heated the bath-house every second day, but my legs stayed dead, naught helped. But help came from the Lord God. He took away my legs and in his mercy he gave me them back.

"There was an old woman in the village, God-fearing and pious she was, all her life she never ate meat or milk, fasting like. They called her Maria of the Fast. And it was this

Maria who told me, 'Stop hobnobbing with the devil, lass, no sweating's going to help you. Your only help will come from the true faith and vows you take.' Well, I cried and I said, 'Oh Grandma, Grandma, I'd take any vow if only my legs would come alive again! ' 'The vow you must take is a hard one; first of all,' she says, 'you must renounce all dancing and games and merrymaking. Have you the strength for that?' 'Aye,' I says, 'I've got it,' though I didn't hear my voice and the light went out 'fore my eyes, for well I knew that if I didn't join in with them things I'd never find me a man. Well, the second vow, to change to the Old Belief, that was sort of easier after the first. That's what I thought, for I was but young and silly-like. But when she told me the third vow I burst out crying. For I was to walk to Pustozerye, where the great martyr Avvakum is buried, and pray by his grave. 'You're making game of me, Grandma,' I says. 'When I go to the outhouse I have to shuffle on my knees, and you talk of walking to some Pustozerye! ' But she says, 'If it pleases the Lord God to accept your vows, he will give you the legs for the pilgrimage. And now,' she says, 'six days you must kneel and pray from sunup to sundown, and you must have it in your thoughts all the time, you must pray that God will give you strength to make your pilgrimage. In all my years on earth,' she says, 'I've never heard of a person going from Pinega to Pustozerye, but you will do it, the Almighty will open the path before you to that holy place where God chose our martyr to pass through the torture of fire and receive the heavenly crown. But mind you,' she says, 'pray with all your heart, let no thought, no sigh be for aught else, so that your whole body burns as if you were in a furnace. Six days you must pray, Monday to Saturday, and on Saturday go to sleep, sleep all you can, e'en all day and all night. And when you waken on Sunday, the day of Christ's Resurrection, cross yourself devoutly with two fingers, and stand up. Your legs will be stronger than before, stronger than wood or stone will be your legs.'

"And it all befell as God's holy one foretold. God in his mercy restored my legs, to this day they serve me, and to this day I follow the call of the Lord."

The old woman turned her head to the east and with dignity and deep feeling crossed herself most devoutly. I waited a few moments and then again gently turned her thoughts to those paths of the distant past.

"Eh, my dear, I could be telling all day and I'd never tell the half of how I walked to Pustozerye. First, d'you know where it is? In them cold parts at the end of the world where in winter there's never day but only night, and in summer no night but only day, with the sun shining all the time. And how should I find my way there, where was the start of a trail? But I had to stand by my vow since I'd made it. So my ma got me ready for the pilgrimage, a wallet with some bread on my back and two copper coins in my pocket, to go and seek Pustozerye. In Pinega town there was the Nikolskaya Fair and folks coming from all over the country, so I thought mebbe someone there could tell me. And in Pinega town they said there were caravans of carts with fish from the Pechora river, I had to go with one of them. Four hundred versts or mebbe more, through forest and tundra, how'd a lone maid ever get there?

"So I went along with one of them trains of carts and I had my baptism of frost and snow, fearsome it was, fearsome the demoniac blizzards, it 'ud blow and blow, nor sky nor earth could you see; five days we hid in a forest hut and could make no move nor stir from there. The fumes from the stove got to us, we kept vomiting, casting all up— a misery it was. And the darkness over the earth—at that time, nigh Christmas, here we do have a bit of light but there in the day there'd be just a sort of dawn and then night again, with darkness thick and black. The men sought for stars in the sky and were guided by them, but I lighted my road with my cross. I gathered my fingers inside my mittens in a two-fingered cross and with that true cross I went forth and I returned. And when I returned folks marvelled at me as at some wonder. Old Believers came from all Pinega parts to look at me. And when I started telling them about my pilgrimage, how I walked, and the sufferings I endured, I could scarce believe it myself. Greater suffering it seemed than those I endured there could hardly be on earth. But no, my sufferings, my torments only began when they married me off into Koida.

"I thought if I might not join with the other lads and lasses when they went a-merrymaking evenings it was my lot to bide a maid till the grave, but no, it pleased the Lord to prepare more trials for his slave. A husband I had but bided a maid, for he had no man's strength to make me a woman. A year I was barren and then another, his father and mother were giving me sour looks and my own mother turned

334

on me wanting to know how long I was going to be a reproach among women. Where was I at fault? Wasn't my lot wretched enough, for two years neither maid nor wife? And I was sorry for my man, a good man he was. Nights we'd both cry, the pillow was wet with our tears. But then the Lord gave me wisdom, he gives the life and he gives the strength. Pray to God, I tells my man, pray day and night. And I will pray. The Lord will hear us. And the Lord heard. One night my man wakes me. 'Rouse up, Solomida,' he says, 'man's power has come to me.' And I roused me and my man did his part.''

I certainly had not expected such blunt frankness from an old woman and coughed to hide my embarrassment. But she divined it at once and with the same tone of simple instruction she continued.

"The Lord God created men and women to be fruitful and multiply and to bless the Lord God with prayer and good deeds. It is no sin to sleep with your husband. It is a sin to commit adultery or to come together in the days of the Passion, but for the rest of the time the world rests on love. All rests on God's word and on faith. God's word sets people on their feet, raises them from their death-bed. With God's word I raised my husband from the dead.''

"From the dead?"

The old woman did not react to my amazed exclamation but continued unperturbed.

"From the time he was a little lad the folks round about hadn't liked my man, and one day to scare off the other lads when they wanted to give him a beating, he bragged, silly-like, 'I'll bring down the hiccupping sickness on you,' and from that day there was no kind of life for the poor lad, and later on for me, his wife, and our lasses. That's what happens when you call up devils instead of calling on God. He wanted to scare off others and brought down a millstone on his own head. He was blamed for all the ills that came, for all taken sick, for all the beasts that fell, and us with him. And there was yon summer when there was a murrain on the cattle and sheep, and not a day but they were dying. My man went off to the haying but I had to stay home, I'd just borne Matrena and it had been a hard birth. When Elias Day came round, all the men came back for the festival, all but mine. Why wasn't he there? A pious man he was, and observed all the holidays. Oh, I felt in my heart something had happened to him. I harnessed the mare, we lived quite well, with two horses, and I started

335

off to meet him. I went on and on and still there was no sight of him. Then I came to some pines and somewhere off to the side crows were cawing as if summer was wrong. I went to that place and there was my man, lying there with no breath in him, and sticks heaped over him. The others had beaten him to death.

"I fell on my knees and prayed to God. 'Lord God,' I said, 'you breathed life into dead clay, you created Adam a man, and am I not your creation, Lord? Is it not your eternal flame that burns in me? Lord God,' I said, 'give me the strength and power to raise my guiltless husband from the dead.' And the Lord gave me strength. I began breathing into my man's cold lips and after a while he said 'oh' and lived again. With the power of God's word I raised him. And times, with that word I tamed a mettlesome beast. Fokta the Horse-Dealer had a horse, a maverick it was, he couldn't break it to work nohow. So he comes to me with 'Solomida, you know words of power, help me, I'll pay all you want.' A dealer. 'There's only one word I know,' I says, 'and that's the word of God. With that word I'll help you. And I'll take no pay, only stop smoking.' And he did, so there was one less in Koida wi' that filthy weed. And I led the horse into the collar, with the help of God's word. For all is subject to that word, man and beast, and the serpent that crawls on its belly. The holy saints who lived in the desert, what wonders they wrought in the olden days! They tamed wild beasts, lions and bears. And by the power of God's word I raised my man from the dead.

"We came near the village, I'd tie reins in one hand and held up my man half alive with the other. And once more death came agin us, men with stakes at the very start of the village, all shouting, 'Kill them! Kill them! ' Oh trouble, oh bitter sorrow, farewell parents, farewell my orphaned daughter. The hour of death is come. There was nowhere to go, if we ran they'd catch us, and go forward, they'd kill us. But then I remembered, I had my protection in the Lord God. If anyone could aid me now it was he the all-powerful, he the compassionate. And I prayed fervently. 'Lord, work a miracle,' I said. 'Many a time you saved me on my pilgrimage to Pustozerye, save us now, I don't ask it for myself, but do not let my guiltless man die and my daughter be left an orphan.' And a voice spoke to me from above: 'A cross and fire, a cross and fire.' But where could I get fire and a cross?—Standing at the edge of the village, facing drunken men with stakes and the dogs all howling. But again the Lord God came to my aid, I pulled a stake from a fence and fastened the whip to it by its lash and had a cross. But fire—I'd taken off my sarafan back in the forest to put round Ivan's head, and now I wound it round the cross and dipped it in a bucket of tar tied to the cart. And when the men started against us with their stakes I stood against them with my burning cross. Stood there in my white shift and the milk poured out of my breasts. With others their milk dries up with fright but things was all diff'rent with me, it was in that moment that my milk flowed. Like as if a dam had burst. All my shift was wet from neck to hem. There I stood on the cart in my white shift and my hands holding that burning cross. 'Down on your knees, you murderous heathens,' I cried, 'swear by God's word that you'll never more lay finger on my man or as God lives I'll burn down the village.'' And they fell on their knees before God's cross and the fire flaming on it. 'Forgive us, Solomida, we'll never touch him more.' The Lord, the Lord God saved me. In his compassion he came to my aid. Would mortal woman have had the strength to go forward alone agin that devil's spawn, with the cross fashioned from a stake and make fire on from her own spirit? But I went agin them in my shift with the burning cross and they saw me like the retribution of God, the Archangel Michael on the Day of Judgement. But where the fire came from I mind not, for in those days there were no matches, we struck fire with flint and tinder.''

"Well, and did the villagers quieten down after that and leave you in peace?"

"Eh, my dear, a man 'ud live all quiet and decent if he'd only an angel to counsel him. But we've a guardian angel on the right and a devil's tempter on the left. So more trials came to me. Whom the Lord loveth he chasteneth. When I worked in the kolkhoz I was allus lone on the field, the bad name they'd given me was like a wall atween me and the other women. If aught went wrong it was allus Solomida who'd spoiled it. And the bosses didn't like me any better because I wouldn't work on Christ's Sunday. I was sent to a camp twice for it. I said to them: give me three times as much to do, and I'll do it. But don't make me trample on Christ's Holy Day. But God did not desert me. And there too, behind barbed wire, I rested secure in God's word. When they summoned us to work on Sunday they told me, 'Old Believer, to the cooler with you! ' Because

I wouldn't work on the Lord's day. They'd push me into the cellar, my teeth chattered and my hands were numb. If only they'd give me a chip to warm me a bit. Then it came to me: but God's word, what is that given me for? And I prayed, I found heat for my body in prayer, I remembered the righteous Avvakum, how they left him to rot underground, naked, tortured with cold, and I felt warmer. God's word warmed me.

"On Monday morn they brought me up out of that cellar, I staggered but I smiled. The chief man bawled, 'What are you grinning at?' and I told him, 'I'm smiling because you gave me a day of suffering, so I could be alone with the Lord God.' And I bowed low before him, and I says, 'I thank you.' So they tormented me all they could, that was the second time I was in a camp, and then they put me out. 'I'm sick of the sight of you, woman. I don't want you to die on my hands. Get out of my sight.' "

"Yes, Grandma," I said, "it isn't an ordinary life you've had but a whole martyrdom."

"Suffering and trials have not been begrudged me. That is good, a sign of God's favour. Through suffering and trials lies the road to God's kingdom. Suffering and trials light the road to the Heavenly City. But one thing I ask, for one thing I pray, Lord God." The old woman crossed herself and suddenly began to cry—helplessly, childishly. "Do not let me die with the scab of devil's slander on me. Take from me the bad name, take from me the millstone. Let it be as I die, let it be as I lie in my coffin, but let all see the truth about your slave Solomida."

I did not know how to console the old woman and could only sigh.

She looked at the sun and began to get herself up from the log.

"Sit a while longer, Grandma."

"Nay, it looks like Matrena won't be here for a bit and it's time to rise for prayers."

"There's time enough," I said, trying to detain the old woman.

"Don't speak them words," she said sternly. "Prayer is of all things the first, the greatest. Strength and wisdom you need all the time and where can you find them but in prayer?"

I realised it was no use trying to keep her. Besides, I could hear the approach of drunken singing; my driver was coming, his arms round a tall heavy-faced young fellow.

3

The next summer, finding myself in my own parts again, I went to Koida to see the old woman.

In the low, old-style hut without curtains, whitewash or wallpaper, only yellowish wood, I found the old woman's daughter, herself pretty old—that same Matrena whom her mother had been waiting for, sitting on the log. Solomida herself had died in the spring.

"It was a good death," Matrena told me, wiping tears from her simple, guileless face, "an easy death. She lived to Easter, broke her fast, and then the angels came for her and her earthly sufferings were over."

"But how did it happen?"

"How did she die? We were sitting round the Easter table. Then she said, 'Go, fetch the old women, I want to take my leave of them.' 'What's got into you, Ma, what have you taken into your head?' But she only said again, 'Go, call them, go quickly.' And warned me again to be quick. Well, so they came. Ma stood up, she was sitting right here on the bench, and she turned to face the icons and crossed herself. 'Soon,' she said, 'I shall stand before the Lord God, without sin against men. All my life,' she said, 'I have lived with God's word on my lips.' And then, before the old women had time to collect their wits, she lay down on the floor here, her eyes on the icons and her arms crossed, and died. And all the women, the old ones and the young, were on their knees before her with 'Forgive us, forgive us, Solomida, forgive us and forgive all who have sinned against you. For all your life long we have trampled and kicked you and made life a misery for your children and now we see a saint lived among us! '

"Well, and wasn't she? When hiccuppers die they are writhing and screaming for days, as devils torment them. But she sighed her last like a dove. With her death Ma showed them all what she was, her death took the bad name from her and from all of us."

In the evening Matrena took me to the graveyard, just as old and neglected as the village; I stood for a long time beside the sandy mound with its pine marker, still fresh and unweathered, which bore not a single letter.

1978

Felt Boots

The Kossov house is prinked out like a bride. All round the house lines are stretched, and on them merrily casting back the sunshine are colourful silk frocks, every possible kind of shawls, scarves and kerchiefs, cotton and woollen dress-lengths, coats, footwear and fur hats.

It is an old custom to air things so as to keep out moths and mice, but at the same time it is a display of the family's prosperity and the dowries of daughters. It need hardly be said that Darya Leontyevna, mistress of all this magnificence, glows and struts. For it is she herself, left without parents at the age of twelve, who has gathered this wealth together.

I am sincerely glad for her, and really enjoy going round this colourful, fragrant exhibition until I notice, by the door, in the most prominent place, two old, worn-out felt boots, the soles practically trodden through.

"How have these smart boots got here?"

Darya Leontyevna laughs youthfully.

"It was with those smart boots that I began to live."

"To live?"

"Aye, really live. They gave me them in the woods, my first bonus. I just can't make up my mind to throw them out."

There are tears in her eyes.

"Eh dear, when I think of all them days, I dunno how I ever got where I am. I was fourteen when they sent me to the lumbering. Well, I come from working in the woods, come to our barrack and they say, 'New Year the morn, Darya.' I must do something to mark the day, but how? There's naught. In them days, in the war, it wasn't only bread we lacked, there wasn't even enough potatoes, not to really feed you. Well, I thinks, at least I'll have my felt boots dry and warm for the New Year. The stove was still warm, I put them inside and lay down on my bunk. I'll

341

lie down a bit, I thought, and then I'll take them out. But I fell asleep and slept to the morn when the foreman banged the iron rail. I jumped up and ran to the stove but there was naught but the tops left of my felt boots. They'd fired the stove real hot. Because the barrack walls were thin, sithee, by the morn the bitter cold would creep in; there'd be drifts of snow in the corners.

"Well, I went a-crying to the manager of the lumber camp. Barefoot through the snow, I mind it well. The office was opposite our barrack. I told him what had happened, how I'd naught to put on my feet. 'What'll I do, Vassily Yegorovich?' But he just says, 'Do what you like but you've got to be at work tomorrow, or I'll take you to court.' It was like that, wartime.

"So I went home, eight versts it was; I cut rags off my ma's coat I was wearing and wrapped them round my feet and went through the woods in them, winter. But what good was it then I did get home? My little sister Katya was in an orphanage, and the house was all cold, colder than outside.

"Well, I just sat me down on the porch and cried. And then Yevgraf Ivanovich happened by, an old man who worked in the stables. 'What's the matter, lass?' he says and I told him, 'I got my felt boots burned. Manager gave me a day to see to it, but where can I get others?' 'Never mind,' he says, 'don't ye cry, come to the stables and we'll think of summat.'

"So I went with him to the stables, it was right warm in there, I just sat down on the floor by the stove, snuggled up agin it like as if it was my own ma, and fell asleep. Slept till eve. And then Grandad Yevgraf woke me. 'Get up,' he says, 'be it good or bad, but I've made summat.' I looked and I couldn't believe my eyes when I saw warm boots—he'd made them out of the felt from old horse collars.

"I put on them boots and ran to the barrack without stopping for breath. It was real dark, just a lonely star winking, but I ran and sang too. I was that glad. I'd be in time and they wouldn't take me to court.

"It was half a year later, spring, when the secretary of the district committee comes, and he says, 'Have you got a real good shock worker?' 'Aye, there's Darya, she's the youngest here but she works real well.' So then he asks me, 'What do you want as a bonus for shock work on the labour front?' 'Give me felt boots,' I says, and he tells me, 'You'll have them, the very best.' And come autumn, he brought these boots you see. Brought them hisself. You could trust him, if he'd promised summat he kept his word.

"I wore them a long time. Took good care of them. For five years I wore them for best, and then I began to wear them every day. That's how I came by them boots."

1974

The Happiest Woman

When Father died he left a whole houseful of childer, and all of 'em lasses save only Tikhon. And not a handful of meal in the bins. Ma toiled and moiled day and night till she was like to have run away in sweat but little did she get by it, the bread-box allus gaped empty.

Well, the long and the short of it was that we had to go out and earn our bread. Tikhon went to town and me, at twelve, I went to be a servant in a monastery. Aye, and it was nine years I was in that hell. Nine years I did all the washing for those bearded devils.

They'd wake me at three o'clock in the morning and I'd stand at that washtub till eight at night, and at the end I couldn't see straight or feel my hands and feet. My hands were raw with lye, red as pigeons' feet. They begrudged soap, them monks did, it was lye all the time. And rinsing in winter through a hole in the ice on the river—a good master wouldn't put his dog out of the house in that frost, and me going to the river to rinse twenty-five wash-basketfuls. And at the end of the month I'd get a ruble for it all.

That's how they treated me in yon holy place. Sometimes Ma would come, she'd cry but she could do naught and she went as she came, because there was naught for me to go home to, anyway.

But mind you, however bad things are, youth is youth, and come Sunday I'd be off out somewhere. You look at me now—a fine beauty I am, fit to scare the crows. But I was a comely wench in those days. When I passed, the labourers would gawk and grin, and going along the monastery corridors them monks would be trying to get a nip at my breast. There was times I gave them such a punch in their hairy mugs, they went down like an ill-made sheaf.

A fine hearty lass I was, I hadn't been behind the door when God gave out health, I could still carry a sack of flour at sixty. But I couldn't hold out against my old man, only he wasn't an old man then, a fine lad he was, and he won me with just a look. I'd tossed off all the rest, the monks and the labourers, like puppies, but he—he just had to look at me and I was his, couldn't move hand or foot.

So I got me a bun in the oven.

Naught to do, my own fault. Ma and I sat and cried—we couldn't do a thing. As for telling Olexei—that's my old man—it never came into my head. His folks was well off, he was the best catch in the village, what'd he want with Olena's lass. No dowry to her, and couldn't keep her gate locked at that. In the old days they were strict about a maid's honour, not like these times.

But Olexei found out and off he went to his parents with "This is the way of it, Father and Mother, I won't have any but Olena's lass."

They tried to talk him out, and his father took the stick to him—he had a hot temper—but Olexei stood firm: there's none comes under my hand save only Okulka.

His father flared up.

"So that's your talk? Go against father and mother, would you? Then live as you will. I'll give you nothing."

He didn't, neither. For three years we lived in a sooty bath-house. For three years we choked on smoke. What d'you think I used for a kneading trough? The tub they washed in.

Before going to bed, Olexei'd say, "Sing, wife! " And would you believe it, all my life I'd never sung like that. All the village 'ud come out to listen. "Naught to wonder at if Okulka sings," they'd say, "why shouldn't she, she's known naught better, a servant since she was a little 'un. But what has Olexei to be merry about?"

Olexei and me, we soon got on our feet. We built us a house. Did it ourselves and 't was a house to marvel at. I worked as his mate, under the logs and on top of them. Aye, I lifted logs together with Olexei and sat with him on the corners with an axe. And folks stared till their eyes popped, a woman wielding an axe—none had ever seen such a thing or heard tell of it.

Well, we'd built the house and we were doing right well, when the old man, Olexei's father that is, came to us.

He'd gotten feeble then and blind too, and who needs one like that? His three sons wouldn't have him, go to Olexei, they said, you haven't lived with him yet. But how could he ask Olexei to take him in when he'd put him out of doors and not given him a brass farthing?

Well, so I comes out one morning and who should I see sitting in the porch? Who but father-in-law. He didn't dare knock, so he just sat there. And it was cold. Winter. The time of the hardest frosts.

I took his hand and brought him in and sat him in the warmest place. And then I gave him something to eat and drink and fixed the bath-house for him to wash because he'd got lice, too, and he cried like a babe.

"Forgive me, forgive me, Okulina", he says, "I done you wrong, I can't reward your goodness but may God reward you."

I don't rightly know if the old man's prayers brought me happiness (he was a very pious old man, not like me, the monastery slavey as they called me in the village), but anyway, the life I've had, I could call myself the happiest woman in the village. I had four men fighting in the war, my husband and three sons, and every one of them came back. But all Olexei's brothers stayed there. And naught strange in that, since only a handful in all the village returned, but mine—all four. Now, wouldn't you call me the happiest woman?

1939, 1980

Wooden Mausoleums

The Novgorod country. The eastern part.

How many times in these days have I passed through deserted, dead villages with their empty houses and long-cold stoves. I was almost getting accustomed to these deserted places going back to wildness, but there was one that particularly moved me. On the house corners I saw small red stars cut from tin, in memory of men killed at the front—a custom fairly widespread in rural Russia.

I learned from the only old woman there (she had come out from town to spend the summer) that the stars had been fixed to the houses by a local teacher and his pupils, and I wanted to meet him; but he lived in a neighbouring village about four kilometres away, the old woman told me, so as it was already evening I decided to put it off until the next day.

My hostess and I had tea by the unaccustomed half-forgotten light of an oil lamp, talking of this and that. Then I strolled out for a breath of fresh air.

It was a beautiful evening. The deep blue sky was thick with great bright stars, and the moon had risen on the left so that the whole street was criss-crossed with deep black shadows.

Stepping delicately through this spider-web of shadows, I passed through the village, came to an old tumbledown fence, and again raised my eyes to the sky.

The stars were brighter still. I gazed at their diamond glitter and a distant childhood memory came to mind, a fantasy that when people die their souls go to inhabit a star, each one its own.

But heavens, I thought, how lonely, how dreary and cold it would be on these stars. And why shouldn't the souls of men from this village who had been killed in battle return to their homes for which they had given their lives?

With that thought the dead houses standing out black against the brilliant diamond-studded sky became for me magical wooden mausoleums, each one of them a resting place for the soul of its soldier-owner, killed in the war. Wooden mausoleums... All over Russia.

1978

REQUEST TO READERS

Raduga Publishers would be glad to have your opinion of this book, its translation and design and any suggestions you may have for future publications.

Please send all your comments to 17, Zubovsky Boulevard, Moscow, USSR.

ИБ № 2708

Редактор русского текста *А. Кудряшова*
Контрольные редакторы *Р. Боброва, А. Буяновская, Л. Киржнер*
Художник *А. Голицин*
Художественные редакторы *И. Трубецкая, А. Суима*
Технический редактор *В. Гунина*

Сдано в набор 18.04.85. Подписано в печать 23.10.85. Формат 84х108/32.
Бумага офсетная. Гарнитура Баскервиль. Печать офсет. Усл. печ. л. 18,48.
Усл. кр.-отт. 64,46. Уч.-изд. л. 21,27. Тираж 13920 экз. Заказ №453.
Цена 2 р. 70 к. Изд. № 1830.

Издательство "Радуга" Государственного комитета СССР по делам
издательств, полиграфии и книжной торговли.
Москва, 119859, Зубовский бульвар, 17.

Отпечатано с оригинал-макета способом фотоофсет на Можайском
полиграфкомбинате Союзполиграфпрома при Государственном
комитете СССР по делам издательств, полиграфии и книжной торговли.
Можайск, 143200, ул. Мира, 93.